DESMOND

DESMOND

A Novel of Love
and the Modern Vampire

ULYSSES G. DIETZ

alyson
books

LOS ANGELES • NEW YORK

© 1998 BY ULYSSES G. DIETZ. ALL RIGHTS RESERVED.
COVER PHOTOGRAPH BY JOHNATHAN BLACK.

MANUFACTURED IN THE UNITED STATES OF AMERICA.

THIS TRADE PAPERBACK ORIGINAL IS PUBLISHED BY ALYSON PUBLICATIONS INC.,
P.O. BOX 4371, LOS ANGELES, CALIFORNIA 90078-4371.
DISTRIBUTION IN THE UNITED KINGDOM BY TURNAROUND PUBLISHER SERVICES LTD.,
UNIT 3 OLYMPIA TRADING ESTATE, COBURG ROAD, WOOD GREEN,
LONDON N22 6TZ ENGLAND.

FIRST EDITION: JULY 1998

02 00 01 99 98   10 9 8 7 6 5 4 3 2 1

ISBN 1-55583-470-1

LIBRARY OF CONGRESS CATALOGING-IN-PUBLICATION DATA
    DIETZ, ULYSSES G. (ULYSSES GRANT), 1955–
        DESMOND : A NOVEL OF LOVE AND THE MODERN VAMPIRE / BY ULYSSES G.
    DIETZ.
        ISBN 1-55583-470-1
        I. TITLE.
    PS3554.I3875D54 1998
    813'.54—DC21   98-12920 CIP

For my partner, Gary,
and our children, Alexander and
Grace, who make life worth living;
and
for Jeffrey,
who made this seem worth writing

"Sometimes a neighbor whom we have disliked a lifetime for his arrogance and conceit lets fall a commonplace remark that shows us another side, another man, really; a man uncertain, puzzled, and in the dark like ourselves."

FROM THE EPILOGUE OF
Death Comes to the Archbishop
BY WILLA CATHER

PROLOGUE

Desmond closed the book and leaned back, stretching, with a long, slow, satisfied sigh. He stared for a moment into the dancing flames in the fireplace. *How nice to have a room like this on a cold gray day*, he thought. Smiling, he glanced across the room at Roger, who looked up from his newspaper and smiled back at him.

"Finished so soon?" asked Roger. "My, my, when you get wrapped up in your reading, you certainly go lickety-split."

"Lickety-split? Lord, where did you pick up that quaint phrase?" said Desmond, getting up from the sofa to replace the book in its spot on one of the high mahogany bookcases. "I wonder where such a silly expression came from?" he continued absently, stretching again as he turned to gaze out the window. "But you're right, I get very intense when I'm reading something that grabs me." He stared absently through the darkening glass, talking as if to himself. "You know how she writes, pulling you into the fantasy, careening across time and space. Heady stuff, if you like it. And I'm a sucker for it."

"*There's* an apt term!" Roger laughed, tossing aside his own reading and rising from the lancet-backed armchair. "I've always thought you the most classic sucker of them all."

"Oh, shut up. No bad puns now; you know I'm always defenseless after finishing a good book." Desmond turned his back to the window, putting on a false scowl as he faced his oldest friend.

Roger approached Desmond and wrapped his arms around him in a playful bear hug. "You're such a romantic. It boggles my mind, since you ought to be a terrible cynic after all these years. How do you stay so wide-eyed and unblemished?" His words were teasing, but the intent was serious.

Desmond pulled back from Roger's embrace, the scowl now exchanged for a quizzical smile. He gave Roger a quick peck on the lips and stepped away from him. "I'll assume you're not just making fun of me. You know perfectly well I've got more than my share of scars. Actually, I don't know why I still get carried away with novels. They've always been able to pick me up and transport me. But only the well-written ones. I don't demand great literature, but I do want good stories well-told. They may not make it to the classics, but they make magic for their readers." Desmond moved to a pier table between the windows that served as a bar. "Want a glass of port?"

"Yes, thanks."

"Actually, in that respect Anne Rice is especially good. She creates whole worlds she's never experienced."

"As far as we know, that is," Roger said with a sly smile. Desmond shot him a look, which he ignored. "Do you think Anne Rice's work will last?" Roger took the proffered glass of ruby-colored port and went to look out the window. Desmond brought his own drink over and stood beside him in the window recess, leaning against the folded-back shutters.

"I don't know. Maybe I have too much of a taste for trash. But I still think Anne Rice has earned her place in popular fiction. That's worth something."

"With emphasis on the word 'fiction,'" added Roger.

"Why do you say that?" asked Desmond, without taking his eyes off the November sun as it disappeared behind the buildings of lower Manhattan.

"Oh, just that even the best of those gothic romances you love— or modern science fiction—no matter how convincingly they're written, never quite work for me because of one detail."

2

"Which detail?"

"It's all make-believe, as you and I know all too well. For instance, does any writer ever give vampires a real sense of humor? Never. The powers of darkness don't have time for fun. All that mayhem to accomplish before daybreak. God, they're all so *serious*."

"Well," Desmond admitted reluctantly, "fictional vampires do all seem to be either mindless killers or constantly depressed about the misery of eternal life. Maybe Lestat has what passes today for wit, but I suppose it's just massive neurosis."

"That's it!" Roger snorted. "They all need analysis!"

"But Count Dracula couldn't have been a librarian or a dairy farmer, could he? He had to be someone suited to the role of 'ancient and evil one.' Come to think of it, I don't ever recall reading about a poor vampire—or a stupid one."

"Perfect—lifestyles of the rich and undead." Roger drained his glass and set it on the center table. "Come on, Des, don't you get tired of reading about vampires as little better than great white sharks? The best I'll do is credit Anne Rice for giving her vampires the common decency to be tortured about it."

Desmond said nothing but regarded his friend through half-closed eyes.

"You tolerate all this bad fiction. But that relentless, ugly mythology is exactly why I can't stomach this rubbish you devour so happily. The authors' fertile imaginations haven't let them take the one step that could change the whole genre: the vampire as nice guy."

Desmond laughed at this. "Oh, please! Admit it—you've loved some of my favorite books. They dream up stuff that's pretty uncanny."

"Yeah—makes you wonder where they got their research material." Roger's deep green eyes gazed steadily at Desmond, whose own hazel eyes locked on his for a long moment, unblinking.

"They always miss the mark a little, don't they, Desi?" he spoke at last, very softly. Then, as if waking, he seemed to shake himself.

3

"Anyway, enough nonsense, my flight's at 6, and I've got to go pack. Did you call a car?"

"Yes, I did, and don't call me Desi. I wish you didn't have to go. It's so lovely when you visit—I revel in the domesticity of it. And then you go back to San Francisco and leave me all alone in this old house." Desmond wrapped Roger in a playful hug, not letting him pull away.

"You'll get over it," said Roger, struggling briefly in Desmond's powerful embrace. He finally gave up and let Desmond hold him, kissing him chastely on the forehead. "Besides, you can always come visit me. Airplanes have made these separations ever so much easier. You know, my friend, it's not healthy to pretend you're married to me. It's a pleasant little fiction, but, not unlike your beloved vampire novels, there's just one little flaw."

"Yes, sir, Mr. Heterosexual!" cried Desmond, releasing Roger and giving him a smart military salute. "I try to forget about that un-happy aspect of your nature. But you always remind me." A smile played on Desmond's lips, but a deep, familiar sadness filled his eyes.

"And with good reason, apparently. I love you very much, Desmond, and I owe you a lot. But I'm never going to be your dream man."

"I know, you cad. Go pack your bags and leave me to my misery. I'll just rattle around here, a melancholy old queen, doomed to spend eternity pining for the one man who can't return his love." He said these last words in a sepulchral voice that made Roger laugh.

"None of that false despair! 'Old queen' has never been some-thing I associate with you. Really, Desmond, you should know bet-ter at your age!" And with this Roger disappeared upstairs to the third floor to pack.

Desmond's smile faded as Roger's footsteps faded above, and he turned back to the window. The sun was hidden now behind the city's superstructure, and cold gray shadows filled the narrow street in front of his house. Looking down from the second story,

4

Desmond smiled again, wondering at the contrast evident from this vantage. The seedy gas station diagonally across from him on the corner of the Bowery was little-changed from when it was built, only now it was run-down and grimy. But just next to it, directly across from his own library windows, was a new restaurant, aglow with pink neon tubing, bright black-and-white–tiled floors, and large potted plants. THE BLUE MOON: AMERICAN CUISINE. A sign of the times, better times, coming back to his old neighborhood. Desmond could remember when American cuisine was the same as English cuisine, which was to say not much to crow about. Originally, the shabby little brick building in which the Blue Moon found itself had been an elegant private residence—not as grand as *his*, perhaps, but eminently respectable. How ironic it was to see the street, this once-quiet and -fashionable street of houses, rise up again from neglect and ignominy. Many of its members had fallen before the wrecker's ball, and others had suffered worse fates at the hands of landlords and uncaring tenants. His house alone had remained untouched. It was his haven in the endless flux of the city around him.

He turned away from the chilly glass and strolled over to the gold-veined black marble chimney piece. Stirring up the fire, he added another small log and ran his hand in an idle caress along the molded edge of the mantel shelf. The revived flames flared up, flickering softly up the flanks of the Gothic colonettes at each side, spreading their decorative warmth through the room. Desmond couldn't imagine rooms without fireplaces, however bad they were at heating. This house hadn't had central heating originally, and yet even his state-of-the-art gas furnace couldn't cast the spell that an open fire could. He let himself be mesmerized by the flames as they danced, thinking back to other times, other fires.

The library had grown dim with the setting sun, lit only by the fire now. It illuminated the deep, figured green carpet and the tufted leather on the high, pointed backs of the armchairs Desmond had so carefully kept and renewed over the years. The octagonal center

5

table, its marble top the same color as that of the bar table and the chimney piece, stood piled with books and magazines beneath the gilt brass chandelier. The whimsical tracery of the pseudo-Gothic panels of the chandelier brought another smile to Desmond's face. How seriously he had taken that chandelier when he had first seen it! How radical and modern it had seemed in this placid classical town house. Once it had held candles, then it had been piped for gas. Now it was electrified, although Desmond rarely lit it. Beneath the table lay Cosmo, a motley tortoiseshell cat Desmond had rescued from a Dumpster on Stuyvesant Street six year earlier. She slept contentedly, curled up amid the clusters of Gothic columns that made up the table base. This was her favorite spot, especially with a fire just close enough to warm her back. Desmond had found her on a night like this—a cold winter night, when Roger had just left after one of his visits.

Roger's right, Desmond thought. Flying helped a great deal. But it didn't make the initial separation any easier. He might joke about marriage and the difference in their sexual inclinations, but Desmond knew that Roger hated the partings just as much as he. They had been too close for too long not to feel it. They were more than married, really; more than brothers. They were soul mates, in the truest meaning of that much-abused expression.

Desmond looked up at the glass-fronted bookcases, their tall pointed doors echoing the design of the chair backs, with hundreds of volumes, ranging from 18th-century calf-bound to modern paperbacks. No title came to him, nothing to curl up with and read after Roger left for the airport. He looked again at Cosmo, sleeping as she always did without any apparent worry in her little nest of columns.

Tonight, thought Desmond, *I'm going to have to find something bigger than a kitten to keep me warm.*

CHAPTER 1

The smell and noise of the bar hit him like an ocean breaker as he opened the soundproofed door, and Desmond almost changed his mind. He turned back to the street but was so stricken by its littered, windswept desolation that he forged ahead into the bar. Once he was inside, his eyes adjusted immediately to the dim, smoky room. It was jammed with people and reeked of cigarettes and beer, neither of which Desmond liked. It was not encouraging. But Desmond knew the sort of people who came here, and they were, when need be, "his type." In this place, that translated to vaguely Ivy League but neither precious nor overgroomed. Everyone in the place, as far as he could see, was dressed conservatively, without much style beyond some brightly colored sweaters and modish haircuts. This was fine by Desmond, who had never taken to fashion very well, preferring good fabric and fit above anything transitory. Careful conservatism had kept his wardrobe functioning longer that way.

But he was not here to make a critique of the patrons' clothing. Ordering a glass of red wine, Desmond burrowed deep into the inner room of the crowded bar. He moved slowly and surely, discreetly surveying the faces around him. One couldn't see much else, given the lighting and the general costume of the clientele, but that didn't worry him. His own 45-year-old body was as trim and smooth as it could be, and his dark hair was as thick as it had been in his youth. No, he wouldn't scare anyone away, with or without clothes.

But he was looking for faces—for *a* face—that would fill the void in him left by Roger's departure.

Loneliness was nothing new to Desmond, and he was better than most at coping with it. Solitude was a way of life and had been for as long as Desmond could remember. Roger had been his best—his only—close friend since they had first met. But for most of their years, they had known as much separation as togetherness. Roger had always mixed more socially than did Desmond, and his life in San Francisco was as full of acquaintances and casual friends as his house on Nob Hill whenever Desmond visited. How different those visits were from Roger's trips to New York; how unalike were Roger's ornate Victorian house and Desmond's cozily luxurious one.

The disparity between their abodes reflected that of their personalities. Roger had always been outgoing and inclined to seek out groups; Desmond had always yearned for intense closeness with one person. The paradoxical result was that they had always maintained a perfect closeness with each other, since Roger's world was built on the superficial socializing that suited him and Desmond's was barricaded within the warm brick walls of his town house. People poured through Roger's big, airy house like water through a fountain. Few people had ever seen the inside of Desmond's house. He was not a hermit, and he did have a small circle of friends for whom he was a charming puzzle. Despite the occasional small dinner, always catered, Desmond's friends were more like close strangers who knew little beyond what they could see.

All Desmond's love was focused—pointlessly, he knew—on Roger. But Roger himself, so surrounded by people, so expert at playing host, had likewise never focused his deeper emotions on any woman, preferring to guard his soul from all eyes—except Desmond's. Thus, they both found comfort in the sweetly sterile domesticity of Roger's East Coast stops. For Desmond, it seemed these were as close as he would ever come to knowing perfect happiness; for Roger, they were as close as he ever wanted to come to fidelity and conjugal bliss.

So, while Roger may have felt a pang at their inevitable partings, Desmond always experienced the desolation he had first felt, so long ago, when he had lost Jeffrey. Roger had not known Jeffrey and could never quite understand to what extent he had soothed the loneliness that throbbed ever so gently, ever so constantly, beneath Desmond's cool, detached surface. All Roger Deland knew was that he owed Desmond Beckwith his life, and that was enough.

In spite of the efforts of the ventilation system, the smoke in the packed bar was overpowering. Desmond felt lucky to be able to breathe easily and wondered how the rest of the men could stand it. The noise level was easy to tune out; his hearing could be very selective when he chose. Likewise, his vision was unimpaired by the darkness and thickness of the atmosphere, and he could watch people without being noticed until he wanted it. A few tossed looks his way. These he dismissed with either a polite smile and a shake of his head or a cold stare, depending on the look.

His uncanny ability to read people's feelings—what people in the '60s had referred to as vibes—was a tool he used with skill, weeding out those approaches he knew in advance to be useless. He exchanged brief words with a few, only to feel his own lack of interest sweep over him like a chilly breeze or to be appalled at the stupidity that lay behind a pair of intelligent eyes. These unsuccessful contacts were taken care of with a mumbled excuse about refilling his wineglass, which he nevertheless nursed carefully through the evening. He needed his wits about him tonight, especially since he was at his most vulnerable.

A flicker caught the corner of his eye, and he turned toward it; someone had passed underneath one of the rare downward-facing lights, someone with fair hair. Desmond froze, electrified at what he saw. The hair he found was not as fair as he'd thought—a dirty blond, in fact. But it was growing softly above a charming face, full of sweetness and wit. It was a face uncannily familiar, like one he had

9

known long ago. As Desmond watched from a distance, he could see the eyes sparkle darkly but could not tell their color.

As the man with fair hair talked, Desmond could see strong white teeth—not quite perfect but just imperfectly enough aligned to seem boyish and natural. A small nose, yet beautifully shaped with a slim, sharp bridge and crisply sculpted tip, rested neatly above a graceful mouth whose bottom lip seemed slightly squared. The jawline was strong, with a gentle chin marked by a mole on its left side. Except for the coloring, Desmond might have been looking at Jeffrey Chapman's twin. He felt the short hairs prickle along the back of his neck. The boy—or man, perhaps, since Desmond couldn't guess his age—talked with several people in a group. His face appeared at ease, his laughter casual and comfortable. And yet his eyes, for all their spark, betrayed an anxiety that Desmond couldn't place.

Such anxiety wasn't entirely unexpected. Since AIDS had surfaced, Desmond had seen much of this sort of suppressed fear in people's faces in the bars. The exuberance of the chase was tempered by caution, and the gaiety of the chatter was tainted by the knowledge that many—too many—of this bar's patrons would meet the specter face to face. Nothing Desmond had ever seen had created such an effect on his world, and yet the gay society he had grown accustomed to in the past 20 years appeared actually to have strengthened under the weight of this calamity. It seemed to Desmond a strange silver lining in a very dark cloud.

Desmond watched the fair-haired man, entranced. He knew they had never met, and yet he felt the stirring of distant memories that usually remained carefully out of reach. It wasn't just that he looked like Jeffrey, but there was even something about the way he moved when he talked that was eerily familiar.

Finally the man (Desmond had decided that he was at least 25) turned away from his group as if to move toward the entrance. His eyes were caught by Desmond's stare. Like a fish drawn to a lure, the man made his way through the crowd, a small vertical line creasing his high, smooth brow even as a flirtatious smile of greeting played on his lips.

"Hi," he began, "I couldn't help noticing that you were looking at me." He seemed embarrassed at this opening and glanced down at his shoes.

"I'm glad you did. It was quite intentional."

"I haven't seen you here before. Are you from out of town?" Then he laughed and added, "That's a terrible line, I realize, but I really do know a lot of the people here, and your face would be easy to re-member."

"Now, *that's* a line, and thank you for it," replied Desmond, tak-ing his turn to laugh but not letting his eyes leave his companion's. "Actually, I live here—and have for more years than you, I daresay. I just don't get out to bars much."

"Oh. Jealous lover, or just not your style?"

"Ah, would that it *were* a lover to keep me penned in. No, it's just the opposite. I don't really enjoy the bars for their social side."

"But sometimes you just need to get out, right?"

"Exactly. I'm Desmond, by the way," he added, extending his hand.

"Tony. Pleased to meet you, I'm sure." The ironic tone of his greeting was belied by the sincerity of his charming smile and the warm strength of his handshake. Desmond flinched inwardly at the human contact and felt a surge of need.

"So, Tony, I take it you're a local boy, since you seem to be at home here. Are you still in some sort of school?"

"Well, yes and no to the local boy, and do I look so young that you need to check to see if I'm of legal age?"

"Not at all, really, but I admit that from a distance I couldn't quite tell if you were man or boy—forgetting, of course, about the legal drinking age. But I really just wondered if you might be in graduate school or something like. There's the air of the scholar about you."

"Damn, it must be these clothes," he returned, looking down at his faded, striped button-down and somewhat rumpled khakis. "I'm giving the wrong impression."

"Not at all. Please don't be worried about that. You have just the right costume for this place, I should think."

"You *are* courtly! Well, thanks, I guess. I was a student fairly recently, but not here. I moved here two years ago, after college. I'm 24."

"I'm not about to tell you *my* age, at least not yet. Where was school and home?"

"Both in Meadeville, Pennsylvania. Allegheny College. You've probably never heard of it."

"I have indeed. A good small school but not too well-known outside the region. You mustn't be so unsure of yourself; it betrays your recent arrival in New York. You should boldly throw out the name like a challenge! *I* went to Allegheny, and I'm *proud* of it! That's the only way to fix those smarty-pants Ivy Leaguers."

Tony laughed again, the anxiety line gone from his brow. He shifted his weight from one foot to another and lowered his gaze bashfully. Desmond smiled broadly at the feeling of desire that shivered through him, accompanied, oddly, by a need to know more. He was drawn to this young man by his resemblance to Jeffrey, startled by a feeling of unexpected urgency. His usual technique would be to charm with soft words, to reel in the fish he had hooked with his eyes. But now he wanted to talk. This was no greenhorn country lad before him. His coyness was not without calculation. Desmond was intrigued.

"Where did *you* go to school?" Tony asked suddenly, before Desmond could speak.

"Oh." Desmond was caught off-guard. "Well, Oxford, if you must know. But I assure you, that's ancient history, and what I want to know is, what did you study?" Seeing the young man's hesitation, he added, "Seriously, I want to know."

Tony looked slightly downcast. "Not that it's done me any damn good, but I got all interested in antiques and their history and the way people in the past furnished their houses."

"You mean the decorative arts, or material culture, as the museum lingo puts it?"

"Right, but I never use those terms, because people always think it means I'm a decorator or an anthropologist. How did you know—do you collect?"

"In a way. I'm also involved with the Museum of the City of New York. My family's lived here a long time, and I'm sort of intrigued by default. Surely you can't get a degree in it?"

"Well, no, but I put together a composite degree in American studies, with some art history."

"How resourceful of you," Desmond said warmly. "Now, I want you to tell me about what you've done and what you liked best. In the meantime, let me buy you another drink." Desmond placed his hand gently on Tony's elbow and steered him toward the bar, astonished at his attraction to this man, simultaneously giddy with physical need and fascinated by the candor and freshness he found there. He had not felt this way about a potential pickup in many years and was all at sea. But more important, he didn't feel his loneliness, and he was determined to keep that feeling at bay for as long as possible.

The two men sat at the bar and talked, some about Tony's schooling, some about his inability to get a job in his chosen profession—museum work—since coming to New York, but mostly they talked about *things*. Desmond's own love of objects had been developed over many years as a collector as he furnished and finished and refined his house. Every object within his rooms had meaning to him, a personal recollection that returned at his touch. For all his distant involvement with the museum, he had never met anyone—certainly no one so young—who appreciated things as much for the stories they told as for their beauty and value. Desmond was as attracted to the young man's enthusiasm as he was to his beauty. This was no superficial style queen. This was a man who saw the soul of an object and could divine its meaning.

Desmond's possessions were a shelter for his past; his house was the shelter of his present. His memories were stored in his things, as

13

if they were dry-cell batteries he could reach for should his energy start to fade. He had never been able to make this understood to his small circle of friends; they had always looked at him as if he were a poor, demented antiquarian, trapped in the past. Tony, however, seemed to understand exactly what he meant—that his objects kept him in touch with the past and at the same time freed him from it. It almost felt as if Tony shared something of Desmond's history— which was patently impossible. The young man knew how liberating knowledge about the past could be, and it gave him an uncanny understanding of history that Desmond had never encountered. Again an eerie sensation of déjà vu lifted the short hairs on his neck. Could it be…?

After an hour of such talk, Desmond was infatuated. He never took his eyes away from Tony's, yet not once did he resort to the seductive banter he was accustomed to using in making a catch. The strange chatter about things had forged a link between them that was as sexual as it was intellectual. The young man was far more than another casual pickup; but just how much more Desmond didn't dare ask himself.

At a lull in the conversation, Desmond turned and placed his finally empty wineglass on the bar and turned back to Tony. "Why don't we carry on this train of thought somewhere else? It's wretchedly late, and the smoke is destroying my eyes." The last was not true, but it was as good an excuse as any.

Tony hesitated, his amiable smile frozen. Then he too put his glass on the bar. When he again faced Desmond, the crease of worry had reappeared on his brow and the thin, tight smile was uncomfortable.

"Sure, Desmond, that'd be nice—really. It's just that I didn't think, uh, well I was so busy talking to you…"

The room seemed to Desmond to have gone entirely dark and silent but for these halting words. He said to Tony in a dead voice, "What's the matter, am I not attractive enough for you? Too old?"

"No, not at all. That's not it—honestly. You're great-looking, really—just my type. It's just that I don't, uh, can't…"

The last words were lost in the crowd owing to Tony's mumbling, but Desmond barely caught them, unbelievingly. "What was that?" he snapped, his voice cold.

"I, uh, don't go for free, Desmond. It would have to be 50."

"Fifty dollars?"

"Yes. Fifty." Tony's eyes once again met Desmond's but then dropped quickly to his shoes.

"I'm sorry, Tony. I didn't understand. I'm afraid I don't play that game." Desmond's voice was icy, but he strained to keep it from cracking with frustration and disappointment. A hustler! In this bar, of all places—and such a man! Desmond's infatuation crashed about him like shattered glass, making his mind reel. How could he have so misjudged? To think that he had been considering asking him to his house! He turned and started to shoulder his way through the still-heavy crowd, his face a mask. He was almost to the door when a tug at his sleeve stopped him, and he turned. Tony faced him.

"Please don't go! I'm sorry! Forget it!"

Desmond was stunned by the change on the young man's face. His eyes were wide, fearful, shimmering now with barely held-back tears. His was the face of desperation.

"Let me come with you. Please, Desmond. It's only that I needed the money. But I just want to be with you now. Forget the money. Please."

Desmond continued to stare, dumbfounded, at the beautiful, wretched face, at a loss for what to say. He raised his free hand and placed it over Tony's, which still clutched at his jacket.

"All right, Tony, come with me. We'll forget the money."

Outside the bar Desmond hailed a taxi and directed the driver to his house. He closed the blurred Plexiglas partition and turned to Tony, who had hardly raised his eyes from his feet since they'd made their exit.

"I'm not quite sure why I'm doing this. Have you hustled before?"

"Not much—not for long. I swear!" Again the pleading eyes looked into Desmond's. Desmond's stare pierced deep and found nothing false.

"But why? You didn't give any indication…"

"I'm no pro. It's just that I've been here two years, working as a waiter or shop clerk. I lost my last job two months ago. Had to give up my apartment a month ago 'cause I couldn't pay the rent. Now I'm in a sleazy hotel—not quite a welfare hotel but not much above. I haven't any money left. So I've been hustling for the past few weeks. Just enough to get by. I'm not very good at it." At these last words Tony seemed to relax, and a small sigh of laughter escaped his mouth.

"Dear God," Desmond said quietly, caressing Tony's hand absently, as a nurse might a patient's. "Don't you know what danger you might be in? Weren't you afraid at all?"

"Not really. That place we were in isn't very scary. My hotel's more frightening by far. Sometimes it was just a relief not to have to go back there, as much as the money."

"What about AIDS, Tony? What about crazies who want to hurt you?"

"There wasn't anything like that, Desmond. I wasn't trying for rough trade. Maybe just a nice older guy—a preppy too far beyond youth to get his ideal without a fee. Really, Desmond, I never did anything unsafe—no one ever wanted me to. They needed companionship, and I needed money. And they were gentle, affectionate. It's a lonely city."

"No need to tell me that," Desmond replied softly. "Why couldn't you have just gone back to Pennsylvania?" His eyes kept probing, looking for evasions.

"Can't. My parents are none too pleased that I'm gay. I told them after I moved here, convinced that I'd be all set in a week. They didn't react very well and still aren't relating to me like a son. They keep in touch, but they say they want me to be cured and that if I would only come home, they'd find me a good doctor, and so on. You know."

"You can't cope with that, I can understand. But you can't go on hustling."

"I don't know what I'll do. I don't see any alternative for the moment."

"There has to be one."

Tony made no response, and they rode silently the rest of the way, Desmond's hand resting gently on top of Tony's in the darkness of the rushing taxi.

In front of the house, Desmond paid the cabdriver as Tony stared up at the brick facade, with its neat dark green shutters and white marble Ionic columns flanking the recessed front door.

"What a wonderful house!" he said softly as Desmond started up the steps, fumbling with his keys. "I didn't think there were any left in this part of town. When was it built?"

"In 1820. It used to be one of a dozen on the block, but it's the only completely intact one left."

"Did you renovate it yourself? It's a beautiful job, from what I can see." Tony came up the steps behind Desmond and stood at his side. Desmond saw him run his fingers down the flutes of one of the columns, like a rancher judging horseflesh.

"Hardly, Tony. It's never been renovated, only kept up."

"What? How do you mean?" Tony turned to Desmond with a quizzical smile.

"I've lived here all my life, practically. An ancestor of mine built it, and it's never left the family."

"Really? That's incredible. This neighborhood's changed so much, I wouldn't have thought there would be any old guard at all. You must be pleased with the way it's gotten trendy again."

"Yes, sometimes. I must say, I miss the quiet of the days when it wasn't fashionable to live off lower Broadway."

Desmond unlocked the tall, paneled front doors and went ahead of Tony into a dark vestibule. He pulled off his tweed overcoat and hung it on a turned mahogany coatrack. A small mahogany bench was the only other object in the marble-tiled entryway. "No closets inside the hall, so just park your coat there."

Tony obeyed, and Desmond ushered him into the hall. With a flick of a switch, a bell-shaped cut class lantern blazed, illuminating a long narrow hall. It too was paved with marble tile, diagonally set in a black-and-white checkerboard. At the left a high narrow staircase with mahogany rails disappeared into shadow. On the right Tony could see two wide double doorways, the mahogany doors closed, the sparkling white of the elaborate classical door frames contrasting with the pearly gray of the walls. The walls themselves were scored to imitate stone. Between the doorways was a long neoclassical settee with caned back and sides, fitted with loose cushions of a dark red wool. Flanking this were two pairs of chairs, similarly covered.

"That's a great sofa. Is it original to the house?"

"Yes and no. It's earlier than the house but came into the house when it was built. It used to be in the front parlor but was replaced by something more modern in the 1850s." Desmond was feeling needful and not a little impatient with Tony's distractions.

"Can I see?" asked Tony, sounding almost greedy.

"Yes, but not right now. We've got other things to take care of." Desmond pulled Tony to him, kissing him with a fervent gentleness that took Tony's mind off furniture. After a brief hesitation the younger man's lips parted, allowing Desmond's tongue to flicker across even teeth. *No tobacco*, Desmond noted with relief, letting the pleasure of the moment overtake his detachment. At last he pulled away.

"Let's go upstairs. If you're a good boy, you can have a tour tomorrow." And he led Tony up into the darkness of the second floor.

Tony's enthusiasm for the master bedroom's furniture was quickly replaced by his physical ardor. Desmond decided to leave no light burning in the room to make sure Tony didn't get distracted again. Off came the penny loafers, the heavy wool socks, and the button-down shirt. Desmond ran his hands slowly down the would-be curator's smooth, muscled chest and belly, thrilling to the silky feel of his skin. He unfastened Tony's belt, then reached around him to gently massage the tight back muscles, starting at his shoulder blades and working his way downward. He slipped his hands into the waistband of the khaki slacks and with a deft motion shucked them off, caressing the warm curve of buttocks as he pushed both trousers and boxer shorts to Tony's ankles. On his knees, he looked up into Tony's eyes and smiled wickedly, then rose and stripped off his own clothes with little ceremony, revealing a trim, taut, ivory-pale body lightly dusted with dark curly hair. His arousal was apparent, and he delighted at Tony's smile. He moved forward and embraced the young man, gradually lowering him down onto the white counterpane of the high-posted bed. The coolness of the linen contrasted with the increasing heat of their mingled flesh, and Desmond gave himself up to comforting passion.

They were like two schoolboys discovering their desire for each other for the first time. They touched, rubbed, and kissed, by turns gentle and ardent. Their lovemaking was like a spring breeze to Desmond's winter-bruised soul. They romped happily and intensely until both were exhausted and content.

Tony lay back on the huge square pillows, dreamily running the back of his hand up and down Desmond's stomach, his eyes half-closed. Desmond too was relaxed, but not somnolent. Sleep would come for him soon, but not yet. He touched Tony's cheek, now feeling the bristle of the next day's beard. Tony sighed.

"Promise you'll take me all through the house tomorrow? I can't even see this bed, and it looks incredible from here." He turned briefly to Desmond and gave him a tired grin before settling back on his pillows.

"I promise, Tony. Right after breakfast."

"Breakfast—so after all this I'm getting breakfast?"

"That's the advantage of not charging, dear boy. It makes you a guest and thus a friend. Breakfast is part of the deal."

Tony looked momentarily pained at the reminder of his unwanted sideline, but Desmond smoothed his worry line with another kiss, and he dozed gradually off to sleep.

Desmond had never before brought a trick back to the house. If his partner's place wasn't appropriate, he had either hired a hotel room or gone without. Any hint of gold digging had always sent him running, for New York was full of pretty boys looking to be kept, and few sugar daddies could offer what he could. So here he was with a would-be curator and an amateur hustler in the heart of his sanctum sanctorum. And it felt exactly right. None of the expected alarm bells. But why?

Tony rumbled quietly as he rolled partway onto his side. His breathing was regular and deep once he settled, and Desmond knew he wouldn't awaken until morning. Sexually fulfilled, Desmond now looked at Tony with a longing that wasn't lust yet was just as urgent. He reached out and stroked the dark blond hair, moving it away from the high brow. He was filled with mixed emotions and hesitated over the urging of an even stronger need than that which Tony had so beautifully answered. Here was a special man, Desmond thought, a man unlike any he'd ever met since meeting Roger, so long ago. He was afraid to go ahead, afraid of shattering the spell that his lonely, loving man-boy had cast over him.

But then, thought Desmond, *perhaps it's just what I ought to do. Perhaps that will be* my *part in the spell.* He hesitated a moment longer; then, his need burning like an inner fire, he decided.

Desmond leaned over Tony's sleeping form and kissed him softly on the cheek. Then, hovering over the man's head, he opened his mouth and drew back his lower jaw slightly. With a mental command that was virtually unconscious, Desmond began to extend his upper canines until they glittered like two ivory pen points in the dimness of the night. Gently, very gently, so as to be precise and painless, Desmond lowered his open mouth to the velvet curve of Tony's neck and answered the inexorable call of his race.

CHAPTER 2

Cosmo leaped up onto the bed, purring loudly, annoyed at having not been fed for several hours. Desmond grabbed her and got off the bed, padding naked into the hall and down the two flights of stairs to the kitchen. Having put out a dish of food for the cat, he ran back upstairs, the chill air of the house shivering across his skin and raising gooseflesh.

Back in the bedroom, he slipped between the linen sheets, pulling the white candlewick coverlet over Tony's immobile form. Desmond snuggled up to the warm body beside him, then, on second thought, reached over and switched on the bedside lamp. Already the marks on Tony's neck were fading, and only a faint bruise remained to indicate Desmond's actions of a short while before. Tomorrow Tony would wear a handsome hickey and might feel a bit sluggish, but no more. Desmond smiled. There would be no need for worry. The blood had been delicious, and he was still tingling from its effect. He snuggled back beside the sleeping Tony, enjoying the radiance of his slender body.

As he called sleep to claim him for the night, he thought again of Tony's face in the bar earlier that evening. That desperate, pleading look had been the key, he realized. He had seen that look before, and only once before, in his lifetime. It had been Roger's face looking at him that way; and it had been exactly 200 years ago.

Desmond Beckwith arrived in Paris in the spring of his 65th year, ostensibly to spend time overseeing the workings of the French branch of his enterprise. This was no great surprise, either to those in the London office or to the servants at Beckwith House in the country. Desmond periodically made trips to the continent to look after his business in the 40 years since he had inherited it from his late father, Sir Charles Beckwith. It was Sir Charles who had founded the small London counting house that had grown into a powerful banking concern with legendary assets. It was Sir Charles who, upon being knighted by Queen Anne for his financial aid to the government, had built Beckwith House in 1706.

He had been just 20 years old when his monetary daring had netted him celebrity at court. Within two years of this initial triumph, he had established his fortune, gained a knighthood, and married the 17-year-old Lady Anne Desmond, a famous beauty and the daughter of a peer.

It was for his young bride that Beckwith House had been built. Sir Charles spent as much time as was reasonable in the country but had never wanted his wife to join him in London, where he lived simply, keeping rooms over the banking house. Lady Anne apparently didn't mind the arrangement and lived contentedly at Beckwith House. The only shadow on the marriage was the lack of an heir—a common enough worry with a large estate at question. But after 18 years the still-young Lady Anne grew great with child and in 1724 delivered a son to a delighted Sir Charles. She was as happy as he with the dark-haired baby, named Desmond; but the birth had taken much out of her, and she sickened in the following year. After an unusually harsh winter, Lady Anne succumbed to a lung inflammation, leaving a tiny son and a bereft husband.

At 41, Sir Charles threw himself into the raising of the boy, with the memory of his beloved wife strong within him. As the boy grew and was educated, he was trained not to be merely an aristocratic dilettante—something much in vogue in those years—but to be a man of business as well. Familiarity with finances and commerce made social roads somewhat rocky, but it gave one an edge in doing business with the landed families. Desmond was educated to be savvy and *savant*. It was with him that the future of Beckwith House lay. And so Desmond Beckwith had fulfilled his father's wish and had readily taken over the banking house upon Sir Charles's death at the ripe old age of 65, in the year 1749.

Desmond had subsequently established the Paris House of Beckwith, and it was Desmond who kept rooms above the bank both in London and in Paris, with Beckwith House as his only seat. But the Desmond who had returned from the Continent in 1747 was not the Desmond Sir Charles had sent away on the Grand Tour in 1745. Sir Charles never knew what had changed his son nor even exactly how he was changed, but the difference was apparent.

On this Desmond mused as his carriage lumbered into Paris in the spring of 1789. He had come to attend to business in the increasingly turbulent city on the Seine. The bank was flourishing and complicated and needed much attending to. But this was not the only reason the younger Beckwith had returned at this particular moment.

He had been warned, many years ago, that his 65th year would be that of his first regeneration, and he was caught up in the fear of what he did not know. Baron Tsolnay had explained much to him but had not been able to elaborate on the details of the regeneration, for the Baron had been almost 70 at the time of his transformation and thus had been doomed to old age for all time. But, he had assured Desmond, the legend was that 65 years was the full cycle of life, and he had heard it from several sources, reliable ones. But he did not know the process or the physical effects or the dangers, and Desmond dreaded the approaching anniversary of his birthday as he had dreaded nothing in his life thus far.

Once established in the sparse, old-fashioned rooms above the bank, Desmond fell into his familiar patterns. He kept no servant, doing what minimal housekeeping there was himself. This caused some comment, but since he was outwardly a man of simple wants and certainly lavish enough with his wealth where others were concerned, no one took it ill. His own reasons were deeper. He had never kept a personal servant, not since his youth, since Jeffrey Chapman. Even more so now, with God-knows-what looming before him, Desmond wanted to be able to be entirely by himself.

At Beckwith House he had had his own apartments—his father's, in fact. He had given strict orders that no servant was to enter his chambers, on penalty of dismissal, and none ever had. He was a good master, and generous in the way he ran the estate. The larders were full, the gardens abundant, the guests minimal. All in all, the staff of Beckwith House could not fault their kind master. If he wanted to make his own bed and dust his own rooms (if he did dust them at all), it was, after all, his house.

So here in Paris the precedent was well-known, and he was undisturbed when closeted in his chambers. He socialized very little but attended concerts, gave small dinners for business associates at which he never ate (complaining of a delicate digestive system), and spent hours reading. He devoured histories, classics, dramas, comedies, and romances, starting with medieval works such as *Le Roman de la Rose*. It was much noted that, for a banker, he was an impressive scholar. He would lose himself in his books, taking journeys back into the past, sharing quests with chevaliers, and savoring the language of the playwright.

His only vice, people said uncritically, seemed to be wine. He loved good wines, sherries, and ports but never touched stronger liquors. He was a puzzle to most who knew him, thought cold by some and arrogant by others, but nonetheless he was respected by everyone and liked more often than not.

The spring and early summer passed without event, Desmond keeping earnestly busy with the bank as well as his regular pastimes. But he had already set the wheels in motion to protect himself from

25

whatever might happen at his birthday. Twenty years earlier he had established a fictitious wife in France, claiming to have had a son by her, named Desmond. As Desmond's own mother had, Mrs. Beckwith lived in seclusion in the country, but no one at the banks ever knew where, beyond that it was outside Paris.

As his birthday approached Desmond prepared a letter for the office manager at the bank, giving instructions for the latter part of July. During this time Desmond intended to visit his wife and son in the country and to bring his son back with him to join the firm officially, now that he was of age. He presumed the visit would be about three weeks, and, since he was feeling a little tired, he would take advantage of the country air to rest a bit before plunging his child into the world of business. And so, three days before his 65th birthday, Desmond Beckwith climbed into a hired coach to spend a holiday in the French countryside with his family.

Of course, no one at the bank knew that he left the coach at the Porte de Vincennes and walked back to his rooms under cover of darkness. Even at 65, Desmond wasn't fatigued at all by the exercise. His eyes were as good as a cat's in the dark, and his acute hearing and smell enabled him to avoid people if he so desired.

But there was one person that Desmond did, intentionally, meet, though he didn't learn his name. In the sultry shadows beneath the clipped chestnuts of the Palais Royale gardens, the elderly Englishman who spoke French so well offered a few coins to a young man loitering in the summer moonlight. Having listened to the older man talk softly and soothingly for a few minutes, the boy had seemed to swoon, and Desmond had helped him to sit on a bench.

Then, had there been anyone to watch, they would have seen the old man seemingly kiss the boy's throat for a few minutes, strangely still, like a statue. Following this the viewer, had there been one, would have seen Desmond gently lay the apparently sleeping boy down on the bench, smoothing his hair with his hand. The boy himself, upon awakening in the morning, would find only an embarrassing bruise on his neck and a number of gold coins in his pocket.

Thus went Desmond's only meeting with a human being on his nighttime return to the Paris bank. He slipped quietly into his upper-floor apartments, double-bolting the doors and windows to prevent any intrusion. For two days, in the shuttered rooms, he read by candlelight, wearing only a nightshirt and dressing gown. He padded about barefoot, lest someone below hear during business hours.

At dawn on July 5, he awoke from his accustomed slumber—six hours of rest so close to death that he feared anyone should find him so. He could will sleep upon himself at any time, but once in its grip he was helpless. He could have gone without sleep but felt, as he had in seeking out the youth in the gardens, that he needed all his strength. This night's sleep had been troubled, filled with dreams and swirling memories of his childhood and youth. He had dreamed of his father and of Jeffrey and of Baron Tsolnay. He rarely had dreams, and never of such vividness. It was a sign, no doubt, of the coming change.

As his wits grew sharper, he was aware that he did not feel as usual; there was a lassitude and at the same time a nervousness quivering within. He rose from the bed and stared into the old gilt looking glass above the dressing table. The familiar face looked back at him: a handsome man for 65, myriad fine lines creasing his eyes, mouth, and neck. Hair heavily streaked with gray. Nothing had changed, not yet.

Just as Desmond was turning toward the basin and ewer to wash his face, he was staggered by a wave of dizziness that brought him to his knees. His vision swam, his eyes unable to focus. As he felt his way along the floor to the bed and pulled himself up into it, he knew that it had begun.

By midday a fever was raging in Desmond's head, blocking out all sense of his surroundings. His whole body seethed with an internal fire unlike anything he had ever known, like molten lead flowing in him. He lay paralyzed, yet strangely not in pain, for an untold amount of time, unaware of what went on around him; aware only of the extraordinary sensations of the transformation within. It was not entirely unlike the first transformation, which had made him as he was. But this was far more powerful.

He could not open his eyes, which saw only eddies of fire and waves of darkness alternating with light. And always the heat, as if the flames of hell were before him and he was coming to Judgment. He knew no fear now, nor any sense of strangeness. As the fever burned and his heart pounded, Desmond felt strangely at peace, letting a new sensation of ecstasy wash over him. Eventually he ceased to be conscious of even these things.

At one point Desmond was wakened slightly from his rapture but could only indistinctly make out noises in the distance. He felt a surge of instinctive alarm within his mind but could do nothing to make his body respond. And so he lapsed back into oblivion.

When Desmond finally came to his senses, he awoke suddenly, with a clarity of vision that made him start. The white hangings of his bed were above him as they had always been. He felt relaxed to the point of inertia, and yet he was vitally aware of his fingertips, his toes, even the disarray of his hair as it lay crushed on the pillow beneath his head.

He could hear the heavy silence of the room and then gradually became aware of a fly buzzing aimlessly in the shuttered window. He still felt the heat and then realized that it was simply a July day in Paris—if indeed it was still only July, for he had no idea of the date. Then he became aware of his own sweat, which had soaked the sheet beneath him and run down his temples into the bedclothes. His nightshirt clung to him unpleasantly, and he longed to be rid of it.

He sat up slowly, testing his movements and finding them easy. He rose, pulled the wet nightshirt over his head, and moved carefully toward the dressing table, hoping only that the water had not all evaporated. As he approached he looked ahead and stopped dead in his tracks. Staring back at him in amazement from the mirrored surface of the glass was a handsome dark-haired youth with long curling tresses and dancing hazel eyes. The wiry, angular body of an old man had been replaced with the supple musculature of a young one. He stepped up to the looking glass, placing his hands on the light stubble that grew on his now firm and smooth face. The hands themselves were unseamed with wear, unspotted with age, and needed only a washing and a manicure to be deemed beautiful. The regeneration was complete, and Desmond Beckwith was again 21 years old.

Both his watch and the clock on the chimney piece in his sitting room had stopped, so Desmond had no clear notion of the time, although from the sun's position he had guessed it to be mid morning. Daring only to open one shutter slightly at the back of his rooms, Desmond shaved and washed himself as best he could with the remains of the stagnant water in the basin. He would have to have a proper bath and have his hair looked to later on, before he made his official return to life—as the son of Desmond Beckwith.

He dressed himself in a plain suit of brown linen so as to attract as little attention as possible to himself and waited for nightfall before departing. In the meantime, he straightened up the rooms and remade his bed in readiness for its new occupant.

Finally the sun settled in the west, and amid the cooler shadows of twilight, Desmond slipped out of the bank as he had entered it. He made his way through the backstreets of the quarter, seeing very few people and none that he recognized. He was struck by the odd quiet in the streets and noted also the unusual litter strewn about. Although the city was no cleaner than most at the best of times, there were signs that things had been dropped—or dumped—in the streets and then simply left where they fell. Sometimes during festival days he had noticed a similar augmentation of the general urban detritus, but he knew of no major summer holiday to which he could attribute this instance.

Once he heard the approach of a rowdy knot of men and women and, wishing to remain unseen, pulled back into an alleyway. As they passed him, shouting and singing with an almost frenetic gaiety, he further noted that they wore kitchen implements as side arms and grimy knitted red caps. They looked like the disheveled members of some outlaw fraternal group, but of a sort Desmond had never before encountered in Paris. A shudder passed through him after they had gone from sight, and Desmond felt doubly glad to have avoided them. He had never seen the common people carrying weapons in this manner and vaguely recalled the momentary disturbance in his regeneration delirium when his semiconscious mind had sounded an alarm to which he could not respond.

With the whole night before him, Desmond sought to fulfill the thirst that began to burn at him as powerfully as the fever of recent days. He made his way to the Luxembourg Gardens and soon found a young man, not unlike the one he had recently met as an old man, and like enough in significant ways. The difference, Desmond quickly noted in this case, was that there was no need to talk of money and that his newly regained beauty was to be payment enough for what they both seemed to need.

As they stood and talked in the deeper shadows of the tree-lined alleys, Desmond's voice beginning its soothing work, his partner softly caressed his cheek and uttered in a low voice, "It was fortunate we found each other. There have been few people to talk to in *le jardin* these past weeks, and I was almost despairing of finding a friend."

"Why so?" asked Desmond with a seductive smile. "I have never been unlucky when I have searched for companionship beneath the trees."

"How can you say this? It seems you have been asleep for a fortnight. But then, your voice tells me that you are not French. Even so, unless you have been under a spell, how could you not know what is going on?"

The strange knot of misbegotten revelers reappeared in Desmond's mind, and a chill made its way up his back. Resisting this hint of fear, he pulled the young man to him, kissing him with a nonchalant passion, and then offhandedly replied, "Ah, well, then, I have indeed been under a spell, as you say. An illness, in fact, which has kept me rather less aware of day-to-day activities since early in July. Perhaps I have not followed closely events from my sickbed. Why don't you tell me what has happened?"

"What has happened, indeed!" said his companion, his tone of teasing scorn softened by Desmond's physical closeness. "No less than the Bastille itself has fallen to the forces of Liberty. The king and his consort are imprisoned, and the aristocracy has begun to flee in panic for their lives. In short, my handsome fellow, we have had a revolution. The France that was is no more."

In spite of his efforts, Desmond stiffened at these words and looked searchingly into the young man's eyes. "Truly, you say? What about foreigners—businesses, I mean—what of them?"

"If that is what you are, then you are lucky. Private businesses held by foreigners are not being touched—that is, as long as they comply with the rules of the new republic. If you are English, as I suspect, then you need not fear, unless you have been working against the republic; and since you have, as you say, been so ill, I doubt you are in danger."

With this Desmond's calm returned somewhat, and he allowed himself to be caught up in the pleasure of the moment. For all the drama of the past weeks, his willing partner seemed more concerned with pleasure than with liberty and responded exquisitely to Desmond's charms. But now the pleasure was heightened, since the newly reborn Desmond did not have to rely so heavily on his hypnotic voice and verbal spellbinding. His renewed youth gave him a new power, one he had nearly forgotten over the past 20 years, and that power made him giddy. Lust had never replaced what Jeffrey had given him, but it had kept loneliness at bay.

As age had burdened him, even the well-kept age to which his nature was inclined, his lust had grown of necessity more one-sided, and the old man had had to employ all his wiles to capture a beautiful stranger. As often as not, he had been expected to offer some remuneration as well, something that had not increased his happiness or pleasure in the moment. This, however, was far different from his recent experience. Here his lust was matched, perhaps exceeded by, this glossy youth. Wandering among the nighttime shadows, this lonely fellow had been drawn to him as to a magnet, and his urgent need was palpable in the heavy air.

The two men kissed feverishly in the still, warm darkness, tongues exploring, bodies pressed together. Such kissing was a delight too little enjoyed by Desmond in recent years, and his fierceness startled his companion, who pulled back, a puzzled smile on his lips. But Desmond had no patience for explanations, so intense were his twin hungers, and he roughly pulled the other back to him, gripping him to his chest with one arm as he wrenched off the other's loose linen shirt, throwing it to one side. He tarried only momentarily, gently nipping at one, then the other of the dark nipples on the man's shaggy chest, and glided his tongue lightly down the middle of his work-hardened belly. Then Desmond quickly dropped to his knees and, impatient with the fastening strings of his partner's homespun breeches, pulled them down around his knees with the sound of rending cloth. Sensing more amazement than fear in his partner's unmoving silence, he hesitated only a moment, eyes flickering upward, before reaching to grip the muscular buttocks and assuaging his desire in the musky sweetness of the other man's loins.

Once the needs of the flesh were satisfied, Desmond's gentle voice continued to caress the youth, sending him into a sleeping swoon from which he would awake with nothing worse than a sense of having perhaps had a drop too much the night before. As the man's breath began to sigh with the regularity of sleep, Desmond laid him gently on the ground and turned his head to one side, revealing the suntanned ruddiness of his muscular neck. He hesitated as a faint guilty pang shivered through him. For all of their mutual attraction, Desmond would take away from this encounter more than he gave.

Sexually gratified and filled with the sense of his own power, Desmond felt the full predatory nature of his being. At moments like this he understood how much his kind would be feared if the world could ever imagine they were more than myth. Somewhere at the back of his mind came the sound of wolves howling, and goose-flesh pricked his skin. He shook himself slightly to rid himself of the sensation. Then, relaxing his jaw, canines extended, he leaned down and carefully attached his mouth to his partner's salty skin. Pressing the tools of his hunger home, he found the great artery that carried blood from the heart to the brain.

The flow of hot blood, without which he had gone for weeks, made his head spin, but he kept his grip so as not to spill a drop. Wave after wave of shimmering redness seemed to pass before his tightly closed eyes, and Desmond felt himself becoming sexually aroused once more. Keeping his fangs embedded in the other man's neck and drinking deeply, he lowered himself still more and pulled the limp body roughly against his own, so that their naked torsos met, slippery with sweat. With each ecstatic draft of blood, Desmond could feel his heartbeat synchronize with his host's. The twin throbbing began to pound louder and louder inside his skull, and for one panicky moment he feared he might drink too much and kill his lover. Again the sound of wolves filled his memory, and as he reached a second fevered climax, he lifted his head and let escape a low feral cry to drown out the ghostly howling. For a moment he lay panting, senses alert, knowing how vulnerable the two of them were, lying unclothed and glistening with the evidence of their secret lives. Then Desmond noticed that the other man was still bleeding from his neck wound, and he bent over him while his tongue did its work. His saliva was potent with a healing agent that would hide the scars of his actions, leaving only a bruise, which itself would disappear in the course of a day.

He left the man sleeping in the grass where they had lain together, a faint smile on his parted lips, as if some happy dream were causing it. Desmond thought briefly about leaving some money to replace the torn clothing but decided against it. The young man had not been seeking gold, and Desmond felt he had gotten everything he had wanted.

As dawn was washing the rooftops of Paris with its sparkling light, Desmond reached an unprepossessing inn on the distant outskirts of the city. He was uncertain as to what sort of reception, if any, he might expect, given the events of the past weeks. He was still not sure of the date and had forgotten to ask his companion in the public garden.

His knock at the door was answered by a middle-aged woman who peered fearfully out of a crack at him before opening to let him enter. He explained that he had just arrived from some distance on foot and needed only water enough to wash, for which he would gladly pay. She seemed relieved at his simple requests and gladly accepted the money he offered. Travelers, it seems, had been few in recent days because of the revolution and the strictures of the republic. Desmond noted a knitted red cap lying on a table in the corner of the kitchen where he waited for his room to be readied. He also found a Paris paper and noted its date—July 26. Three weeks he had lain in his bed as his years had fallen away and his youth was revived. He was still not sure of what those three weeks had done to France, although it seemed that his bank would possibly be unaltered.

He washed carefully, dressing his hair simply with a black ribbon to hold the queue. He was glad that, even as an old man, he had never affected powdered wigs, which he knew would be dangerously aristocratic now, and that he had chosen a simple costume for his arrival at Beckwith's Bank, Paris. Asking his hostess about hiring a carriage, he was greeted with a confused story about the difficulty of such things but finally managed to arrange to have a neighboring shopkeeper drive him into the city in a grand carriage that had clearly not always belonged to him. As Desmond settled somewhat gingerly inside the carriage, he noted the damaged panel on the door, where the paint had been recently scraped away. The interior was none too clean, despite evidence of not-too-distant luxury in its appointments. Desmond guessed that this was the conveyance of some unlucky noble and that the marred door indicated the removal of a family crest. Desmond wondered whether the carriage was all this unhappy aristocrat had lost and shuddered inwardly at his own instinctive answer.

The hired coachman held up his end of the bargain and managed to get Desmond through the confused streets of the city. Desmond noted many of the knitted red caps and kitchen weapons on the populace of the new republic. He also noted a total absence of the conspicuously fashionable people Paris normally exhibited. In one instance, as they passed the facade of a noble private hotel, Desmond saw the ominous wording of a placard pasted to the door, declaring the house to be property of the nation.

As the carriage finally pulled up before the street doors of the bank, Desmond alighted and paid his driver, who only muttered his thanks before lurching away into the teeming street traffic. Taking a deep breath and pulling out the papers he had prepared while still in England, Desmond Beckwith the younger entered the place of business he had just inherited.

The clerks and other staff in the bank were not surprised to meet the younger Mr. Beckwith, although they marveled at the striking likeness between father and son. They were, however, dismayed at the news that the senior Beckwith had fallen ill while visiting his wife and son and had died after lingering for nearly two weeks. He was buried, his son said, in the village churchyard. Desmond embroidered his prepared speech, adding that the tumultuous events of July 14 and the fall of the French monarchy had been a fearful blow, and concern over the fate of the bank had most likely hastened his untimely end. As his only heir, Desmond explained, he knew his duty was to carry on in his father's place, as the senior Mr. Beckwith had wished. To this effect he drew out the letters outlining the late Mr. Beckwith's wishes as to his son's duties, stating that he had full confidence in his abilities and business sense.

At the end of his first day, Desmond ascended to his rooms, leaving the bank staff with the comforting sense that things were going to continue smoothly despite the death of their employer and the fall of their host government. The appearance of the younger Beckwith had reassured the bank, and Desmond was pleased with the way his plans had come off.

And so the new Desmond threw himself again into the routine his elder self had pursued over the years on his sojourns in the French affiliate of the London bank. He began to slowly reacquaint himself with those people who had known his "father" and to become a known quantity in the troubled city, as his "father" had. The business needed much tending to, and just as some of those with whom the old Desmond had associated had just disappeared, so did the French Republic have its influence on the running of the bank.

Although the bank itself was not threatened by the political chaos and anti-aristocratic hostility that boiled like venom in the streets of the capital, a good sum of the assets of Beckwith Bank was aristocratic. These assets, when impounded by the republic, usually remained in the safe council of the Beckwith Bank. When Desmond met with government representatives who wished to withdraw the accounts of an imprisoned nobleman, he had remarkable success in persuading them that this English bank could care for the money of *la république* as well as it had for that of *monsieur le marquis* and that wouldn't it be easier all around to keep the funds secure where they were? Insecurity usually won out over nationalism, and only a few of the aristocratic accounts were lost. Moreover, much of what Beckwith held was tied up in English properties and thus physically out of reach. In these cases it made complete sense to maintain the Beckwith management.

Beckwith's lack of interest in court life under the old regime stood him in good stead during the new. He had always found the French aristocrats who were his clients to be dissipated and prone to extravagant self-indulgence. He had been irritated by their waste of money and appalled at their lack of feeling for those they called their inferiors. Apparently, his feelings had been shared by a great many Frenchmen.

Late in 1789, firmly established in Paris, Desmond left the bank in the hands of his staff and returned to the English headquarters he had supposedly never seen in order to establish himself there as well. The same papers drawn up for the Paris office had been made for the London house, and once again the staff was reassured by the younger Beckwith's presence and startled by his likeness to his late father. Beckwith House too was regained, and after a solemn period of official mourning for the dead lord of the manor, the younger Desmond Beckwith took his rightful place as head of the house. Since the curious habits of Desmond Beckwith had become so much a part of the tradition of the house, Desmond's continuance of his presumed father's solitary life pleased rather than disturbed the people on the estate. His good looks and charming manner swept away doubts that might have lingered about this French-born and -raised son of whom no one knew very much. Moreover, he so reminded the servants of the old Mr. Beckwith that they could only shake their heads, smiling, and tell each other that the apple never falls far from the tree.

CHAPTER 3

For the next few years, Desmond carried on the routines of city and country life, fulfilling his roles as country squire and London banker. But in the winter months of 1792, he began again to hear frightening rumors from the Continent, rumors that suggested that the revolution of 1789 was not only not over but that it was about to enter its worst phase. Fearing for the Paris bank, Desmond once again made his way to France, prepared to do what he could to preserve the interests of the London firm.

In Paris he found that the bank was still untouched but that the staff were terribly concerned for their own safety. No threats had been made, but the atmosphere of the capital was charged with blood, and everyone said that this was just the beginning. And so it was. What would come to be known as the Reign of Terror burst forth in 1793, washing the cobbles of Paris with a wave of death that would redden the Seine as at no time since the Middle Ages. The guillotine raised its sinister silhouette, and the glittering blade soon became the nightmare vision of all whose republican sentiments were in question—and that meant almost everyone. The prisons were full, kept from overfilling only by the tumbrels that daily carried their tragic charges to the scaffold. The excesses of the Bourbon dynasty were soon matched by those of the Directory, and the city of Diderot became a den of political intrigue and public betrayal. The Age of Reason became an Age of Madness.

But life went on in Paris; people of all stations continued to move from day to day, hoping that each would not be their last, generally getting by as people do in times of crisis. So too did Desmond, although his intellectual pursuits were limited and his social life truncated. The public gardens continued to provide him with sustenance, despite a distinct aura of fear that had never existed before. Desmond noted this constancy with some wry amusement, realizing that both of his unorthodox needs placed him so far beyond the pale of government concern that he was in no danger from that quarter. He knew that in this time and place, his inclinations toward those of his own sex would undoubtedly lead him to the guillotine; but he also knew that the republic had bigger game to kill than those of his stripe. As to the other side of his nature, he doubted if it could even be conceived of by the minds who now ran this country—or any other country, in fact.

Imagine his horror one day when, working at his desk in the bank, he was brought the following note, sealed with black wax and written on plain foolscap:

My Dear M. Beckwith—

We have observed with great interest your activities in Paris and would greatly appreciate the opportunity to meet with you at your earliest convenience.

There was no address and no signature. The hand was bold and old-fashioned. Desmond's secretary told him that a messenger was waiting for a reply and ushered in a wizened old man at Desmond's demand.

Alone in the office with the messenger, Desmond began coolly, "I do not think I understand the note your employer has seen fit to send me. Perhaps if you could explain it more fully, I might know then how to respond."

The old man, black eyes shining with a cunning that both chilled Desmond and made him somehow sure that the government of the republic wasn't involved, replied simply, "I can say no more than you read in the note there before you. If you wish to accede to my master's wish, I will return to take you to him this evening. If not, I will trouble you no further."

"But how does your master know me? What does he refer to in the letter?" Desmond asked, concern and curiosity mingling.

"I can say nothing, good sir, beyond what I am ordered to say. I will say, however, that you need not fear my master; that was not the intent of the communication."

"What time, then, should I decide to come to your master?"

"Midnight, sir, as is customary."

"Midnight, customary? I am curious to see what sort of man receives guests at such an hour." After a momentary silence Desmond said to the old man, "Tell your master that Desmond Beckwith looks forward to making his acquaintance."

The little man bowed slightly and smiled. "Very good, Monsieur Beckwith. I will come to fetch you a half hour before the appointed visit to convey you there." And with that he left.

Desmond sat, unthinking, at his desk for some minutes after his visitor's departure, staring at the note in his hands. At last, rising, he crumpled it and threw it into the fireplace. He then settled back at his desk to finish his business.

At 11:30 that evening Desmond was waiting nervously in his sitting room. He had dressed carefully, putting on a dark blue silk suit with linen that was simple but fine. Fashion in Paris these days was austere, which was perfect for him, but he had the impression that he was going to meet someone unusual this evening, to say the least. The plain elegance of the suit, together with his pale skin and dark hair, made him a striking figure. This costume, Desmond reflected, also gave him a somewhat businesslike appearance, in addition to being more appropriate in the tenuous society of republican France.

It had occurred to Desmond, who had read and reread the anonymous note before he burned it, that maybe he was simply dealing with a terrified nobleman who was trying to protect his property through some English business connection. That might explain the vague wording of the note and the strange hour at which he was to meet its author. The more he considered this, the more it seemed logical to him. He began to think that his mind was simply infected with the unreasoning fear that was all too common in Paris these days.

Desmond's thoughts were interrupted with a knock from the street, and he threw on a cloak before going down. In the street his earlier messenger waited for him beside a lumbering old coach of a style not much seen in Paris's more fashionable quarters, even before the revolution. Certain old families used such elderly conveyances as state coaches, but this had none of the pomp of those examples. High-wheeled and boxy, his mysterious host's carriage was painted black and was ornately lined in very worn velvet of the same color. Desmond climbed in, aided by the old messenger, who then surprised him by jumping up on the box to drive the two pawing black horses.

They moved through the quiet Paris streets, for the moment undisturbed by the riotous mobs of people who filled them each day with their calls for blood. Carnage was tiring work, and those citizens most deeply involved savored their sleep, so as to better enjoy the pleasures of the guillotine. Desmond had little followed the progress of the Reign of Terror, noting occasionally the death of a former Beckwith Bank client, whose money had usually been already appropriated by the republican government. He knew slightly of the absurd impromptu courts, which arrested, tried, and condemned people of all stations of life, who may (or more likely may not) have been guilty of anything, to feel the fatal kiss of the maiden of steel. But, sheltered as he was by his nationality and his financial necessity to the republic itself, the gore of modern France had not touched him.

Starting from his reverie after a jolt on the rough paving stones, Desmond peered out of the drawn curtains and was surprised to see

41

that they were lumbering past the ruins of the Bastille. How ironic it was, Desmond mused, that of all the prisons of Paris, the Bastille had in fact been the least used and the least brutal. Whatever the truth of the prisoners' tales of the Bastille, it was more a symbol than anything else. The carriage lumbered on through the even more quiet streets of the Marais, the part of Paris that had been fashionable in the age of Molière. Ancient *hôtels* lined the streets near the Place des Vosges, and it was before one of these that the driver stopped. The old servant leaped with surprising agility from the box and opened the door for Desmond.

The house before them was tall and dark, grand but seemingly ill-kept; it was of the style of François Mansart and certainly dated from the first half of the past century. No light escaped from its shuttered windows. But for the bright brass lion's-mask knocker on the huge entrance door, the house might have been abandoned. Producing a massive iron key fitted with an ornate ormolu grip, Desmond's guide now unlocked that high door and ushered him into the house.

He walked up a wide marble stairway, now lit only by a massive church candlestick that his guide had found burning at the foot of the stairs. Inside, the house was clean and smelled not at all of the must of unused buildings. But everything showed signs of great age. A massive gilt lantern hung, lightless, from a grand stuccoed ceiling, dimly visible in the shadows. At the top of the main staircase, Desmond was shown through a pair of high carved oak doors. As he entered, his cloak was taken and his guide disappeared quietly back into the shadows of the hall.

The scene before him was like a tableau from the past, calling to mind an engraving in the library at Beckwith House. The room was lofty, with an elaborately stuccoed ceiling and elaborate *boiserie* in dark wood on its walls. Two massive ormolu lusters hung, 50 candles burning in each, from the time-tarnished gilding of the ornate plasterwork. The windows—or at least what Desmond presumed to be windows, since all were heavily draped—were hung with black Genoese cut velvet with a ground of gold. The drapery, like the carved and gilt consoles that punctuated the perimeter walls and the dozen or so armchairs of throne-like form, all reflected the taste of the court in the early years of the Sun King. Gilt torchère stands, spaced evenly around the walls, held ormolu girandoles with dozens more burning candles. A fire blazed invitingly in the monumental black marble chimney piece. Tall looking glasses above the consoles doubled the pinpoints of candlelight, to splendid effect.

Ten people were assembled in the vast, strange room talking softly as Desmond entered, falling silent upon seeing him. The strangers ranged in shape, size, and age, two being women, but all wore costumes of modern design, and all wore only black. At the moment he had made his appearance, they were all but one standing. The exception was an obese old man seated in one of the great velvet-covered thrones. He raised his hand in greeting as Desmond approached, taking him for the host.

"Welcome to my home, Monsieur Beckwith. We have been long looking forward to meeting you. I am Gregory Charlon."

Desmond bowed and at a gesture from his host turned to the remaining guests. They greeted him with a cool friendliness and an expectant attitude that seemed to be shared among them. Some bowed with great formality, including one of the women, while others shook his hand in a more modern, casual manner. All of the guests appeared to be younger than the host by a good margin, but only one seemed to be a youth of Desmond's years. He was the lone person who did not show even the shadow of a smile upon taking Desmond's hand in greeting but instead looked intently at him with what seemed a mixture of curiosity and fear. His eyes, which caught the firelight, were dark olive-green, and his hair, severely tied back with a black ribbon, was a deep polished auburn. Despite the pallor of his skin, freckles showed unfashionably on his high cheeks, and he blushed strongly when Desmond returned his look with a stare of surprise.

A suppressed titter rose from the other guests at this blush, and Desmond turned his eyes back to his host in confusion, embarrassed at having been caught in such a lapse of manners. But it was not, apparently, Desmond's faux pas that had caused the amusement.

"You must excuse Roger Deland, Monsieur Beckwith. He has been with us only a few short years. He has not quite learned his manners. You see, his father was—is, I daresay—a successful merchant in Bourges at the outbreak of this unhappy state we call the French Republic. Roger had rather a bad falling-out with him at that time and came to Paris. It was only in the fall of 1789 that I took him under my care and made him a part of our little circle."

At this moment the old servant entered, now dressed in elaborate black livery trimmed with gold, as antique in style as the room itself. He carried a silver-gilt waiter laden with Venetian goblets, all filled with a deep ruby-red liquid.

"Some port, Monsieur Beckwith? I have heard that you favor it and have brought out one of my finest old bottles for the evening."

Desmond took one of the delicate glasses and held it before the fire, its deep color glittering in the flickering of the flames. Each of the party took glasses in turn, and then the host turned again to Desmond.

"To Desmond Beckwith, then, with our greetings and best wishes for the years to come."

All hailed the toast and drank. Desmond followed suit, puzzled at the meaning of this affable toast but enjoying deeply the richness of the port and the fire with which it warmed his body. Encouraged by the wine, he gestured to the other guests and said with gentle humor, "I must confess, I am rather at a disadvantage here and do not quite understand why you have called me to join you. Surely I am glad at the invitation but puzzled to know how and why you sought me out. I had suspected it might be in regard to my banking, but that now seems unlikely."

"Ah, Monsieur Beckwith, surely you can guess? No, it is not *les affaires* that made us seek you, although I am certain all of us could be aided in that quarter in this troubled time. No, I am afraid we have been watching you without your knowledge for quite some time, Monsieur Beckwith, and have only just been able to decide to ask you to know us."

Desmond felt a thrill of fear shoot through him, remembering his nocturnal wanderings in the public gardens of Paris. But how would they know this? And why propose such a toast after bringing him here? Was this some sort of society of people who yearned for their own sex? If so, it was an ill-assorted group to make such a society. And why the midnight hour and the strange funereal pomp? He spoke to the room at large, but looking at his host, hiding his fear, and using as lighthearted a voice as he could muster: "I am still uncertain of what you mean, Monsieur Charlon. I have only been in Paris since this terrible bloodletting began, and before this only at the outset of the republic in order to secure my bank's interests. I have not provided, I fear, much opportunity for clandestine surveillance.

"Surely again, Monsieur Beckwith, you are joking! We have watched you these 40-odd years on each of your visits to this great city, from when you first began your banking house here. Indeed, we saw you on your very first visit to Paris before the banking house was even in your mind."

Desmond's mind raced at this revelation, inevitably focusing on the one conclusion he dared not make. Faltering, he said, "But you must refer to my late father, Monsieur Charlon."

Charlon snorted impatiently and then smiled benevolently up at Desmond from his throne as he finished off the last of his port. "Not at all, Monsieur Beckwith. It is indeed you we have watched all this time, ever since Baron Tsolnay gave me warning of your transformation and your impending arrival in France."

Desmond felt his knees weaken and moved to one of the velvet chairs, on which he sank, pressing his free hand to his brow. So these people were like him in their thirst for blood! The baron had told him there were others but had not seemed anxious to have him contact them. He had come through Paris on his way back to England in that dark year of 1749, having left his beloved Jeffrey and the life he had known behind in Tsolnay's desolate mountain village. They had seen him even then—warned by letter? They had watched him on all of his trips to Paris in the 40 subsequent years and had noted his regeneration in the year of the revolution. They had waited all this time—for what?

One of the women, a younger one, perhaps 40, came over to him with another glass of port, murmuring comforting words. The auburn-haired man, Roger, had started toward him but held back at a gesture from Charlon. Desmond looked at Deland and saw the sympathy, mingled with anger, in his face. The woman who had brought Desmond the port then went to Deland and took him by the arm to the other side of the room.

"But why did you seek me? Why am I of such interest?" asked Desmond of no one in particular.

"Because," replied one of the men, "there are few of us in the world, and we were curious at seeing someone so new."

"We could not be sure," added the older woman, who seemed to be about 60, and, Desmond realized, near to her own time of re-generation. "We have to be very careful before we try to know any-one. You were here so infrequently!"

"And for short times. We could not take the chances to spy on you without the greatest care, Monsieur Beckwith," elaborated Charlon, "for Tsolnay had given us only the barest description. He had not, apparently, been sure of you himself."

"Or of you, Monsieur Charlon." This came from Desmond, with a coolness that startled even himself.

"Perhaps you are right in that, Desmond—may I so address you? The Baron and I have known each other for a long time—since long before this house existed. We were created together, in fact, in the time of the Turkish invasions of the eastern European principalities. We have had little communication since then, for many reasons. To my knowledge, you are the only creation he has made. This in itself might have caused him to contact me. I know not what other reasons he may have had in being less precise."

"But of course they were not sure you would return, Monsieur Beckwith." Roger Deland spoke out from across the salon, where he had been whispering with his female companion. "They were afraid that, having set the bank to rights and made your first regeneration successfully, you might disappear back to England and never return—or at least until the republic fell, which is the same as never from where we sit now."

"Come, come, Roger, you do not know this; how can you, so new, tell Monsieur Beckwith of our feelings? You do not know our feelings." Charlon spoke with the strained patience of a schoolmaster who is tired of a bright but troublesome student.

But Deland continued, seeming agitated beneath his calm surface. "But I do know your feelings, Gregory, and now I understand." He broke away from the woman, and walked quickly across the vast polished floor to Desmond. "Don't you see, Monsieur Beckwith, they were distraught at your departure after your regeneration—they must have been! It would have been only logical. After so many years of waiting, watching, being careful, with the hope that, after a century's tedium, they might add another to their party. Once you disappeared, they were despondent, certain that you would stay safely in England."

"Roger, please! Monsieur Beckwith doesn't want to hear your ramblings!" Charlon's voice was edged with anger now, and Desmond saw the other guests looking nervously toward him.

"But he does, Gregory, and you should as well, for I have just realized for the first time why I am here." He looked fervently into Desmond's eyes and then wheeled to face Charlon, his voice slightly giddy as he continued.

"It was just after you left for London, Monsieur Beckwith, that Gregory Charlon befriended me. He found me wandering amid the political turmoil of Paris, estranged from my family, penniless and terrified about my future. He brought me to this very salon, introduced me to this very group of people. He persuaded Emilie," Deland looked at his companion, who looked down at his glance, "to seduce me, to play at being my *amante*, to make me appreciate him and his circle. You understand that I was quite dazzled at first. Then he told me of his nature—of the immortal life of those in this house. He regaled me with stories of eternity and his adventures since his transformation. With the world I knew crumbling around me, Gregory turned my head to another world. In this very house I crossed from my world into theirs." His glance swept the little assembly and stopped at Desmond, looking him straight in the eye. "And now I see that it was only because they were all bored with each other and had just lost you, their new plaything, to England."

His deep green eyes stayed locked on Desmond's, softening into a wistful expression, a wry smile on his lips. "And then you came back when the blood started to flow from the guillotine, again to protect your bank. I have not turned out as they wanted, am not the companion they wished me to be. I do not want to join in their morbid games and live my life as if in a perpetual stage play. They are unhappy with me, Monsieur Beckwith, and I now see that you are to be my replacement."

"Nonsense!" roared Charlon, who heaved himself out of the gilt bulk of the velvet-covered throne and moved heavily over to Roger's side. Placing a hand on Roger's shoulder, he smiled at Desmond reassuringly.

"Monsieur Beckwith, Roger is simply overwrought, as we all are from the strain of introducing a new member into our circle. It is true that he does chafe at our rules—we are very old-fashioned. But we all love Roger dearly, do we not, friends?" He turned his smile on the guests, and all assented in union. "You see, Monsieur Beckwith, we are delighted to have you among us, as is Roger, who is simply newer than we others and rather prone to exaggeration."

A soft general laugh erupted from the guests, and the woman

called Emilie came and again took Roger away, caressing his cheek and kissing him playfully.

Charlon turned to the wizened servant. "Ivan—more port for the company!" Then, to the guests, "Let us pull the chairs into a more comfortable arrangement, so that we may talk with our new guest."

The great thrones were pulled into a rough circle near the fireplace, and company settled down with their glasses of wine, chattering softly to one another.

"So tell us," began one of the older men, "what is the state of your banking business in this tiresome republic?"

Desmond was taken aback at the banality of the question but answered as best he could. He found that talking of things in his day-to-day world calmed him, as did the superb port. He even noted young Deland watching him intently, hand interlocked with that of Emilie, who was indeed a beauty. He expanded on his business affairs, then, at further questions from the guests, told them of his English bank, of Beckwith House. He talked of his father and mother and in some detail of his motherless upbringing. He finally talked of Jeffrey, hoping perhaps to shock the audience with his candor, but was surprised to find nothing but sympathy in the faces of his listeners. One of the guests asked him to tell of the fateful trip to Europe, but at this Desmond demurred.

"I say, this is unfair to a new guest!" cried Roger. "We should tell him about us!"

"Yes, do, Monsieur Charlon, I should like to know about your customs, your history. Like Monsieur Deland, I too am a relatively modern youth, in spite of having lived a lifetime already. I have always been alone in the world and have never had to bend to rules of another, aside, of course, from my King's."

"Well, Monsieur Beckwith—Desmond—if you insist. We shall tell you." Charlon settled himself in his chair and finished his glass, setting it on a gilt gueridon at his side. The servant took the silver waiter and disappeared from the room.

"I founded this little *société*," Charlon began, "many years ago. Ivan had been my faithful servant in my old life and came with me to the new one. We both of us, Monsieur Beckwith, were transformed as old men. We are thus, perhaps sadly, doomed to maintain the physical states in which you find us now. But you know all this through your own experience. Ivan is surprisingly strong, as am I, in spite of outward appearances. Would that, in life, I had been a bit less of an epicure, I might myself be lighter on my feet!" This last was spoken with a chuckle, which released a soft laugh from his audience.

"Ivan and I moved about a bit in those days, after leaving behind your friend Baron Tsolnay in the East. For a while Macedonia, then the Italian peninsula, finally north to France, where we set up house here in the 1630s. Now, you understand, Ivan is a good servant, the best indeed, but hardly an intellectual companion. So, along the way, I added my friends, Emilie being the most recent before Roger. All of my companions, Monsieur Beckwith, are different ages now, but all share your lucky state of regeneration, since all were in younger years than I when transformed. Tsolnay, Ivan, and I all must live out eternity as old men, and I wouldn't want that inconvenience forced on anyone."

Desmond was intrigued and ever more curious. "But tell me, why the black clothing, the midnight meeting? I am so used to dealing with humanity on its own terms. Of course, the night is helpful, especially for those of our nature..."

"Indeed, Desmond, helpful for those quiet meetings under the chestnuts of the Tuileries?" he added slyly, making Desmond blush. "But you recall that I have confessed to being old-fashioned. When transformed, I knew nothing of my new state other than that I was both dead and undead. I did not feel I could deal with mankind any longer on its level. I still do not. Thus, we wear the raiment of the funeral and keep to ourselves. The hours of darkness are the best, as you say, for the hunt, for we can see well and few people are out to disturb us—even in times like these."

The elder woman spoke now, expanding on Charlon's theme. "I was 18 and unmarried when Gregory met me in Venice during the 1560s. At that age I was desperate for a wealthy husband and saw none in sight. Gregory offered me a world I couldn't conceive of—and his rules were not so terribly difficult. I accepted them then, as now, gladly."

The murmured assent of the group was broken by Roger, who spoke softly yet with mischief in his voice. "Yes, Monsieur Beckwith, and I am the only dissenter—the troublesome black sheep. I haven't got the lofty intellect of the others or the complex background. I am a bourgeois youth who wants only to enjoy the endless life I have been granted."

"Granted by *me*," said Charlon icily.

"Yes, Gregory, granted by you but my own nonetheless."

"And do we not let you have your way, Roger? Do we not let you wander among the peasants and populace of this mad city? Do you not watch the trials and executions, the madness that grips this country in the throes of republican butchery?"

"Yes, you allow me, and for it I am grateful. Mad as France is, she is still my country. At least the people are alive."

"But you must admit, Roger," quipped one of the men, "once they've kissed *la guillotine*, they are far deader than you!"

Roger blushed again at the general laughter, and Desmond felt his heart go out to this handsome man who seemed so ill at ease among his otherworldly family.

"But we forget ourselves, Roger, all of you!" Charlon again rose and spread his arms toward Desmond. "We have a treat for our new guest. It is late, and we must not delay too much. Come!"

With that he turned and lumbered toward the far end of the long room, throwing open a pair of doors that mirrored those through which Desmond had entered. Desmond and the rest of the group followed.

The room they now entered was smaller than the last, square, but just as high. No candles burned from the luster above—only a pair of massive silver candlesticks flanked what appeared to Desmond to be an altar. Before he could look closely, Charlon spoke.

"We wish to welcome Desmond Beckwith to our midst and to make him feel comfortable with us. But we also wish to be finally assured that he is indeed one of us. This may seem unnecessary, given what we know and what we have heard, but we shall all take pleasure from this little surprise. Now, Monsieur Beckwith, you will see how well we have watched you!"

And with those words Charlon moved over to the altar, which Desmond now saw was draped with a black damask cover. Motioning to Ivan, Charlon took one end of the cloth and, with a dramatic flourish, they drew it aside.

An appreciative intake of breath came collectively from all present, but Desmond's was more of a gasp. There, lying on a polished black marble tabletop, was a naked youth. Almost transfixed, Desmond moved closer. He was young, perhaps 18, and looked as white as boxwood in the dim light of the two candles. Heavily muscled arms and legs and a sharply defined abdomen identified him as a working man. Few gently raised boys were so strongly made, having not the benefit of physical labor. His hands, though clean, were blunt-fingered and gave witness to hard work. His dark hair was carefully brushed back from his eyes, leaving his white forehead bare. His lean stomach rose and fell almost imperceptibly, suggesting a deep, narcotic sleep. Desmond looked up at Charlon uncomprehendingly.

"He is our gift to you, Desmond. We have seen your taste and know he is to your liking. You have not drunk the blood of life in several days, Desmond, and you must be thirsting. Take him as a symbol of our new friendship and our eternal kinship. Show us what your transformation has made you. Share with us the gift given you by Baron Tsolnay."

Desmond looked around in confusion, suddenly horrified at the macabre spectacle of the offering and at his own surging lust at the sight of the beautiful boy. Roger moved quietly to his side and whispered in his ear, taking his arm. "Do what he says; you certainly need it, and to refuse would cause needless offense. Please…I understand, Desmond."

A look of annoyance on Charlon's face changed to one of despotic benevolence as Desmond collected himself and moved slowly toward the bier. Roger's words had made Desmond realize that this gruesome voyeurism was just one of Charlon's customs, rooted in some long-established cult. Desmond knew he could play a part as called to and was strangely moved by Roger Deland's support.

The cold marble of the tabletop was just at Desmond's waist level, making it easy for him to bend forward gracefully to the peasant boy's bared throat. He turned the head to one side, inhaling rapturously the fresh scent of youth and vigor. He ceased all pretense, letting his instinct and his innermost needs surface. His lower jaw drew back, the canines grew, and Desmond lowered his lips to bestow for his audience the skillful kiss of the vampire.

As always, Desmond was good and careful and gentle. As the boy's sweet blood filled him, he reveled in the synchronization of their beating hearts and almost lost himself in the close, sexual power of his smell. In a different setting Desmond would have wanted more than blood from this boy, but he was unable to completely forget his audience and only allowed himself to fleetingly caress the soft warm skin beneath him. When he finally drew back from the sleeping youth, two tiny incisions were fading rapidly and a pale bruise showed on the boy's neck. Desmond's heart pounded with the influx of fresh blood, and he smiled luxuriously at Roger, who returned his smile with the complicity of a friend.

Charlon came over to him, clapping him on the back and exclaiming, "Well-done, my friend, well-done. Such elegance, such grace. You are an artist!"

His praise was interrupted by a small cry from behind, where Emilie was bending over the naked youth. "Gregory, he still lives!"

"What?" Charlon turned back to Desmond, perplexed. "You have not killed him?"

"Of course not. Why would I?" Desmond was again horrified and turned back to Roger, whose face was darkened with anger.

"It is the custom to kill the offering. The boy is a peasant—he will not be missed, especially not during this bloodbath. He is our gift!" Charlon seemed upset and angry, as if Desmond had breached some social delicacy.

"If he is your gift, then he is now mine!" Desmond said stiffly, turning as he spoke and looking at each of the guests in turn. "I may do what I like with him. I have, for our mutual pleasure, enjoyed his beauty and his blood, and for that I thank you all. I have savored the life he has given me without his consent. Peasant or not, he is a human being. I will not take his life; I do not take human life when I drink. He is mine. I give him his life in exchange for his blood. That, Monsieur Charlon, is *my* custom, and it will not be altered for anyone!"

The circle of vampires watched him in startled silence.

"You were not always so careful in your feeding habits, Monsieur Beckwith," Charlon said in a low voice that was almost a hiss.

Desmond froze and cast a quick look at Roger, whose eyebrows were now raised in confusion and surprise.

"What do you mean, Charlon?" he asked, fearing the answer.

Charlon smiled with narrowed eyes, and his tongue flickered over his teeth, as if anticipating a delicious treat.

"I seem to recall an instance a long time ago—you might say a lifetime ago—right here in Paris, in fact." Charlon paused for effect, and he turned to face not Desmond but Roger. "I remember a rather handsome young man, fair skin, golden hair—quite coarse, perhaps, but alluring, if one likes that sort of thing."

He paused again, a sneer on his lips, and would have said more, but Desmond interrupted him, his voice barely controlled.

"Since you seem to have been watching so closely, then you know full well that I was attacked. I was forced to defend myself."

"Defend yourself?" asked Charlon incredulously. "You, a vampire, the progeny of Baron Tsolnay, defend yourself against a mortal?"

"If you saw, then you know I speak the truth."

"I saw it all, Monsieur Beckwith, and I must say, you were magnificent. A snarling panther in the shadows of the Bois de Boulogne, acting on instinct and making short work of your hapless victim. I was quite moved by your gifts, Desmond."

"Enough! Speak no more of victims. I'll not have you pervert my past for your own morbid delectation, Charlon."

Desmond moved quickly around the bier and picked up the fallen cloth from the floor. This he threw over the recumbent figure, wrapping it in a bundle, and lifted the boy off the marble slab.

Charlon and two of the men moved as if to stop him, but Roger interposed himself with his arms folded. His head held high, his eyes glittered like serpentine in the flickering light.

"Let him go! He has done what you asked. You may not force him to go against his own soul to satisfy your archaic cruelty. The boy is his—let him go!"

Charlon and the others halted, and Desmond, mind awhirl, carried his burden to the great salon. Old Ivan caught and passed him, with a whispered instruction to wait for the coach. More footsteps, rapid ones, came up and fell in step with him as he walked steadily down the long room toward the staircase. It was Roger Deland.

"God be with you, Desmond Beckwith. Go quickly. Charlon is not your friend, I fear, and he is no man to have as an enemy. But perhaps he is just angry with me for now, and that will spare you." He spoke in a low voice that was breaking with excitement.

Desmond looked at him, seeing the exultation in his eyes. He stopped, leaned forward, and kissed Roger firmly on the lips.

"You may be a man who loves women, Roger Deland," Desmond said softly, "but I know that I already love you for what you are."

And with that Desmond left Roger behind and descended the echoing marble staircase to the waiting carriage.

CHAPTER 4

The next morning the boy awoke on the settee in Desmond's sitting room. Desmond had not allowed himself to sleep that night, watching the boy as he slept. The youth, truly a peasant but not bloody-minded like many of his peers, was confused and remembered only being attacked the night before. Desmond told him that he had found him, lying unconscious, in an alleyway. His clothes had been dirty and torn, Desmond also told him, and thus he was to have a suit of plain brown linen, which would do well enough. The boy seemed to accept the Englishman's charity with muddled good humor and shook Desmond's hand gratefully after being given a few pieces of gold. He wandered off whistling into the busy morning street outside the bank.

Desmond watched him go from the window above and wondered to himself, *They would have had me take his life! Baron Tsolnay warned me, and yet I never really understood. How many have they killed in their lives? And how many have they made Roger kill in his turn?* His mind pictured the smooth dark red hair, the green eyes, and the pale freckled skin, and Desmond shuddered.

Several days passed uneventfully, and Desmond fell back into his routine, working long hours at the bank, calling sleep to him late at night. He did not venture forth to the gardens, still too shaken by his soiree at Charlon's to brave the task. Sex he could live without, but his thirst would eventually drive him to seek fulfillment. Until then he preferred the solace of fasting.

Even while he was immersed in accounts and correspondence, Desmond's thoughts were never far from Roger Deland, whose breathless parting words remained with him. He had seemed thrilled at Desmond's challenge to Charlon, as if it had been something Roger himself had never dared to do. How much imprisoned Roger must be in that house, how much in Charlon's thrall! Desmond began to try to plan some way to free Roger from Charlon's spell, trying out schemes in the back of his mind as he worked.

Money, of course, was the root of an answer. Charlon was clearly of vast wealth. Desmond knew how much help his own great fortune had been to him. Roger was torn from his family and had no resources of his own. Perhaps if Desmond could give him some measure of independence... It seemed, at least, a logical beginning. Roger was an independent soul, and Desmond could no more replace Charlon's influence with his own than replace iron shackles with gold, but maybe he could grant Roger Deland his freedom.

Accordingly, Desmond withdrew from his own Paris account the sum of £5,000, which he deposited into an account made exclusively to the name of Roger Deland, citizen of France. Once this was done the money was no longer Desmond's at all but legally and finally Roger's. It was a small fortune and enough to allow Roger to decide how best to lead his own life, free from the malignant presence of Charlon's morbid society. Roger could not turn down the money, since it was his already. And certainly it was a fitting gift for his assistance to Desmond. Of course, Roger could try to give it back, but Desmond could refuse and then persuade him to reconsider.

But how to communicate to Roger and to meet with him? Desmond cringed at the thought of returning to that dark house but realized it to be the only possible way. If the household all slept during the day, perhaps then he could somehow get a message to Deland. The old servant, Ivan, had helped him with the carriage that night. He might again be of some assistance.

But just that same afternoon, Desmond's work was interrupted by his secretary, who reported that the same messenger from before awaited him in the antechamber. Desmond had him shown in immediately.

Unlike his first visit, this time Ivan seemed nervous and almost afraid. He spoke in his low, shaky voice before Desmond could even ask his business.

"I am at risk coming here without specific orders from Monsieur. He and the others are at rest, and I avoided it myself so that I might have the chance to come to you. You must not let anyone know of my presence here. Swear it!"

"Ivan, please, you need not fear my indiscretion. I so swear! Now, tell me! What is the trouble?" Even as he asked, Desmond had a chilling premonition of the truth.

"It is Roger Deland, Monsieur Beckwith; I have overheard my master talking with the others. I fear they have denounced him to the republican government, and he is to be arrested, if not already in irons at the *conciergerie*!"

"Denounced him! For what?" Desmond rose from his desk and, taking Ivan by the arm, forced him to sit in a leather chair by the empty fireplace. Crouching beside the shaken old man, Desmond pressed: "Speak, Ivan, what is their plan?"

"Their plan, Monsieur, is already done. Roger has been allowed to keep a small apartment in a quarter near the *hôtel* Charlon. It is just one of the many things he does that angers Monsieur but which he nonetheless has been allowed to do. Apparently, watching him closely, one of the household has slipped into his rooms while he was out and has left documents there that incriminate him in antirepublican sedition."

"Has the evidence been found yet, Ivan? Is Roger arrested?" Desmond felt panic clutching at his heart and fought to remain calm.

"I fear so, my lord. From what I could hear, it sounded as if they were very pleased with their success. Only Madame Emilie was angered and was apparently not part of the plan. But she fears to do anything that might displease Monsieur Charlon."

"I must go to the *conciergerie* at once. Will you accompany me, Ivan, and assist me?"

"I cannot, sir—I fear for my own life if I remain any longer. The household will awaken before long, and I must be back at my post beforetime. If you can do anything to save Monsieur Deland, it will be worth a lost night's sleep to me, my lord."

With these words Ivan turned from Desmond's pleading look and scuttled out of the office, disappearing into the crowded street as quickly as if he had been a phantom. Desmond ordered his secretary to let no one disturb him, then sat down heavily behind his desk, head in his hands.

So this was the price Roger would pay for defying Charlon and for humiliating him before a guest! Vampire or human, the guillotine cared not. Her kiss would end an immortal life as easily as a mortal one. And in this time of madness, there would be no possible defense for Roger Deland. Such trumped-up charges were common currency among the revolutionary hordes, and many innocent heads were on pikes for no better reason than jealousy or political rivalry. The existence of any evidence would matter little; the accusation, especially from a prominent figure, would carry its own weight.

Desmond ran from the bank, hurrying through the streets on foot. Gentlemen on foot were no surprise in Paris, but the look of fear in this gentleman's eyes would have possibly been noticed. Those who did, and who remarked on the direction in which Desmond went, would have understood both his destination and the reason for his fear.

As Desmond approached the Ile de la Cité, he could hear the roar of the crowd. He fought his way through the throngs before Notre-Dame and into the courtyard of the *conciergerie*. The great Gothic bulk of the cathedral loomed helplessly before the prison, the heads of its ancient saints lopped off as brutally as those of Paris's citizens, by a mob just as unthinking. It seemed to Desmond that the power of God had abandoned Paris. The aristocracy had been bad, per-haps—but was this better?

An impromptu courtroom had been erected in the courtyard of the *conciergerie*, complete with jury box, accused's dock, and a bench for the self-styled magistrates. There, huddled in a small group to one side of the dock, Desmond could make out the bowed auburn head of Roger Deland.

The trials were efficient and summary. Evidence was read, usual-ly inaudible amid the cries of the reeking audience. The jury con-ferred for a few moments, then wrote a decision on a slip of yellow paper, which was then handed to the judge. The verdict was read, and the judge, standing, announced sentence. Some of the cases caused some discussion, and once a young woman was even acquit-ted and set free; but the overwhelming number of the accused were condemned and sentenced to die on the scaffold.

Roger's case was little different from the rest. He was pushed rudely up to the dock, where he stood with bowed eyes throughout, probably unable to hear what was said about him. The prosecutor waved some documents and pamphlets before the jury, all of whom scowled in anger. Then the documents were waved before the audi-ence, who screamed in unison, chilling Desmond's blood. The jury's conference was brief, and the sentence a foregone conclusion. The handsome, well-dressed young man was the ideal scapegoat for the mob, his hands unmarked with labor, his clothes those of the bour-geoisie, not the people. The judge stood and added the name of Roger Deland to the guest list of the maiden of steel.

It was approaching dinnertime at this point, and the court ad-journed its bloody business until the next day, when today's con-demned would meet their fate. The crowd waited while the convicts were led away and into their cells for their last night on earth. Insults were hurled into the faces of the terrified victims, most of whom kept their faces downturned to avoid the spittle that often accompanied the shouts. But Desmond couldn't take his eyes off Roger's smooth red hair and neat black ribbon. As he passed the spot from which Desmond watched, Roger looked up and caught Desmond's eyes. A fleeting look of surprise flashed across his face, was replaced with another just as fleeting, and then his gaze returned to the filthy pavement as before. The massive oak door of the prison closed with a solemn thud upon the backs of tomorrow's victims.

Long after the crowd had begun to disperse, Desmond stayed rooted to the spot, eyes unseeing, mind churning feverishly for some course of action. In that brief moment, that instant when Roger had recognized Desmond in the howling mob, he had given Desmond a look of such agonizing fear and pleading that Desmond could not ignore it. Even at the cost of his own life, he would try to save Roger Deland from a place where no one had ever escaped. As Desmond turned and hurried from the courtyard, his thoughts raced with ideas, and he desperately tried to imagine a way to get Roger away from here alive.

Desmond passed out of the narrow street and stepped onto the Seine embankment. Lost in thought, he followed the pavement along the high, brooding walls of the *conciergerie*. The dark bulk of the Louvre loomed ahead of him across the river, the setting sunlight glinting off its windows. Suddenly a massive gate in the wall of the *conciergerie* was pulled inward with a great screeching of rusty hinges. Startled, Desmond stepped back as a high, crudely constructed wooden cart rumbled through the opening and onto the roadway. Massive wooden wheels thundered over the cobbles, and rough planks formed a rickety superstructure. A single overworked draft horse pulled the cart, which was driven by a sullen soldier and carried a handful of dirty, frightened men and women. The cart turned in the direction Desmond had been walking. Desmond's eyes widened. He knew where this tumbrel was going, and he followed in horrified expectancy of its destination.

The tumbrel and its miserable passengers rattled down the Seine riverbank until the last long arm of the Louvre was behind it. Then it turned and crossed over a stone bridge into a vast cobblestone plaza. Desmond had followed as if compelled, keeping his distance but unable to tear himself away. As the cart approached the bridge, Desmond caught a scent in the twilight air—the smell of fresh blood. The men and women in the cart had been silent all this time, but as they entered the Place de la Concorde, moans of fear escaped. The guard snarled at them, and they fell back into hopeless silence. One of the women began to weep softly, and another tried to comfort her with shackled arms. Desmond glanced beyond the tumbrel and saw, standing in the center of the open space, a high wooden scaffold and upon it the tall silhouette of the guillotine. The sharply angled blade, drawn high in its parallel tracks, caught the light of the setting sun.

A sizable crowd was gathered around the scaffold, talking animatedly and making a good deal of noise. Only when the tumbrel was upon them did the throng part to let it reach the scaffold steps. Desmond stayed back, losing himself in one of the quieter pockets of onlookers. From where he stood the smell of blood was more distinct, and he could see, even in the fading light, the dark, glistening smear below the opening at the guillotine's base. The sun was at the horizon now, and it bathed the city in a strange ruddy light, as if the fires of hell were peeking up to check on their handiwork.

The crowd began to call for dispatch, that they might witness a few more beheadings before darkness spoiled their fun. As if to appease them, the guard brought the tumbrel to an abrupt halt at the base of the steps, roughly herded his charges out, and presented their condemnation papers to another guard seated at a desk by the stairs.

The first of the condemned, a young man with long dark hair and an open shirt, was shoved up to the desk. The charge and the sentence were read aloud to the jeering and taunts of the crowd, punctuated by an occasional *vive la république*. Then he was pushed up the stairs, where the executioner, head masked in a black hood, placed him with surprising gentleness facedown on a bench—a bench, Desmond realized, that would be wet still with its last occupants' blood. The man's head was placed in the semicircular opening at the base of the blade's tracks. A word from the guard at the desk, and the executioner pulled the rope. The blade fell quickly, with only a metallic hiss and a crisp *chunk* as it found its mark. The young man's head fell out of sight into a bloodstained wicker basket, and his body, blood gushing furiously from the great arteries in his severed neck, was flung unceremoniously off the other side of the scaffold into a second waiting tumbrel. The executioner then lifted the dripping head from the basket and raised it for the crowd to see. Their enraged cheers filled the darkening plaza, and Desmond turned and began to push his way out of the crowd.

As he reached the edge of the Place de la Concorde, Desmond's carefully controlled walk turned to a run. He was filled with horror, not because of what he had just seen but at what he was feeling. He was horrified at his own blood lust, which now surged through him like a fever. The image of the young man's headless body, blood pumping, was vivid in his brain, and the image filled him with insatiable hunger. He ran and ran and ran, along the immense length of the Louvre, keeping to the shadows. There were few people in the vicinity of the ancient palace, and Desmond finally slowed, gasping for breath. He continued on, mind buzzing with thirst and dread. As he passed one of the high archways that led into the palace's inner courtyards, he noticed a republican guard standing indolently on duty in its shadows. Desmond stopped and walked quickly toward him.

"I have just witnessed something terrible," he said, his voice low and feline. "I need to report it to someone." His eyes were locked on the guard, who could barely see him in the dimness.

The guard, who had not been paying much attention to his duty, was suddenly alert. "Halt. Come no further. Identify yourself. Show your papers." He raised his musket, his voice quivering. Desmond thought to himself that the king's guards would never have been so slatternly. He ignored the belligerent gesture and moved up to within inches of the guard's face. Desmond could smell his fear—and his blood.

"Do not resist me, and I shan't hurt you." He gripped the guard's hand with viselike strength, forcing him to drop the musket with a clatter. Then, clasping him fiercely in his arms and crushing him in a powerful embrace, he lowered his canines and plunged them into the terrified guard's neck. Desmond drank deeply, scarcely conscious of his host's weak struggling. As the blood streamed into his own veins, he began to feel his hunger abate and his heartbeat begin to slow, bringing with it the mortal's own rhythm until they sounded a gentle tattoo in his blood-filled brain. At last he felt the guard's body grow slack, and he lowered him to the pavement.

"I could just as well have killed you, *mon bon citoyen*," he sighed softly, looking down at the unconscious guard, "for all it would matter to anyone in this bloodthirsty city. But you may just consider yourself lucky that I am not one of Charlon's compatriots." Desmond turned and walked calmly out into the evening.

The bank offices were long closed by the time he returned. Desmond set about working on his project. It all depended on Roger's wit, and Desmond knew too little about him to be sure. A vampire in prison was a vulnerable creature. But since Roger would have been locked up for only a short while, the chances were good that neither his thirst nor his need to sleep would have been pushed to their limits. Desmond prepared a few notes for his secretary with explicit instructions and left the bank again. Moving quietly and quickly through the silent streets, Desmond returned to the *conciergerie*.

Guards at the gate of the prison stopped him, but they were not Desmond's concern.

"Let me pass—I am English and a banker. I have urgent business with a client incarcerated within. Let me speak to the commandant!" Desmond's voice was cool and authoritative.

"If you need to see your client so desperately at this hour, then he must be taking a short trip tomorrow!" sneered one of the guards. "Pass, then, Englishman." And he did.

Once inside the guardroom of the prison, Desmond had a trickier story to tell. He approached the table where the chief warder sat, surrounded by piles of papers. Numerous sullen and unkempt guards lounged about the room on bare benches, playing cards and drinking. The chief warder looked up at him suspiciously.

"What is your business?"

"I have come to confer with a client," replied Desmond, handing the warder some papers. "I am an English banker—Desmond Beckwith, to be precise. Monsieur, or rather, Citizen Roger Deland has an account with my concern, and I must, understandably, consult with him as to its disposition." Desmond was aware that the republic could impound such money, especially when belonging to a traitor, but hoped that this operative would not be aware of that financial detail. Much of the impounded aristocratic money had never in fact found its way into the state coffers, and thus Desmond suspected that relatively few people knew of this admirable republican system of wealth redistribution.

"Going to the guillotine tomorrow, eh?" asked the warder with something between a friendly smile and a hungry leer. "All right, then, go ahead." He turned to a guard at one side of the room. "Hey, Robert, take this Englishman up to cell 48. It's the traitor Deland's banker to see him. Fat lot of good it'll do. Guess he wants to say good-bye to his money, eh?" A shared cackle of coarse laughter rippled through the room.

The grubby guard took a key ring from the warder and led Desmond down a series of dank, foul-smelling corridors and up a staircase, lit only with a few pine-knot torches that smoked terribly.

At length they came to cell 48. The key turned in the lock, the door swung open, and Desmond entered. The guard slammed the door behind him, locking it. "I'll be just outside," he bellowed.

In the half-light of the cell, lit from the corridor by the flame of a single pine torch whose feeble flickering barely passed through the grille of the door, Desmond could hardly see Roger. But his eyes adjusted quickly to the darkness, making even the torch's poor glow more than enough. Roger sat on a crude straw mattress that lay on a plank bed in one corner of the cell. His head had been sunken on his chest when the door had opened, but he now looked up and rose with a start when Desmond entered. Recognizing a friend—indeed, his only friend—Roger flew at Desmond and wrapped his arms around him in a desperate hug.

"Oh, my God, Desmond," he sobbed. "What am I going to do? I shall die tomorrow as sure as that bastard Charlon has wished it these past few months." He trembled with fear, and Desmond stroked his hair with gentle yearning for a few moments before speaking softly into Roger's ear.

"Roger, I learned of everything this afternoon. I am not your only friend, but only I could come to see you. Charlon has had his revenge on you indeed, but perhaps we will have the last laugh. Do you speak English?"

This last question made Roger start, but the guard, if he had been watching through the door's grille, wouldn't have seen it in the mortal darkness. Roger looked deeply into Desmond's eyes and whispered his one word reply. "Yes."

Desmond began to talk softly in English, sure that even if the guard had some rudimentary knowledge of it, he would not be able to understand their muffled conversation.

"Roger, you have not slept since you were taken away?"

"No, not a bit. I have dared not, as I was unsure of when I might be moved."

"Good. You understand that you can call sleep to you at any time?"

"Of course, and also that I may not awaken from it for six hours after it has begun. That was my fear."

"You understand also that our sleep is like death in its stillness? Or so it would seem to mortals?"

"Again yes, Desmond. But why do you ask this?"

"Because, Roger, you must die tonight in order that you do not die tomorrow at the guillotine!"

"What? What do you mean to do? Tell me, Desmond!"

"First let me explain to you a few small things. I am your banker, which might surprise you. You are the happy possessor of a fortune of £5,000, which is in your name at the Beckwith Bank. Therefore, as your executor in this matter, I can rightfully claim other legal rights in the absence of any family. Therefore, dear brave Roger, you must call sleep to you at once, pretending first as if you feel faint. The guard will think you dead, and I will not disabuse him of that notion. Then, as your executor, I will take it upon myself to return your earthly remains to your family in Bourges. Do you understand?"

"But Desmond, what if they don't believe you? You are taking a terrible risk!"

"No more of a risk than you took for me at Charlon's that night—indeed, far more of a risk than either of us understood at the time. Remember, Roger, you are still young, both as a man and as a vampire; but we are immortals, and humankind does not readily believe in our existence. The guards will not suspect the truth of your slumber, and even these bloody citizens will take no pleasure in beheading a dead man! Are you game, my friend?"

"Yes, Desmond, I am."

"Good, let us begin. We should sit, as if for your fainting spell." They moved back toward the pallet, and Roger, closing his eyes, moaned softly, and sat heavily. Desmond leaned over him, with concern, crying out his name: "Monsieur Deland!"

"Monsieur Beckwith, I feel great pain and dizziness," mumbled Roger, placing his hand on his brow and slumping backward onto the mattress as if in swoon. He called sleep to him, and Desmond sat beside him, hovering over his face, repeating his name, softly at first, then more loudly, as he saw the stillness of sleep settle over Roger's pale features.

"Monsieur Deland! Monsieur! What is wrong? Please awaken—get up!" Desmond turned a panic-stricken face to the faint outline of the grille in the door. "Guard, Monsieur Deland is ill! Come quickly!"

The door was unlocked and thrown wide, and the guard rushed in. Bending over Roger's recumbent figure, he slapped his face several times, as if rousing a drunken man. Desmond winced at the blows but kept still. The guard then felt first for breath, then for pulse, and, finding none, as Desmond knew he would not, he ran out of the cell, leaving the door open. Desmond fought his instinct to carry Roger out, waiting in the cell for the return of the guard.

The warder accompanied the guard on his return, out of breath, from the guardroom. He burst into the cell angrily, his quiet evening upset for the moment. "What has happened here, Englishman?"

"My client, Mon— Citizen Deland, has collapsed as we were speaking. I fear he is very ill."

"Ill, nothing, Captain," retorted the guard. "He's dead as a fish, if I know anything!"

The warder bent over Roger's body, making the same checks as his inferior had, and finally stood up, facing Desmond.

"Looks like your client's gone and cheated the steel maiden, mister banker. He'll do you no good now, nor you him."

"Dead…but how?" exclaimed Desmond in mock horror.

"No matter to me," answered the warder, "but I'd gather fear might have done it or some disorder that neither you nor I knew of coupled with it. Final word is, Englishman, that he's dead, and you'd better take him away."

"Me? Now?" Again Desmond feigned surprise, hoping for the correct response.

"No use in our keeping him, is there? I'll sign him out as deceased, and you can cart him off."

"But shouldn't a doctor make sure of his death officially?" asked Desmond, aware of the need for the formalities.

"If you like. There's a doctor about the prison; we can call him for a certificate."

Desmond agreed, and a litter was brought to the cell. The warder ordered two guards to carry the lifeless body to another, barely better, cell, which served as the office for the doctor. This latter, a poorly groomed individual of dubious training, had the pleasant duty of affirming such in-house deaths. Given the terrible rations and filthy conditions that abounded in the prison, he was not without business. After a brief inspection the underling physician duly filled out a death certificate, which was signed, dated, and notarized, declaring that one Roger Deland, late of Bourges, had died of natural causes on this day in the year 1793, aged 25 years, at the *conciergerie* in Paris. The document was handed to Desmond, who crowed with inner triumph that his plan had, thus far, worked perfectly.

Some further negotiations brought assistance in the form of a rude cart in which to lay Roger's body and a still ruder citizen to drive the remains and Monsieur Beckwith back to the bank. Since Roger officially had no relations at all in Paris, returning with his body to Desmond's apartment was the only possible course of action for the time being. Once there, Desmond further prodded the driver of the cart, with the aid of a few coins, to help lift Roger from the cart, carry his inert form up the stairs, and lay it to rest on the settee in Desmond's sitting room. Desmond could easily have carried Roger all the way from the prison, but he wanted to arouse no suspicion. It was important for all to believe Roger Deland dead, for escape could come only after some preparation, and no undue haste could be seen on the part of the English banker.

Desmond gently unwrapped Roger's body, which had been roughly shrouded in a coarse blanket, and looked lovingly at the young man. The haggard expression he had seen in the prison cell, the terror he had seen in his eyes for that tiny moment in the court-yard, all that was gone. In its place were the serenity and peace that sleep gave. To mortal eyes, this sleep looked like death; to those of Desmond's sort, it spoke of blissful rest. Desmond leaned impul-sively over Roger's lips and kissed him softly, almost furtively. He immediately withdrew in embarrassment, wondering if Roger was aware of it. Desmond had never been conscious of anything in the outside world during sleep, but then nothing had ever happened to him during those six hours of vulnerability.

Another fear crossed Desmond's mind, however. What if some member of the Charlon household was still watching him? They would surely know that Roger could not die a mortal death. Desmond had seen nothing to indicate spies, but he had never known that he was being watched by Charlon for all those many years. The only answer was to move as quickly as possible, to get Roger out of Paris soon, under the guise of returning his body to Bourges for burial. He could do no more for now but lock the doors securely and make sure he and Roger were safe for this night. They would have to depart the next day.

Desmond made his final preparations, packing some small articles and clothing in a portable trunk but leaving most of his things as they were. He didn't know when he would ever return to Paris, realizing that here, now, an enemy perhaps awaited him. Once back in England, he would eventually have to send for his other things. But that was all in the future; for now he too needed rest if he was to protect Roger in his flight. And so Desmond drew the shutters and bolted them, then lay down on his own bed, keeping the sitting-room door open, calling sleep to bring him six hours of escape from the brutal world of humankind.

Desmond awoke quickly, feeling rested and alert, to find Roger's smiling face looking into his. Roger's smile widened upon seeing Desmond's eyes open.

"So here you are, slugabed, back from the dead at last. I don't know how to thank you for what you've done."

Desmond returned the smile and pushed Roger aside, climbing out of bed. "Don't thank me yet, Roger; there is much to do. You must be dead for some while more so that we can carry your body away from here. To England, in fact."

"England! Why?"

"You forget, Roger, that you have been condemned by the republic. They won't let you just reappear without some questions. You must leave France forever—at least the rest of this lifetime."

"And beyond that," Desmond continued, splashing water on his face, "I wouldn't be sure Gregory Charlon will be at all fooled by your unfortunate and untimely death. Once he catches the scent of what we've done, he'll most likely be after you." He lathered his shaving brush and soaped his face.

"You're right, of course, Desmond. But what will I do in England?" Roger watched as Desmond shaved in the looking glass.

"What did you do here?"

"Nothing. Charlon took care of everything—even my *apartement* near his house, the one he used to betray me!"

"No, I mean before you met Charlon."

"Again, nothing. I had worked for my father, a merchant, as Charlon told you, in Bourges. But after that I merely drifted."

"Did you enjoy business?"

"I didn't dislike it. Father was—is, rather—very rich and skilled at what he does. It had its moments of excitement. Most of it was rather mundane."

"Well, if you didn't absolutely hate it, perhaps you could work with me. As you might imagine, if you've given it any thought, working as much in the mortal world as I do, I could certainly use a close compatriot of my own nature." Desmond straightened up, face half lathered, looking directly at Roger as if suddenly struck with the idea. "You could be of vast assistance to me, Roger."

"And then," added Roger softly, as if thinking, "there's that money you came to the prison to see me about."

"Oh, yes, the money. I certainly didn't do that with any idea of making you a sluggard and give up all thought of work."

"Why did you do it, then?" This was even softer and made Desmond look up at Roger's reflection in the glass, razor poised.

"To set you free, Roger. That money was—is—to give you a chance to live your life—your many lives to come—as a free man, just as I have lived one lifetime and begun another. I wanted to get you away from Charlon and the morbid influence of his funereal world."

"I am glad that is the reason, Desmond. I confess I feared for a moment that there might be other reasons." Roger paused, embarrassed.

Desmond suddenly turned back to the looking glass, razor in hand, soap drying on his half-shaved face. He looked back at Roger with an expression of mixed pain and amusement.

"Roger, you must know now that I never for a moment had any intention of trying to replace Charlon with myself. It was to liberate you, not exchange one enslavement with another, however well-intentioned, that I set up the account. I confess, without shame, that your beauty and your courage have affected me more deeply than any man since…since I was a youth. It *is* my inclination to love men, Roger, just as it is yours to love women. But I would never try to force that on one for whom I care as much as I do for you. Those with whom I have met in the gardens of Paris have always been willing, Roger. It may be that I have taken more from them than they might imagine in their darkest nightmares, but I have always given pleasure, with the knowledge that I needed more from them than they knew."

"I know that, Desmond, and I knew it the moment I saw your face at Charlon's when he threw the cloth off the bier. That's when all the instincts I had about you were proved; that's when I found the courage to stand up to Charlon at the end. I understood then that you were a different sort of vampire than the model Charlon had always held before me. You are a different sort, even, than Charlon himself has ever met. I think he was as afraid of you as you were of him. You surprised him completely!"

"And for that I must be thankful. I had little teaching from Baron Tsolnay, but that little has never failed me. I was afraid it had that night when I saw that naked youth laid out like a banquet before me. But you helped me—you let me know that my heart was right. You gave me the courage to challenge him."

"So it seems we were mutually beneficial, my friend." Roger now spoke with a relaxed smile on his features, though he still stood unmoving, facing Desmond before the dressing table.

"And we still could be, Roger. Although our hearts and bodies yearn for different loves, we are both of the same race. We both need to quench the thirst of our kind in order to live. We could protect each other, support each other, as immortal friends and partners. I don't ask for your love, Roger Deland, but only your comradeship."

"And you have it, Desmond Beckwith, my comradeship and my love—the love of a brother." Roger stepped forward, and placing his hands on Desmond's shoulders, kissed him tentatively on the lips. "I would rather a thousand times be your slave, Desmond, than once more be Charlon's friend."

The soapy razor dropped to the floor with a small clatter, and Roger stooped to pick it up, handing it back to Desmond.

"Dead men don't need to shave, but you'd better finish. I imagine we've a lot to do today before we leave. You have made plans?"

"Yes, many, and if my secretary is as good as I think, they will be under way at this moment." Desmond turned back to the looking glass and finished his morning preparations.

Once ready for the day, dressed in an appropriately sober black linen suit, Desmond explained his plan to Roger in detail.

"You must remain dead to the mortal world throughout the voyage; it is our only hope of eluding detection. You can remain in sleep for only six hours at one time, but you can, as you know, recall the sleep as many times in succession as you wish. Have you ever slept in a coffin?"

"No, never. I don't think I'd much like it." Roger shuddered.

"Well, I'm afraid you'll have to, like it or not. I promise I'll not for a minute leave your side—or at least not when your time to awake comes near. It will take us a very long day to reach Le Havre from Paris, and then who knows how long before we can get on a boat for England. You will have to be nailed into your coffin. People might suspect otherwise."

"It is the only way, then?"

"The only way, Roger. You do not need to fear."

"I wish I could drink once before this starts; I have not since before I was arrested."

"That is impossible. You are too well-known; you would be recognized immediately. There is one way, though…"

"What is it, Desmond? It would make it so much easier for me."

"You could drink *my* blood, Roger."

"No! It would kill you."

"No more than it killed that boy at Charlon's, and it would affect me even less, I imagine. Did Charlon tell you that to take blood from one of your own is deadly? Well, it is not true."

Desmond crossed the room, where he fussed needlessly with some papers on his writing table. "Of course, I've never done it, but the Baron told me it's a way one of our kind can assist another who is somehow imprisoned and cannot hunt for himself."

"And you would do this for me, Desmond?"

"To make this terrible voyage less so? Of course. I can always find ways to get sustenance along the way. The sailors on these boats are remarkably indulgent with the whims of a wealthy passenger." He now turned a mischievous smile on Roger. "Well, where shall you have it?"

"What?"

"Neck or arm—either is possible; the former is faster, the latter less intimate if you are squeamish." His look of sly complicity roused Roger's humor.

"You must think me completely spineless. I'll take the neck and enjoy every drop, just to show you up!"

"All right, then, we must make haste." Desmond quickly stripped off his jacket and waistcoat, opening his shirt enough to bare his neck. He lay down on the unmade bed, closing his eyes. "I won't look so as not to fluster you," he teased.

"Just keep quiet, I'll manage all right." Although he was following Desmond's playful lead, Roger was hesitant and not a little afraid. He had never taken blood from another man, nor indeed from anyone of his acquaintance. He knelt by the side of the bed and grasped Desmond's hand, feeling comforted by its firm pressure. Then, leaning over Desmond's bared neck, his breath short, he fixed his mouth on its target and drank deeply.

As the life-giving blood flowed into his being, Roger felt suffused by more than the energy and strength that drinking gave. As their heartbeats began to pulse in unison, he felt overwhelmed by a sense of love and kinship that he had never known, not even in his mortal being. This man, who had saved his life, now placed his own immortality in Roger's hands. Such faith, such unflinching trust was something Roger had never seen. His mind reeled with the experience, and he gripped Desmond tightly as his heart filled, its beat becoming stronger with the influence of the older vampire's potent blood.

It was over in a short time, and Roger withdrew. The faint marks, which remained visible in mortal flesh, disappeared as he watched, and no bruise even left a hint of what had happened. Desmond opened drowsy eyes and looked at his friend.

"Well, dear man, feeling stronger?"

"Yes, Desmond, much." Roger stroked Desmond's forehead.

"Tell me, Roger," asked Desmond softly, murmuring as if half asleep, "how many has Charlon made you kill since he transformed you? Don't be afraid, you can answer me; it doesn't matter now."

"None, Desmond, I swear. I would never do it, even though he said it was the custom. It was one of the things he hated in me, one of the ways I disappointed him."

Desmond smiled and brushed the back of his hand across Roger's cheek. "That's what I had hoped. Now, my friend, I owe you an explanation for what Charlon said about my past."

Roger placed a hand on Desmond's lips. "You have no need to explain."

Desmond grasped his hand gently, kissed it, and removed it from his lips. He sat up slowly. "I wish to tell you. I can trust you. It was shortly after I was made a vampire. I was on my way home to England and had only been in Paris a short while. I was still quite unused to what I was and rather giddy with my power; but I was equally astonished at how easy it was to hunt in Paris."

He stood and walked over to the looking glass above the chimneypiece. He looked at his own reflection, running his fingers absently over his face. "In the evening shadows of any large public garden or park, men were drawn to me as if by magic." He smiled at Roger's reflected image. "Of course, they were looking for something other than blood, and that is what took me by surprise." He turned and looked intently at Roger, who returned the look with frank sincerity.

"In all my life to that point, I had had carnal knowledge of only one other human being. You heard me speak of Jeffrey Chapman at Charlon's. His loss to me was still recent, and my grief was likewise fresh. My need for blood forced me to hunt, but I was unprepared for the sexual urgency that hunting in Paris aroused in me." He paused and asked, "Am I shocking you?"

"Not at all, Desmond. Please go on."

"One night on that first visit to Paris, in the Bois de Boulogne, just as Charlon said, I met a young man who reminded me of Jeffrey.

Although I was hunting to drink, all thought of blood vanished when this man caught my eye. His blond hair, his blue eyes, his fair, smooth skin unleashed in me a lust more fierce than any I'd known since becoming a vampire. Our encounter was of a purely sexual nature, the first I'd had since losing Jeffrey, and I was completely caught up in my mortal physical senses. Our mutual abandon was so great that, once spent, we lay side by side under the trees, gasping for breath." Desmond placed his hands over his face, shuddering, and Roger rose and went to him. He put a comforting arm around his shoulders.

"It was then that it all went wrong. Suddenly my erstwhile lover, still slick with the evidence of our passion, jumped up and began to hurl wild insults at me, calling me a vile catamite and other hateful names. He said I was an instrument of the devil and should be destroyed in the name of God. Then, as I lay stunned and apparently helpless on the ground, he pulled a knife from within his discarded boot and leaped on me, stabbing me repeatedly in the chest and stomach." Desmond's voice had grown small and tight, but it never wavered. Roger pulled him close in a comforting embrace.

"Blood began to pour from my wounds, and my screams of fear and pain quickly became screams of rage. I must have let him stab me a dozen times before I grabbed his arm, stopping him without great effort. At that point my forgotten blood lust exploded with my anger, and rather than throw him off I pulled him down on top of me and sank my fangs into his neck. It was like drinking from a terrified animal. He struggled wildly and vainly against me, his heart pounding frantically. As I drank and drank and drank, I could feel the flow of blood from my wounds slow and cease. I also felt my attacker's heartbeat slow from frenetic hammering to match my own pounding rhythm and then slow further until—at last—it stopped altogether. Before I even knew what I had done, he was dead, soaked in my blood and semen and drained of his own vital fluids." Desmond pulled gently away from Roger's embrace and stared into his deep green eyes.

"By the time I stood up, trembling, my wounds had all begun to heal, and that beautiful young man lay still, a bloodied carcass, blue eyes wide and staring. I buried him in a shallow grave in the woods and went back to my rooms to bathe. I doubt that I shall ever wash off the horror of that night."

"I can't believe you acted so coolly when Charlon brought it up. How he taunted you! I would have struck him." Roger's voice rose in anger, but Desmond startled him into silence with a kiss.

"We have finished with Charlon, Roger. It has done me good to tell my tale, and now that you have regained your strength, you must once again die so that I may begin my work. We must go."

And so Roger, lying down and allowing Desmond to again wrap around him the blanket from the prison, called the sleep of the undead to him. Desmond dressed and, checking his watch, went quickly downstairs to the banking house. His secretary was already in full action, although extremely puzzled by his employer's request.

"Is the coffin I ordered from the undertaker here?"

"Not yet, sir, but it will be directly. I do not think I understand, sir, but it is done. And the funeral carriage is ordered, although they squirmed a bit when I could not give them a destination. Is it a churchyard in Paris, sir?"

"Neither churchyard nor in Paris. I am taking the mortal remains of a deceased client home to his family in Bourges. I went to him in prison yesterday, the *conciergerie*—and you know what that means. The poor soul, unjustly accused and despicably convicted of a crime he did not commit, died in my arms in the squalor of his cell. At least it was a better death than this damnable republic would have given him today!"

"I see, sir. Where, ah, if I may ask, sir, is…?"

"The body is in a blanket in my sitting room. I will see it wrapped properly in a winding sheet, which we can improvise from my bed linens, and placed in the coffin. I need your help in making sure the other arrangements are completed."

"Very good, sir. I have the letter of account for the London bank, transferring Monsieur Deland's £5,000 there. I also have your transport papers here so that you may move about the countryside unmolested by guards. Will you be taking luggage, sir?"

"Just a few small things; they too are up in the sitting room."

"If there are inquiries, sir, what shall I say?"

"Say nothing at all, beyond that I am gone for a few days. I will return before long. That is all anyone need know. The fewer people who know about this poor soul's end, the better."

"Very good, sir— ah, here is the undertaker."

A shabby black funeral cart had pulled up before the bank, and a black-garbed driver climbed down off the box. A lean but well-cared-for black horse pawed impatiently at the pavement as the driver climbed down. Desmond went out to greet the driver and surprised him by helping him lift a plain new coffin out of the carriage. The two men carried the coffin up the stairs to the apartment and placed it on the floor next to the now blanketed body of Roger Deland. Together, the undertaker and Desmond moved the body to the bed, where they rewrapped it in one of Desmond's fine linen bedsheets. The body was then placed in the coffin, and the undertaker nailed the lid shut. The loaded coffin, along with Desmond's bags, was carried back to the street and lifted onto the waiting hearse.

"Where to, sir? Your man didn't tell me," said the undertaker. He had read the death certificate and understood the need for discretion.

"I'll tell you as we go, good man, but drive as quickly as possible. Start off this way." Desmond pointed down the street and joined the driver on the seat. The carriage lurched into the morning traffic and joined the throng of Parisians going about their daily life in spite of the madness that eddied around them.

Desmond reflected with a wry smile on the ironic contrast between the bright cloudless sky above and the somber appearance of the hearse and its three passengers. Looking around him, he marveled at how utterly *normal* everything looked, when in fact things were about as abnormal as they could possibly be. No one seemed to notice their presence—but death was a constant companion to the republic now. The little funeral party was just another unremarkable bit of the everyday scene. Desmond smiled again. If only they knew what this cart *really* carried.

He closed his eyes and let the sun's rays warm his upturned face, wondering how Charlon and his band could turn their backs on the glory of the day. Hunting at night was proper, but for practical reasons. Shadows could protect, and darkness was a highly useful shield—but shuttering oneself away in a crumbling old *hôtel* seemed a stupid waste of a precious gift. No wonder Roger had chafed at their rituals.

The driver began to realize that they were heading the wrong way if Citizen Beckwith really intended, as he had said, to go toward Bourges. His qualms were quickly assuaged with a generous pouch of gold, which also purchased the promise of silence.

And so the carriage with its mournful burden departed from the capital of the French republic by the Porte D'Asnières and began its journey to the port of Le Havre. They traveled slowly but uneventfully throughout the day, finally stopping at the driver's protest that he needed rest and refreshment. A roadside inn at the small town of Elbeuf provided their shelter, or at least the driver's, for Desmond refused to leave the coffin unattended and the innkeeper refused to allow the remains of a traitor within his walls. So Desmond sat on the driver's box through the night, sometimes taking short walks on the road to exercise his legs. He could not sleep despite the weariness he felt, especially after the blood he had given to Roger. He comforted himself with the thought that once on the boat for England—assuming they could find a boat leaving quickly—he could at least breathe a little easier.

At dawn the undertaker returned to take his seat on the box, and they continued on the last leg of their journey. Their departure was momentarily checked by the arrival of a messenger on horseback who pulled up to the inn as they were preparing to leave. Clearly the rider had been at it all night and was covered with road dirt from hours of hard riding. He hailed the undertaker to find if he was cognizant of an Englishman by the name of Beckwith. The driver nodded silently toward Desmond. The messenger withdrew a letter from his pouch and delivered it. He received his pourboire from Desmond civilly and went inside the inn to recover from his night's labors.

The funeral cart lurched northward toward Le Havre as Desmond opened the sealed letter with curiosity. No signet or imprimatur indicated that it was from his bank. He wondered who could have sent it and was only slightly surprised when he recognized the hand of the writer. A chill passed through him as he read the old-fashioned script.

My Dear Beckwith—

Congratulations at having accomplished what I suspected you would try. I cannot say I grieve, for to lose Roger to the republican rabble in that way would have been tragic indeed. It was a bit of rashness on my part, I confess, and I am not unhappy to see it thwarted. Roger is no doubt better off with your guidance, and in England. Our circle here was apparently too confining for one so new and so full of modern ideas. Please, dear sir, let us not, however, part on other than amicable terms. Our race is too small and scattered to maintain enmity within. We may never meet again, but it is my sincere desire to clear the air between us and to assure you of my unswerving admiration.

It was signed merely "C," lest it fall into republican hands, and Desmond was forced to smile as he read it. "So Roger was right, he *was* afraid of me!" At least here was one direction from which they never again need fear reprisal. Roger, then, was a tabula rasa, a new man. Free of his past life, he could start a new one, with Desmond as his comrade, in England. Desmond glanced back at the coffin. There had been no indication of trouble from within, but Desmond knew that Roger must have awakened at least twice since their departure. "Just lie quietly, Roger my friend. Your trials will seem like a momentary darkness once we reach England. I will show you how happy we can truly be." His words were scarcely more than thoughts, spoken so softly as to be inaudible. The driver paid no heed, mindful only of getting his charge to Le Havre as soon as possible.

Even in those days of turmoil, boat traffic across the channel was only slightly diminished. Desmond's papers were in good order, and his odd luggage was far outweighed by his generous purse. He readily found a small Dutch vessel sailing for Portsmouth and booked a cabin—the captain's cabin, in fact. He needed sleep and would not leave the coffin in the hold with the other cargo. So, for a sum, the captain turned over his own cramped but comfortable cabin, and into it Desmond's few pieces of luggage and Roger's coffin were loaded.

Stopping only to write a hasty letter to the Paris bank, he explained that he had decided to return to England. Requesting that his belongings be sent on to the London office, where they would be placed in his rooms above, Desmond boarded the boat with a lightened heart. He offered the captain a bottle of fine port in thanks for his cooperation and shared a glass of it with him before sailing. He explained that he was taking the mortal remains of this unfortunate associate back to family in England rather than let him be buried in the hostile land that had, in its way, caused his untimely death. The captain was most understanding, made even more so by the gold the young banker had given him. As the tide dropped and the boat prepared for sailing, the captain left Desmond in the cabin, promising that nothing would disturb him until they landed in Portsmouth.

The captain gone, Desmond leaned over the coffin and spoke, knowing that Roger wouldn't hear him but feeling the need to reassure him. "Fear not, my friend; we are off, and soon we'll be home."

He carefully bolted the cabin door, then, undressing, lay down on the narrow bunk that served as the captain's bed. At least the linen was good, for the need to call upon sleep overwhelmed Desmond rapidly. As he began to sink ever more deeply into stillness, he thought once more of the look on Roger's face that day in the courtyard of the *conciergerie*. Then the vision faded to blackness, and Desmond felt only the swaying of the waves as they rocked the ship gently on its way to England.

CHAPTER 5

Desmond swam upward from the darkness of sleep to the sound of his name. He felt himself being shaken and heard again his name, called as if in fear. "Desmond! Desmond!"

He opened his eyes and was staring up into the frightened, sleep-disheveled face of Tony, whose fear gave way to a smile when he saw Desmond's eyes open. Desmond returned the smile and reached up to caress the soft stubble on Tony's jawline. "Can't a body get a good night's sleep around here?"

"Sorry, Desmond, but you were so still! I just woke up a little bit ago and was lying by you when I realized you didn't even seem to be breathing. It scared the hell out of me. I'm sure glad you woke up— I was about to call an ambulance!"

"Well, that would have been a charming good morning!" joked Desmond, who at the same time felt a sickening alarm at the back of his mind. He had let himself sleep all night with a mortal! Of course he had seemed dead: He *had* been—and no mortal had ever witnessed that sleep. But it had been such a joy to nestle up to another man, to not sleep by himself! But what if Tony had realized his deathly stillness an hour earlier? What if he *had* called an ambulance? Desmond shuddered at the thought. Two centuries of safety shattered by one night of careless passion. How could he have been so stupid? His racing thoughts were interrupted by the sight of

Tony's naked backside as he padded out of the room toward the bathroom at the end of the hall. His heart leaped, and Desmond understood that last night had been unusual in other ways as well. Tony was something he had never expected, and he was still not quite sure what it was even now. But he had brought Tony here intentionally and had slept with him knowingly. The man was here, and Desmond could not deny the fact that it gave him a feeling of joy to see him.

"Great bathroom!" came the cry from down the darkened hallway. Tony had obviously just discovered the ultramodern marble and mahogany bathroom Desmond had installed in the 1880s, finally convinced that running water and flush toilets were advanced enough to be worthy of the investment.

Desmond climbed out of bed, piling the covers on the sleeping form of Cosmo, who responded merely by purring for a moment. He went down the hall and nuzzled up behind Tony, who was urinating happily into the elaborately enameled porcelain toilet bowl. Desmond had never seen anyone enjoy a bathroom more.

"You're certainly an ideal guest—everything makes you so happy!" Desmond said, resting his chin on Tony's shoulder and whispering into his ear.

"Thanks—but this is so great. It all looks like new. You take good care of it."

"Yes, I always have. These bathrooms were my— ah, my great-grandfather's pride and joy. The only additions to the house that he made. The one upstairs on the guest floor is a little plainer but still pretty nice. Would you mind very much using that one while I get ready? I'm a little private about morning ablutions."

"No problem. We've all got our quirks. Is it just over this one?"

"Yes, and you'll find soap, towels, and even a toothbrush in the cupboard inside the door." Desmond had had guests rarely in his house, but he always kept prepared in case. It made him feel more part of the world to maintain his house as a mortal might, even if he had seldom met anyone with whom he felt secure enough to allow to invade his sanctum. Roger, of course, always stayed upstairs during his visits and always teased him about his domestic fussing. It was part of their game.

As Tony's lithe form disappeared up the stairway to the third floor, Desmond called out after him: "And no peeking! I promise I'll give you a tour after I'm dressed." He waited to hear Tony's distant acquiescence before shutting the door and setting about his own morning preparations.

Most of Desmond's toilet was unremarkable—showering, shaving, brushing his teeth—but he knew that he would never have been able to explain one thing. As Desmond stood over the Victorian toilet bowl, he released a stream of what at first looked like blood. It was in fact only the red wine from last night. As with anything Desmond drank, only the alcohol was absorbed by his body; everything else passed through his system unchanged. This was one thing he didn't want Tony to see. If he'd had white wine, it might not be so strange, but Desmond favored port and red wines and figured that separate bathroom facilities were easier than other precautions. He just hoped Tony didn't find his whims too peculiar.

Back together in the sun-filled master bedroom, Tony exclaimed again over the furniture. Aside from the high-posted mahogany bed, there was a marble-topped dressing table with mirror between the front windows, a tall wardrobe, a chest of drawers, and four side chairs. All of the furniture was of the same dark shiny rosewood, inlaid with classical designs in polished brass.

"This can't be American, can it?" asked Tony.

"It is—made by a French immigrant, Charles Honoré Lannuier, about 1810. It was made for my great-great-great-grandfather, for the place he lived in before he built this one. He never replaced the set since it was so good. It's been right here in this room since 1820."

"I've never even heard of an entire bedroom from Lannuier's shop. It's worth a fortune today!" Tony moved from piece to piece, stroking them as if they were alive. His unclothed body glowed in the dappled sunlight slanting through the muslin curtains. His feet were slim and high-arched, his long-fingered hands elegant and graceful. Desmond watched with mingled lust and consternation the unlikely image of this delicious Ganymede inspecting his bedroom. So conscious of money—of Desmond's money. Was this a bad omen? Desmond shook off his doubts.

"Well, I've been lucky. My antecedents have been very conservative, and nothing's been lost. They came from England in to New York in 1798 but apparently didn't bring anything but their money with them. They wanted to be Americans but also wanted English-quality goods, and they got them. Local craftsmen could do anything, really, but most of their customers didn't want to pay for the highest quality. I guess my family was an exception."

"What were their names?"

"Oh, all the men were Desmond—I'm actually the sixth of my name."

"What about their wives?"

"Wives? Oh, well, I don't really know. Things all passed down through the men, you see, so…"

"Pretty sexist, weren't they? Maybe that's why you turned out a woman-hating fag!" Tony laughed as Desmond tried to swat him, ducking out of the way.

"I'll have you know I revered my mother—her name was Anne."

"At least you know *one* name. But your *mother*, Desmond, that's so Freudian!"

Then Tony grew serious and looked thoughtfully at Desmond. "Your folks are both dead?"

"Yes, a long time ago."

"Then you're an orphan."

"Well, I'd never really thought of it that way. I *am* an adult, Tony, and I was always pretty independent."

"I know. I'm sorry if I offended you. You obviously take family seriously, and I didn't mean to make fun."

"That's OK, Tony. My mother died when I was very little, and I didn't really know her. My grandmother was gone long before I was born. My father died back in 1964, when I was 21. I've been on my own here ever since."

"Since I was born!"

"Thanks for depressing me about my middle age!" Desmond leaped on Tony, pushing him down onto the bed, and quieted him with a long kiss. Then he rolled off him and said, "I forgot to buy any food. You want a tour before or after we eat? Because we've got to eat out."

"Before, definitely. Food can wait," Tony answered eagerly.

"But first," Desmond said with mock seriousness, "we've at least got to put on robes. Seeing you naked is much too distracting. I don't think I could make it out of this room with you this way." Desmond smiled and lazily ran a finger down Tony's soft belly, mentally making a note to stock the kitchen with basic breakfast things. He opened the wardrobe and took out two long silk robes, giving one to Tony. Then, with the formality of a guide in a country house, he started his tour.

They did the house in reverse, since they were already halfway upstairs. The third floor consisted of two large guest bedrooms, each with a severely classical gray marble mantlepiece. A bathroom and a third, smaller, bedroom completed the guest quarters. These rooms had once been sparely furnished but had grown more lavish over the years as Desmond had moved things from the ground floor parlors up to the guest rooms. The mate to the cane-seated settee in the front hall was in one bedroom, as were several ormolu-mounted Empire chairs that had come from the front parlor. The original carpets were still in place on the floors, colors still bright. Tony marveled at everything.

The second floor consisted of Desmond's own bedroom and bath at the back and the big Gothic library, which stretched across all three bays of the house on the street side. This he had redecorated in 1845, when the craze for Gothic was just beginning to crest. The old classical furnishings had been moved to the guest rooms—all but the bookcases, which had been refitted with Gothic-style glazed doors.

"Who did all this? Meeks & Co.?" Tony now spoke like a connoisseur.

"No, Alexander Roux, actually. My great-great-grandfather didn't like their designs as much as Roux's, which were more sophisticated. Roux didn't do much Gothic—this is probably his best surviving interior. His descendants did the bathrooms on these two upper floors. They'd become decorators by the 1880s."

"Everything is in such great shape!"

"Well, you see, I've had some things redone—the curtains and carpet in here, for example. This room was used more than others, and the originals had begun to wear badly. They saved samples of the originals for the reproductions. I've got them all stored in the attic, labeled. All the bills for each generation's changes are in my files."

"Could I look at them sometime? Most people think old documents are a real snore, but I love them."

"We'll see, if you're a good boy." Desmond swatted Tony's behind and shooed him out of the room, wondering what he'd started.

The tall, narrow staircase had a thick mahogany handrail supported by carved balusters. It flared outward slightly at the bottom, ending in a heavy carved newel post topped by a faceted cut-glass knob. The first floor was the parlor floor—long double parlors, front and back, were divided by paired Corinthian columns. The rear parlor, set up as a dining room, still had the black marble chimney piece from 1820, its simple broad shelf supported by two slender Ionic colonnettes.

The front parlor had been redecorated in the modern French mode of the 1850s. Here the mantelpiece was a sculptor's confection of snow-white Carrara marble. A nest in high relief, complete with a clutch of eggs, served as the keystone to the arched firebox, while two ghostly birds seemed to flutter in attendance amid scrolling vines, grape clusters, and rose blossoms. Some of the more severe Empire furniture had stayed, including a coffinlike pianoforte and a pier table with a narrow looking-glass between the tall front windows. The elaborate rosewood center table, sofa, and chairs were, however, as curvaceous and flamboyant as the mantelpiece. A tall rosewood étagère stood to the left of the fireplace, its mirrored back reflecting a collection of porcelain enameled with vivid floral bouquets.

"Belter—fantastic!"

"No, those are Meeks & Co. Look closely—you can tell the difference." Desmond warmed to Tony's keen interest. "Meeks is much overlooked today, since Belter's name is so revered in the marketplace. But they sure knew their way around the rococo." Tony gave Desmond a curious glance, and he quickly moved on.

"The dining room has all its original pieces from 1820, plus the chairs and table from the earlier house." Desmond gestured to the rear room and smiled at Tony's expression of disbelief. It looked as if his eyes were about to pop out of his head. Two big mahogany sideboards, brass-inlaid and elaborately carved, flanked the fireplace. These were laden with silver, most of it in the heavy classical style of the 1820s. Below each sideboard was a matching cellarette for wine bottles, shaped like a miniature Greek sarcophagus. The dining table was opened up only enough to accommodate six chairs. These were of a graceful, classical *klismos* form with lyre-shaped back splats. Six more like them were placed discreetly around the walls of the room.

"You're kidding—you don't have a dozen Phyfe lyre-backs!"

"Oh, yes, I do. They came from the Pearl Street apartment my great-great-great-grandfather had before he built this place. That apartment—rooms, really, above the offices he kept—was designed for a rich bachelor's entertaining. The bedroom, sitting room, and dining room were all he had, so he did them up well. I've still got the bill from Phyfe for this set. His shop was just down the street from the flat.

"And the sideboards?"

"Michael Allison. We had them modeled after one owned by a grand Jewish family in Philadelphia named Gratz, who were business connections. They were made for the room, as were the card tables in the parlor and the marble-topped mixing tables in here."

Tony stopped roaming the room and turned to fix a warm smile on his tour guide. "You're as into this as I am. You'd better feed me soon, Desmond. I'm going to pass out if I see anymore!"

"Good, we'll go. There's only the kitchen below us here, and it's new. My father did that back in the '40s—actually, that's probably an antique to you. I've got an office down there, for homework, and there's the laundry and such. But, since there's no food in the larder, we'll breakfast out. Any ideas? I don't eat out much."

Tony suggested a place in the Village to their west. They dressed quickly and grabbed their coats, heading out into the bright November morning. As Tony wolfed down a massive breakfast, Desmond drank a glass of apple juice and watched him in wonder.

"Why aren't you hungry?" asked Tony between mouthfuls. "I've been starving since we woke up."

"I have strange eating habits and as a result tend to eat on my own schedule. It's basically a very weird metabolism, and I've always had to keep a strict diet. I've managed to handle it by eating on my own and just being a spectator when other people are eating. They all think I'm crazy, but it works for me."

"Well, if you've got no choice, who can complain? It must be some sort of allergy."

"Sort of, or at least in that if I ate what most people ate, I'd get very sick." Desmond could say this with truth. Wines and filtered juices were simple enough to pass harmlessly through his system, as were distilled liquors. But his mortal gastric system had been drastically altered during his transformation, and any solid food made him deathly ill, since his body rejected it. He remembered having once eaten a full meal, sometime in the 19th century, buzzed on too much wine and thinking that the aftereffects wouldn't be too severe. He had learned a hard lesson that night and had created his dietary fiction to avoid such problems in the future.

Desmond also felt another qualm arise. Tony was bound to notice inconsistencies if he spent any time at the house with Desmond. This would always be something Desmond would have to watch for. Suddenly Desmond realized he was planning a future he had no idea about, and he nearly laughed out loud.

"What's so funny?" asked Tony.

"I'm sorry, I just look at you, and find myself thinking things I've never thought before—or at least not since I was your age." *And,* Desmond added silently, *that was in the 1740s!* Could this handsome young man really be to him what Jeffrey Chapman had been two centuries ago? And even if this could happen, how would it work; how *could* it work? How could Desmond ever tell this serious, intelligent, modern person that his lover was an ancient English vampire who sucked blood out of sleeping boys? It all seemed so ridiculous, one of the very things that had always kept Desmond distant from friendships. And, for that matter, how did he know that Tony wasn't just another impoverished pretty-boy gold-digger, on the lookout for a sugar daddy? What in heaven's name would Roger say?

"Desmond," Tony began, setting down his fork and knife on the clean plate, "I'm really glad I met you last night. It was so awful when you turned away from me. I'm glad I didn't let you go. Something made me go after you, in spite of how badly I'd messed things up."

"Me too, Tony. I was surprised at myself at the time, but now it seems to make perfect sense. I'm happy you stopped me. Last night was special. Thank you."

Tony smiled across the table, then reached for his coat on the seat beside him.

"I'd better get going, Desmond. I have to be at the employment office by 10—or the unemployment office, I should say."

"OK. I've got to get going today too, despite my instincts to goof off all day with you. You're a good influence on me already." Desmond felt a pang at the impending parting but kept his voice light and cheerful.

As they got up from the table, leaving money with their bill, Tony turned to Desmond. "Does that mean you want to see me again?"

"Of course—if it's all right with you." Desmond's heart leaped at hearing Tony's interest. "Will you call me?"

"Sure. There's no phone in my fleabag, and I certainly don't want to entertain there. But I can call from a pay phone."

"Here's my number, and you know where the house is. If you can't get me by phone, you could leave a note, or something."

"It may be a few days, Desmond. Things are pretty hairy now. But I will call, I promise. You're the nicest thing that's happened to me in months—maybe years."

"Thanks, Tony. Same here. Let's make it soon—as soon as you can."

"Absolutely, Desmond."

Then, out on the sidewalk, Tony gave Desmond a quick affectionate kiss and headed off down the street. Desmond looked after him, bemused. These young people were a lot different than they'd been in 1965 when he'd started this life. Then suddenly he called out:

"Tony, wait!"

Tony stopped and turned.

"What's your last name? I never asked!"

"What's yours?"

"Beckwith, Desmond Beckwith. The sixth!"

"Chapman, Anthony Michael, the first!" And with a laugh he turned and continued on his way down the busy Village street, leaving Desmond openmouthed and speechless behind him.

CHAPTER 6

Desmond did have a busy day ahead of him. Back at the house his basement office waited, with its computer, fax, and telephone. As CEO of Beckwith Investments, the evolutionary offspring of the original London banking house, Desmond Beckwith had to keep in contact with his operatives in Paris, London, San Francisco, Hong Kong, and New York. He was not as active in the company as he had been early on, but he kept his fingers on its pulse every day. Back in Georgian London, the office had consisted of a dozen men with quill pens and pots of black ink. Today, "it" numbered hundreds of people around the globe.

Telecommunications had made expansion and diversification possible in ways Sir Charles would never have imagined. The money generated through his immense holdings was his security, and he had to plan for many lifetimes—five so far. He had also gotten adept at planning for the passing of one Desmond's reins of power to the next. His technique varied from generation to generation, but there was always a son to carry on at the death of one 65-year-old Desmond Beckwith. Desmond had always been careful to follow any tax laws to the letter—he had, after all, seen most of the modern-day Internal Revenue Service created in his time. The last thing his world needed was the scrutiny of the government. His money was his shelter but also his burden. He hated to see huge sums lost to estate taxes when, at the times of his regenerations in this century, he had been forced to "die" and to reappear as his own heir. But honesty was the only practical policy if he was to live out his lives quietly and unmolested by outsiders.

On his way back to the house, Desmond stopped and stocked up on eggs, milk, bread, bacon, maple syrup—anything that seemed as if it might appeal to Tony's taste. From what he'd witnessed over breakfast, Tony was easily pleased. And again he wondered at Tony's name—Chapman. Surely this was a good omen! Coincidences rarely interested Desmond, since the world was too full of them; but this one he grasped greedily. He needed assurance that this impulsive feeling was right. He had brought an unknown man to his home and had invited him back—almost urgently. He had never opened up his life to anyone in this way, and it scared him. The fact that Tony so closely resembled Jeffrey *and* that they shared a name—albeit not a very rare one—made him feel that fate was, after all, behind this.

Desmond also purchased a quantity of organic foods from a health food emporium, thinking this would be adequate to keep Tony's curiosity satisfied on his dietary issue. He would have to plan out his strategy more carefully, but for now he could just keep the larder believably stocked and put things down the disposal when Tony was gone. He hated the idea of such waste but decided it was a necessary evil.

Once the kitchen was filled with its new accoutrements, Desmond went upstairs and made the bed. He still did his own housework, not wanting anyone to invade his privacy. He then spent a couple of hours in his office, handling the details that needed his businessman's attention.

By the middle of the afternoon, Desmond's routine work was done. He now turned to other things. He left the house and headed uptown to a hospital on the East Side. Here he played another role, one that gave him spiritual, rather than financial, comfort. In the hospital he took the elevator up to the isolated little room he had been coming to faithfully for the past four months. With a quick knock on the door, Desmond went in before waiting for the reply. There, sitting up in bed, was a slender dark-haired man with large dark eyes and a small mustache. At first glance he looked older than he was, but the drawn features were the result of illness, not age.

"I'm sorry I'm late, Louie. I got wrapped up in work."

"Hey, no problem, Des; I got nowhere to go anyway. Good to see ya."

Desmond leaned over and gave him a gentle kiss on the forehead.

"How are you doing today? Things more or less normal?"

"Not bad. You didn't check with the nurse?"

"I will on the way out. Why don't you tell me what you've been up to the last day or so. I've been really busy, but I want you to go first, then I'll talk, OK?

Louie agreed readily and began to chatter away animatedly. Desmond settled into a chair by his side and listened intently. Although Beckwith funding supported a hospice program in the city, Desmond had wanted to do something personal. Louis Lambruso was the third person with AIDS for whom Desmond had acted as buddy in the years he had been involved with the volunteers of Gay Men's Health Crisis. The other young men, in their 20s, like Louie, had already died. Desmond had grieved at their losses, but he feared more the inevitable outcome of this particular man's battle with the disease. Since he had first met Louie, in this very room, he had felt an empathy with the young man, partly because of his isolation. Of the other people with AIDS Desmond had comforted and counseled, one had been surrounded by family at the end and the other had had a lover by his side most of the time. But Louie was alone, more terribly alone than Desmond could imagine.

Born and raised in a strict Catholic family in Brooklyn, Louie had lived a double life, trapped by the blue-collar morality of his family and the reality of his homosexuality. He had lived a furtively gay life, knowing that side of his life only through frequent and superficial contacts made at New York's many bars. He had never been a part of the so-called gay community in New York until he had been caught up in the grim specter that haunted all gay men. The response from his family on learning that Louie had AIDS had been all too swift. His brother had beaten him up, badly, almost to the point of death. Hospitalized, he had to depend on state support, since his family had refused to cover any of the expenses. His mother threatened him if he dared to press charges against the family for his beating and then threw him out of the house after his release from the hospital.

Louie had lived by himself on the streets for some weeks until he finally stumbled into the GMHC offices, seeking help. He had been very ill and was put into the hospital with an attack of *Pneumocystis carinii* pneumonia, which he managed to survive. Desmond had been assigned to be his buddy, and he had been coming to this room ever since. He had also been personally covering Louie's hospital costs.

As Desmond listened to Louie's painstaking account of every little humdrum detail of his unchanging days, he thought back on his first encounter with people in such desperate need. It had been during the Civil War, in the middle of 1863, when he had heard of the great influx of Union wounded into the train depots in Newark, New Jersey. No stranger to death, with nothing to fear for his own safety, Desmond had volunteered to try to help the overworked physicians care for the multitudes of maimed soldiers, for whom there were as yet no hospitals in New Jersey. His experience in revolutionary France had not prepared him for the gruesome sight of the depot packed with dying men. At least the guillotine had been efficient and clean. Medicine as it existed was no match for the results of newly invented war machinery. Here was the stench of hundreds of undressed wounds and the cries of agonized voices. Desmond had continued to help, financially and personally, throughout the war, to the amazement of his rich acquaintances in

New York. It was one thing to give money for such things, but to actually go and do them! But Desmond had persevered, knowing all the while that all the money in the world wouldn't spare the men a moment's agony. Perhaps human contact; gentle, if helpless, hands; and comforting—sometimes even hypnotic—talk might remove their minds from the pain and distract them at least for a while, until they received proper attention or died.

And always Desmond was aware of the irony of his position, now as he watched Louie's eyes sparkle with talk, and then as he had seen pain-clouded eyes look up at him with thanks for the little he did. Desmond knew that he could save Louie, as he could have saved some of those Union soldiers, but only in a way neither they nor the world around them would ever have understood. He could have transformed them, causing their limbs to heal rapidly, driving disease out of their bodies with miraculous speed. But then they too would have joined the undead, and Desmond knew that he could never do that. The Baron had tried with Jeffrey and had failed. Desmond had never forgotten that failure.

Louie drew to the end of his account, and Desmond took up the train, telling him all about Roger's visit, his departure, and the subsequent foray into the bar. Louie looked on in delight as Desmond told him about Tony, and Desmond himself took secret pleasure in being able to share such a story. He had never had a romance to share with a client before, and he reveled in it.

"Hey, he sounds real nice, Des. You gonna see him again?"

"I sure hope so, Louie. He's a special man."

"Well, be good to him, and make sure he don't get what *I* got!" Louie pointed his thumb at his chest and smiled widely. Desmond winced at the idea but smiled outwardly at Louie as he bent over to kiss him again.

"I'll do my best, buddy—you can count on it." His kiss changed to a warm embrace, and Louie clung to him for dear life.

As Desmond pulled away and stood to go, he noticed the gold crucifix Louie always wore on a chain around his neck. It nestled crookedly in the sparse chest hair peeking up from the opening of Louie's pajamas.

"Louie, can I ask you something?"

"Sure, shoot, Des. What?"

"Why do you still wear the crucifix? I mean, after what Cardinal O'Connor's been up to and your family and all that...?"

"Well, I figure, Des, that Jesus didn't suffer any less than I am, and He died for me anyway. I can't blame Him if the church doesn't always act so Christian to guys like me. So the least I can do is keep Him near me when I'm sick. Anyway, you wouldn't understand, since you're not Catholic. Once a Catholic, always a Catholic."

"No, I understand, Louie. At least, now I do. Thanks."

"Anytime, buddy, anytime."

Desmond left him there, smiling, birdlike in his frailty. He checked Louie's chart at the nurse's station, his heart falling at what he saw. Then he went downstairs and back out into the painful brightness of the winter sun.

Friday evening Desmond had an affair to go to, a small dinner party. After the emotional turmoil of the week, he looked forward to an evening of talk and wine. He wanted to at least mention Tony to his few close friends, and they would most likely all be there. He relished the idea that they all would be fascinated that he, the aloof and untouchable Desmond Beckwith, actually seemed to be smitten, and would tease him mercilessly. Of course, even this circle of friends didn't know him very well. All of them he had met after his last regeneration, in 1965. Before that time he had been more reclusive than now, shunning most human company except in the most superficial of social or business settings.

But he had been caught up in spite of himself in the gay rights struggle of the late 1960s, and had witnessed with a strange awe the drag queens battling the police at the Stonewall Inn on Christopher Street. From these heady days of revolution—and though it was so much less violent and so minuscule compared with the French Revolution, in its way it had had an incredible impact on his world—he had moved into a greater awareness of the gay culture around him in his city. His life in Europe and in early America had always revolved around silent and solitary meetings in public parks and isolated quarters. His inclination toward his own sex as well as his need for blood had always gone hand in hand. Both had seemed attributes society couldn't understand and would certainly have destroyed had people known of them. Some of the notorious Marquis de Sade's writings had intimated that at least one of Desmond's needs was not unique to him alone, but then Desmond had also shuddered at the violence of that French nobleman's sexuality.

Throughout the 19th century in New York—and even in San Francisco, where he and Roger had gone for their regenerations in 1921—he had not moved in any sort of subsociety for men who longed for other men. This was partly due to the fact that Desmond always maintained his careful fiction of a wife and heir, which, combined with his own natural aloofness and secrecy, might have put off anyone trying to seek him out. After all, Charlon had waited over 40 years before approaching him! And Roger was no help, as he chased women with the joyous abandon natural to him. Roger too had few close friends, but his acquaintances were legion.

So it was in the post-Stonewall years of the early 1970s that Desmond fell into a small circle of educated professional gay men, all torn between fear for their careers and anger at the way their kind was treated by society. They had befriended and supported one another, rather like a therapy group. They had encouraged one another's little forays out of the closet and had sympathized when fear made one of them retreat. None of them had ever understood Desmond's real secret, and he couldn't imagine ever telling any of them. Gradually, as the decade had passed and Desmond's circle had all approached middle age together, they had begun to "come out" within their own worlds, leaving behind the deceptions of the past. Desmond had joined in this evolution, but as his own boss he hardly had the same fears. Only Desmond's secret hunger had never come out, and this remained the one region of darkness on which his friends had never been able to shed the faintest light.

One of these friends, the host of tonight's party, had come closest to breaking down Desmond's barrier. Bill Lawrence had known Desmond longest, and they had vaguely lusted after each other early in their friendship, to no avail. Bill was the youngest son of a large, prosperous Bermudan family that traced its roots to free blacks in the 17th-century settlement of that island commonwealth. He had come to college in the United States in the early 1960s, thinking that opportunities for black men would be better there than in England. He had gone to Columbia University, then to New York University's law school. He and Desmond had met at the bar in Julius's in Greenwich Village in 1965, just after Desmond's last regeneration.

Desmond had been fascinated by and strongly attracted to this dark-skinned, elegant, almost foppish man, with his clipped British accent and college-boy manners. In all his lifetimes Desmond had never been close to any people of color, whose world had been completely alien to him. His first attempt to seduce Bill among the shadows of this backstreet bar, however, had been bluntly countered with a startling—and somewhat drunken—legal polemic against Anglo-American racism. Desmond's hypnotic voice seemed to have no effect on Bill's sharp, finely tuned mind. So, abandoning his efforts and putting his thirsts in abeyance, Desmond joined in, and they had argued and talked at length on the parallels between racism and antigay prejudice. They had quickly become friends, and lust had given way to a brotherly affection. One evening, quite tipsy, they had returned to Bill's apartment from a night of barhopping. They were both frustrated at coming home empty-handed, and Desmond's thirst for blood was exacerbated by his attraction to his friend. They had nattered on for hours with each other, bemoaning their ill luck and the fate of gay men in general. Bill had complained how no one's life was more lonely than his, and Desmond had been on the verge of spilling the beans when he noticed that his friend was snoring peacefully on the sofa. At first angry, then frightened at what he might have said, Desmond had instead taken the drink of life from his sleeping friend. No mention of the evening had ever been made since.

As Desmond rode up to Bill's little flat in the silent elevator, he anticipated the evening happily. Bill had gotten his law degree but had thrown over that profession after passing the New York State bar exam in favor of journalism. He had become a respected investigative reporter at *The New York Times*. In recent years his presence as a more or less openly gay man on the paper had actually begun to do him good rather than harm, as the editors' stance on gay issues slowly changed for the better. In the past five years, he had advanced more than in the previous 15, and the small but glamorous penthouse was one sign of his elevated status. Having Desmond as a friend and financial adviser hadn't hurt either.

The apartment on Madison Square was modern and glossy—Bill called it "totally un-Bermuda"—with a wall of glass looking over the cityscape and including in its dramatic vista both the Chrysler and Empire State buildings. Desmond, once the flurry of greetings was over, escaped to the windows with a glass of wine. He wryly suspected that Roger would live in such a place if he had stayed in New York.

"So, Desmond, can you see your tenement from up here?" Bill came up behind him and gave him a jovial slap on the back, followed by a chaste peck on the cheek.

" 'Fraid not, Bill, but the view is gorgeous. A little too high for me, though. I'd probably get nosebleeds."

"What do you mean, 'tenement'?" asked a guest Desmond hadn't met before.

One of the others piped up. "Haven't you seen Desmond's house? It's a palace!" he said, proceeding to fill him in. Bill was in fact one of those who had actually been to Desmond's quite frequently over the years but still felt it to be as distant and enigmatic as Desmond himself. Desmond turned to his old chum.

"So how's the paper doing—from your end?"

"Great, keeping me busy. More than ever, really, since they've given me more and more AIDS pieces to do. Since they got over their gay problem, they've gone the other direction entirely."

"Exhausting, huh?" teased Desmond, knowing well that Bill enjoyed every bit of his new status.

"Yeah, and it looks like it'll get more so before it cools down. They want me to do some reporting into things other than just AIDS, like changing attitudes, backlash, things like that."

"What 'things like that'?" Desmond could sense a suppressed excitement in Bill's voice. "Something new?"

"Well, for example, and this isn't official yet, there's a case that's just beginning to surface. It's a murder, in fact, maybe more than one. They're not sure, but from what the police say, it might be gay-related. I've been asked if I'd cover things and do some digging."

"Sounds gruesome. Why do they think it's gay-related?" Desmond didn't read newspapers as much as he supposed he should.

"They just found out that one of the victims, the latest one, was HIV-positive. It's given the cops a new slant on the other cases that might tie them together.

From across the rooms a loud voice called out, "Do you mean that the vampire slasher is *gay*?"

Desmond looked around, startled, and scowled at the friend who had produced the outburst. "Where did you get that awful name, Chris?"

"Right out of the glorious *New York Post*. VAMPIRE SLASHER CLAIMS THIRD VICTIM! screaming from the newsstands. You really ought to slum more, Desmond—you'd know more about the real world."

"You forget, Chris," Bill said, "Des *lives* in a slum."

Desmond joined him in the general laughter at his expense, thinking to himself that the *Post* he had read regularly in the 1810s was a far cry from the lurid tabloid of the present day.

"Is that right, Bill? Is this the case they've put you on?" Desmond was troubled by the idea of both sides of his nature being coupled in this grotesque way; it seemed like a personal affront.

"I'm afraid so. The *Post* must have gotten their hooks into a few police reports. It's no great secret, just a theory that hasn't been codified. The *Post* doesn't tend to expend too much time researching this sort of thing."

"But why 'vampire slasher'?" asked Desmond, shuddering at the ugly images the words evoked.

Chris interrupted Bill, enthusiastically giving his own report: "It seems that the three victims have all been attractive males in their 20s. There wasn't any evidence of sexual activity, so this threw off the cops for a while. All of them had apparently been stabbed repeatedly with an ice pick—or something like that, sharp and slender. The choice detail is that each was stabbed in the neck at least twice. Hence the charming nickname. Sure sells papers."

"Didn't the police make the connection between the murders right away?"

"Well," answered Bill, "the first two were similar, so this aroused suspicion. The third one seemed to clinch some sort of a link. The last one's being HIV-positive added a whole dimension. The *Post* grabbed at what the police had and ran with it."

"When are you going to start on it?"

"Probably tomorrow, even though it's Saturday. I would have waited until Monday, but this *Post* headline puts more pressure on me to get started.

"Well, enjoy yourself. Not the sort of thing *I'd* want to deal with." Desmond suppressed a flush of anger, knowing that no one present would possibly understand the source or depth of his feeling. He felt slandered and, at the same time, threatened.

"Let's talk about something more fun," he said suddenly, turning away from Bill's puzzled face. "Say, Chris, how's your love life?"

"Shitty, now that you ask, Desmond. But, more to the point, *why* do you ask? You couldn't care less about anyone's love life. So what gives?"

"Well, it just so happens I've got a new wrinkle in the fabric of my life."

"Really? No kidding!" Chris drew him away from Bill's side, a solicitous hand resting on his arm. "Tell us more. This is going to be better than the *Post*, I can just *feel* it."

The rest of the evening revolved harmlessly around romance, work, and life in the city, just as Desmond had anticipated. He felt almost human.

Desmond left Bill Lawrence's earlier than the rest of the company, who all seemed determined to drink themselves through to the next morning. In another time they would have all gone out to the bars to drink and cruise together. These days most of his circle were more inclined to stay home. The bars had lost a good deal of their attraction. So had the baths, which had once been Desmond's favorite source for sustenance. He had particularly liked the popular St. Marks baths, partly because he remembered it back in the days when the building had still been James Fenimore Cooper's house. He had eventually stopped going entirely. Although at no risk of disease himself, protected by his kind's unique blood, he found himself dwelling morbidly on all those men who seemed to have no care for precautions, no fear of AIDS.

It was ironic, he thought, that although he could neither infect others nor get infected himself, he could derive no pleasure from his hunting when he saw that others had so little regard for their own safety. Even in the vital search for blood, the specter of the plague haunted him.

This night, buzzing pleasantly from the good wine Bill always provided, Desmond paid a visit to a bar he hadn't seen in quite a while, a far cry from the one in which he had met Tony. Here the clientele was more prone to denim and leather, more inclined to attitudes of overt toughness. These men were not really Desmond's style, but he found that his seductiveness worked especially well in an atmosphere so charged with fantasy. He knew what he needed and had no intention of wasting time over polite chitchat.

He plunged into the beer-soaked atmosphere, its stygian dimness moist with breathing. Loud rock music pounded the leather-clad men into submission, making everyone seem to move in slow motion. Desmond was wearing his own leather jacket, an old one from the '30s, sufficiently worn to admit him to this place. He completed his armory of props with a glass of straight vodka, which he drank as if it were medicine. He couldn't order red wine in a place like this and couldn't stomach beer. So he kept his edge on with this smooth liquid fire. His acute hearing tuned out the thumping of the sound system, and his feline vision searched the darkness for likely faces.

Within a half hour of prowling slowly through the paced rooms, Desmond had lured a companion to his side. He had consciously chosen someone as different from Tony as possible. Wavy black hair and a dark two-day-old beard gave this man a sleazy eroticism. His tight, tattered jeans and steel-studded jacket covered only a thin ribbed undershirt. Despite the man's muscles, which were all too apparent beneath, Desmond couldn't help thinking that he was far too lightly dressed for a cold night like this. Spurred on by the vodka and his growing thirst, Desmond put his mouth to his new friend's ear and talked to him soothingly, caressing his thinly veiled chest. Gradually the pair moved into a far recess of the noise-filled bar, where they were shielded from what little light made its way through the smoky haze. Passionate encounters in dark corners were nothing new in this establishment, and Desmond felt no fear; only a pounding excitement edged with hunger. He whispered feverishly into his companion's ear, occasionally nibbling an earlobe or flicking his tongue over the man's neck. All the while his hand caressed taught muscles, dropping lower and lower until he managed to stir the dark man into a near frenzy of expectation. The man groaned with pleasure and murmured to Desmond, "Oh, man, *do* it!"

Desmond pressed him suddenly to the wall and, canines extended, gripped the man's neck with hungry passion. The man went rigid with surprise, then grew limp as Desmond tenderly supported his swooning form. After a few minutes, satiated, heart pounding, Desmond released his grip, running his tongue one last time over the rapidly healing wounds. He offered a sloppy kiss to his barely conscious partner. Then, supporting his weight easily, Desmond helped him back to the front bar, where he plopped him onto a stool.

"Bartender, I think this guy's had a little too much. You'd better let him sleep it off awhile before you send him home." And with that he was out on the street, pulling his collar up to fend off the November wind.

Desmond walked the long trek home to sober himself up and to savor the solitude of the nighttime streets. He feared no muggers but kept an eye out for unwanted company. He could outrun most and overpower others. He had been remarkably lucky in his many years. Only once in this century, here in New York City, had he felt the cold flash of a knife blade cut through his flesh. He had not returned the attack that time but had fled like a wounded animal. In terror he had used a washcloth to stanch the copious bleeding once he had gotten home, actually fainting from exhaustion and loss of blood. When he had awakened from this involuntary sleep, the wound had completely healed. Despite this inhuman power he shunned danger; the pain had been human enough. Desmond had known this city for so long that he couldn't bring himself to fear it. What he feared more was his own power and what he might do. He was adept enough at life in darkness to protect himself, cautious enough to avoid trouble. He never again wanted to unleash the panther from the Bois de Boulogne.

By the time Desmond approached the familiar brick front of his house, it was early morning but still dark. The wind howled down the narrow street, scattering papers and whipping the branches of the few meager trees. His heart warmed to see home even as it beat with the vitality of new blood. He yearned to take a hot shower and to climb into his big bed, nestling in the linen sheets. His thoughts were on this happy prospect as he climbed the marble stoop and took out his keys. As he reached the top step and held his key up to the lock, he froze and his heart leaped. The door was ajar.

Charged with the power of his recent conquest, Desmond decided on a bold, if reckless, action. He stepped back, and with all his force kicked the paneled door open into the vestibule. A dark figure crouched on the floor, and as the door flew inward it flew back with a wounded cry. The light from the streetlamp behind Desmond shone over his shoulder and illuminated the terrified face of Tony Chapman, cowering like a cornered animal by the coatrack.

Instantly Desmond was on his knees before the shivering form, folding it in a comforting hug.

"Jesus, Tony, I didn't know it was you! I'm sorry."

"Desmond, you scared the hell out of me! I was asleep on the floor when the door exploded. God, I thought I was going to die!"

"Tony, Tony, forgive me!" Desmond felt the tears on the younger man's cheeks and wiped them away, kissing Tony's sobbing mouth. "What are you doing here? At this hour!" He hugged Tony tightly to him, quieting his shaking.

"I...I couldn't stay at the hotel. It's so depressing. I've been miserable all week. I lost your number, so I couldn't call, and you're unlisted. I just came over tonight, hoping you'd be home. You weren't, but the door wasn't locked—at least, not the outside one. It was so cold, I thought I'd just sit inside, out of the wind. I guess I fell asleep. I felt pretty safe here—better than *that* horrible place, anyway."

Desmond helped Tony to his feet, unlocking the inner door and bolting the street door behind them. He wondered at the fact that he'd left the door unlocked. He hadn't done that in decades! He was always extremely careful about his security. He switched off the burglar alarm, hidden in its niche to one side of the door. The vestibule wasn't wired to this, to allow him time to get through both doors before setting it off. It was almost as if he had expected to see that face staring up at him from the vestibule floor! A sudden flash returned the events of the evening to him, and Desmond felt a blush of shame rise, a blush Tony wouldn't see in the darkness. He pulled off Tony's coat and let it drop to the floor; then, with another warm kiss, he lifted Tony and carried him lightly up the stairs. He carried him into his bedroom and put him on the bed.

"Wait right there. I'll be back in a flash." He went down the hall to the library and poured a glass of brandy. Bringing it to the bedroom, he found Tony lying back, caressing Cosmo, who had come up from the kitchen and was purring loudly in hopes of food.

"Here, drink this. It's brandy. It'll calm you down and warm you." Tony took a sip, then a gulp, coughing a little at the potent liquor.

"Hey, don't chug it—you'll pass out!"

"I'd love to pass out!" He pushed Cosmo off the bed, and the cat yawped angrily and stalked out of the room.

"I'd better go feed her, or she'll bother us all night."

Desmond went down to the kitchen to attend to his duties as pet owner. Noise in the pipes indicated that Tony was using the bathroom. By the time Desmond came back upstairs, Tony was in bed, naked, smiling and looking much more relaxed.

"Better?" asked Desmond, sitting on the bed.

"Yes, now that the fear for my life has passed." His taunting tone cheered Desmond. The worst had already faded.

Desmond quickly went to brush his teeth, eliminating a large quantity of red wine from his system. Undressing with a rapid carelessness as Tony watched with hooded eyes, he climbed under the covers and snuggled up to the young man.

"You've got a nice body for an old guy," teased Tony.

"And you've got a sharp tongue for a vagrant! Here I rescue you and sweep you into my castle, and all you can do is make jokes about my age! Such gratitude!"

"Gratitude! After you practically frightened me to death, I should sue you."

"Sue me—for what?"

"Breach of contract."

"What contract?"

"Knights in shining armor don't kick doors down while threatening to kill innocent damsels who happen to be sleeping on their floors."

"That's a contract?"

"It's in all the books—just look it up."

"Sure, and you've got a nice body for a moron," said Desmond as he rolled on top of Tony and locked their lips in a long kiss. The earlier passion of the evening's hunt faded to nothing as Desmond felt his soul explode at the sensation of Tony's lithe frame beneath him. They wrestled together for a while, again exploring each other's bodies as if neither had ever before encountered a naked man. Desmond sighed as he kissed Tony's smooth, curved instep, then his ankle, working his way up past the smooth muscles of his thighs to nuzzle in the dark golden hair at his groin. Tony rubbed his back, thrilling him with his soft, precise fingertips as he caressed the ridge of his spine all the way to the downy swell of Desmond's firm bottom. As he slipped his fingers into that warm crevice, Desmond groaned and turned to look into Tony's eyes.

Wordlessly, Tony kicked the bedclothes to the foot of the bed and turned, opening the drawer of the mahogany nightstand. Turning back, he placed a small box of condoms and a tube of lubricant on the sheet beside him. He smiled shyly.

"Are you ready for this? I thought, just in case…" his voice trailed off, and Desmond could see a flush rise up his pale neck. But no embarrassment could hide the physical fact of Tony's readiness, and Desmond laughed softly.

"Always prepared, just like the Marines. Or is it the Boy Scouts?" Then, more seriously, "I'm ready, Tony. But I want you to know that this is a two-way street. If you're ready for me, I'm ready for you."

It was Tony's turn to laugh. "My, what a coy metaphor. Well, then, let's get going. We've only got all night." Then he lay back, stretched luxuriously, and raised his arms to welcome his lover's embrace.

Once they had settled down, Tony began to doze off, drained and content. Desmond realized that he too was very tired and needed rest. How could he put Tony out of the bed and send him up to the cold guest room on the third floor? He did not want to leave Tony here by himself after what they had been through this evening. He still didn't know what lay behind Tony's coming here so late. He struggled for a short while, then nudged Tony.

"Hey, before you go to sleep, will you do me a favor?"

"Yeah, sure, what?" Tony rubbed his eyes sleepily.

"Don't try to wake me up in the morning, if you're up before me. You don't need to panic if I seem really out of it—it's just the way I sleep. Very deep. If you try to wake me, I just get cranky." He scanned Tony's eyes for a reaction and found only curiosity.

"So I should just let you lie there like a corpse, huh?"

"Right. Often I don't sleep well, so I need what I can get."

"OK. I promise. If I'm hungry, can I go down and fix breakfast?"

"Fine. The kitchen's all stocked. I tried to imagine everything you might like."

"Gee, you must be rich! I'm a big eater."

"Just go to sleep. I'll see you in the morning." Desmond switched off the bedside light and moved in as close to Tony's backside as possible, wrapping his arms around the younger man's slim torso. Gradually, as Tony dropped off, his breathing slowed and evened out to a regular sigh. Once he was dreaming happily, Desmond rolled onto his back and, composing himself, sank peacefully into his own slumber.

CHAPTER 7

Sunlight was filtering weakly through the closed shutters when Desmond's consciousness surfaced the next morning. He couldn't remember what time he'd gone to sleep but noticed that the sheets beside him were cold. Exhausted as he had been, Tony hadn't topped Desmond's own six-hour requirement. Desmond got out of bed, pulled the long wrapper from the wardrobe, and went downstairs. As he reached the parlor floor, he could smell bacon—something he couldn't ever recall smelling here in the morning. Tony was sitting at the white-enameled kitchen table, munching on fried eggs and the bacon Desmond had smelled. He jumped up, gave Desmond an eggy kiss on the cheek, and resumed his meal.

"You didn't sleep very long. You OK?"

"Great! Do I look that bad?"

"No, you look lovely. It's just that I slept only six hours, and you've been down here some time."

"Couldn't sleep any more, and the way *you* sleep makes you about as cuddly as a stiff, so I thought I'd drown my sorrows in cholesterol. Sure you don't want any?"

"Positive—with that menu I'd spend my day with my head in the toilet bowl upstairs for sure."

Desmond poured himself a glass of cranberry juice from the refrigerator and sat down at the table with Tony. Tony, still barefoot, had pulled on his shirt and slacks from last night. Desmond watched him eat for a few minutes, then asked: "Am I that unpleasant when I'm asleep?"

"No, not really. Just very still. I mean, it's like you're not even breathing." He looked at Desmond. "Like a house with nobody in it."

"What?"

"A line from a corny Joyce Kilmer poem I learned as a kid—

> I suppose I've passed it a hundred times
>
> but I always stop for a minute,
>
> And look at the house, the tragic house,
>
> the house with nobody in it.

I thought of it while I was sitting in your vestibule last night. Didn't realize it was still in my memory, even. Your house must have dredged it up. I'm sorry, I didn't mean to hurt your feelings."

"No offense taken, Tony. I'm not used to having people sleep with me. I've never been reviewed before, that's all."

"And anyway, what you do when you're awake is more important, and I've got nothing to complain about there!"

"That's more comforting." Desmond laughed and got up from the table. "Any plans for today?"

Tony stopped chewing and looked up. The old worry crease had reappeared on his brow. "No, why?"

"Well, I just thought you might want to spend some time with me, if you're not otherwise engaged."

"Now, what would be otherwise engaging me? Look, Desmond, not to cast aspersions on your smarts, but I am an unemployed, impoverished noncurator with no home but a disgusting furnished room in a urine-stained hotel. A handsome executive type with a gorgeous town house full of antiques carries me up the stairs to his bedroom, sweeps me into sexual bliss, provides me with a pig-out breakfast, and then wonders if I want to spend the day with him? Are you nuts?"

"My, you do go on; but I'm flattered. You forget, Tony, you are also a gorgeous guy with charm and brains, and one can't sleep with a town house full of antiques."

"No, but I'd like to sometime." Tony leered up at Desmond, who smiled wistfully at him.

"I've done it, Tony, for too many years. I guarantee, it's more fun sleeping with you."

"Yeah, well I've been sleeping with me for years, and I'm bored. Want to trade?"

"You for the house? It's a deal."

They both laughed, then Desmond turned, tossing back as he walked down the passage to the stairs, "I'm going to get ready. You know your way to the third floor?"

In half an hour they were both in the library. Desmond was putting the newspapers in a rack by his favorite chair, and Tony was holding Cosmo, who purred with gratitude.

"This is a wonderful room," mused Tony, half to himself. "I'd love to curl up in here with a good book and a fire."

"Just what we'll do this afternoon, if you like. I usually spend my Saturday afternoons reading in here."

"What do you have in mind for this morning?"

"Oh, nothing specific. Just some shopping, walking. Show you a few things I like. That sort of thing."

"Sounds great."

"Good, let's go. Dump the cat and get your coat."

Tony's jacket was on the floor in the front hall where Desmond had dropped it the night before. In the vestibule was a knapsack, lying under the mahogany bench.

"Oh, there it is. I'd forgotten I'd brought it."

"Just leave it on the bench. We'll come back."

"Remind me—I brought something for you."

"A present…for me?"

"Something to read. A paper I did in college."

"Oh, I see, you want me to read your term papers, is that it?"

"I just thought you'd enjoy it; it was my senior thesis. I think you'll like it. It's *very* scholarly." Tony's mock seriousness revealed to Desmond the sincerity of his intent.

"OK. When we get back we'll light a fire, and I'll read every word."

"Thanks, Desmond." Tony flashed a grateful smile, and they went out into the day.

Desmond had more of a plan in mind than Tony knew, and he gently steered the young man through the course in his mind without making it too obvious. Walking over to the West Village through Washington Square, they talked of sundry things. Tony sketched his childhood and family life in Pennsylvania. Desmond told of his business, his involvement with GMHC, and the party the night before.

"You really told your friends about me last night?" Tony seemed genuinely flattered.

"You bet I did—it was a historic moment for me. Someone tried to engrave an inscription on one of the goblets with his diamond pinkie ring to commemorate the historic occasion. You see, I'm not known for my passion."

"They don't know you very well, do they?" Tony's shy grin made Desmond blush, and he ran his hand across Tony's shoulders.

"No, they don't, Tony. That's a fact."

"You know, I've read your friend Bill's articles in the *Times*. He's good. I didn't realize he's gay."

"Neither did the *Times* until a few years ago. He was terrified that he'd get fired, but they kept him. At first—at least Bill thinks so—they kept him on because he was black. After a while, they realized how very good a reporter he was and what his gay perspective could bring to his work. Now he's vital as their link with the gay community."

"How does he feel about this vampire-slasher story they've got him on?"

"I don't know. I didn't probe too much. The whole thing gives me the willies."

"I know, and now that this HIV thing's cropped up, they'll probably call it the *gay* vampire slasher just to sell more papers."

"God, I hope not! The last thing we need now is some deranged gay guy running around stabbing tricks in the neck."

"But didn't he say there didn't appear to be any sex involved?"

"Right, but you've got to admit, the pattern, small as it is, points to someone who has a taste for pretty young men."

"Like you, huh?" Desmond was so startled at this that he missed Tony's mischievous look.

"What do you mean? Why do you think I'd go after—"

"Hold it, Desmond, calm down. I was just kidding. You know, you and me. I'm younger, not hideous—get it?"

"Oh, oops. Sorry; I told you it gave me the willies."

"No problem." Now it was Tony's turn to give Desmond a side-long hug as they walked.

"I guess I'm afraid it *is* someone like me who's doing this," Desmond admitted.

"How so?"

"Well, middle-aged, maybe lonely. Maybe rejected by too many pretty boys at too many bars."

"You couldn't ever hurt anyone, Desmond. I'm sure of that."

"How can you be sure? You don't know me, Tony."

"I think I do, Desmond, I really think I do."

Desmond smiled at him uncomprehendingly, and they walked on in silence.

As they started down Christopher Street, Desmond excused himself. "Just for a minute, Tony. I've got to talk to someone."

"Hurry back!" Tony called after him as he disappeared inside an apartment building. Tony studied the building a moment, realizing that it had probably been something else once, for it was a lot older than most apartment buildings. It looked vaguely institutional and probably of the same vintage as Desmond's house. Then his mind drifted to the various distractions in Greenwich Village on a cold, bright winter day. He wandered down the street a little, peering in windows, shopping the way someone with no money shopped.

A tap on his shoulder startled him, and he turned to find Desmond smiling at him.

"Browsing?"

"You bet. It's all I can do."

"Let's go in. You don't have to buy to go in. This city's full of deadbeats who shop for hours without buying. I love shopping, and I hardly ever buy things."

"Does that make you a deadbeat?"

"Ouch! Wounded by my own sharp tongue!"

They went into the shop Tony had been staring at—a boutique selling modern household goods geared at a young professional crowd with more flair than space in their cramped city quarters. Desmond and Tony compared all sorts of folding and collapsible furniture, critiqued flatware and kitchenware, acting for all the world like a newlywed couple shopping for their first apartment together. Desmond noticed that Tony looked at everything, even brand-new things, with the same sort of critical historical eye he used on old things. He was fascinated by functional design, practicality, quality of construction, and finish. He also made note of the things Tony liked best as they made a game out of selecting their favorites.

"Desmond, let's get out of here," Tony whispered. "It's too depressing when you can't buy things."

"Nonsense, it's like going to a museum. Do you get depressed looking through the American wing just because you can't buy what you see?"

"You bet I do!"

"Oh, I forgot you're a curator. In that case..." and he hustled Tony out of the shop so quickly, they both broke into laughter on the sidewalk.

"Now I'm really embarrassed. We'd better move on!" Tony laughed as he took Desmond's arm and pulled him away from the store.

"Tell me, Desmond," Tony started as they sauntered aimlessly down Christopher, "why do you even look at modern things, with that house full of goodies?"

"I don't know, just interested. Remember, everything was modern once. When my ancestors put in that Gothic library, it was the cutting edge. Just because I hold on to the stuff from the past that I've inherited doesn't mean I don't care about what's being made today."

"Then why don't you redo your kitchen? It's like walking onto the set of *Leave It to Beaver*."

"What are you talking about?"

"Good God, don't you know who Beaver is?"

"Aside from the furry animal who eats trees and makes a good hat?"

"Where have you been all your life—but you don't have a TV, do you?"

"No. Never wanted one. I've always been a reader."

"Didn't your folks let you watch ever?"

"Uh, no—that is, it never really came up."

"But you have heard of TV?"

"Of course! I'm not a hermit. Some of my best friends have televisions."

"I'm afraid you're just another intellectual bigot. I've been a TV fan all my life, and I can read too. Television only warps your mind if your mind is weak to begin with."

"Don't get bent out of shape, I don't look down on TV fans. It's just that I'm so used to reading for my escape from the real world that I've never felt any interest in television. Besides, books let you enrich the fantasy your own way. Anyway, you're wandering from your point, which was to make fun of my kitchen."

"Oh, right. Well, why don't you update it?"

"Because it would be a waste of money. It doesn't get used that much, especially with my eating habits. An occasional catered dinner and things like that. Everything works, so why change it?"

"Now you're sounding like the person who only believes in the good old days, and you said you like what's being made today."

"I did, and I do. There's a brand-new heating system, not to mention the burglar alarm and smoke detector. I mean, I did replace the gaslight with electricity. It's not a complete dinosaur."

"You replaced the gaslight?"

"My great-grandparents did. Stop picking on me!" Desmond gave him a gentle punch on the shoulder.

"Sorry, it's fun to tease you. It's just that you *are* very wrapped up in the past. Your whole family must have been. Except for the bathrooms, that whole house is frozen, as if time stopped in antebellum New York. I mean, I'm really into the past too, but in a detached way. You seem so steeped in the atmosphere of your house, it's like you've lived there since it was built."

Desmond smiled nervously. "I guess I do get a little caught up in it. But that's only because I've never had as good an audience as you. Most people don't want to hear me talk about my house. They couldn't care less. I swear, I'm not crazy." Desmond wanted to steer Tony away from this line of thought.

"Do you travel at all?" Tony switched topics abruptly.

"Of course I do. I keep a suite in the Connaught in London, in fact. And one in the Georges V in Paris. I go to visit my friend Roger in San Francisco. We go places together."

"Roger? Who's he, an old lover?"

"No!" Desmond blushed, realizing he'd opened up something he hadn't intended.

"I'm sorry—again! I don't mean to bring up painful memories or anything. You just made yourself sound so isolated, and then you bring up this guy Roger."

"Roger's straight, and we've been close friends for longer than anybody else we know. He's also my business partner, although we're not as active in business as we used to be."

"Retired early, huh? Is he as nice as you are—or as handsome?" Tony's voice was sly, distracting Desmond from his embarrassment.

"Yes—*I* think he's very nice. And handsome. We're just the same age. He's got dark red hair and freckles and green eyes. French, but he looks Irish."

"Sounds adorable." Tony was silent for a moment. "Also sounds like maybe you were in love with him once."

"I was and, frankly, still am in love with him. But I knew right off that friendship was as far as it would go. He loves me too, in his way; I know that."

"It's funny for a straight man to be so close to a gay man, especially in, uh, your, ah, generation."

"*My* generation? You hateful child. I'm only 45!"

"Ha! I made you tell me your age!" Tony ducked as Desmond tried to box his ears and ran ahead of him, laughing.

Desmond caught him and kissed him, ignoring the startled looks from a pair of elderly ladies passing them on the sidewalk.

"Let's go uptown."

"Why?" asked Tony.

"I want to show you my museum."

"Your museum?"

"The Museum of the City of New York. I mentioned it the other night. I'm a trustee."

"Sounds great. Let's go."

Desmond stepped out into Seventh Avenue and hailed a cab. As it pulled up to the curb, Tony said, "But still, Desmond, it is neat to have a straight friend who's that close to you—and rare for a gay man."

"You're right, there, Tony. Roger is a rare man indeed. But we've got something deeper than sexuality that ties us together."

"I'd like to meet him someday," said Tony hesitantly.

Desmond looked at him thoughtfully. "I hope you will."

And he opened the car door to let Tony in.

They spent two hours up on 103rd Street, wandering through the grandiose neocolonial building that houses the Museum of the City of New York. They pored over the remarkable collection of New York silver, from the 17th-century Dutch-born silversmiths to the products of Tiffany & Co. They talked about the furniture on display, inspected the period rooms, the costumes, the paintings. They laughed at the dollhouses and the huge variety of toys. They bought a postcard to send to Roger and then crossed Fifth Avenue to wander around the Vanderbilt Gardens. All the plants were dormant and the trees leafless, but the formal layout of the garden was still beautiful.

"Those," said Desmond, pointing to the massive stone-and-iron gates they had passed through from the avenue, "came from in front of the Cornelius Vanderbilt house on the corner of Fifth Avenue and 57th Street, where Bergdorf's is today. It filled the whole block."

"It must have been a palace," said Tony, slightly awed.

"It was. But that didn't stop them from knocking it all down in the 1920s and shipping the rubble to the meadowlands in New Jersey." Desmond's thoughts reeled backward. He had been invited—just once—to a ball in that house, thanks to a piece of advantageous financial advice he had given the great commodore's son. It had been a splendid, if overblown, party. Desmond had danced a bit, drunk a lot of champagne, and—to his surprise—met a pretty young man there, the son of a very grand beer brewer in Newark. They had left the party somewhat early, ostensibly to talk banking, but it had gone further than that. Afterward they had kept in touch in a casual way. Desmond had even been to dinner at the brewer's grand mansion in downtown Newark. Ultimately, however, they had moved in different circles and had lost contact. Eventually the young man had killed himself, or so the gossipmongers had said. Desmond had always wondered why.

"I'm glad my family never moved uptown and never built a fancier house," Desmond said, finally breaking his reverie. "Even I wouldn't want to maintain a 50-room mansion in this city today. My neighborhood has changed a lot, but nothing like what's happened uptown."

Tony said nothing but reached out and took his hand as they headed out of the garden. They walked down Fifth Avenue, then over to Lexington to take the subway downtown to Desmond's house.

As Tony started to make coffee, Desmond shut himself in the office near the kitchen. "Just going to make a few phone calls. I'll start a fire in a minute."

By the time Tony carried the coffee tray up to the library, Desmond had already gotten a fire crackling in the fireplace. Cosmo snoozed happily in her usual nest among the columns of the library table as Desmond looked through the newspapers.

"Do you drink coffee?" asked Tony.

"Yes, black, with a little sugar."

"My, my. Some strange diet you've got, if you can drink coffee with your delicate constitution."

Desmond peered at him over the top of the *Times*. "It's just sugar and water with some flavoring. So shut up and pour, doctor."

"Can I get a book out and read?"

"No, of course not. They're only for decoration," Desmond replied with sarcastic emphasis.

Tony stuck his tongue out and turned to the high, glass-fronted bookcases. He opened one and studied the books for a long time, occasionally pulling one off the shelf to look at it. Desmond continued to read the paper, absorbed in the news.

His concentration was interrupted by a quiet exclamation from Tony. "Good grief, Desmond, you've got incredible books here. So many are original editions—even 18th-century ones. Voltaire, Molière—but that's 17th-century, isn't it?"

"An 18th-century edition, but you're right. The first really funny playwright—if you forget about Aristophanes. Molière always cracks me up."

"And you've got Sir Walter Scott, James Fenimore Cooper, Dickens, Hawthorne, Melville. This is remarkable."

"It's not just me; these books were all bought new. They're only first editions because my family has always read what's current."

"My, my! Here's your creepy shelf!"

"What's that?" Desmond's eyebrows went up.

"All of Edgar Allan Poe, Mary Shelley's *Frankenstein*. Have you read *Frankenstein*?"

"Yes."

"Did you like it?"

"Yes, but it's not at all what most people today expect."

"That's for sure. I thought it was sort of tedious."

"Fair enough. Certainly not like the movie."

"Who's Sheridan LeFanu?"

"A now-obscure writer from the 19th century. He wrote what is considered the first classic vampire story, *Carmilla*. He was very popular in his day and is now, with his own following of devoted, if peculiar, readers."

"And *Dracula*." Tony pulled a fat volume from its place. "Autographed! Wow! Where'd you get this?"

"From Bram Stoker, I imagine. My family went to London a good deal. *Dracula* was a best-seller in its time, you know. Are you surprised, or did you really think Bela Lugosi created the character?"

"No, I'd heard of the book, but I've never read it. It would be fun to read a first edition—actually signed by Stoker. Is it good?"

"I loved it when I first read it. It's pretty Victorian in its sentiments—lots of high moral tone—but incredible as a story, anyway. Go ahead."

"Thanks." Tony settled down in one of the big dark green leather chairs next to the fireplace, opposite Desmond's own, and opened the book. Desmond, watching him, recalled his brief meeting with Bram Stoker in London and remembered well the tall bearded Irishman's serious face. They had talked over brandies in a dark little pub in the theater district, where Stoker worked as the stage manager for Gilbert and Sullivan. Desmond had quizzed him about his research and had brought out a finely bound copy and asked him to sign it. Stoker had been flattered by Desmond's sincere and knowledgeable interest in his work. Desmond was fascinated by the author's keen insights into the mythology of the Eastern European vampire and his skill as a storyteller. Stoker had never suspected how close he had been to a real vampire nor how different that creature was from his fictitious count. This book had long been a key piece in Desmond's collection of tales of the occult and the mysterious, which he had continued adding to right to the present day with Anne Rice's contemporary vampire chronicles. These too were signed by the author. Desmond had traveled to New Orleans expressly to meet her in her romantic, moss-draped villa.

Tony will never know, Desmond mused silently, *how thrilling it was to find my first vampire story, regardless of how inaccurate and penny-dreadful it might have been. He'll never understand the pain of seeing your own race described by people who know nothing of you, who make you a child of Satan because they cannot comprehend your existence in any other terms.*

Desmond's eyes were fixed on Tony's bowed head when he looked up and caught Desmond's stare.

"So aren't you going to read it?"

"Read what?"

"My paper. You said to remind you. I'll go get it." He darted out of his chair and was down the stairs in a flash. He returned a minute later with a tidy dark green folder, which he handed proudly to Desmond.

"*Status, Style and Technology: Chair-Making Practices in Nonurban Areas in the Delaware Valley, 1700–1800.* Hmm, sounds gripping." Then, seeing Tony's face fall, he added quickly, "I'm sure I'll enjoy every word. Now, you sit down and read so I can get started."

Tony settled back into his chair and picked up the book again. Desmond watched his dark eyes lock on to the page, the little crease of concentration between his sandy brows. His one free hand absently caressed his own jaw, the slender fingers moving gently as if to some unheard rhythm. Once Desmond could tell his attention was firmly focused on the book, he turned to the term paper and dutifully started to read.

It was not exactly like reading a novel, but Desmond was impressed by the elegance of the language and the level of scholarship. Dry bones to some people, but Desmond was fascinated by the vivid, if somewhat economically slanted, picture of life in the past that Tony had managed to paint by using a group of surviving artifacts and related documents. This young man was no slouch. Here was someone who really knew his business and could, moreover, express himself in well-wrought English. Desmond looked up from his reading about halfway through Tony's paper, only to find the younger man oblivious to his presence, deeply wrapped up in the fantasy of Bram Stoker's prince of darkness. Desmond smiled with a quiet satisfaction and turned back to his reading.

The fire had burned low, and the evening shadows were enveloping the room in darkness by the time Tony roused from his book. He put it down on the table beside his chair and rubbed his eyes. "What time is it?"

"Only about 6, but late enough."

"What should we do about dinner?"

"*We're* not going to do anything. I'm kicking you out." Desmond stood up and stretched, catlike, with Cosmo rubbing at his ankles.

"Huh?"

"You've got a lot of work to do at home."

"What are you talking about? The only thing I can do in that hotel is kill cockroaches and watch the walls crack."

"That's not your home, but you will have to get your clothes at some point."

"Sorry if I seem obtuse, but I'm lost."

"Tony," said Desmond softly, getting up and going over to him, "I did a few things this afternoon for you. I didn't tell you because I didn't want to argue with you."

"What things?" Tony looked curious, a tiny bit worried.

"Remember when I stopped by that apartment? Well, I own that building, and I knew there was a studio unoccupied. The last tenant died of AIDS three months ago. I knew him slightly and hadn't been able to bring myself to let anyone show it yet. You were in such terror over that hotel you're in last night, I decided you really needed the space, someplace clean and safe."

"But Desmond, I can't afford it, and I've got no furniture—"

Desmond silenced him with an upraised hand. He knelt down by Tony's chair and kissed him softly.

"It's paid for, for the next three months. And I also had the guys in that shop we were in this afternoon deliver all the things you liked best. There's a sofa bed, tables, chairs, bookcases, dishes, and the like. I forgot a TV, sorry."

"Desmond, you can't—this is too much!" Tony's voice rose, and Desmond was startled to see tears well up in his eyes, glittering in dim light. "I didn't come over here to play on your sympathy, honestly! I just needed to see you again, to be with you. I wasn't fishing for, for…"

He looked at Desmond with a plaintive expression. "I wasn't looked to be *kept*, Desmond!"

Desmond winced at the word, then put his hands gently on Tony's shoulders still kneeling before him.

"I'm not keeping you, Tony, I'm taking care of you. You definitely need taking care of. Your parents can't or won't do it, except by their own terms. I want to, Tony. I care about you. When you caught my arm in the bar that night, I didn't relent just because I wanted sex with a handsome guy. You needed my help, maybe more than you knew. I knew it then. Then, when I saw you shivering in my vestibule last night like a whipped puppy, I knew you needed more than just my companionship."

"But Desmond, the money…" Tony began.

"No buts, Tony. The money is nothing. I'm loaded, remember? And as for the furniture, you can pay me back, if you want, once you get a job."

"Yeah, a job, like when Hell freezes over."

"Don't be so glum. I read your paper. It's good. You've got a scholar's mind. You're ideal for museum work. It'll never make you rich, but it'll make you happy."

"I've been trying to get a job for two years! That's why I'm scraping bottom like this."

"So keep trying. I'm here to make sure you don't hit bottom again. I'll protect you. I'll be your friend."

"Oh, Desmond, I'm just so uneasy about accepting all this from you with nothing in return."

"Nothing? Bullshit, Tony. You've given me more than you know in the past 24 hours. Roger worried the same way when we first met, when I helped him. He gave me something that I've always treasured and always will."

"Roger—your straight, cute, redheaded friend Roger?" Tony's worry seemed pushed aside by curiosity at this.

"Yes, that Roger. Now he's got his own big house in San Francisco, and he's as rich as I am. His friendship over the years has more than paid back everything I ever did for him. So let me do this for you, OK, Tony?"

Tony pulled Desmond into a hug. "OK, Des, OK. Take care of me. Thank you." They held each other for a few moments in silence.

"And now, out you go!" Desmond stood up and pulled Tony to his feet. You've got a new house to unpack and a bathroom to clean. Towels to fluff and fold, blinds to hang. Go nest!"

"When can I see you again?"

"As soon as you get a telephone. Call me. But seriously, maybe give us a couple days at least to cool off. I'm a little giddy over all this, and I know I've rushed you into something you weren't expecting— nor was I. Think things over. How you feel about this, about me."

"I think I know," began Tony.

Desmond held up his hands, "Think about it anyway. Time, kiddo, we both need time. I need to settle back into my routine. You do too. Look for a job. Get used to things. Then call me."

"Right, Des. I'll do that." He took Desmond's hand, and they went down to the hall. Tony pulled on his jacket and knapsack. Desmond handed him the key to his new apartment.

"It's 4C. One room, kitchenette, and bath, on the corner. All yours."

"Thanks, thanks a lot." Tony looked briefly awkward, then gave Desmond a deep kiss and rattled out the door into the dark street.

CHAPTER 8

Sunday, Desmond telephoned Roger from his office. He felt Tony's absence terribly but steeled himself to being alone to let Tony think the situation through. He had never felt this way about any one person, not even Roger himself. Only Jeffrey had given him such love, and even that had been considerably different.

Roger answered with a cheery hello despite the still-early hour on the West Coast.

"Hi, it's Desmond."

"Well, hello, partner. How are you? I didn't get any panicky, depressed calls last week and wondered if I'm losing my charm after two centuries."

"No, nothing like that. It's just that I've been busy."

"You're always busy, Desi. Now, what gives?"

Desmond told him, roughly outlining the entire week.

There was a short silence at the other end, then a loud hoot from Roger. "You're kidding. Desmond Beckwith is in love!"

"I didn't say 'love,' Roger."

"Oh, yes, you did, but not in so many words."

"Do you mind?"

"Mind, whatever for? I've always said all that predatory tricking wasn't good for you, with your romantic heart pining away for a rose-covered cottage for two. I'm a slut and always will be, but you're a different kettle of fish, my boy. Now maybe you won't keep playing Joan Fontaine when I visit. At last I'll have my best friend and not a surrogate wife!"

"I'm relieved. I was afraid you might be angry."

Roger's tone became serious, for he understood Desmond's depth of feeling. "Look, Desi. You are *the* person in the whole world who means most to me. This has been so since we met. You are the rock my whole life has been anchored to. Nothing would give me more pain than if we were ever, for any reason, to part as friends. Nothing would give me more joy than to have your life fulfilled in the way you want it to be. Clear enough?"

"Perfectly. Thanks, I needed that."

"Good. I suppose he doesn't know?"

"Know what? That I'm a vampire?"

"Well…"

"Oh, sure, Roger, I'm really going to tell this young man I've all but picked up out of the street, who is still scared of me anyway, 'Oh, by the way, I'm a 250-year-old vampire, and I sucked your blood the night we left the bar together.' That would be a marvelous way to smooth out our relationship."

"You drank from him?"

"Yes, didn't I say that?"

"No, you didn't. Was it good?"

"Stupid question. It was bliss, but you're leaving the issue. You've never told anyone—any mortal—have you?"

"Sort of."

"*Sort of?* Roger! How could you risk it, even today? We're not exactly something the world is prone to take lightly, right up there with extraterrestrials and the Loch Ness monster."

"Don't worry. It was just a deranged queen, years ago."

"Assuming you don't mean royalty, I didn't think queens, deranged or otherwise, were your line."

"Not that way, Desi. This was back in the '60s—lots of drugs, you remember? This guy was someone I did business with a lot, and we were stoned at a huge party here one night, and I sort of came out to him."

"As a vampire? And his reaction?"

"He thought I was some religious cultist. Made the sign of the cross at me and passed out."

"Beautiful. This is the sort of business you do for *our* company?"

"Relax, he's very mainstream now, Desmond. No risk to our good reputation. And he's probably forgotten my little confession."

"I hope so."

"But that doesn't change things, friend. If you're going to get close to any mortal, you'll have to face this someday. They'll grow old and die; you'll just keep going through the same old cycle."

"I know, but I don't want to think about it yet. We'll cross that bridge when we get to it. I've only known him a week."

"Yes, Desmond, and I've never *ever* seen you, or rather heard you, act this way. This is serious, isn't it?"

"I think it could be. Roger, he looks just like Jeffrey."

The only reply was a low whistle.

"Will you help me?"

"Me? How?"

"Just be there, like always."

"Like you were with me, back in '93?"

"Well, yes. If need be."

"Consider me there, then. But I'm not due back East for a visit until spring. Can you cope?"

"Of corpse."

"Gad! Talk about deranged queens. You're too much."

"Sorry, couldn't resist. Thanks, Rog, it means a lot to me."

"No problem. Keep me apprised of the situation.

"Will do."

"Bye, now."

"Bye-bye."

Desmond rang off, then sat back in his desk chair, staring thoughtfully at the painting over the fireplace opposite his desk. It was an oil on panel—a portrait, so to speak—of Beckwith House.

Painted in the early years of the 18th century just after the house was built, it was all that remained from his father, Sir Charles. It had been installed over the chimney piece in Sir Charles's office at Beckwith and was the only piece Desmond and Roger had brought from England when they had sold the estate and come to New York in 1798. He stared at it, eyes unfocused as his mind whirred and his fingers drummed absently on the desktop. Finally, coming out of his reverie, he turned on the computer and began to type.

Monday morning Desmond called the Museum of the City of New York. The operator recognized his name as a trustee and cordially put his call through to the curatorial division.

"Hello, Vivian Lake speaking."

"Vivian, this is Desmond Beckwith."

"Mr. Beckwith, what a pleasant surprise. What can I do for you?"

"Call me Desmond, to start. I hate formality on Mondays."

"Sure, Desmond. What's up?"

"Well, I'm a little embarrassed, but I've got an idea I'd like to run by you. Got a minute?"

"Of course; you, for one, never waste my time!"

"I'm flattered. Here it is."

Desmond had known Vivian Lake since her arrival a few years after he had filled the vacant place on the board of trustees left by his "father's" death in 1964. They were the same age, and he had become one of her allies on this very conservative board. She was the curator of the decorative arts collection at the museum and struggled to keep her department secure as well as to preserve and enrich the varied collections in her care. In spite of the institution's august history, there was stiff competition in New York's museum world, and it was a constant struggle to keep moving forward. Desmond, whose own passion for things made him her obvious ally, had always supported her when the chips were down. Vivian had developed a soft spot for the aloof Mr. Beckwith, who seemed so much older than he was.

With powerful places like the Metropolitan Museum's American wing courting the Beckwith bankroll, Desmond had remained faithful to his family's tradition, and Vivian Lake respected him for his fidelity. Neither knew much about the other outside of this trustee-curator relationship, but within that context they were good friends.

Desmond had a plan, and he knew it was the sort of thing that smacked of influence pushing and undue pressure. He laid it out candidly to Vivian, warning her that he knew its flaws but stressing that he would leave the final decision to her."

"Can I be honest with you, Desmond?"

"Certainly. That's why I called you and not your boss."

"It sounds fishy. You want to provide money for a curatorial assistant and you want to have us hire some unknown kid from Pennsylvania to fill the space?"

"You make it sound so slimy, Viv!"

"OK, Desmond, make it sound better!"

"Look, all I'm asking is for you to interview him. You do need help, don't you?"

"Of course. I'm always bitching that I need an assistant, especially for research. We just don't have the money."

"Good, that's all set. I'll provide the money. Just set a salary that's appropriate for such a position, and I'll promise it for the next, say, three years."

"What about the kid?"

"Anthony is no kid. He's 24 and a college grad. I've read his senior thesis, and it's damn good material-culture scholarship. I know you don't know him, but with my say-so, would you at least pretend there's a job open and talk to him? If you don't like him, you don't have to hire him."

"And we don't get the assistant money, right?"

"Uh…oh, I see. Well, yes, you will. How about that—I'll promise a three-year grant for the salary and benefits of a research assistant for your department, provided you see Anthony Chapman first.

"Are you serious, Desmond? That's a lot of money."

"Absolutely. Does it sound fishy anymore?"

"No; it sounds like I've backed you into an expensive promise."

"I guess so."

"Send the guy in anytime this week—no wait. Wednesday morning. I'll put him through his paces and see how smart he is. Fair?"

"Fair."

"Good. This is rather exciting, Desmond, come to think of it. Will you send a written proposal to the director, with a copy to my office?"

"In the mail this afternoon, I guarantee."

"Great, and thanks, Mr. Beckwith."

"Thank *you*, Ms. Lake. And one more thing, Vivian. If you like him and he gets the position, he mustn't know the source of the money. I must be anonymous."

"Discretion is my middle name."

"Thanks. Bye now."

Tuesday evening Desmond was about to walk over to the Village to visit Tony, wondering how to ask him about the interview without arousing his indignation or suspicions. Desmond had never known poverty or powerlessness, but he remembered the pall Charlon's influence had cast over Roger's spirit. He knew Tony was smart and able but wanted to give him a chance he wouldn't get otherwise. Too many smart and able people crashed and burned in New York. It was part of life in this city and had been since Desmond and Roger first set foot in it.

Just as Desmond was putting on his coat, he heard the telephone in his office ringing distantly. He raced downstairs and picked it up.

"Hello?"

"Desmond? It's Tony."

"Tony! You've got a phone already? I was just coming over."

"Please do, but first I wanted to tell you some big news. I got a call from a woman at the Museum of the City of New York this afternoon, named Vivian Lake."

"Yes, I know her; she's nice."

"She seemed very amiable to me."

"Well, good. So what's up, a job?"

"Maybe—an interview at least. It seems they've got some extra money from the city and can afford an assistant to help this Vivian Lake in the decorative-arts department. Isn't that great!"

"Yes, fantastic." Desmond was actually a little puzzled. "*How* did they get your name?"

"Through an old job application."

"I didn't know you'd applied there."

"I applied everywhere two years ago. There wasn't anything available, so they just filed them."

"So when's your interview?"

"Wednesday morning—tomorrow."

"Good luck."

"Thanks. But aren't you going to come over anyway?"

"I'm supposed to be cooling off, but I confess that talking to you isn't helping. I'd love to see your flat."

"It's cute. I love all the stuff."

"You should—you picked it all out."

"Come quickly, please?"

"In a flash." Desmond rang off and almost forgot to set the security system in his haste. He leaped down the front steps and walked rapidly westward to the little apartment building on Christopher Street.

Tony buzzed Desmond up, and he rode the tiny elevator to the fourth floor. Tony opened the door before he pushed the bell and wrapped him in a fond embrace.

"How do you like it?"

"Very nice—the stuff we picked out fits perfectly." And it was true. The spacious, high-ceilinged room was spare, to be sure, but Tony had arranged all of the things from the shop artfully, making it a comfy place. Desmond noticed just-washed dishes by the sink and that the bed was unfolded from the sofa and made up with fresh sheets.

"You've eaten?"

"Yeah. I knew you would have, so I ate quickly."

"Still no TV? I figured as much, since you weren't likely to steal one. So I brought this."

He took out the autographed copy of *Dracula* that Tony had left in the library and handed it to him. "To while away the hours without *Leave It to Beaver.*"

"Wonderful; I promise I'll take good care of it."

"You damn well better. I don't lend books lightly."

Tony laughed and drew Desmond close to him again. "But I'm not planning on reading right away." He kissed Desmond hungrily and pressed his body against him with such force that Desmond could feel his ribs through the shirt.

They separated momentarily and began to undress. As Desmond unbuttoned his shirt, he worried as he watched Tony pulling his own over his shoulders, revealing his smooth rippled belly and willowy arms. Physically, Tony satisfied him more than any man had ever done. But what about his thirst? That couldn't be denied for much more than a few days at a time. He must hunt; he must drink. Alone. How could he ever explain this to Tony?

He'll just think I'm out prowling for sex, and I won't be able to tell him otherwise, Desmond thought. *He could never understand or even believe the real reason. I'll just have to try to keep it from him for as long as possible.*

Desmond realized that this new little flat was the best thing for Tony as well as for him. Tony needed someplace to establish his own identity rather than get swallowed up in Desmond's memories. Beyond this it would give Desmond the latitude to attend to his own vital needs without upsetting Tony and without being forced to try to explain.

But even so, wondered Desmond, *how long can that last? How long before Tony notices something?* His thoughts were brought up short as Tony tackled him around the knees and pulled him heavily onto the bed with a laughing cry.

"You're standing there like a zombie! I need you *right now*!" Tony crowed with husky glee. Desmond's flesh shivered at the touch of Tony's body, and his eyes sought out his lover's sparkling dark gaze. He smiled at his young man, then gave himself up to pleasure, letting his worries fall away like so many tattered garments, unheeded and, for the moment, forgotten.

Wednesday morning Desmond awoke to the sound of the distant telephone. He jumped out of bed and ran down the two flights of stairs to his office. He wondered briefly how long the phone had been ringing or how many times the caller had tried him.

He took a deep breath and answered.

"Hello?"

"Desmond Beckwith?"

"Speaking."

"Mr. Beckwith, this is the floor nurse at Lenox Hill Hospital. I'm calling in regard to Louis Lambruso. He's very bad. It's pneumonia again."

"Will he die?"

"It looks like it this time. I'm sorry."

"Is he conscious still?"

"Yes, that's why I called so early. He wants to see you."

"Of course. I'll be right up. Thanks for calling."

Desmond rang off abruptly. He had completely forgotten Louie yesterday, and now the poor guy was going to die alone. Desmond cursed his own selfishness as he raced back upstairs to hurriedly slip on slacks and a pullover. He locked up the house and ran over to the Bowery, where he hailed an uptown cab.

When Desmond got to Louie's room, he found the nurse and a young doctor there with him. The doctor, who Desmond knew was gay and had taken good care of Louie all the time he'd been there, looked up as Desmond walked in.

"I'm glad you got here, Mr. Beckwith. Louie's hanging on, but there's not much more we can do for him. He's not responding to any treatments.

"Can I stay alone with him?"

"Certainly, Mr. Beckwith. Just buzz if you need us or if there's any change."

The doctor and nurse left Desmond in the room. Desmond pulled a chair up by the side of the bed and took one of Louie's hands, careful not to disturb the intravenous tubes that snaked out of his arm. Louie looked unconscious, but Desmond felt a slight pressure on his hand and saw Louie's eyelids flutter, indicating to Desmond that his presence was known. He had not, at least, been too late.

He sat this way for a while, looking silently at the gaunt little face he had come to know so well. The naughty smile was replaced by a rictus that required effort at every breath, and the flashing black eyes were hidden beneath the dark eyelids. Desmond noticed for the first time how long Louie's eyelashes were and irrelevantly wondered if Louie's mother had been envious of them. Louie's mother! The same woman who had thrown her desperately ill son out of her house and had left him to die alone in a hospital room. Tears burned in Desmond's eyes, and he gently dropped his head onto the blanket to stifle his quiet sob.

A hand stroked the back of his head, and he lifted it to find himself looking into Louie's smiling face.

"Hey, Des. Glad you could make it." The voice was a whisper.

"Louie, I'm sorry I didn't come yesterday. I got all caught up in things…"

"Don't worry, Des. I understand. Your new boyfriend, huh?"

Desmond choked a laugh and nodded. "Yeah, sort of."

"Good. I hope he keeps you busy and vice versa."

Desmond could only smile and grip Louie's hand a bit tighter, which made the man smile through his labored breathing.

"Des, I was kinda anxious to see you before…well, you know. I remembered something you said last week. You know, about my cross?" He fingered the small gold ornament on its thin chain.

"Yeah, I remember, Louie."

"I want you to have it, Des. As a souvenir, like."

"But Louie—!"

"Who else do ya think I'm gonna leave it to anyway? No, seriously, I want you to have it. Maybe the cardinal hasn't been any comfort, nor the church either, but this guy's given help when there wasn't anyone else around. Remember like I said, Des—"

"Once a Catholic, always a Catholic. I remember." Desmond smiled in spite of himself.

"Can ya help me get it off? My fingers aren't too steady."

"Sure, Louie, just take it easy." Desmond stood up and leaned over Louie. He pulled the chain around gently until he found the clasp, then undid it and pulled the necklace away.

"Put it in your pocket, so's the nurse don't think you robbed me or nothing." Desmond placed the chain in his shirt pocket.

"Good. Now I can rest easy, Des."

Desmond only smiled in reply and once again held Louie's hand. Into the afternoon Desmond sat in the hard little chair by Louie's bedside, listening to the younger man's stertorous breathing. The background noise of the hospital and the traffic in the busy city below faded into a hushed murmur. The winter sun streamed in through the windows, heating up the room like a greenhouse. Desmond let a bead of sweat run down his cheek but didn't move to wipe it away.

He remembered that hot July afternoon in his bedroom over the bank in Paris when he had awakened to his second lifetime. How the world had changed since then! And yet how it hadn't changed at all. Even with the tremendous knowledge gained during this century, stupidity and selfishness and neglect of others still prevailed. Well, he had saved Roger, at least. He hadn't been able to save Jeffrey, and he couldn't save Louie. Maybe, though, he had saved Tony. Two lost, two won. Maybe, Desmond thought, that wasn't such a bad score for five lifetimes.

The sudden awareness of the room's silence made Desmond start. He realized Louie had stopped breathing. He stood, leaned over, and put his ear to the man's lips. The emaciated hand was limp in his grasp, the body as still as Desmond's own in sleep.

Desmond placed his hand gently over Louie's closed eyes, then bent and kissed his immobile lips, feeling one last time the tickle of the little black mustache. He stood, straightened his shoulders, and went out into the corridor.

The nurse at the floor station looked up as he approached the desk. Her look indicated that she knew why he was there.

"He's gone. Just now, very peacefully."

"I'm so sorry, Mr. Beckwith. I'll call the doctor."

"I'm not going to stay right now, nurse, but I want to make sure all the arrangements are taken care of."

"Yes, Mr. Beckwith?"

"His family won't want anything to do with him. I'd like to have him cremated, however that's done."

"We can do that, Mr. Beckwith. Mr. Lambruso left no orders for next of kin, and since you were his closest contact, we can give you authority."

"Send me the bill for whatever costs are incurred. Can you have his ashes delivered to my house?"

"I would think so, Mr. Beckwith; I'll check."

"Good, and thank you, nurse. You were good to him. He appreciated that, you know."

"Thank you, Mr. Beckwith. I'm glad you think so."

"And the doctor too. Give him my thanks when he gets here. I've got to get outside for now."

"I understand, Mr. Beckwith; I'll tell him."

On the sidewalk Desmond turned westward toward Fifth Avenue. His feet pounded the concrete steadily as he walked rapidly to the busy avenue, then crossed it, heading into Central Park.

On this cold, blustery day, there were few people out, and the park's winter aspect was bleak despite the sunshine. Desmond walked deep into the park. He gradually made his way to the complex network of picturesquely curved paths, dotted here and there with rustic gazebos and little bridges, known as the Ramble. Desmond remembered when this charming part of the park had first been built. He remembered walking with Roger through the young trees amid the great glacial boulders that littered the site. With all the restoration that had been done in recent years, it didn't look all that different from those many decades ago but for the litter that was scattered about among the brown leaves and the rats that played happily in the undergrowth like urban squirrels. But there were people in the Ramble even on this uninviting day, and they were there for reasons unimagined by the park's designer.

Not many men sauntered along the winding pathways, but there were enough for Desmond to notice and to draw him out of his sad thoughts. Frequently enough he had joined the furtive hunters here, even in the early days of the park's creation. Throughout his lifetimes Desmond had always found that those of his inclination sought release and closeness in places like this. Those who had haunted these places seeking love or romance had been disappointed, perhaps, but for those with less lofty ideals, these havens of green shadow offered something potent to slake their thirst. Thirst for sex or thirst for blood—it mattered little; the hunt itself could be great sport, and there was no questioning the intense pleasure.

Desmond smiled to himself, recalling the pleasure; but today the presence of these men also dredged up anger. Here they were, looking for sex, in such weather, in such a place—with Louie's body not yet cold in his hospital bed! How could they? Would these men be seeking safe sex? Desmond doubted it. He feared that those desperate enough to cruise the Ramble on a day like this wouldn't be much inclined to take precautions. They were looking to feed a hunger so deep that it didn't consider matters of safety and health. As Desmond walked, passing men of various ages and races and modes of dress, his anger grew—and so did his thirst. Here he was among them, seeking what they sought, and they knew nothing of who or what he was or what he might do to them.

A man perhaps a decade his junior caught his eye. Beautiful, with chiseled features and windswept blond—*real* blond—hair. He might have been a model. He wore a bulky denim jacket and a long knitted muffler. Expensive cowboy boots and sexily faded jeans completed the outfit. He looked like a Ralph Lauren advertisement. He smiled at Desmond in passing, then stopped at Desmond's own smile. They exchanged a few words of polite foreplay, then moved off the path. Desmond led his partner, who smiled encouragingly with perfect white teeth, to a spot secluded from view, ringed with a small stand of dense evergreens. They sat close together on a sunwashed rock, and the blond kissed Desmond suddenly, with an urgency that startled him. But for all the man's beauty, Desmond could taste the cigarettes in his kiss, and anger simmered along with his craving. Somewhere deep within, the panther growled.

They kissed awhile longer, then the blond lay back on the rocky outcrop, reaching forward to undo Desmond's belt. As he did so Desmond grasped both his arms and pinned him beneath his own weight. The blond, at first startled by the suddenness of Desmond's actions, relaxed and smiled at this show of apparent lust. Then his look changed again, more gradually, to one of confusion, and then of worry, as Desmond spoke fiercely, in a hissed whisper.

"You exquisite idiot! Why do you *do* this? How do you know who I am or what I've done? Why do you risk your life this way?"

The blond just lay there beneath him, staring up in astonishment at the vehemence of the words. Suddenly Desmond found himself looking down into Tony's face, wide-eyed with fright and yearning as he had seen him cowering on the vestibule floor. He suppressed a gasp of surprise, and his voice cracked.

"I'm not going to hurt you. I just don't want you to hurt yourself! Stop doing this, please! Stop doing this!"

There was no reply from the confused beauty, who only fixed his wide blue eyes on Desmond's face with incomprehension. Then Desmond did something he hadn't done in years; he reached up and gripped the man's neck with his right hand. With Desmond's powerful grasp on the carotid artery, the blond's head slumped to one side in a moment. Desmond waited a few seconds to make sure blood flow was restored, and then pressed forward to quench his thirst.

As the unconscious man's blood pumped into him, Desmond's anger was displaced by a dizzying passion. The rhythmic duet of their heartbeats washed Desmond with waves of heat, and he felt himself getting aroused. But the stirring in his groin was quickly overwhelmed by the familiar sensations that coursed through his entire body like flames following a trail of spilled oil. From his lips to the soles of his feet he tingled, a hot ticklish delight suffusing him. The blood was everything. This went beyond sex. This thirst for lifeblood went to the white-hot core of his being. The union Desmond felt with his blood host was consuming, more complete than any sexual union could be.

Unable to turn his head for fear of wasting even a drop, Desmond grappled blindly with the man's clothing. He tore open his own jacket to better savor the man's warmth, and to feel the palpitation of his heart through the fragile partition of cloth and skin and muscle and rib. The pounding of their mingled blood in his veins and the beating of their hearts echoed in Desmond's brain like a syncopated drumbeat.

It was over as quickly as it had begun. His bloodlust sated, he let himself collapse gently onto his unknowing lover, mouth still firmly on his neck, healing the wounds with his powerful saliva. Their hearts continued to beat together for a few moments as they lay chest to chest, with Desmond on top, catching his breath.

A few minutes later Desmond strode out of the park and back onto Fifth Avenue, flushed with fresh blood. He knew the blond would awaken in a short while with only a headache but hoped that he might also have something else; enough fear to keep him out of the Ramble. He hadn't used the old hunting technique for a long, long time. Desmond always preferred to seduce, to combine his sexual urges with his need for blood. He wanted to give pleasure to his providers, to return as much as he took from them. The Baron had taught him this more efficient technique, warning him that seduction was never foolproof and that charm wouldn't always work. He had used the knockout pressure only in moments of desperation or at times when he had himself feared losing control. It had been a useful fallback in his older years. This time there had been no fear; only anger. He hoped the beautiful golden-haired man wouldn't end up in a solitary hospital bed like Louie, even if it took fear to prevent it. It was a nasty sort of good deed, and even the rich new blood did nothing to lift Desmond's bruised spirit.

A sound came to him on the wind, and he stopped, realizing that he was in front of St. Thomas's Episcopal Church. The sun had dipped below the false horizon of the West Side, and twilight washed the city with deep blue light. Inside the huge church, the evensong service was under way, and as the street doors opened to let people in or out, Desmond could hear waves of choral music. He went in.

The cavernous splendor of the church was warm and filled with the achingly sweet voices of its celebrated boys choir. Candles blazed on the altar before the pale carved stone of the Gothic reredos. Desmond slipped quietly into a back pew and knelt, listening to the singing. The boys' voices soared to the vaulted roof of the nave, and Desmond felt his heart well up to meet the music.

He reached into his shirt pocket and pulled out the thin gold chain with its little pendant crucifix. He held it before him, watching the cross spin and waver, reflecting softly in the gentle light. Desmond smiled in spite of his sadness. How laughable to think that this was supposed to repel him. Images of Bela Lugosi snarling and shielding himself from Van Helsing's crucifix flickered through his mind. He remembered seeing *Dracula* with Roger in 1933, both of them biting their lips to keep from laughing. This tiny gold cross was no weapon against creatures of their kind. It couldn't vanquish the feeblest newborn vampire. No, not a weapon, yet something far more powerful. It had conquered hatred, ignorance, and fear and had helped a gentle man greet death with a peaceful embrace.

Desmond had not been in a church since his transformation except as a tourist. His indifference had grown out of the knowledge that immortality had not changed him, had not made him any wiser as to the workings of the divine being, if there were one. For two centuries he had seen the church, in all its denominations, struggle to resolve questions for which there were no mortal answers. He had seen it formulate answers that were cruel and unfeeling to questions that were asked incorrectly. He had seen the church fail as often as it had succeeded in its purported goal of doing good. He had come to lose all sense of the distinction between what the church could do and what man could do—for good or ill—in the secular sphere. He had left the church, in short, because he had felt it to be irrelevant. Immortality had given him no easy answers, no ready platitudes with which to console himself during long decades of loneliness. Desmond had ceased to feel any need for institutional guidance beyond his own principles of goodness and integrity.

Now, as he knelt in the soft golden light of this vast Gothic hall, listening to the choir sing, Desmond watched the little gold cross twinkle before his eyes and wondered at the faith that had kept Louie strong throughout his ordeal. Abandoned and brutalized by his own family, struck down by a plague he had never heard of before, left to die in a sterile white room with a near stranger as his only friend; Louie had given this fragile symbol of his faith to Desmond, needing only this to willingly give up the battle he had valiantly fought for so long.

Desmond pressed the cross to his lips and placed it safely back in his breast pocket. The boys choir reached a crescendo; their crystalline voices, untarnished by time and trouble, echoed throughout the church, reverberating to a silence as heavy as death itself. And as the quiet descended on all the assembled congregation, Desmond lay his forehead on his arms and wept as he had not wept since Jeffrey's death.

The house was dark and cold by the time Desmond returned. Usually impervious to both, Desmond felt an almost desperate need to bring life into the house. He turned up the thermostat and went through all the rooms on the main floors, turning on every lamp and chandelier. The whole parlor blazed with light, the rosewood surfaces reflected it, and the brass fittings and great plate-glass mirrors sparkled with it. Breaking his usual custom, he lit a fire in the elaborate white marble fireplace. Once it was burning steadily, he went down to the kitchen to feed Cosmo, who had greeted him hungrily at his return, yowling her usual protests.

The telephone rang as he was opening Cosmo's can of food, and as he picked it up, he heard Tony's cheery voice sing out, "Desmond, is that you?"

"Yes, who else?"

"I've been trying to get you for hours. I got it, Desmond."

"Got what?" Desmond stiffened, before realizing that Tony's voice was much too happy to be announcing bad news.

"The job! I had my interview this morning with Vivian Lake, and she said I'd be perfect for the job. I start Monday."

The job—Desmond had entirely forgotten the interview! "Tony, that's wonderful! We should celebrate. Can you come over?"

"Can I? You couldn't keep me away. A real job, and in a museum! I can't stand it!"

"Have you eaten yet?"

"No. Do you want to go out?"

"Let's stay here—I just lit a fire in the parlor."

"The parlor? You must've guessed my good news."

"Maybe. So could you perhaps pick up something on the way over? I've got champagne here. I didn't think about food."

"No problem. I'll find something. See you soon."

He rang off, and Desmond slowly replaced the receiver in the cradle. Cosmo yawped from the kitchen, and he went back to finish feeding her.

By the time Tony rang the doorbell, Desmond had dressed in dark gray flannel slacks and a bottle-green velvet smoking jacket with wide quilted black satin lapels. The front was closed with three large black silk knots. He had bought the jacket in the 1850s when this parlor had been finished. Having been worn rarely, it was still as good as new. Desmond thought Tony would appreciate it. He opened the front door and ushered in his friend with a kiss.

"Wow, don't you look elegant! Where'd you find that jacket?"

"It's part of the furniture. My great-great-grandfather's."

"Why, it looks brand-new, and it fits you like it was made for you!" Tony hugged him and pulled back, smiling. "So where's the champagne?"

"In the freezer, chilling. It wasn't cold when you called."

"Great. I brought Chinese food. Not elegant, but better than pizza, right?"

"Infinitely. At least we can use china and the proper utensils. I've got it all set up. This way, please."

And with a mock-formal bow he ushered Tony into the parlor. The fire blazed away in the fireplace, and Tony all but clapped at the spectacle of the room lit as if for a party.

Then Desmond gestured to the dining room, and Tony saw that the long mahogany table had been set for a lavish dinner—for one. A huge white damask cloth covered the wood, and a single setting of white porcelain, painted with floral sprigs, sat at its far end. Heavy silver flatware with the monogram DB flanked the dinner plate. Hexagonal Bohemian goblets with a matching gilt monogram completed the setting.

"All for me? Oh, Desmond, this is great!"

"Just what you deserve for joining the ranks of the employed."

Tony kissed him again, then moved around the room, touching things lightly like a child in a toy store, unable to decide which attracted him most.

"Go sit in the parlor, and I'll be right back with the champagne." Desmond disappeared into the hall.

A few minutes later he returned to find Tony parked happily in one of the ornate rococo armchairs by the fireplace. Desmond poured out the sparkling wine into more monogrammed glasses— tall, slender flutes this time.

"To Mr. Anthony Michael Chapman, future head of the American wing!" Desmond toasted.

"Let's limit that to my first week on the job—I don't want to jinx myself," Tony laughed.

"Fair enough." They touched glasses and drank.

Tony proceeded to relate his day with an enthusiasm that swept away any remaining doubts Desmond might have had that his actions were for the best.

"Mrs. Lake and I got along really well. I showed her my senior thesis, which seemed to impress her. At first she was sort of cool toward me, but she warmed up as we talked."

"That's a good sign. Vivian doesn't warm up quickly with anyone. She doesn't warm up at all if she doesn't like you."

"You know her?"

"How do—I'm a trustee, remember?" Desmond had decided to be relatively candid here, lest Tony suspect too much. "She started

148

as curator nearly 20 years ago, just after I joined the board. We were about the same age and both loved the same sort of thing."

"So you're friends?" Tony was curious but no more. Desmond noted that with some relief.

"Well, yes and no. We're pretty close as these trustee-curator friendships go; but on the other hand, she's never been here, and I know virtually nothing about her private life. So I guess you'd say we're business friends."

"She didn't mention you."

"But she doesn't know you know me. Anyway, even if she did, she keeps me anonymous to outsiders."

"Why?"

"Well, I keep a low profile there. I've helped them out over the years with objects for the collections—silver, furniture, that sort of thing. I've helped her get things that other board members disapproved of because they didn't fit into their image of the museum. All the gifts are listed as anonymous in the labels. So she maintains that fiction in conversation as well. That keeps us both out of trouble."

"I see. Will you tell her you know me?" Tony flushed a little, and Desmond realized that his concern didn't even brush on the source of the funds for the job.

"I hadn't thought about it; but I suppose I should call her and congratulate her on a wise choice. I don't think she knows I'm gay." He hesitated before continuing. "But she does know about my son."

"Your son?" Tony's eyes widened, and Desmond regretted saying anything. It had been an impulse to try out this fiction on Tony, but he now wished he'd waited for another moment.

"You never said you had a son." Tony seemed almost hurt, and Desmond understood why. He resented having to make up an heir, but his reasons were practical, not camouflage. This fictitious heir was his only means of keeping his lifetimes linked financially as well as historically. He had worked out five such stories before, and all had served him well. He looked at Tony and realized that here was

149

a son to whom he could gladly leave his empire but also that it was too impossible an idea to accept. Desmond had to be his own heir, and that was that.

"It's not quite what it seems, Tony. You know, I've got a family streak in me—I mean a sense of history, continuity. It always bothered me that I've never had a child, someone to carry on the name, the company. The house."

"Sure. You're not alone in that. No siblings at all, then?"

"None. I'm the only one. The last Desmond Beckwith. So last year, when I went to London for a while, I met a lesbian—a high-powered executive. She'd had the same ideas, and we sort of decided to have a baby together—artificial insemination. She's got a baby to raise, and we both have an heir. It was all very friendly."

"Desmond the seventh?"

"Right. Gross, isn't it?"

"Does he look like you?"

"Well, it's hard to say, but he's got dark hair." *Tony wouldn't believe how alike they'd look eventually*, thought Desmond.

"Hey, have you actually seen him?"

"What?"

"I mean, if he was conceived just last year, he can't be very old."

"Oh, right. I've only seen pictures." Desmond felt a flush creeping up his neck. What stupidity to get caught on this detail!

"Can I see?" asked Tony.

"See? The pictures?" Desmond repeated stupidly. "Uh, sure. I'll need to dig them out of my files. I'm not quite certain where I stuck them," he finished lamely, cursing himself.

"Maybe we could go visit him sometime—when I can afford to take a vacation." Tony's look had again become one of interest and enthusiasm. "I'd love to know a child of yours, Desmond. To watch him grow up."

Desmond agreed heartily and suddenly felt his heart sink within him. He himself would never see a son grow up. But what if he and

Tony *did* become a couple? Here he had lived 5½ lifetimes and hadn't even considered the next 20 years! If, with luck and effort, he and Tony made it as a couple for 20 years, then Desmond would die, again, at 65. The seventh Desmond Beckwith would then take over the house, the business, the life. And Tony would be all alone, a middle-aged man. And he would meet the new Desmond Beckwith and see that he was identical to his supposed father. Then what? Desmond had never seriously considered these possibilities. Back in his 20s, in the late '60s, he had thought only of being part of life. He had never made close friends because of his need for distance from the mortal world. But this go-around he had come closer to true friendships than in all his previous lives. Someday he would have to face separation from all of these people and start anew. The thought horrified him.

"Hey, Des, you look sick." Tony tapped him on the hand.

"Oh, it's nothing. Just wandered off." Desmond smiled wistfully at Tony and stroked his hand. "I'm sorry. It's just been a long day, and I'm feeling my mortality. Louie Lambruso died this afternoon. I'd just gotten home when you called with your big news. I'm afraid I just lapsed a little."

"Desmond, I'm so sorry. I didn't know. And here I've been blathering on about my good luck while you watched a man die!"

"No, really, Tony, it's good for me. Your new life balances out Louie's lost one. At least I can believe there's some happiness in the world with you here."

"Good. I'm glad I make you happy. Do you want to tell me about it?"

And Desmond told him, editing the day's events. Tony listened, eyes glistening, his hand holding Desmond's, his own joy forgotten in sympathy with the tragic curtailing of Louie Lambruso's young life.

When Desmond had finished his abbreviated account, he rose and sent Tony into the dining room to sit while he readied the meal.

Tony settled into the lyre-backed armchair at the head of the table, the ormolu chandelier glowing softly above him, and sipped more champagne. In a few minutes Desmond returned with a great silver waiter laden with covered porcelain serving dishes filled with take-out Chinese food.

"Culinary delights for the young master," intoned Desmond solemnly, making Tony smile gleefully.

"Oh, Des, this is great. I'm starved!"

Desmond served him with the reserve and efficiency of a well-trained butler; then, setting the tray on a sideboard, sat down in an adjacent chair with his own glass of champagne.

As Tony ate they talked of small matters, with bits of information about the new job, the things in the room. Then Desmond reached into one of the big pockets of the smoking jacket and pulled out Louie's gold chain.

"Tony, would you wear this for me? Consider it a new job present."

"A cross—how did you know I'm Catholic?"

"I didn't—you are?"

"Yeah, my mother's Irish. Her family insisted. Not that I ever learned much about it from either parent. They haven't been to church in aeons." Then Tony stopped and cocked his head at Desmond.

"But you didn't know I had the job until this afternoon." He paused. "It's Louie's cross, isn't it?"

"Yes. If you don't want to…"

Tony reached over and took the chain gently from Desmond's hand. He slipped it over his head and arranged it so the little cross lay nestled against his white chest, glinting in the lamplight. Then he leaned toward Desmond and kissed the hand that had held the cross.

"I'll always wear it. For you and for Louie. It'll remind me what a special person you are and he was."

"Thank you, Tony." Desmond felt his throat tighten and didn't dare try to say more. Tony didn't respond either but gave him a tender look and continued to eat his Chinese dinner with gusto.

That night Desmond didn't send Tony packing to his new flat after they made love. He needed warmth and clung to Tony with the intensity of a frightened infant. Once Tony had dozed off, Desmond too could call upon the release of sleep.

The following morning Desmond rose early, leaving Tony to rest in the big bed, and attempted to prepare the way for breakfast. He had never learned to cook, having no need—not just because he didn't eat mortal food but because in his youth this sort of thing had always been taken care of by servants. But he delighted in following directions in his new copy of *The Joy of Cooking* and felt he had acquitted himself pretty well by the time Tony wandered in, tousled and sleepy-eyed. Desmond quietly enjoyed the domesticity for which Roger had always chided him.

And so it went in the days and weeks that followed. On those nights when either Desmond or Tony felt a special need, the other would stay in whoever's place they happened to be. At first Desmond felt the strain of trying to time his sleep so that Tony would witness his deathlike slumber as rarely as possible. Once he had awakened early in the morning to find Tony, fully dressed, sitting in the darkness in one of the stiff sidechairs, staring blankly at him, as though in a trance. When he realized Desmond was awake, Tony had muttered an excuse about being unable to sleep and not wanting to disturb him. Desmond, however, had suspected that his method of sleeping had somehow frightened Tony. Unwilling to start a discussion, Desmond had coaxed Tony back into bed and had held him close until the workday forced them to part.

Eventually, though, as Tony made no further mention of those occasions when he did rise before him, Desmond ceased worrying. But on many nights, and at least one night a week, they slept apart.

To some degree this was part of establishing their ties while keeping independence. Desmond didn't want independence, but he needed it. Tony, Desmond felt, was better off for the separations. Once his job began, his mornings were geared to getting ready for work, and it was best for him to launch himself into each new day from his own space. Desmond, all other considerations aside, had a routine for his days that had been built up over many years and still felt comfort in it. For all his loneliness, Desmond relished his solitude as much as he treasured his house and the things that filled it. Tony was a distraction, albeit one that made his heart ache with joy and longing. But the most practical aspect of this solitude was that Desmond still had to hunt every few days to remain fit.

Christmas came and went. For the first time since the early 1850s, when he had forced Roger to help him decorate a tree in the parlor, Desmond went through the full Christmas ritual in order to please Tony. Roger, the Frenchman, had scoffed at this Germanic custom, which the young Queen Victoria had started at Windsor Castle in homage to her beloved German-born husband. Desmond, still English at heart, had pleaded and cajoled and finally gotten Roger to go along, if only for the sake of the novelty. But Roger's resistance had spoiled the fun, and Desmond hadn't attempted it again.

Desmond always enjoyed shopping for friends, although he himself was notoriously difficult to buy for. This year he felt a special joy in buying Tony presents, without any fear of the younger man's hesitation over taking gifts. For his part, he insisted that Tony should buy him only a token. The token, as it happened, was a slender gold chain, finer even than the one Tony wore. Tony blushed as Desmond opened it, declaring jokingly that it represented the chains that bound them together. They laughed together at the jest, but Desmond could tell that the feeling behind it was heartfelt. He accepted the chain with delight in his eyes but made no allusions to its meaning. Desmond saw it for what it was, something neither of them was yet able to articulate. The last thing he wanted to do was to frighten Tony away.

New Year's brought the usual urban hysteria and two major events for Tony—a New Year's Eve party at Bill Lawrence's and a surprise visit from Roger. At the former he was at last introduced to Desmond's select circle and tacitly approved by all. Desmond bridled with pleasure at being seen as part of a real couple, no longer the old maid hungering pointlessly after his straight best friend from childhood. Roger's arrival at Desmond's sanctum on two days' notice was, for the first time in Desmond's memory, the source of mixed emotions. As always he longed for Roger to be there, but this time he nearly dreaded it as well, for fear that Roger would dislike or disapprove of Tony. Too young, too pretty, too dull, too mortal.

But in truth Roger liked Tony immediately and threw Desmond a sly wink. This unleashed such a startling rush of jealousy in Desmond's soul that he was for once relieved that his old friend was so utterly heterosexual. Tony too was fascinated by Roger and quizzed him at length about San Francisco, his work, and his younger years as Desmond's friend. These questions Roger answered with great pleasure, doing his best to come just near enough to over-revelation so as to keep Desmond in a near-dither.

"I love red hair. Is yours naturally curly like that?"

"No, actually, I have it permed now and then, for variety. It's really straight. Ask Desmond; when we first met, he can attest, I wore it very long with a bow."

"Like a queue, or hippie-style?"

"Hippie-style—never! That's when I first curled it. No, I mean more Thomas Jefferson–like, you know."

"He had red hair too!"

"All this talk about hair," Desmond would interrupt, glaring at Roger, "makes you sound like a couple of silly queens. Can't we get a little more intellectual?"

"Are you guys the same age?" Tony would then start off.

"Tony! That's rude." Desmond would fold his arms threateningly.

"It doesn't bother me at all. It's just that I'm so much better preserved than Desmond is, and he's jealous." Mischief flashed in Roger's eyes.

"Jealous? Of what? I'm actually some months younger than you."

"Well, depending on how you count it."

"What's that mean?" Tony would ask, all innocence.

"If you count lifetimes, Desmond's much older."

"Roger, what the *hell* are you talking about?"

"You mean like Shirley MacLaine?"

"Exactly. Desmond's been lots of people in past lives. Beneath that handsome middle-aged veneer lies the soul of Dorian Gray."

"All scarred with past evil?" Tony played along.

"Hideously disfigured. Did you ever notice that there are no family portraits around, and none of Desmond either?"

"That's right!"

"It's because they all made Quasimodo look good. Couldn't pay an artist to sit in a room with them. Just wait till Desmond hits 65, he'll start to decay like those Nazi goons at the end of *Raiders of the Lost Ark*."

"Ugh, I hope I'm not in bed with him when it happens."

At this point Desmond could only stalk out of the room, leaving Tony to stare after him, surprised.

"What's wrong with him?"

"No sense of humor. You haven't improved him much in that respect. You should work on it." Roger sipped his wine, eyeing Tony innocently over the rim of his glass.

All was perfectly peaceful when conversation stayed on general topics, and for the most part it did just that. The weeklong holiday ultimately made Desmond feel better, knowing that Roger and Tony would be friends. The night Roger left, he made his good-byes in the marble-tiled vestibule as the car waited on the street.

"Bye, Tony. It's been great to meet you," he said, shaking hands.

"Same here, Roger. I'm happy to have a face to put with your name." Tony gave him a boyish, impulsive hug.

"More than just a face, I hope." And at Tony's smile of agreement, he added, "Take care of Desi, Tony. He's an armful, let me tell you."

"I will—I promise."

"And you, Desi, keep this boy happy. He's a gem."

"Will do, chum. Come back soon." And the two older men embraced and kissed.

Once Roger's car had pulled away, Tony turned to Desmond.

"I can see why you fell in love with him."

Desmond only smiled. For once, Roger's departure didn't leave him desolate.

CHAPTER 9

Two months later Tony was asked to act as courier for the Museum of the City of New York. He had to carry a rare piece of colonial silver for an exhibition at the Smithsonian Institution. Normally this was a privilege reserved for the curator, but Mrs. Lake was tied up, and Tony got to go. He planned to visit college friends for a couple of nights and do some research in the Smithsonian library.

It was the first real separation they'd had, and Desmond found himself stewing over Tony's absence as if they'd been spending every minute together. It was the same sort of feeling of being at loose ends that Roger's departure had always given him. To complete his foul mood, the late-winter weather was repulsive as only New York can be: temperatures hovering just above freezing, with a pouring rain that chilled through the heaviest overcoat.

Standing in the library window, Desmond stared out at the reflections of the streetlights and traffic signals in the glistening pavement. A sense of abandonment swept over him. He had not felt this way for so long, it seemed, and the contrast irritated him even more. He needed to drink. It was a good time to go out. The bad weather and his bad mood would sharpen his hunting skills, increase his efficiency. Make it seem less like cheating.

He donned his black leather jacket, and, pulling the collar up to protect his neck from the cold, he set out into the dripping night.

Walking rapidly uptown, he perversely enjoying the clammy cold-ness. He wanted to be mean tonight, not happy. He didn't want to flirt, to cajole. He wanted to stalk, lure, and savor his thirst. There was an edge to his craving tonight, and he wanted to make the most of it.

His destination was an enormous club where hundreds of young people of both sexes and various orientations exhausted themselves through long nights of dancing, drinking, and drugs. Beneath a planetarium dome that exploded with lasers and false stars, Desmond worked his way slowly through the gyrating mass of slen-der arms and legs and bodies. The smell of this place was so differ-ent from the smoky, beery, beefy atmosphere of the denim and leather bars. Likewise, it differed from any of the gay bars Desmond knew or had known. There was no smell of fear in this place, none of the electricity of the survival instinct in the air. Everyone here was here for one reason: to have fun. Even the specter of AIDS didn't dampen the pansexual youths' enjoyment; it just made sex a less sig-nificant option, leaving them free to concentrate on drinking them-selves stupid and dancing until they passed out.

Desmond ordered and drank down a shot of vodka, then ordered a second vodka on the rocks, which he carried with him. He moved slowly throughout the club, letting the mechanical pounding of the music work its way into his system with the alcohol and catch the rhythm of his heartbeat. As he watched the dancers from the half-light of a balcony, Desmond zeroed in on a boy below him. Accom-panied by a girl, the boy danced with his eyes closed, so absorbed in the movement of his own body as to be unaware of her presence. Thick black hair was swept back above his forehead. His olive skin glowed darkly in the black lights, which made the thin cotton of his sleeveless white undershirt an iridescent violet. A tiny rhinestone stud glinted in one ear, and Desmond realized that this was most likely a straight boy, according to the peculiar realities of teenage fashion.

Desmond went back down to the dance floor, watching the boy as he and his partner continued to dance, ignoring each other. At a break in the music—or really a shift, since the music never actually stopped—Desmond caught the boy's eyes, icy blue in the murky atmosphere. He gulped his drink and set the glass aside, sidling onto the dance floor, where he began to move with the music, copying the boy's own motions. Desmond never had enjoyed this modern sort of dancing for its own sake but well understood its sensuality.

Loosened up by the unaccustomed intake of vodka, Desmond was a good mimic. At 45 his slim, tight body moved well, with all the tensile grace inherent in his race. For him, age was mere surface. He knew from past experience that he wouldn't start to age noticeably until his mid 50s, and then even at the end of his lifetime people would remark at how young he looked. There were limits to his physical allure, he understood. But he had ways of making up for any deficiencies.

Desmond danced with conscious self-absorption for a while, then slowly opened his eyes, knowing that he would be looking directly at the blue eyes of the dancing boy. He was right, and they were trained on him. The eyes flitted away, toward the girl, but she was not paying any attention, and the boy's eyes had no place to return to but Desmond's sleepy gaze.

This continued for a while, then Desmond simply stopped dancing and walked off the floor, with a final riveting look at the boy. The blue eyes made one more attempt to make contact with the girl, who remained oblivious, and then followed Desmond to the dim sidelines.

Having reeled in his catch, Desmond had to land him. He started to talk to the boy, getting him a beer, from which he drank greedily. Desmond found out everything about the boy but remembered nothing. The talk was to draw the boy out, relax him, close in on him. Desmond spoke in an intense low voice, deep as a panther's purr, which cut through the surrounding noise like a scalpel, reaching the boy's ears alone. They gradually moved closer together and farther from the writhing bodies on the dance floor until Desmond could feel the boy's heat through the thin undershirt against his hand. Desmond could almost hear the boy's heart pounding, his eyes locked on Desmond's smiling gaze, his body tensed but unable to move.

Desmond whispered ever more intently.

"You're a good dancer. You've got the perfect body for it. You must practice a lot."

The boy dropped his eyes, just for a moment, and smiled, embarrassed.

"Yeah, thanks."

"You always dance with the same girl?"

"Uh, no, not always."

"Always with only girls?"

"Yeah…uh, no. Mostly."

"Sometimes with guys?"

"Yeah, sometimes—But I'm no fag." The boy's expression became suddenly hard.

"You, a fag? Just because you like to dance with sexy guys now and then, in a place like *this*?" He responded coolly, his tone faintly mocking, but inwardly Desmond winced. How he disliked these homophobic boys who flirted shamelessly with gay men, pretending they weren't attracted. Outwardly his eyes merely narrowed as he fixed the boy with his stare.

"Well, no, I mean…" The boy flushed, and his blue eyes stared unblinking into Desmond's.

"Did they ever do this?" The catlike purr became a soft guttural growl. Eyes locked with the boy's, Desmond ran his hand ever so gently down the front of his belly, making him shiver.

"Or this?" Desmond just grazed the boy's crotch. Another shiver.

"Or this?" Desmond softly gripped the boy's crotch and leaned forward to give him a flirtatious kiss, flicking his tongue against moist lips, teasing.

"Oh, God!" mumbled the boy, responding to Desmond's kiss and letting himself be pulled closer until their bodies were pressed together. Now to set the hook.

Desmond massaged the boy's crotch gently, and the boy let his head fall to one side, eyes closed, with a gasp. Then, unexpectedly, just as Desmond was preparing to release his canines, the boy's blue eyes popped open, filled with a hard expression somewhere between anger and fear.

"Hey, back off, faggot. I don't *do* that shit!" The voice was tight with loathing. One muscular hand suddenly gripped Desmond, squeezing his arm hard, as if to inflict pain.

Desmond paused only an instant, momentarily startled. Then in another fleeting moment his imprisoned anger bubbled up and he snarled, enveloping the boy in a crushing embrace and baring his fangs quickly. Before the boy could utter a protest, Desmond fixed his hungry mouth on the slick, fragrant skin of the other's throat. Holding him tight, he drank deeply. The smoky noise of the whirling bar receded to nothingness around them. The boy's struggle soon abated, and Desmond was alone with him, with his blood, with the fire that danced in his veins.

In a minute it was done, and Desmond, suddenly afraid, managed to pull away before he went too far. The boy's eyes were closed, and his body heavy against Desmond's shoulder. Desmond steered him obligingly to a banquette by a far wall and sat him down. He leaned the inert form against the seat and turned away into the throng, leaving the boy in near darkness to sleep off his little adventure. His anger was now appeased, and Desmond noticed with some pride the dark patch that stained the boy's gray slacks.

Well-done, Desmond old boy, well-done! he thought. But as he headed out into the rainy cold to the haven of his home and his bed, he couldn't escape the eerie sense that, somewhere in the city, wolves were howling.

The wretched rains of late winter gradually changed to the gentle rains of spring, their moisture soothing the spirit as their warmth urged on the renewal of life. Tony flourished on the job, and Desmond could hardly recall the desperate, panicky young man whose hand had so fervently gripped his sleeve back in November. Desmond himself was occupied with his business and mixed into the familiar routine of his life the happy presence of Tony's unprecedented influence. Their daily routine together was largely determined by Tony's job and his need to keep regular hours to be his best at it.

On weekends they continued the tradition they had started of reading together in the Gothic library. Tony mined the riches of Desmond's bookshelves, gratifying his vanity in this regard in a way Roger had never approached. Roger had always teased Desmond about his passion for novels, especially the more arcane ones; yet Tony seemed to appreciate the taste reflected in these volumes and shared Desmond's own literary favorites. Desmond was somewhat relieved to see that, after *Dracula*, Tony's interests turned to Edith Wharton, Henry James, Nathaniel Hawthorne, Dickens, Thackeray, Trolloppe. Unlike Desmond, who had read these books as contemporary fiction, Tony saw them as time machines, letting him travel into a past long gone yet perfectly preserved on these pages. Desmond could amaze Tony with insights the younger man couldn't have conceived himself, but he always felt like a cheat. Tony read voraciously and would regularly borrow books to take home on those nights when they were apart.

A fine mist was falling on a silky April evening, the sun just setting, as Desmond rang Tony's bell. They were going up to have dinner with Bill Lawrence, as they did occasionally, making the relationship a sort of platonic triad.

As he greeted Desmond, Tony seemed more subdued than usual, but Desmond put it off to the gray weather. His little apartment was full of his personality now, the walls hung with museum posters and piles of books, bought with his salary, littering the shelves and tables.

Tony had no apparent interest in nonpractical objects for his own place, preferring to immerse himself in Desmond's house when he spent any time there. His interest in the house was intense but clinical, detached—so unlike Desmond's own emotional attachment. Desmond had even agreed to have him begin an inventory of the house, room by room. Tony had been horrified to find that Desmond had no such document. Desmond, of course, knew every minute detail about the house, right down to the cost of the nails in the floorboards; but he could hardly explain that to Tony.

So part of every weekend was devoted to making further entries in the computer, using special inventory software that Desmond had gotten through his business. Tony himself would write a short description of whatever it was they were looking at, then turn to Desmond, who would supply historical information as to where and when and by whom. Tony had also pored through some of the files of 19th-century billheads, all but drooling over the unheard-of documents he found there. These he cross-referenced into the computer database as well.

On this warm, damp evening, Tony seemed not quite morose but thoughtful as they headed out. When they reached Sixth Avenue, Tony suggested they walk part of the way to Bill's, and Desmond agreed.

"Is everything all right at work?" Desmond ventured.

"Sure, great. Viv is wonderful to deal with. She's so glad to have me to help, she doesn't know where to start."

"You get along well, then." Desmond knew they did; Tony and Vivian had both reported as much. But he guessed that Tony wanted to talk about something tied to his job.

"We're real friends by now. It's funny; she's not used to having someone assisting, and so she almost apologizes when she asks me to do something for her! I have to tease her about it, to ease her up. She laughs at me and calls me her 'willing slave.' But overall she's just grateful."

"That's good. I'm glad you like each other. Not liking your boss must be terrible."

"God, yes." Tony paused, then, with a quick sidelong look at Desmond, continued. "She asks about you sometimes."

"Me?" Desmond feigned nonchalance, but his senses were at once on alert.

"Yeah. She had mentioned you a few times, and I said I knew you. It didn't seem to surprise her. Then, after a few days, she'd just ask a question about you."

"What sort of question?"

"Oh, innocuous things. It was like she was trying to find out what I knew; not so much to find out who *you* are but how you know me. How often did I run into you. Did we go places together."

"Nothing about my family or my house?"

"Such vanity! No, I guess she knows all she wants about that." Tony gave Desmond a sly smile.

"She doesn't actually know anything about that. And what do you tell her?"

"Whatever she asks. It's never very personal. Just like she's curious."

As well she might be, Desmond thought. *Here I foist this boy on her, and she's just interested in why I focused on him in particular.*

"You said once that Vivian doesn't know you're gay, right?" Tony asked.

"Well, she didn't then. It looks like she's getting an idea. I just hope she doesn't get any wrong ideas!" It was Desmond's turn for a sly smile. "Remember, I called to congratulate her about hiring you, as your friend. And I've also told her about my son and nonwife in England. Maybe she's started to put things together. You've got to admit, I'm a puzzle."

"I'll say. So you think she's getting the picture about us?"

"Looks like it, from what you're telling me."

"Does that bother you?"

165

"No, I don't think so. It's never come up before." Desmond looked intently at Tony. "You don't think I'm in any way ashamed that she might figure out you're my boyfriend?"

"No, not at all. But I'm glad to hear you say it outright."

"It's so new to me. It's nice to be linked to someone and to have people know it." They shared a smile, and then Tony grew serious again.

"She told me something else today. Something I gather you didn't want her to tell me."

Desmond didn't reply but just looked at Tony.

"She told me that since we were friends, she didn't think she ought to keep this from me. Also that she didn't want any secrecy getting in the way of your friendship with me."

"She told you about the interview?"

"Yes. That you asked her and that you're putting up the funding for it—for me."

"That's true, Tony." Desmond didn't know what more to say. They walked along awhile in silence, eyes on the pavement, before Tony spoke.

"Why, Des?" He asked softly.

"Why did I arrange an interview, money for a job that didn't exist? Why did I force a friend of mine on Vivian Lake, using my position as a trustee and my financial clout? Because. Because you needed a job, and she needed help. And I needed to help you."

They walked on in silence. Finally, Desmond continued.

"And because I knew you were worthy of the job. Worthy of my inexcusable pushiness. I knew she'd like you, and I knew you would dazzle them with your brains."

Tony didn't answer but kept his eyes on the sidewalk.

"There's one more reason, Tony. Because I love you."

"What?" Tony's head shot up, his brow creased in the familiar way.

"You heard me. Because I love you. I think I have since I found you curled up like a starving dog in my vestibule. I knew you'd hate

166

it if you found out, which is why I asked Viv to keep it very hush-hush. I guess Viv decided that you were self-confident enough to take the truth and also that the deception was potentially more dangerous than the facts."

Desmond stopped and put his hand on Tony's shoulder.

"It that right, Tony? Was Viv right?"

A smile slowly worked its way across Tony's face, and he wrapped his arms around Desmond, hugging him fiercely.

"Oh, Des. I love you too. Thank you for interfering. I was just afraid it was out of pity or just to keep me happy."

Desmond murmured into Tony's damp ear, holding the embrace. "There was pity, at first. You *were* pitiful, tragically so. But all the good things about you so overwhelmed me, I couldn't *not* do anything I could to help you."

They pulled apart and held each other at arm's length.

"Do you forgive me, Tony?"

"Of course I do. Do you still love me?"

"With all my conniving, deceitful heart."

"So be it, lover." And Tony kissed him.

They had walked well out of the Village by this time, and their kiss was greeted with a loud volley of "Faggots!" from a passing car. Tony and Desmond ignored it and completed their kiss with a final brief peck before turning to head uptown again.

"Maybe we'd better get a cab, now that the air's clear," suggested Desmond.

"The air, maybe, but not the weather. A cab it is!"

Desmond stepped to the curb to hail an uptown cab, but Tony pulled him aside.

"Look at that!"

"What?"

"In the newsstand, the *Post* headline."

They looked, reading in three-inch high block letters across the top of the front page: VAMPIRE GAY KILLER CLAIMS FOURTH!

"Oh, no," groaned Desmond.

"Oh, yes. Poor Bill. He's going to be completely depressed by this."

"Do you think he's seen it?"

"Maybe not. Should we buy one? Too cruel?"

"He'll see it anyway. Better he not spend his own money."

So they bought a paper and climbed into a cab to read the grisly story on the way to Bill's flat.

"Gee, thanks for the nice present. So much more thoughtful than flowers or wine." Bill folded up the *Post* and threw it dramatically into the trash can in the kitchen.

"Sorry, Bill. We just thought you'd at least want to see it."

"I appreciate the thought, guys. But I knew all about it already. They found the fourth body early this morning. I've interviewed the family and have a piece in tomorrow's edition. Mind you, not as colorful as that," he added, gesturing to the trash. "You want drinks?"

They both ordered wine and followed Bill into the kitchen.

"You interviewed his family?" Tony quizzed.

"Yup."

"Was he gay?"

"Yup again. What's more—and worse, really—is that his folks knew about him and were tremendously supportive. The murder has blown them away completely. They've done everything to make sure their gay son knows they love him, to make his life as untroubled as being gay *can* be, and then some psycho stabs him with an ice pick. And twice in the neck, just like the others."

"That's horrible."

"No more, basically, than the other murders. Just a lot sadder," mused Desmond aloud.

"What about the other families?"

"What about them?" Bill led them into the living room and settled down on one of the sectional leather sofas. The lights of the city blazed beyond the windows.

168

"The gay angle," Tony continued. "Have you talked to them again in light of this new focus on the victims' all being gay?"

"Yes, but to what advantage I'm not sure. The parents of two of the victims, Michael Bauer and Jesse Hernandez, denied vehemently that their murdered son could have been gay. The third guy, Larry Vitelli, was HIV-positive, so his family got the double whammy of that. They did admit to me that they had suspected he was gay. It hadn't ever been discussed among them, however."

"Who was the last one?"

"Frank O'Rourke. Beautiful Irish redhead from Queens. Just 21."

"Do you have a picture?" Tony asked.

"Tony! You're ghoulish!" Desmond chided.

"In fact, I do. I'll get my files." Bill left the room and returned from his study with a shabby leather satchel. He had carried the sorry excuse for a briefcase since his 20s, Desmond remembered.

"I've got pictures—snapshots, really—of all of them." He pulled out a folder full of color snapshots of varying shapes and sizes. Each had a small, typed stick-on label with the names on it: O'Rourke, Hernandez, Bauer, Vitelli. "Here's O'Rourke."

Tony took the picture and looked at it closely under the lamp by the sofa. Frank O'Rourke, a full head of carrot-red curly hair, dark eyes, flashing white teeth. He stood with his arms around the shoulders of two older, slightly shorter versions of himself—his mother and father.

"Cute, wasn't he?" commented Bill quietly.

"I slept with him once," said Tony.

"What?" Desmond's brows arched.

"A couple of years ago, right after I got to New York. He was in school—Hunter College, I think. He was fun. Didn't see him much after that. Now and then in a bar."

Tony stood up and stared out the windows as the city sparkled wetly beneath in lowering spring sky. "It's so weird to think of him after all this time. To remember what fun he was, how sexy and cute. Now he's been killed by a crazy."

"I'm sorry, Tony," Desmond said softly, standing to hug him from behind.

"You don't mind?" Tony asked.

"Mind, why? You certainly didn't expect me to think you were a virgin when I met you. I'm just sorry this has hit you so closely."

"Not as closely as it hit his folks."

"That's for sure."

"It seems so unfair. Here's a kid who's got all his shit together, and his folks are behind him. And this. What would my folks think, I wonder, if..."

"Don't even think about it," Bill interrupted. "Desmond, you'd better take care of this boy."

Tony pulled away from Desmond and sat down on the sofa again. "It's no more unfair than Louie, is it Des? He had nothing going for him, and then AIDS took what little he had—his life."

"None of it's fair, Tony. Gruesome things happen. You can't blame the victims of AIDS any more than you can blame murder victims. And for the moment it looks like no one can stop either one of the killers. At least Frank O'Rourke's parents will be able to grieve knowing that their son knew he was loved. What sort of hatred and pain did Louie's family feel, if they ever felt anything?"

"What did you ever do with Louie's ashes, Desmond?" asked Bill, refilling his glass.

"We put them in the garden behind the house," Tony piped up. "He'll always have friends there." He cast a weak smile to Desmond, the troubled look gradually lifting from his face. "Can I look at the rest of the pictures?"

"Sure."

Tony studied each one in turn. All of the murdered men were in their early 20s and fairly slender in build. Michael Bauer was blond and blue-eyed, athletic-looking. Jesse Hernandez was a light-skinned black man with a carefully clipped mustache and a pretty smile. Larry Vitelli was a romantically beautiful black-haired Sicilian with a come-hither glint in his jet-dark eyes. They posed in these snapshots with their families, some with siblings, some with parents. Hernandez's parents were a mixed-race couple, his father Hispanic, his mother a tall, elegant black woman. Vitelli's siblings looked like they were cut from the same cloth, just as Bauer's parents and sister matched his athletic, blond good looks.

"How old was Michael Bauer?" asked Desmond.

"Twenty-two, why?"

"How old's his father? He looks young."

"Hmm, let's see…" Bill rummaged in his files. "Forty-one."

"Then he was just 19 when his son was born. He's younger than I am now." Desmond looked at Tony.

"And you're thinking that you're old enough to be my father," laughed Tony. "Look, Des, I hope you're not going to be hung up on this age difference between us. My father's 60, so I don't see you as a surrogate daddy."

"Yeah, Desmond," Bill chimed in. "Tony's father could be your father too."

"At 15?" Desmond asked archly.

"Well, you know those country white trash…" Bill ducked as Tony pretended to throw his wine at him.

Tony sat down next to Desmond, took his hands, and looked earnestly into his eyes. "Desmond, Bill had better hear this officially and tell all your friends. I love you, 45 or not, and I don't worry one whit about the gap between our ages. When you're 60 I'll be, uh, 39, and it still won't make any difference." Then he kissed Desmond solemnly on the lips.

Desmond kissed him back with the same solemnity but couldn't help thinking, *When you're 45, Tony my boy, I'll be 22 again, and won't that be interesting!*

What he said was, "I love you too, little boy, and I will do my best not to dwell on my potential senility before you hit middle age."

They all laughed at this, which broke the spell and cleared the tension from the room. Tony refilled his wine, and Desmond looked through the photos again.

He suddenly looked up at Bill quizzically.

"Did you get personal-property lists from the victims at the police station?"

"You mean what they had in their pockets when the bodies were found? Yes, they're right in here. There was no robbery evident with any of them." He handed Desmond a few sheets of photocopied paper.

"What's up?" asked Bill.

"Just an idea." Desmond scanned the lists.

"There we are," he muttered.

"What? What you got, Des?" Bill asked with interest.

"Look at these—and that, Bill," he said pointing at Tony.

"I don't get you."

"What religion were these guys?"

"I don't know, it didn't come up. They're not any religion once they're dead, are they?"

"That's not what Louie said to me, Bill. He said, 'Once a Catholic, always a Catholic.' "

"So?"

"Look at this picture of Larry Vitelli. He's got a gold cross around his neck."

"You mean like the one Louie gave you, the one I'm wearing?"

"Exactly."

"So Vitelli's not a very WASP name, Desmond. Is this a surprise to you?" Bill looked bemused.

"No, not at all. But according to the lists, Frank O'Rourke had a cross, a silver one on a chain, that he probably wore. *And* Jesse Hernandez, also a gold one, like Louie's, only bigger."

"Did Michael Bauer have one? It's a German name. He might be Protestant—Lutheran, I'd imagine."

"No, but look at that picture." Desmond held up the snapshot of the blond Bauer clan. There, on the wall behind the senior Bauer, was a crucifix, its Christ figure hanging in agony on the black wooden cross.

"I've never seen a Protestant household with a crucifix like that on the wall."

"And your conclusion, Sherlock?" asked Bill.

"All of the victims were Catholics."

"So?"

"Isn't that peculiar," asked Desmond, "especially since three of them wore crosses? Bauer might have had one, for all we know, and it was taken by the murderer."

"You think there's a connection?" asked Tony, looking at Bill and Desmond in turn.

"I don't know. I just think it's a strange coincidence, that's all."

Tony nodded. "Four young gay men, all Catholic. Maybe all wearing crosses."

"Perhaps," said Desmond. "What do you think, Bill?"

"I think I don't like the idea. Some deranged Episcopalian queen out to kill Catholic boys?"

"There wasn't any sex involved, remember, or at least that's what it looks like," Tony commented.

"Right."

"A priest, then?" suggested Tony.

"Oh, God, that'd be just wonderful," groaned Bill sarcastically. Then he rubbed his eyes wearily and stood up, scooping up the papers into his file and stuffing it all back into the battered briefcase. "Look, guys, you've played amateur sleuth enough for now. I, for one, would like to eat, and at least Tony will be glad to join me in a bite, right?"

"I'm starved!" Tony stood and looked down at Desmond. "You?"

"I'm not hungry. I'll just drink myself blind."

"Good, then let's get going."

Together Tony and Bill dragged Desmond up off the couch and out into the April night.

CHAPTER 10

By the end of April, winter was already a vague memory in the minds of most New Yorkers. Fresh greenery was beginning to fill the parks in earnest. The air became balmy and, for New York, almost sweet. The little garden behind Desmond's house blossomed with late daffodils and tulips, and a virtual hedge of azaleas filled the space with glowing color. Desmond and Tony altered their winter routine, sitting together in this miniature paradise for their weekend reading sessions. Desmond himself had never spent much time in his garden, preferring to look at it from inside the house. Others came and weeded, planted new flowers, kept it tidy. Tony teased him about being a mole and forced him to admit that the spring breezes, the smell of the plants, and even the muffled sounds of the city traffic all were pleasant and refreshing.

He joked about Desmond's inability to get any color from the sun even as his own cheeks grew rosy and his high cheekbones glowed from the gentle spring light. Desmond laughed this off as an attribute of his tough middle-aged complexion. Inwardly he understood the reason exactly: tanning was simply the sun's rays reacting chemically with the skin's melanin, darkening the skin's appearance. Like any such physical alteration that took place in Desmond's body, this too reversed itself in a short while, leaving him bereft of any color he might have gained in the course of an afternoon's sunbath.

Desmond loved the warmth of the sun against his skin and had no fear of skin cancer. However, it all seemed pointless because, for all his efforts, he retained his normal healthy pallor.

While his resistance to sunbathing seemed only to amuse Tony, it worried Desmond, who feared Tony might begin to question the reasons too closely. Even as he luxuriated in the intimacy of Tony's closeness, he often felt surges of panic at the thought of his secret being somehow revealed. Desmond was very careful, but his fears kept up a constant muted continuo in his mind.

Tony carried on with his inventory of the house, growing more and more intimate with the possessions with which Desmond surrounded himself, even as their love, now put into words, deepened its roots and grew with the season. Tony was surprised to learn, through a chance remark at work, that Vivian Lake had no idea of the treasures in Desmond's house. He mentioned this to Desmond, who extracted a promise from him that he would say nothing to her. Desmond still saw his house as a sacred precinct. His friends saw it mostly as another rich queen's hoard; only Tony had understood the historical import of the objects and their related documents. Vivian Lake would see it in the same light, and Desmond had always avoided inviting her to the house for that exact reason. He didn't want the outside world getting too interested in his home or its owner. Tony was the only exception to this rule, and he was, in his own and Desmond's mind, hardly an outsider anymore. Long gone were Desmond's shadowy doubts about Tony's motivations. His consuming interest in Desmond's possessions was a professional one, and his interest in Desmond was unquestionably personal.

It was early on Friday evening, at the end of a spectacular April day, when Desmond returned home from his business office downtown. He rarely made these trips to the New York headquarters of Beckwith Investments, usually keeping tabs on things from his basement office. But today he had been needed to sign some papers and had gone to the home office on Wall Street to take care of it. These visits caused quite a buzz with the employees, most of whom had never actually seen *the* Mr. Beckwith, and Desmond enjoyed playing the role to the hilt.

He always hired a limousine to drive him there and to wait while he was inside. He dressed in his most conservative suits and generally carried himself the way he thought people expected he should. His executives knew only his telephone number and a post-office box number, not his address. For the most part they dealt with him by telephone. They knew of his New York house and of the hotel suites in Paris and London but only by repute. No Beckwith employee had ever been to any of them—except, of course, Roger, who was Desmond's only partner. Roger's huge house in San Francisco, like his life, was an open book, but this was as close to knowing Desmond Beckwith as the Beckwith staff had ever come.

Desmond unlocked his front door, having sent the chauffeur off with a generous tip, chuckling to himself over his afternoon's performance. He always enjoyed playing his own impostor, realizing that the semifictional Desmond Beckwith his people knew was far more acceptable than the true man. A little eccentricity and a lot of money were the perfect combination to keep the world at arm's length.

As he was feeding Cosmo in the kitchen—Tony had finally stopped nagging him about modernizing it—the study phone rang. It was Tony. Desmond could hear repressed emotion in his voice.

"Hi, love, what's up?" Desmond asked, curious.

"Nothing in particular; I just thought we might go out to dinner tonight, it being Friday and all."

"Of course. Where did you have in mind?"

Tony named a hot new restaurant on the Upper East Side and hastily added, "It's my treat."

"Your treat? Why, you know I don't eat out. Since when do I make you buy your own meals, anyway?"

"This is special—I've been saving. And I'll compensate you while I pig out by getting the best red wine in the house for you."

"Now, I don't want you squandering your savings on wine. Second-best will do." Desmond was puzzled by this sudden and uncharacteristic extravagance, but he didn't want to quash Tony's obvious pleasure. He detected a note of excitement but also—and oddly, Desmond thought—a hint of fear. "I'll tell you what: You get over here as soon as you can, and we'll go from here, OK?"

"Great. We don't have reservations until 8, and even that might be a little early for this place."

"All the better. We can dine in solitary splendor. See you soon." And Desmond rang off. He quickly picked up the receiver again and called the car service, to have the chauffeur he had just let go come back and get him at 7:30. If Tony was going to splurge, he wasn't going to do it in a cab.

When Tony arrived at 6:30, he was, like Desmond, dressed in a dark suit, looking older than usual and, Desmond thought, gorgeous. A sudden mental image of Jeffrey dressed in his dark blue livery leaped to mind, and Desmond had to close his eyes to dispel the vision. They kissed in the vestibule, and Desmond led Tony into the parlor, where champagne was waiting on the marble-topped center table. He had also phoned out and had gotten a quantity of spring flowers sent over, which he had arranged in vases around the room. He couldn't remember the last time he'd had flowers inside.

"Oh, Des, it looks beautiful," said Tony softly. I've never seen flowers in here—and champagne!"

"Well, you seemed so fired up, I thought we'd better do it right. I've called back the car I hired this afternoon to deliver us and pick us up. No grimy cabs tonight, lover."

Tony gave Desmond another kiss but this time an affectionate, almost brotherly peck on the cheek. He seemed subdued yet somehow radiant. Desmond poured them champagne, and they clinked glasses.

"Desmond, we look like a couple of Wall Street banker types."

"Well I *am*, at least. Why are *you* getting into the role so suddenly? I mean, why this celebration?"

"Well, two reasons, actually. Tonight's an anniversary for me."

"An anniversary?" Desmond quickly thought back over the past months, and came up with the answer: "Oh, I *see*, our six months! Oh, Tony, I'm sorry I didn't think of it myself!"

"Don't be sorry. It's just that I happened to think of it a while back because it's also my birthday. I'm 25 now."

"A whole quarter of a century! Any signs of decay?"

"Not a wrinkle. Must be my bone structure," Tony said with a short laugh. He eyed Desmond over the edge of his glass as he sipped.

"I'm sorry again—I didn't know it was your birthday. I haven't bought you anything. Let me pay for dinner."

"No way—it's on me tonight. That's why I kept it mum. When I realized that my 25th was also our six-month anniversary, I decided to keep the secret and surprise you."

"Well, you certainly succeeded there. I'm ashamed at being so careless of dates."

"Don't be. By the way, when's your birthday?"

"Mine? July fifth."

"How patriotic, right after the fourth!"

"It wasn't particularly important back then anyway, and I've never paid much attention to it."

"Back then?"

"I mean in England, when I was a child. You know the Brits don't share our love of Independence Day."

"I didn't know you spent your childhood in England. You always make it sound like you've always lived here."

"I did, I have. It's just that we spent time in England too, in the London house. My father always downplayed the Fourth of July bit with me in a sort of deference to his English ancestry." Desmond ended lamely, feeling his usual thrill of panic, hoping this would cover his stupid blunder. Of course, in his first—and only—childhood, the fourth of July had been just another day, followed by his birthday. It wasn't until he and Roger had come to the United States in 1798 that the patriotic holiday had become known to him, and he had never paid much attention to it.

"Anyway, let's not dwell on *your* age, Desmond. It always upsets you, being so old and all!" Tony taunted, pouring more champagne into both their glasses.

They talked of other things, warming under the effects of the sparkling wine, until the doorbell rang, announcing the arrival of the car and driver.

As they motored quietly uptown, Tony seemed ill at ease, not quite able to enjoy the ride. Only when they were halfway uptown did he break the silence.

"This is the first time I've been in a limo since my grandfather's funeral. It's funny that limousines are most associated with weddings and funerals nowadays. Chauffeur-driven cars used to be just one of the basic props of upper-middle-class life."

"Like maids, cooks, gardeners," Desmond added. "The whole labor force that's disappeared as the world has changed. Once even middle-class people had a servant or two. It was assumed. Only the poor did without any help." He eyed Tony's face, amused at this strangely formal small talk.

"Why do you do without, Desmond? I mean, you could afford a car and driver full-time—and a housekeeper. Why do you do all the housework yourself?"

"Privacy, self-protection. I don't want outsiders in my house. Never have. My father was the same way."

"He did *his* housework too?" Tony's tone was incredulous.

Desmond looked at his lover and decided that a lie would be safer than evasion, as much as he regretted it.

"Well, he did have a cleaning woman. But he made me clean things myself, to teach me the value of caring for fine objects. I guess he taught me better than he thought." Desmond was satisfied despite the white lie; his father had done so, back at Beckwith House.

He had first instilled in Desmond the care for beautiful things and their maintenance. Of course, he had never done any of the actual cleaning himself, but those had been different times.

"Anyway, Tony, it's much simpler not to have people working for you. I can always hire a car—or a housekeeper, for that matter—when I need one. The rest of the time, it lets me be free. Money can be a burden if you let it be. I make sure it's a tool to keep me *un*-burdened.

"That makes sense, sort of." Tony settled a little more deeply into the wide leather seat and lapsed again into silence as the city sped by silently through the tinted windows. Desmond reached over and took his hand, holding it for the rest of their trip uptown.

The restaurant was spare and elegant, lit discreetly so as to let you see your food without dissipating a sense of privacy and quiet opulence. The menu was short and the wine list extensive. Tony selected a simple, elegant meal for himself and then a lavish bottle of burgundy for Desmond to enjoy. The uniformed waiter was amiable and solicitous. The wine was brought to the table and opened. Tony let it sit while he worked on his appetizer. As he ate, Desmond watched him with pleasure. He always liked to watch Tony eat; he so relished his meals that it almost made up for Desmond's not being able to join him.

Desmond had carefully kept up his fiction of having a strange and restricted diet, which he prepared and ate alone. Whenever they ate together, whether it be breakfast or dinner, Desmond drank something, juice or wine, and regarded Tony with detached affection. At first Tony had been a little self-conscious; it was like being a pet dog doing something cute while his master looked on with admiration. But, as with so many of Desmond's quirks, he had grown accustomed to it and now seemed to like it. Somehow his meals with Desmond were more flavorful, more sensual, he had told Desmond, because he knew he was giving the vicarious pleasure of eating anything he wanted to someone who couldn't. From Desmond's perspective, food was the one mortal function denied to those of his race that he actually missed.

Watching Tony's beautifully shaped jaw move, watching his lips savor what was set before him, watching his beautiful hands handle the utensils deftly and gracefully—all had become one of the little joys Tony had added to Desmond's life. Tonight was no exception, although Desmond noted an unusual formality in his eating rather than the usual full-tilt enthusiasm. Tony described the dish to Desmond as he ate, and Desmond smiled indulgently over the table at him.

After his appetizer and salad had been removed, Tony gestured to the waiter to start the wine. He indicated that Desmond should taste it, and a small amount was poured into Desmond's glass. Desmond pronounced it perfect, and their glasses were filled with the deep red liquid, which sparkled darkly in the candlelight.

Tony's main course was set before him, and Desmond reached for his glass to propose a toast to the birthday boy. But Tony stopped him.

"Not yet, Des. I have something for you."

"For me? It's not my birthday, silly, it's yours. First you buy yourself dinner, and now you're going to give *me* a present?"

"*You're* being silly. You've given me more than anyone else in my life has, even my parents, over the past six months, Desmond. I wanted to give you something, something special. I hope it will be precious to you, as you are to me. Even though your money funded my job, I have earned my salary, and I wanted to use it to repay you."

"But Tony, you mustn't…" Desmond began, but Tony waved him off.

"Don't interrupt me with your scruples. Do you love me?" Desmond was startled by a carefully controlled edge to Tony's voice.

"Of course."

"Then hush up and let me do this." There was a look of such intensity in his eye that Desmond felt a thrill, somewhere between pleasure and fear. Tony was up to something.

Tony reached into his jacket pocket and pulled out a small gray velvet box, such as jewelers use for rings.

"An engagement ring?" Desmond asked with a smirk. Tony replied only with a mysterious half smile.

"Open it; you'll see what it's for."

Desmond hesitated, then took the box from Tony's outstretched hand. He opened it and stared at its contents.

There, nestled against the dark gray velvet, was a tiny gold bat. Its wings were outstretched, maybe three quarters of an inch across. It was minutely detailed in gold, the surface of the wings enameled in translucent lavender. In each eye was a tiny emerald. Its mouth was open, and two microscopic fangs glinted. A small ring was attached at the back of its neck. Desmond looked at it for a moment, then up at Tony, who smiled at him.

"It's an antique—to go on the chain I got you at Christmas."

"A bat? But Tony, I don't…"

"You don't know what to say?"

"I don't understand."

"Yes, you do, Desmond." Tony's smile vanished, and the look of seriousness returned. "You just don't want to believe it. I didn't want to believe it either at first."

Tony paused and took a swallow of his wine. Then he set his glass down and leaned slightly forward across the snowy linen, speaking slowly and softly.

"I know who you are, Desmond. I know *what* you are. There's a lot I don't know right now, but I do know that." Desmond noticed that Tony's hands, pressed against the white linen tablecloth, were trembling.

"You know!" Desmond could barely whisper; his throat had suddenly gone dry. The muted continuo of panic with which he had lived these past months suddenly became a deafening crescendo. He felt beads of sweat form on his forehead.

"I know you're a vampire, Des. I couldn't believe it—didn't want to believe it—at first, but there's been too much evidence." Tony rattled on, speaking more and more quickly, the words spilling out of him as if a dam had finally burst. "At first I thought I was crazy, but facts don't lie, even as careful as you've been to hide the truth from me." Tony's eyes fluttered, and he smiled self-consciously in spite of his apparent anxiety.

"It's just that I've got a good memory. You were always so careful, but then there would be some little thing that didn't quite make sense, and I'd remember it. Bits of information would suddenly fit into the puzzle in my mind and reveal part of a picture."

"Like what?"

"Your strange family, for one. All this business about your father, grandfather, and so on. You're the same Desmond Beckwith that built the house, that came from England—with Roger Deland, probably."

"Roger?"

"He was driving you nuts with his teasing. Then the business about his long hair but not in the '60s. I suddenly had a flash of the two of you with queues in the 18th-century style, and it made *sense*. And other things, harder to pinpoint. Your books. That library is tremendous, but it doesn't have the *feel* of a library that's been built up by different generations of the same family. It's more like an individual collector's books. This wouldn't have puzzled me if the books hadn't all been first editions and so many of them signed. No family is ever so consistent over generations. Your library is so much *yours*, only you could have built it up. And you're only supposed to be 45!"

"What else?" Desmond finally allowed himself to smile faintly at Tony, who reached over to stroke his hand timidly. Desmond realized that he too was trembling.

"Well, this stupid diet business. You've clearly never done this routine before with anyone as elaborately as with me. It's one thing to tell people you don't eat normal food; it's another to keep up the physical trappings of a weird diet. That health-food crap you've been buying—and probably throwing away—since you met me wouldn't have kept a gerbil alive. You're in beautiful shape for a middle-aged man—or however old you are. Your body's firm and strong, your skin clear, your energy high. You have none of the symptoms of a fragile metabolism."

"Was it that obvious?" Desmond asked.

"Not really, just that it didn't make sense. Why would you be lying about food, of all things, unless your source of sustenance was something you couldn't tell me about."

"Drugs?"

"Really, Des, even you couldn't afford to live on drugs, as if anyone could stay alive on drugs!"

"Yes, I guess that's naive."

"Of course, reading all those books you have really got my mind going. I mean, plenty of people read vampire stories; but you seemed to have a family tradition of it. That was all part of the library puzzle—why would your grandfather have bought a signed copy of *Dracula*, and then you buy copies of Anne Rice's books signed by her? A family vampire fetish?"

"Well, in a manner of speaking." Desmond felt himself relaxing and chuckled.

"Exactly. A one-man family fetish." Tony took another gulp of his wine, and Desmond followed suit.

"And then there was your odd schedule, not to mention your strange sleeping habits. Your need to be alone on certain nights, at least once a week. Your anxiety about waking up before me. You really are dead when you sleep, aren't you?" Tony cocked his head.

A nod from Desmond. "More or less."

"I caught you once when you didn't know I was there."

"What? When?"

"That night I supposedly went to Washington and I was supposed to be away on one of our regular nights together?"

"I remember. I was miserable."

"I came straight back from Washington because my friends were suddenly called away, and I thought to hell with the research I'd planned to do. I came over to your place late that night and saw you leaving from the end of the street. You never saw me."

"You followed me?"

"Yes, but not for the reason you think. I had pretty much suppressed any suspicions I may have had about who you were, but I was sure you were cheating on me—tired of me physically, looking for love elsewhere. Remember, you'd never said anything about love to me."

"My mistake. I did love you then, you know."

"I'm glad. But that night I was sure that was it. So I trailed you up to that club and skulked in the shadows, watching as you picked up that straight boy. I couldn't imagine what you were going to do with him. He was so unlike your type."

"Unlike you, you mean."

"Well, yes, I suppose. Was I jealous! Then you got him aside and into that clinch in the shadows away from the dance floor. And all of a sudden, you just park him on a bench and disappear! I couldn't understand it."

"Did you follow me home?"

"No. I went over to where you left him. He was kind of woozy, like half asleep. There was this weird hickey on this neck." Then Tony gave Desmond an embarrassed little smile. "You made him cream in his pants."

"I know. I was proud of that at the time. Now I'm mortified."

"At first it didn't mean much, but I couldn't figure why you'd just neck with the guy and dump him without getting anything out of it—other than soothing your ego, which didn't follow. Then all of my carefully locked-away fears and doubts began to rattle their tin cups on the bars of their cells. All those little bits of evidence began to clamor for attention."

"So what finally set them all free with the answer?"

"Bill Lawrence."

"Bill?" Desmond was startled.

"Not the way you think. We were just talking one night at his place, during one of his parties. I was helping him in the kitchen. I know you've known each other for 20 years, and he's handsome, like you are. I just casually asked him if he'd ever slept with you."

"You didn't. What a nosey parker!"

"Sorry, it's my generation. Sex isn't all that private to us. Anyway, he said no. You guys had been sort of turned on to each other way back in the '60s when you first knew each other, but it hadn't developed into anything. But he did tell me about one night when you'd been on the verge of doing something when he passed out."

"*That* was drugs."

"I would imagine. But he said he woke up the next morning with a strange hickey on his neck and figured you'd made out with him while he was asleep."

"It makes me sound like a necrophiliac."

"But in this case it's the dead doing it with the living, right?"

Desmond blushed at Tony's quip. So Bill hadn't forgotten about that evening, even after all these years.

"The first night you brought me home, you did the same thing to me, didn't you? I had a hickey the next morning."

"Yes."

"Why that night and not again?"

Desmond hesitated. There was now a look of fear deep in Tony's eyes, which were wide and fixed on him, waiting for his reply.

"I had gone out that night to hunt. I needed to drink. Roger had just left after a visit, and I was terribly lonely. I hadn't expected to fall in love; I'd never, ever brought a trick back to this house. Then you were there, asleep beside me in my bed, something I'd never experienced. I wanted to cast a spell on you, to make you part of me somehow. I knew it wouldn't hurt you, and I was famished anyway."

"And not since then? Why?"

186

"Because you became my lover, not my feed bag!"

"You've never drunk from someone you know?"

"Aside from Bill, no. I let Roger drink from me once." Desmond's memory flickered back to that July night in Paris.

"Roger. Your straight friend. He's beautiful. He's wonderful. And he's…"

"A vampire, just as I am."

"How long have you known him?"

"You ready for this?"

"As ready as I'll ever be."

"I met Roger in Paris in 1793. I had come back to Paris on bank business. He was exactly my age, but he'd only been a vampire for a few years. It's a little complicated."

"Paris? In 1793, you mean as in the Reign of Terror?"

"Exactly."

"Good grief! How did you meet?" Desmond could see the curator's professional curiosity push the fear out of the way.

"Initially, at a party of sorts. Then I sort of saved his life. We went to England, and then after a few years decided to start afresh. America was the place of choice then. I sold the family house—the one that's in the painting in the study downstairs—and we moved to New York, lock, stock, and barrel."

"And the rest is history, as they say."

"Right."

"Wait a minute. You *sort of* saved his life? What's that all about?"

"Oh, God, Tony, it's a long story."

"Well, I've got a big dinner getting cold here. I'll shut up, and you can talk."

Desmond was silent. He had never told anyone this. But then, no one had ever known about him. Only Roger. He felt dizzy and a bit sick to his stomach.

"Are you sure you want to know all this?"

"Absolutely."

"Well, then, let's go." Tony picked up his knife and fork and started in on his dinner, now with something more of his typical gusto. Desmond poured himself some more wine and began his story. If anyone in the restaurant were paying them any attention, Desmond, for once, was unaware.

The sleek black car brought Tony and Desmond back to the house well into the evening. They were silent in the car, Tony lost in thought, digesting both his meal and Desmond's story. Desmond was feeling surprisingly calm, almost relieved, but could not read Tony's emotions. He seemed withdrawn. They let themselves in and stood awkwardly for a moment in the dim stairway hall. Then Tony grabbed Desmond in a passionate kiss, releasing him just as quickly and walking down the hall a few paces. Suddenly he turned and blurted out:

"Desmond, I've got to tell you, I'm still freaked by this. I know I spilled all this out like some sort of legal case to convict you of being who you are. I may have sounded like I knew what I was doing, and I guess I thought I did. I mean, I've been planning it for weeks, but I still don't know—I need to know—if we're OK. If *I'm* going to be OK. That is, with you." He stopped abruptly and hugged himself as if he were cold, looking small and frail in the shadowy, high-ceilinged room.

Desmond stood at the doorway, frozen, staring. "What do you mean, 'OK'?"

"I—I mean, I've *unearthed* you," Tony stammered. "Found you out. Exposed you. I know what Lestat would do. Or Count Dracula. Or even Miriam Blaylock in *The Hunger*. But I don't know what *you're* going to do." He paused, standing at the foot of the stairs, and licked his lips. "What you're going to do with me." His voice cracked, and Desmond could see tears shimmering in his eyes. All the self-control he had witnessed all evening was falling away, and Desmond realized that Tony was terrified. Terrified of him.

"Dear God, Tony—do you think I'm going to hurt you?" His voice was barely more than a whisper. "If you did, then why not just leave, run away?"

Tony only shook his head, looking into Desmond's eyes. Then, in a small voice, he said, "I couldn't. I loved you too much. Needed you too much. I couldn't leave. I had to try, to see what you'd do. Now that I've done it, I'm afraid. Tell me what you're going to do, Desmond."

In a voice so soft, he wasn't sure even Tony could hear him, Desmond said, "This is what I'm going to do." And he quickly walked down the hall and caught Tony up in his arms, lifting him up off the floor as easily as if he were a child. He cradled him in his powerful vampire embrace for several minutes, Tony's blond head on his shoulder, his own lips near Tony's ear. At last he felt Tony's quivering body begin to calm, and felt his taut muscles relax. Finally he set Tony down on his own two feet and looked into his eyes.

"Tony Chapman, tonight you have given me a gift beyond all price. By taking on the burden of my history, you have set me free for the first time in two centuries. I love you; don't ever be afraid of me."

They kissed for a long moment. Tony broke the embrace gently and walked back to the vestibule, taking off his suit jacket.

"I can't believe I'm in love with a 200-year-old vampire," he said, almost to himself, dropping the jacket on one of the chairs.

"Do you want another drink?" asked Desmond solicitously.

"No, I'm fine now. And tired, though. Can we go to bed?"

"You have to ask?"

"Just polite, I guess."

They climbed the stairway, grabbing Cosmo as she scampered up from the kitchen to join them. Inside the master bedroom Tony looked around as if he'd never seen it before.

"And to think that you saw this furniture when it was *new*! It boggles the mind." Then he turned to Desmond. "Was it different then?"

"Different? I don't really remember. The changes have been so gradual. I guess it was, well, *fresher*, crisper. It's softened with time, somehow. Mellowed, you might say. I do remember when it was new, though. I was very pleased with it; it was mighty grand for its day."

Then Desmond stopped and laughed. "I can't believe I've just told you about my life as a vampire and you're still interested in the fucking furniture!"

"Hey, I'm a curator, get over yourself. So what was Lannuier like?"

"Like? I haven't the faintest idea. He was a furniture maker, not a friend, Tony. I met him a few times. We did business. I didn't really know him."

"Didn't know him—how could you not know him? Think of the people you could've met over the years, the things you know…!"

"Hold it, kiddo. I hardly planned to unveil my past life to a 25-year-old history freak in 1989 when I ordered this bedroom suite in 1810. Roger and I never planned our lives that much in the future. We lived—and live—our lives in the here and now. We just have more memories than most people."

"That's the understatement of the week!"

"Got me there."

"Can you tell me about it?"

"It?"

"Your whole life, things in the past. More than your meeting Roger."

"All at once, no. But you must have talked over the past with old people in your family, as a kid."

"My grandparents. They would talk about the '20s and '30s, when my parents were small."

"That's all I can do; I just have a larger stockpile of past. Give it time, Tony, there's a lot to tell you. I've never told anyone about my life. Only Roger knows it all. We'll just have to handle things as they come up."

"Can I ask questions?"

"Anything. Now that the secret is out, there's nothing to hide."

"Nothing?"

"No. What are you thinking about?"

"Your nonhuman life—the vampire side of things."

"If you want, I'll tell you about that too. It's not so astounding—once you've accepted the basic concept, of course."

"Is it like the books say?"

"No, but sometimes yes. Given that those books were all written by mortals with vivid imaginations, it's remarkable that any of it makes sense. But then the legends must have appeared out of some grain of truth so ancient that *I* don't know it."

Desmond stood by the bed, looking at Tony, who had untied his tie and was slowly unbuttoning his shirt. Once more he sensed something behind these perfectly reasonable questions. Desmond sighed and decided to take the bull by the horns.

"Perhaps I didn't make something clear when I told you how Roger and I first met. Vampires don't have to kill to feed. It's part of the mortal myth about us but in fact totally impractical. Blood regenerates in a living body, and killing would be wasteful. Neither Roger nor I have ever killed to drink. In that way we differ radically from the books. We can't change into bats or wolves or rats. We can't climb brick walls with our bare feet. We don't shrivel up before the sun or a cross. We're not magical. Actually, we don't really know *what* we are."

"Another kind of creature entirely, like Miriam Blaylock in *The Hunger*?"

"Perhaps, but I was born a mortal, as was Roger. It's something we were made into, something given to us by others of our kind."

"That's like the books, then."

"Yes, that's like the books. But it's logical, isn't it?"

"I guess, in a crazy way." Then Tony's thoughts seemed to shift, and his eyes brightened. "Hey, are you going to put my present on?"

"Of course. Here, I'll do it now."

He removed his tie and undid his collar button. Pulling the slim gold chain out, he unfastened it and took it off. Opening the box, he held the tiny enameled bat in his hand.

"Where did you find it?"

"I found it in a jewelry store in the Village. I asked if he had any bats. He didn't think I was crazy, because apparently bats were big at the turn of the century. I told him you were a *Dracula* fan."

"Little did he know, eh? It's beautiful, Tony, and more precious to me than I can tell you."

"I'd hoped it would be. Here, let me put it on you." Tony moved forward and helped Desmond slip the chain through the link at the back of the bat's neck. Then he solemnly lifted the chain over Desmond's head and fastened it.

"With this bat, I thee wed," he uttered jokingly, unbuttoning Desmond's shirt.

"You still love me, fangs and all?" Desmond asked.

"Fangs? Can I see?"

"Now?" Desmond rolled his eyes in mock exasperation.

"Just once. I hadn't thought of it." Tony was like a child. Desmond was glad to see his eagerness return.

"OK, just once." He dropped his lower jaw, and—his first time with an audience—extended his canines.

"Wow, that's incredible!"

"They do their job—ow!" Desmond had never tried to talk with his teeth in position and gashed his lip. He ran his tongue over the cut to ease the pain.

"You all right?"

"Yes. Guess I can't talk with my mouth full."

"Sorry."

Desmond looked at Tony, his eyes questioning. "You didn't answer me."

"What? Oh, yes. Yes, I do still love you. And I always will."

"Always is a long time," Desmond said, not without irony.

"You'd know better than I." And they both laughed.

Their lovemaking that evening was fervent and yet tentative, as if each were seeing each other in a totally new light. Desmond again wondered at the glorious feel of Tony's warm body, thrilled at the curves of his flesh, the softness of his lips, the sound of his breath. He was in a state of wonder that here was a living, breathing mortal man, his declared beloved, who *knew*. They were fully together, and nothing separated them but for Desmond's immortality. There would be much ground to cover in the time to come, but for now Desmond felt a peace he had learned not to hope for.

As they lay snuggled next to each other against the big down pillows, Tony idly fingered the lavender bat on its golden chain as it lay on Desmond's chest.

"Des?"

"What is it, Tony?"

"There's something else I'd like to know about."

"What?"

"Who's Jeffrey?"

Desmond looked at Tony in surprise. "Jeffrey?"

"You called me that once while we were in bed. At first I assumed it was a past lover, but then later I figured out that it wasn't anyone around now. You've never mentioned the name in conversation. Is he—was he—a lover?"

"Yes, Tony, he was. In fact, you remind me of him."

"Really? Was it a long time ago?"

"Very long."

"Before Roger knew you?"

"Before Roger."

"I thought maybe that was it. Would you tell me about him?"

"Tony, that's an even longer story than Roger's. Could we put it off until tomorrow? You must be exhausted. I *know* I am."

"You promise, tomorrow?" Again the excited child.

"Yes, tomorrow, little boy. *If* you're good."

"Can I watch you sleep?"

"What?"

"I want to watch you go to sleep."

"It doesn't look like much, really."

"Please?"

"For Pete's sake. Oh, all right." Desmond gave Tony a petulant little kiss, then pushed him away.

"Brace yourself, it doesn't take long. See you in the a.m."

Desmond lay back on the pillow, composing himself comfortably. Then, for the first time with an audience in his 265 years, he called up the sleep of the undead and sank peacefully into six hours of oblivion.

Tony lay alongside Desmond's body, feeling it go still as the ordinary signs of mortal life disappeared, leaving a handsome corpse in its place. He shuddered slightly, as if he had just watched Desmond die, then reached out a tentative hand and stroked the unlined brow, the immobile belly, the quiescent hands.

It's unbelievable, Tony thought. *A moment ago he was warm, vital, alive. Now he's dead. And he's completely unprotected. I could kill him, end his immortal life right now. He trusts me with his life.*

Tony bent down and kissed the lavender bat and Desmond's cool lips. Then, pulling the covers up under his chin, he settled down to guard his beloved as he slept.

CHAPTER 11

Desmond Beckwith was almost ten years old before he ever met a child his own age. After the death of his mother, Lady Anne Beckwith, the infant Desmond had been raised entirely within the precincts of Beckwith House and its park, deep in the rolling Berkshire countryside. Sir Charles, having replaced the bitter grief at his young wife's death with a stonelike determination to do well by his only child and heir, took on the boy's education with a fervor that Desmond would always look back on with amazement. As soon as Desmond was old enough—about five years—he was taught to write, read, and understand logic and basic mathematical principles. With an eye to his social as well as his business acumen, Sir Charles wanted Desmond to know literature as well as foreign languages. Accordingly, as soon as he could learn, he was taught French, German, Latin, Greek, and Hebrew. But every one of the many private tutors Sir Charles brought to Beckwith House was an adult.

There were young people about the estate—mostly children of servants and tenants—but all were in their teens by the time Desmond was of teaching age. Some were, it is true, impressed to join in games with Desmond, lest he have no sense of fair play or athletic interest. But Sir Charles took on himself the duty of teaching Desmond gentlemanly sports, such as horsemanship, shooting, and the like. And so for the first ten years of his life, Master Beckwith saw the world only through eyes older than his own and only from the perspective of his father's estate.

Not that this was a bad life for a child, even if it did somewhat rob Desmond of the innocence that siblings or childish playmates might have given. Beckwith House was a genial hothouse for the optimum growth of such a rare bloom as Sir Charles's only son. The house itself had been built for Desmond's mother, who had lived her entire married life within its walled park. Sir Charles's marriage to Lady Anne Desmond had been a great social coup, but it had also been a love match. Lady Anne had been quite content to remain in the country while her husband pursued his business in London, and the house had been designed to give her every pleasure. Outwardly it was a typical, moderately large house of its day, with mellow red brick walls trimmed with tawny dressed stone. A long rectangle with two high principal floors and a shallower third, it sat on a high basement with broad staircases centering the two long facades.

Its rooms were arranged in the formal, processional way peculiar to the time. Both of the main stories had their suites of sleeping chambers, each attached to a dressing room and closet or private study. Sir Charles and Lady Anne had matching suites on the upper floor, flanking the long saloon. Desmond's nursery had initially been in a large spare bedroom across the stair landing from his mother's room, but at her death his cradle had been moved to a suite of smaller rooms adjacent to his father's apartment. The state rooms, just below Sir Charles's and his wife's quarters, were used for visiting dignitaries, which at Beckwith House usually meant potential clients for the bank. Some of the visitors were titled, and just as many were not. But all of them were rich.

Desmond's earliest memories were of running through the many variously sized rooms with a tutor or nurse in laughing pursuit. He adored the great wide staircase, cantilevered out from the walls, with its richly carved oak balustrade. He loved the polished floors of the reception rooms and the lush carpets in the private chambers. He loved the high-posted bed into which he was moved once the crib was deemed too small, with its colorful embroidered hangings and vast white featherbeds. Most of all he loved the daily ritual of scampering across the narrow vestibule to his father's cabinet to surprise him while he was being shaved early in the morning. There his father, still lathered with imported French soap, would grab him and kiss him, lifting him high up in the air. Then he would shoo Desmond away to his own childish toilet, and they would not meet again until dinnertime, at noon.

Desmond's nurse would wash and dress him and give him the spartan breakfast thought fit for children in the time. Then he would climb the narrow back staircase to the third level of the house, where lay his schoolrooms, the bedrooms of his tutors, and those of the upper-house servants. There, by a fire in winter or an open window in fairer weather, he would go about his various studies. As many as three tutors were kept on hand at all times for little Desmond Beckwith, with strict orders to treat the boy gently but firmly and above all to teach him everything possible. It was an easy job for the tutors, for not only did they have each other's society but their charge was a bright and amiable child and, generally speaking, a pleasure to teach.

If Sir Charles was not in London, as was often the case, Desmond would join him for the midday meal in the withdrawing room, where a large square table would be unfolded and placed at the room's center, set with the proper linens, silver, glass, and porcelain. Sir Charles, ignoring the general practice of keeping children away from adult activities until older, coached his son from the age of six or so to know his manners and to eat as befitted a gentleman. Sir Charles had not been highly born, but he had learned the rules by which one transcended any limitation of birth.

After the dinner was done, the outdoor sports would be turned to if Sir Charles was in residence. In those lonely times when Sir Charles was in London, Desmond would return sadly to the top floor to continue more studies under the gentle prodding of his pedagogues.

By the summer of his tenth year, Desmond was allowed relatively free reign of the park without being attended by a nurse or tutor. He had his own gray pony, which he rode with expert ease. Although with the farms the estate ran to over 5,000 acres, the park was bounded by walls and was just 300 acres. This in itself was plenty of ground for an imaginative boy to explore endlessly.

It was this same summer that saw the arrival of a new steward for the estate. For Sir Charles, this was a drastic change, and the settling in of Horace Chapman and his family was of great import. The steward of an estate this size had great power. Although technically a servant, an estate steward held the reins, for it was he who oversaw the management of the tenant farms as well the home farm, and these together brought in thousands of pounds in income each year. It was the steward who saw to the maintenance of the park, gardens, and house itself, and it was he who saw to the work of the grooms, stablers, coachmen, gardeners, bricklayers, and gamekeepers.

In short, second only to Sir Charles himself, it was to Mr. Chapman that the people of Beckwith House looked. Even with the most talented of masters, no great estate could run without a skilled and honest steward. Sir Charles was doubly aware of this, since his banking kept most of his energy focused on London. He placed great store in Horace Chapman's abilities and was never, it must be said, disappointed in the least.

The arrival of the Chapman family at the estate had an entirely different meaning for Desmond, however, for the family consisted of several girls and two boys. One of these was just Desmond's age. Desmond had heard about this monumental truth from the housekeeper and had ridden cautiously down to the lodge on his gray pony one summer afternoon. Beckwith Lodge, which sat squarely beside the high stone gates, was a miniature version of the house, comprising six rooms, and was a feature of great status for the estate.

The Chapmans deemed themselves luxuriously situated in this solid little brick dwelling.

Desmond watched from a distance for some time, keeping to the woods behind the lodge as if trying to catch sight of an exotic bird. Little activity betrayed the new tenants, but finally, after nearly an hour among the trees, Desmond felt his heart jump to see a slight figure emerge from the kitchen door of the lodge and run across the yard to the garden fence. It was, without question, Desmond knew, *the boy*.

The boy was of Desmond's height and build, which is to say wiry—not yet awkward as in adolescence, no longer plump as in infancy. His most startling feature, from this distance, was his hair, which was a brilliant, almost snowy gold. It flashed in the June sunshine like a candle flame. Although he knew himself to be this boy's better, Desmond was afraid to approach. To him, the boy was something long desired and little hoped-for: a friend. He was afraid he might scare him off.

Finally, fearing more to waste the opportunity, Desmond dismounted and led the gray pony out of the trees and into the meadow behind the lodge. The towheaded boy caught sight of him at once, resting motionless at the garden gate as Desmond approached slowly.

Desmond's heart pounded in his rib cage as he walked the pony ever forward. At least the boy hadn't run away or done anything to indicate unfriendliness. As he neared Desmond could at last see his features. Small and regular, almost pretty, with a button nose and bright blue eyes, the boy stared solemnly at the oncoming stranger. Surprising in one so fair, no freckles blemished his tanned cheeks.

Drawing up to within a few feet of the gate where the boy stood, unmoving, Desmond stopped, unsure of what to do next. He had no way of knowing that the boy might be as afraid as he, which was indeed the case. Nor would Desmond have known then, although he did learn it later, that the boy held the same hope of friendship, for he too had heard that Sir Charles had a young son just his age.

After some awkward seconds had passed in silence, Desmond spoke.

"Hello."

"Hello, sir."

"I'm Desmond Beckwith."

"I know, sir. I'd been told, sir."

"What's your name?"

"Jeffrey, sir. Jeffrey Chapman."

"Why do you call me sir?"

"Because, sir, your father's my father's master, sir. My mother told me always to call you sir, sir." At this the blond head bowed slightly to conceal a sheepish smile. Desmond caught sight of even white teeth.

"Well, please don't, since I don't think I'm actually your master, at least not yet. What age are you?"

"Ten, sir."

"I too! Or at least almost. My birthday is July fifth."

"Mine's April the 20th."

This brought their conversation to a halt, and Desmond felt he wasn't doing very well. But at least he hadn't scared him away. Then he thought of something.

"Do you ride?"

"A horse, sir?"

"What else, of course! Well, *do* you?"

"I've been on one, sir, but I've no training."

"Would you like to ride my gray? She's very gentle."

At this the boy's eyes lit up, and he smiled for real.

"Would you let me, sir?"

"Certainly. Perhaps we could ride together for a while, then I can give you a lesson, if you like."

"That'd be lovely, sir. It's such a pretty horse." The boy came out of the gate and approached the pony. "May I pet her, sir?"

Desmond nodded assent, and Jeffrey timidly reached up and stroked the velvet front of the pony's nose. The gray snorted softly and nuzzled the blond boy's hand.

"See there, she likes you!" exclaimed Desmond.

"I guess she does!" Jeffrey beamed with pleasure.

"Shall we go, then—does your mother mind?"

"If you want me to go with you, sir, I don't think my mother would have much to disagree with."

"Would you ask her, please? I wouldn't want you to get into trouble."

"All right." Jeffrey turned and ran back through the gate across the kitchen garden and into the lodge. In a moment he reappeared with a youngish blond woman, drying her hands on an apron. She curtsied and smiled at Desmond.

"Are you sure he'll be no trouble, Master Beckwith?"

"Not at all, Mrs. Chapman."

She turned to her son, who was fairly bursting with excitement.

"Go on with you. Do as he says!" And off he went.

Desmond helped Jeffrey up onto the saddle, then climbed up behind him.

"It'll be easier if I ride behind. That way you can pay attention to what I do, without me blocking your view."

"That's fine, sir."

"One thing, I insist."

"Yes, sir?"

"If you are to be my friend, as I hope you are, you must cease calling me 'sir.' My name is Desmond."

The blond turned his head and looked for a moment into his master's hazel eyes and saw there no mockery, no pride.

"As you wish, Desmond."

"Thank you, Jeffrey. Now, let's go."

And with that Desmond kicked up the graceful gray, and they flew across the fields of Beckwith House as if before the wind.

From that day on Desmond Beckwith and Jeffrey Chapman were virtually inseparable. The joy of a playmate overwhelmed Desmond and was barely less intense for his friend. Before long Desmond had asked for Jeffrey to have his own small brown mare, and they would ride for hours through the park, creating fantasies in the woods where the two boys became knights-errant or great hunters. Sir Charles indulgently shared his son's training with the steward's son, so apparent was the kinship between the two, and Desmond arranged to have Jeffrey join him in his lessons. Although the tutors objected at first, Sir Charles smiled at his son's wish. Having risen from modest beginnings himself, Sir Charles appreciated his son's ability to ignore class—or birth—in favor of other qualities. Indeed, Jeffrey was already literate, one of the benefits of being the son of an estate steward. His mind seemed as ready to learn as Desmond's, and they advanced steadily together. Once their daily studies were done, and when they were not riding the park, the boys would play in the maze of rooms inside the house, having mock sword fights in the echoing great hall or playing hide-and-seek among the many store-rooms of the cellars and stable yards.

On his 13th birthday Desmond was called into his father's closet, where Sir Charles sat at his writing table. As his father finished a letter, Desmond looked around at this little-visited room, his father's most private space. It was a small room but luxuriously fitted out. Blue and white Chinese porcelains filled the shelves above the little corner fireplace. Engravings in black and gold frames covered the walls, which were hung with indigo cut velvet. Eight high-backed upholstered chairs, covered in the same fabric, were ranged against the walls. Blue silk festoons were drawn up above the tall corner windows, which overlooked the wide smooth lawns and geometric flower beds of the gardens.

Finally Sir Charles turned from his work and cocked his head. A smile of pleasure and pride flickered about his lips. From his expression one could see that, even without his beloved Anne, he thought he had not made a bad job of it so far.

"Desmond."

"Yes, Father?"

"I have made a decision regarding Jeffrey Chapman."

"Sir?" Desmond felt his throat tighten with fear. Was his best, his only friend, to be taken from him?

"I have decided," Sir Charles continued, aware of Desmond's reaction and relishing it with a sly benevolence, "that you are now of age to have a personal manservant. One to be in your attendance night and day, as befits a gentleman."

"Yes, Father?" Desmond, now merely puzzled, was curious.

"I think Jeffrey would be the ideal candidate for this. He is by now far too educated to send back to the farm. His elder brother will eventually follow Chapman as the steward of Beckwith House. It seems to me that with Jeffrey's training, and with his attachment to you, he would serve you well in this capacity."

He did not have time to ask Desmond's opinion of this idea, for the boy had thrown his arms around his father with a cry of joy.

"Oh, Father! That is wonderful! I know he would be perfect for me. He knows already my every habit—he can almost read my mind."

"I daresay," said Charles, chortling as he gently pushed his son away. "But you mustn't carry on like this. You're not a child anymore, you know."

Desmond regained his composure and stood tall before his father, drawing his chest up in what he presumed was an adult stance.

"Yes, Father. I agree with your decision. Jeffrey Chapman should make an excellent manservant for me. When do you wish him to begin at his post?"

"Straight away. I've called Chapman and the boy to my office. They await us downstairs."

He rose and led Desmond, who now walked a little stiffly, suddenly aware of his adulthood, down to the cluttered business room adjacent to the back staircase on the main floor. It was from this room that Sir Charles reviewed the workings of the estate, and here that Horace Chapman made his reports to his master.

As they entered both Chapmans rose. Desmond quickly glanced at Jeffrey, whose own panic was as plain as Desmond's had been. Desmond winked at him and saw Jeffrey's engaging features relax into their normal demeanor. Sir Charles seated himself at another writing table, in this case a plainer and more functional one than the brass-and-ebony–inlaid *bureau mazarin* that served upstairs in his closet. Desmond remained standing by his side, trying with some difficulty not to smile.

Sir Charles gestured to Horace and his son to draw up two of the stiff-backed cane chairs that lined the dark wooden walls of the office. Horace Chapman fingered his cap nervously.

As Sir Charles outlined his plan for Jeffrey's promotion to personal manservant to young Mr. Beckwith, Desmond and Jeffrey exchanged several short looks. Jeffrey would share Desmond's rooms next to Sir Charles. Desmond would be moved into the spare room atop the secondary staircase, and his present bedroom would become his dressing room. His former dressing room would become the cabinet, and the late cabinet would become Jeffrey's chamber. Jeffrey would continue his education in the capacity of Desmond's companion.

Mr. Chapman agreed heartily to the entire plan, honored that his son should have grown to be so close to the future master of the estate. Jeffrey himself said nothing, but Desmond could tell from the glimmer in his eyes that his happiness was great.

The two Chapmans were dismissed to fetch Jeffrey's belongings from the lodge, and Sir Charles called the housekeeper to arrange for Jeffrey to be measured for the proper clothing and to have Desmond's rooms rearranged according to the plan. They would be installed, master and manservant, by the evening.

So Desmond's high-posted bed was dismantled and moved into the adjacent guest chamber, which connected with his own former bedroom. His furnishings and personal paraphernalia were reordered to suit the new setup, and a small camp bed was brought down from the attic and installed in the little room adjacent to the cabinet. In the cabinet, Desmond realized, Jeffrey would someday shave him every morning—when his beard began to grow in earnest. Jeffrey would arrange his clothes in the dressing room, lay out his writing implements, make his bed, and generally see to his comfort. How grown-up it was to have one's own servant, one not an elderly nurse! And to have one's best friend as well. It was almost too much for Desmond to bear.

That evening Desmond dined with his father, accompanied by several local people and two prospective clients from London. These were eventually shown into their respective suites on the main floor. Desmond dutifully kissed his father good-night and then raced up the stairs to his new bedroom. There, as he opened the door, he found Jeffrey laying out his nightshirt.

Jeffrey turned with a smile as Desmond entered.

"I think I've got everything right, sir. The housekeeper's just been teaching me what to do."

"Dear Jeffrey, I suppose you'll have to call me 'sir' now, since I really am your master after all. But only when we're in company. When we're in here together or outside alone, you must keep calling me Desmond."

"I promise, Desmond." And Jeffrey welcomed Desmond's open arms in a warm hug.

Thus began their life together and Desmond's happiest years. They now grew used to each other as master and servant as well as friend and friend. The sudden underscoring of their difference in station was awkward at first, but soon Jeffrey took great pleasure in being the perfect valet, and Desmond equally delighted in being able to act as his father did, to rule his little three-room kingdom. But their friendship for each other was overarching, and each felt a deep-seated love for the other grow to maturity.

In time, and with no sense of surprise or dismay, they uncovered the mysteries of physical pleasure with each other. As their bodies matured, their already-present love drew them together naturally. Many times as little boys they had swum in the park and had seen each other's unclothed forms. As boys in their teens, each discovered a keen physical attraction to the other, which in that time and place seemed only logical. Their relationship as man and servant was in no way unusual for the time, and they had no reason at first to believe that their sexual relationship was any more unusual. Both had certainly been aware of the expected role of women in their lives. Desmond had heard many times of his mother's beauty and had seen her portrait in the suite of rooms no one had occupied since her death. Both he and Jeffrey had watched the younger servant girls and farm girls about the estate and had even glimpsed a group of them bathing in the stream at the far side of the park. But when the first stirrings of sexual maturity worked their way into Desmond's soul, it was to Jeffrey's willowy golden body that they drew him. And when Jeffrey first experienced the power of an erotic dream, it was Desmond's beautiful face and dark hair that aroused his ardor.

Gradually, as years passed, Desmond and Jeffrey realized that the expected attraction to the opposite sex was not likely to appear. This caused no alarm for Jeffrey, who could remain a bachelor servant all his life. But for Desmond, it was distressing, since he, as his father had been, would be expected to produce an heir for Beckwith House.

This one dark spot hardly diminished the joy of Desmond and Jeffrey's life. But Desmond dutifully played his part as the young squire, gallantly hosting the daughters of the neighboring gentry as wonted his role as Sir Charles's son. After all, Desmond Beckwith was an unparalleled match in the area, with the prospect of a great house and ever-greater fortune to accompany it. Sir Charles, for his part, seemed in no hurry that Desmond should marry, at least until he attained his majority. Assuming that one day his son would marry some young lady and bring her to Beckwith House, just as he had brought Lady Anne in his turn, Sir Charles indulged his son's freedom.

For Desmond, this long-range prospect was less pleasant, for he realized that his marriage, inevitable though it might be, would be little more than a sham compared to the enduring love his father and mother had shared. His love for Jeffrey was solace to him, but he could hardly conceive that it would please his father! In spite of these qualms, he determined to enjoy the time he and Jeffrey had alone together before they should be forced to share their life with another. In his heart Desmond already pitied this unfortunate lady, whoever she might be, for she would undoubtedly ever feel herself alone in this unnatural triangle.

Chapter 12

Following his ambition for his son's education, Sir Charles sent Desmond to Oxford. Desmond leaped at the chance to see something of the world beyond the walls of Beckwith's park. Until this time he had never even been to London. Jeffrey, of course, accompanied his young master to the university. Their relationship, happily concealed by their differing positions, not only flourished but ultimately protected Desmond from the worst influences of university life. Drinking to excess, gambling, and the sort of dissipated wastrel living that caused many a noble parent endless grief—none of these touched the close domesticity of Master Beckwith and his manservant. Indeed, Desmond was teased by his classmates about his abstemious habits and his chaste manner of living. Desmond laughed off their taunts in a good-natured way but continued to keep his own counsel.

Most of these privileged young men liked Desmond in spite of his oddities, for he was intelligent, kind, and generous. If any Oxonian took notice of the handsome golden-haired servant, it certainly never occurred to them that all of Desmond Beckwith's passions were aligned in that direction.

In 1745, the year of Desmond's 21st birthday, it was arranged that he and Jeffrey should take part in the ritual of the grand tour. Sir

Charles, seeing it as both a business and a social opportunity, suggested an itinerary that focused on the great cultural and political centers of the day. Thus, he reasoned, Desmond might both learn a great deal about the world and meet many of the young Englishmen who would someday be, like Desmond, heirs to great fortunes—and who might then seek the advice of a London banking house. Enough time and capital was allowed so that Desmond, attended by Mr. Chapman as secretary and servant, could plan his own route in the course of the year abroad. Sir Charles made no secret of the vicarious pleasure the tour afforded him; he himself had never left England, so busy he had been building his name and fortune.

As spring was creeping across the British Isles, Desmond and Jeffrey boarded a ship at Portsmouth bound for Amsterdam. From this sleepy capital, with its curved canals and gabled houses nestled together like hens in a coop, they made their way south to Cologne, with its great Gothic cathedral. Thence to other German cities, each one bearing the distinct stamp of the region in which it lay. At the great baroque abbey of Ottobeuren west of Munich, they saw the newly decorated Benedictine basilica, resplendent in its bright frescoes and gilt plasterwork. But it was to the remnants of the classical past that Desmond was drawn rather than to the modernism of the rococo, and they traveled southward through Austria to Verona, Parma, Florence, Siena, and Rome. As any educated Englishman, Desmond knew of the great modern houses of England, modeled on the theories of the 16th-century Italian architect. He longed to visit the sites that had first inspired Andrea Palladio and thereafter his English disciples. They sought out the Roman gates in Verona, its little coliseum an echo of the great one in Rome. They explored the glories of Caesar's capital, embellished by the builders and artists of the Renaissance.

Desmond and Jeffrey wandered in awe through the vast nave of Saint Peter, which dwarfed in size and splendor any building in England. The Continent was Desmond's first exposure to the art of

Catholicism, and he was overwhelmed by the creations of Europe's faithful. In Florence they found Michelangelo's *David*, keeping his ever-watchful eye to the left, on guard against some unseen Goliath. They marveled at this homage to the boy warrior who became a great Hebrew king and recognized in it an artist who reveled in the beauty of man. Even at the Vatican, before the Pietà, as they gazed in reverent silence, they were struck by the physical beauty of the dead Christ. His holy mother looking down on him in her serene sorrow, his limbs and hair and face exquisite despite the agony just ended. How different this image of death from the bloody and gaunt German examples they had seen! How pure and spiritual and—yes, *sensual*—was Buonarroti's translation of the Passion. As they looked on, Desmond and Jeffrey exchanged a glance and a clasp of their hands, understanding the unspoken union they felt with this long-dead sculptor who so gloried in the male anatomy and who could use it to express the deepest feelings of the human heart.

The two young men continued their journey northward to Padua and thence to Venice, where they were overwhelmed by the city of the doges and its fading splendors. No longer a center of power like Rome, Venice remained romantic and mysterious. From this city of canals, so unlike its prosaic cousin in the Netherlands, they moved eastward through Trieste and then south along the Dalmatian coastline of the Adriatic Sea. At the ancient port city of Spalato, they stopped, not sure whether they should continue their southward journey to Greece or to return to the Italian peninsula.

They settled into a snug inn that catered to foreign travelers. From the inn they could look out over the shimmering bay upon which the city was set. At their backs the Dinaric Alps rose like a jagged blue wall in the summer sunlight, guarding the mountainous lands of Bosnia beyond. Desmond and Jeffrey explored the old city and the new town, with its bustling fishing boats and curly-haired blue-eyed sailors, descendants of the race of Alexander. Desmond took tea with other English travelers in the ruined hall of the great palace of the emperor

Diocletian, its tall columns and Roman arches supporting only the sky for a roof. Jeffrey kept to the background, attending to his master's needs with a readiness and solicitousness that made others envious.

Throughout their journey Desmond and Jeffrey had shared quarters. It was not unusual, since every gentleman traveled with a servant, and in places where accommodations could be at times difficult to find, there were many arrangements to be made on a daily basis. Inns and posthouses generally supplied quarters for servants, high in the roof beams or buried below street level in cellars. Desmond, however, always insisted that a camp bed be arranged for his manservant in his own room, ostensibly so that he could be near at hand at all times.

The truth of the matter was that Desmond and Jeffrey always slept together, as they had since their early years as master and servant at Beckwith House. Desmond could not bear the thought of being by himself at night, and Jeffrey was nearly as adamant as his lover. Whether the ever-present camp bed fooled innkeepers or chambermaids, they never knew. On occasion there were no spare beds available, and the English gentleman was forced to make space in his bed for his servant. Perhaps the innkeepers did take note of the fact that this particular Englishman made no fuss at all about this situation— an unusual circumstance for the English, who were notoriously fussy travelers. As always, Desmond and Jeffrey were in public as they were expected to be: Desmond the gentle and considerate master, with Jeffrey his solicitous and efficient assistant. But once they were shut off from the eyes of the world, they met each other as equals, embracing in trust and love as if they alone understood the meaning of the words. As happy as their days of travel were, it was the nights they treasured. Then, in each other's arms, they knew the harmony of two souls united, and the worries of the future could not burden them.

The August sun sparkled across the bay early one morning as Jeffrey packed a small trunk with enough linens and other sundries for the short excursion they were going to make. Desmond had decided to take a trip into the mountains to explore the picturesque terrain. They had heard of a beautiful little church from the 15th century nestled in an unlikely little village high up on the rocky slopes, and nearby the castle of the local baron was said to have remarkable baroque frescoes in its medieval hall. The trip would take perhaps two days, and they would picnic along the route. Accordingly, Jeffrey purchased wine and such implements for eating as they would need and hired a coachman and carriage to take them. The grizzled driver, not young but not yet old, spoke broken German but communicated well enough with his temporary employer. He stocked his carriage, an old-fashioned but well-kept affair, with tools and torches and provisions of his own. The mountain roads, he said, were rough and towns few and far between.

They set off to the east, the coach's springs creaking in protest. Leaving quickly the lush coastal fields, they rose into the foothills and then the mountains themselves. The leafy deciduous forests of the lower hills gave way to the darker, harsher green of the pine forests, and above them bare rock glittered with snow under the blazing summer sun.

At the end of a long day of travel, which was interrupted only by a brief meal en route, the coachman slowed his horses and hailed his passengers, who leaned out of the windows. He pointed up ahead to indicate their destination.

They were in a descent, and below them lay a narrow green valley, rich with farm fields and bright with summer flowers. At the far side of the valley, they could see the road again wind up into the mountains. There, perched on an outcropping like some tawny bird of prey, was the village of Tsolnay. Slightly above the village, protected from behind by a craggy mountain lightly peppered with conifers, sat Castle Tsolnay, once a fortress, then home to the Barons of Tsolnay. Its walls looked white from this distance, the stucco reflecting the waning sun. Desmond waved the driver on, and they approached the village in the golden twilight of early evening.

The village was clustered about a cobbled square, and even in the fading light Desmond and Jeffrey could see that the narrow medieval houses were freshly whitewashed and bright with boxes of flowers. An ancient octagonal wellhead stood at the center, its wrought-iron superstructure creating a delicate tracery in the violet shadows. At the eastern side of the square, an arched gateway, its iron gates closed, revealed a paved roadway, which sloped upward and out of view. This, the innkeeper explained as he warmly greeted the unexpected guests, was the entrance to Castle Tsolnay. The Baron was away at present, in Spalato, in fact. Although he would not be back until at least the next day, he would most certainly be more than happy to show the foreigners about his ancestral domain. In the meantime, the comforts of Tsolnay's solitary posthouse were at their disposal.

In no time Desmond and Jeffrey were established in a comfortable suite of rooms, with Jeffrey's bed set up in the sitting room, while Desmond had a massively carved bedstead recessed into a corner of the adjoining chamber. Both rooms were heated by tiled stoves into which logs were fed through iron doors in the outside hallway. The two men had the low-beamed dining parlor of the inn to themselves, with an open fire in the antique hearth to stave off the encroaching chill of the alpine night. Jeffrey served Desmond the various hearty local dishes brought to them by the innkeeper, then joined him at the table with his own meal. They spoke little while they ate other than to review their plans for the next day's journey.

After dinner they withdrew to their rooms, and Jeffrey began his nightly routine of arranging Desmond's nightclothes as well as those for the coming day. He worked with his back to Desmond, who idly watched from the sitting-room door. His look lingered on Jeffrey's expert hands as they folded linens and rearranged various necessary articles in the traveling cases. As always, his long golden hair, pale in the light of a single candle, was pulled back tightly into a queue. Suddenly Desmond stepped across the room and wrapped his arms around Jeffrey, pinning his arms to his side.

"Enough of this. You've done nothing but care for me all this long, tiresome day."

"That is my job, Desmond." Jeffrey turned and smiled, eyes heavy with fatigue.

"Not tonight. I am your servant this night." Then he released his grip and pressed his mouth against Jeffrey's soft pink lips, probing hungrily with his tongue, lingering over the warm response.

They separated, and Desmond went to draw the bolt on the door to the narrow corridor. Telling Jeffrey to stay put, he fetched a circular japanned bath from the bedroom cupboard and set it down in front of the tiled stove, which gave off a surprising amount of heat. He pulled off his coat and threw it over a chair. Rolling up his sleeves, he went to the dressing table, on which was a washbasin and a large ewer of hot water left by the innkeeper's wife. These he placed next to the bathtub by the stove. Next he went to his own boxes and rummaged about, unearthing at last his sponge and soap.

"Now," he said to Jeffrey, "undress and stand in the bath." The words were a command but spoken in a low, husky voice that suggested ardor rather than authority.

Without a word Jeffrey removed his dark blue linen coat and vest, folding them carefully and laying them on the chair with Desmond's coat. He bent down and pulled off his boots, standing first on one foot, then the other. Next he unfastened his knee buckles, slowly and deliberately drawing off his white silk stockings. His bare feet shone against the dark stained boards, and the corn-colored hair on his calves glinted in the faint candlelight. Unfastening his breeches, he slipped them down and off with a graceful movement and threw them onto the chair with the other garments. This too he did with his underclothes, leaving only the long linen shirt and neckcloth that were part of his daily uniform.

Untying the neckcloth, he dropped it on the floor by his stockings. Then he reached behind his head and undid the black grosgrain ribbon that held his queue, adding it to the rumpled pile at his feet. Finally, crossing his arms in front of him and bending slightly to grasp his shirttails, he pulled the shirt up and over his head. As the shirt settled in unruly folds on the floor, Jeffrey stood naked, his shining yellow hair cascading about his shoulders, revealed in all his beauty before his lover's yearning eyes. Still silent, he walked over to the bath and stepped in, standing with his hands at his side, his blue eyes on Desmond's, a smile playing at his lips.

Desmond poured water from the ewer into the basin and lathered up the sponge with lavender-scented soap. He started at Jeffrey's broad shoulders, rubbing the soapy sponge over the smooth, rose-tinted golden skin. He washed his back, massaging the tired muscles and his chest and stomach, unable to resist kissing the small pink nipples, taut from the contrast of warm water and cool air. He worked his sponge down the long, slim arms, rubbing the sinews, and then rubbed each slender finger between his own, even to the translucent oval nails. The sudsy, perfumed water made a glistening, bubbled sheen down Jeffrey's curving backside, causing the gluteus muscles to quiver like the hindquarters of a well-bred horse. Desmond paused to caress their firm roundness and then carefully washed Jeffrey's private parts, noting with pleasure the evidence of arousal yet ignoring it, as was seemly in a good servant. Finally, half-drenched himself, Desmond sponged the strong thighs and calves, then worked his fingertips between each toe, making Jeffrey lean on him so that he could lift his feet and rub the soles and heels. At the end Desmond rose and poured the remaining water over Jeffrey's body, so that his flesh shone like a newly polished statue of golden Siena marble.

Trembling with desire, unable to carry the charade any further, Desmond grabbed his still-wet lover about the waist, lifted him out of the shallow bath, and carried him, dripping, to the bed.

Later that night, as they lay dozing in the curious old bed, moonlight streaming through the open window, they could hear the distant mournful wail of wolves echoing across the valley below.

"Why do they howl so?" asked Jeffrey absently, stroking Desmond's dark curls against his shoulder. "Are they baying at the moon, as dogs do back in England?"

"Perhaps," replied Desmond softly. "Perhaps it is just their way of speaking to one another."

"It sounds so sad, so painful," mused Jeffrey. "It's almost as if they're lonely or lost or frightened."

"They are much feared hereabouts, for they take sheep and other cattle—even children have been said to have fallen prey to the mountain wolves in harsh winters. The innkeeper seemed not to have much sympathy for their howling when I mentioned it earlier." Desmond yawned and stretched luxuriously against the warm golden skin.

"Then they are like us," breathed Jeffrey.

"Us? How so?"

"They live according to their nature, doing what they must only to survive." Jeffrey continued stroking Desmond's head as he spoke, lulling his master and lover with his gentle voice and reassuring hand. "And yet they are hunted and killed and reviled by the people for being what they must by God's intent be."

"And how is that like us, dear one? We do not kill sheep or carry off children."

"But we are considered to be monsters, creatures of Satan, condemned to hell for the love that only God could have placed in our hearts. If our kindly innkeeper or our coachman knew us for what we really are, do you suppose we would be treated any better than the wolves?"

"I think that as long as we had gold to pay them, we could *be* wolves for all they care. Beyond that I shan't venture to guess. Anyway, you shouldn't concern yourself with this. As long as we've each other, we need not bay at the moon, for we will not be lonely or lost or frightened. You must sleep, my beloved."

"Yes, Desmond." Jeffrey bent his head forward and gave Desmond a kiss on his forehead. He then lay back, his long golden

216

hair spread across the pillow. The rhythm of Desmond's breathing gradually began to match his own, and in a short while they were sharing the dreamless sleep of the exhausted traveler.

The next morning, after a breakfast of still-warm bread and very strong coffee, they explored what there was of the tiny village. The populace of Tsolnay was surprisingly large, but few of the people actually inhabited the village proper. Most lived in the valley below, much of which was owned by the Tsolnay family. The region was prosperous through farming owing to the sheltered setting in the mountains and the fertile fields that flanked the river. The Baron himself was apparently a benevolent lord and much-praised by the populace. Desmond and Jeffrey inspected closely the exquisite little 15th-century church set in the town square opposite the gate to the castle. More French than Eastern European in style, it seemed a curiosity to the Englishmen, out of keeping with the architecture of the region. The elderly priest who showed them through the church explained it readily.

"Ah, but Herr Baron is much-traveled. He has brought a great deal from the outside world to this village."

Desmond looked perplexed. "Surely you don't mean the present Baron?"

"Of course not, milord, I meant the Baron and his ancestors." But the quickness of the priest's answer and the sly little smile that played about his lips did not go unnoticed, and Desmond decided he would very much like to meet the Baron.

"And, of course, the castle itself shows much outside influence, despite its exterior crudeness," continued the prelate, pointing upward. Desmond and Jeffrey followed his motion and looked up at the castle. The massive walls, plastered over, were pierced here and there with windows, which had brightly painted shutters. The pointed turrets and high-peaked roof of the main block were sheathed with red clay tiles from the local kilns.

"The ancient hall, completed in the 15th century, was redesigned in the 17th. Italian artists came to paint the new vaulted ceiling and to produce the plasterwork. It is said to be as fine as any of its type in Italy."

"I do hope we'll be able to see this and to meet the present Baron," said Desmond.

"Perhaps, milord. The Baron is expected back today from Spalato."

"Then we should put off our departure until tomorrow, Jeffrey."

"Do you think, Father, that the Baron will receive strangers so soon after returning from a trip?" asked Jeffrey.

"Most certainly, sir. Herr Baron is most interested in strangers. As I said, he and his family have always been open to ideas from the outside. He enjoys visitors greatly, and they are relatively rare."

"The Baron has no other family at the castle, then?"

"None, Herr Beckwith. He has lived alone there since I can remember, and I have lived here most of my life." With this the priest excused himself to attend to something within the church, leaving Jeffrey to rouse the coachman from the livery stable where he had passed the night.

"Mr. Beckwith has decided to remain here for one more night in hopes of seeing the castle and paying his respects to Baron Tsolnay tomorrow. I shall arrange with the innkeeper and prepare some provisions for today."

"Today, sir?"

"We would like—that is, Mr. Beckwith would like—to take a further excursion up into the woodlands and make a picnic. We will do some walking, so you needn't go too far with us."

Mid morning saw them on the road again, passing around the mountain on which the village sat and into another range of peaks with a wondrously varied landscape. The coachman drove them for some distance into the uninhabited countryside. They stopped for a picnic on a rocky outcrop overlooking another green valley with its rushing ice-cold river and verdant farms. Bottles of wine, kept cool in a lead-lined chest; fresh bread and butter; as well as boiled meats, eggs, and cheese from the innkeeper's larder fed their hunger and made them drowsy in the dappled sunlight. The driver settled back on his box to nap while Desmond and Jeffrey walked into the woods to look for interesting plants and wildlife.

"Mind you be back before too long, Herr Beckwith," he called after them, "we don't want it getting dark before we leave."

Desmond turned back to him with a questioning look, then understood his meaning. "Ah, the wolves," he said with an understanding wave.

They walked for a long time, breath straining as they moved uphill over the rough ground. They picked leaves unfamiliar to them, pressed small wildflowers in a notebook Desmond had brought from England for the purpose, and exclaimed at the views they seemed to uncover at every turn. Sitting to rest in a little clearing with a thatch of dry grass covering the rocky soil, Desmond took Jeffrey's hand in his and gazed silently into his lover's bright blue eyes.

"Here we are, my love, all alone with no one to trouble us. As free as the birds around us, we are complete unto ourselves." He then kissed Jeffrey's smiling lips with gentle ardor, arousing his partner's desire. They made love there in the clearing as they had not done for many years, unfettered by the trappings of human society. As the mountain breezes stirred the yellow grass about them, they dozed in its caress.

Desmond awoke with a start and shivered at the chill in the air. The sun was still in the sky, but it was much lower than it had been.

"Come, Jeffrey, we must make haste back to the coach. The driver will be fretting over us surely."

They scrambled back down the mountain, paying close attention to the landmarks they had passed on their way up. Their return was much quicker than their ascent, but the shadows were slanting ever more sharply by the time they reached the coach. The driver was agitated but much-relieved to see them.

"I was afraid I'd lost you, milord. All the same, we'd better begin in good speed. I don't relish driving these roads in the dark." So they bundled into the carriage and set off back to Tsolnay. Once settled back into the comfortable coach, both Desmond and Jeffrey dozed again as the scenery drifted past the open windows of the carriage.

Jeffrey was jolted out of his nap and thrown against Desmond as the carriage lurched violently to one side and stopped. They could hear the driver curse in his native tongue as he climbed off the box. Climbing out of the listing coach, they could see in the weakening light that one of the rear wheels had split.

"It could have been worse, and I expected we might have some trouble on these roads," explained the driver. "It's going to take some time to repair this, but I've got enough equipment to do the job. Meanwhile, milord, you will have to stay outside, since I can't work with your weight." He then went to the back of the carriage and began to rummage about in the box tied to the frame. First he pulled out a tinder box and lit the two-carriage lamps at the front below the driver's box. Then he pulled out two iron spikes to the ends of which were fixed rope torches soaked with pitch. These he also lit, and soon their smoky light was brightening the deepening shadows of dusk. He planted the iron spikes in the ground near the broken wheel and set about his work as Desmond and Jeffrey stood and watched in silence.

He worked for some time, not speaking, grunting occasionally and now and then muttering an oath in a dialect unknown to the Englishmen. Suddenly, out of the stillness of the deep blue twilight, a piercing wail rose up, soon accompanied by a chorus of others like it.

"Wolves," said Desmond, turning to Jeffrey, whose brows had risen in surprise.

"They sound so much closer than last night," observed Jeffrey.

"Aye, and that's because they are. We're not in the village now, gentlemen, and I suggest you stay within the circle of light thrown out by the torches. Wolves won't approach fire." Then, without further elaboration, he went back to his task at hand.

Desmond stared as if mesmerized at the grizzled head of the driver as he worked with dexterity on the broken wheel. He had no sense of time passing until another, more distant, wolf cry made him look up. His heart jumped as he realized that Jeffrey was nowhere in sight.

"Jeffrey!" he cried out into the blackness behind him.

"Over here, Desmond! It's just the wine from earlier. I'm not far off." Jeffrey's voice sounded embarrassed at being caught.

Desmond smiled and scanned the invisible woods as he turned back to the light. His smile froze when, far off among the shadows of tree trunks, something green glinted in the night.

He wheeled around in the direction from which Jeffrey had called. Before he could call out, he heard a rustling in the underbrush, followed by a low growl.

"Jeffrey!" he screamed. "A wolf!"

There was no answer but a crashing and a strangled yell together with the muffled snarling of the wolf. Desmond, without thinking, grabbed one of the spiked torches from the ground and rushed into the forest as the coachman looked up at him in panic.

He made his way, blinded both by the darkness and by the focused light of the torch, toward the sound of the struggle. When he reached the spot, the pitch flames flickered across the chilling scene of Jeffrey on the ground, locked in battle with a gray wolf the size of a mastiff. Desmond leaped forward and flashed the torch at the beast, singeing its fur. With an angry yelp the wolf turned from Jeffrey and lunged at Desmond. As the full weight of the huge dog hit Desmond's chest, the torch flew out of his hand and landed in the brush. Desmond's head hit the ground with the absurd thought that the torch might start a forest fire. Then the wolf's slavering jaw, foaming with rage and evilly red in the torchlight, loomed over his face. He shut his eyes to ward off the sight, shielding them with his arm. Pain tore through his wrist as the wolf's teeth ripped through his jacket sleeve. Then an explosion shattered the night, and suddenly the weight of the wolf was gone with a quivering wail. Desmond looked up and saw the coachman standing over him, holding a pistol. The wolf lay, still twitching, between him and Jeffrey's limp form.

He groggily rose up and stumbled over to where his lover lay. He put his ear to Jeffrey's lips and felt the warmth of his breath.

"He's alive yet!" he cried to the coachman, who plucked the fallen torch and planted it next to the two young men. Frantically, Desmond looked for Jeffrey's wounds. His right arm was torn and bloody. More frightening was a deep wound in his thigh, above the knee, from which pumped deep red blood. An artery had been cut. Desmond pulled off his linen neckcloth and, tearing it in strips, bound up Jeffrey's leg, slowing but not entirely stopping the flow of blood. He next bound the lesser wound on the arm. He was puzzled by the blood on the bandage, which seemed not to be seeping through, then realized that it was from his own wound, which had been bleeding freely the whole while. The driver pulled off his own neckcloth and bandaged Desmond's arm, adding another layer to the more serious of Jeffrey's injuries.

Together they carried Jeffrey to the carriage and placed him inside, despite the broken wheel. The driver continued on with the repair work as Desmond stood helplessly by.

It was not long until the wheel had been fixed and the carriage righted. The driver motioned Desmond inside, where Jeffrey half lay, half sat across the seat. Pulling a flask from his coat pocket, the coachman offered it to Desmond.

"This'll put a bit of color in his cheeks, milord. Brandy."

Desmond put the lip of the flask to Jeffrey's mouth and got him to accept some of the fiery liquor. Taking a swallow for strength, he tried to hand it back to the driver, who refused it.

"Better keep it—you might need it as we go." And, turning, he clambered up onto the box and geed up the horses.

The return route to Tsolnay seemed torturously slow to Desmond, who held Jeffrey's head in his lap, oblivious to any impression that might make. Jeffrey groaned from time to time, and his face looked pale and drawn in the faint snatches of light from the flickering carriage lamps. Desmond laid his hand across Jeffrey's brow and felt it to be cool and dry. He stroked the soft blond hair and the fine stubble on the unblemished cheeks. Once he reached down to feel the bandage on Jeffrey's leg and shuddered to find it wet with blood.

At length they rumbled into the cobbled square of the village. At the sound of the carriage wheels on the stones, the door of the inn flew open and the innkeeper came out to meet them.

The coachman hailed him as they approached. "There's been an accident. Herr Beckwith's servant was attacked."

The innkeeper was horrified. "Attacked!"

"Yes, wolves. We were stopped to repair a wheel."

The innkeeper wrung his hands and clucked fearfully. Desmond noticed that the servant girl in the doorway behind him crossed herself when she heard of the wolf.

"This is very bad! But we are lucky. Herr Baron has returned within the hour and is at the castle. You must take him there now." He exclaimed again upon seeing Desmond's bandaged arm. "But you are hurt was well, milord!"

"Not too badly, I think. Why should we go to the Baron?"

"Herr Baron is also a physician. He has cared for the villagers for many years and has a surgery at the castle. He will know what to do."

At Desmond's nod the coachman climbed back up and headed the exhausted horses through the castle archway, whose great iron gates were now open. They wound up a steep stone-paved incline until, passing under a tower with a portcullis dimly lit by two torchères embedded in the stone walls, they entered a courtyard. The coachman pulled the carriage up before a massive pair of carved wooden doors with broad strap hinges flanked by two more flaming iron torchères. As he stepped down from the coach, Desmond noted an elegant carriage, still with its sleek chestnut horses, standing off to one side of the courtyard. The Baron must have indeed just returned.

As Desmond approached the doors, one of them opened and a plump elderly woman peered out at him. Seeing he was a stranger, she spoke accented German. "What do you want?" She seemed suspicious but not unfriendly, and Desmond realized that he must look terribly disheveled, with his queue awry and his arm bandaged.

"I am Desmond Beckwith, ma'am. My servant and I were attacked this afternoon by a wolf in the forest; he is badly wounded, and the innkeeper told me the Baron is a doctor." His shaking voice and pleading look seemed to galvanize the woman, for she threw the door completely open and rushed forward.

"Please, bring the man inside." She peered into the carriage and gasped at the sight of Jeffrey's bloodied leg. Despite the bandaging and Desmond's efforts to keep him immobile, a pool of red glistened on the floor of the carriage at Jeffrey's foot.

"I will go tell the Baron." She turned and darted back inside.

The coachman and Desmond carried Jeffrey as gently as possible into the castle. The vast room into which they entered was sparsely furnished and dimly lit. As he surveyed the shadowy space, Desmond realized that this was the great hall the priest had told them of just this morning. A wide carved-stone fireplace stood empty at one wall. Of the frescoes themselves, he could see nothing in the scant candlelight. A door opened at a far corner, and the old woman returned, followed closely by a tall elderly man with white hair. As they came nearer Desmond could see a high forehead; an aquiline nose with a high, almost Semitic, bridge; and a wide, gentle mouth. Most striking was the expression of concern in his deep brown eyes ringed with white lashes. He looked very old yet moved with speed and grace, gripping Desmond's hand warmly in a clasp of strength.

"Please, Mr. Beckwith, bring your servant into my surgery. I am just glad that I had returned." He turned and led the way back toward the door through which he had entered, Desmond and the coachman following, Jeffrey groaning slightly in the coachman's arms.

The doorway led through a long passage and then down a spiral stone staircase. Narrow windows, once arrow slits, made Desmond realize that they must be on one of the outside walls of the castle. They reached a landing at which a small arched door led into a high oblong room, brightly whitewashed. A large wooden refectory table stood at its center, and the walls were lined with row upon row of wooden shelves, upon which endless bottles and flasks and beakers twinkled in the light of a simple iron chandelier. High up one wall Desmond could see two tiny arched windows. This had once been a dungeon, he guessed.

"Please, place Mr. Chapman on the table. We must inspect the wounds." The Baron spoke in English with gentle authority. Desmond realized with a start that he had known both of their names, yet Desmond had not mentioned Jeffrey's name to the housekeeper, as she indeed appeared to be.

As the coachman laid Jeffrey on the table, the Baron motioned to the housekeeper, who led the coachman out, leaving Desmond alone with the doctor.

"Mr. Beckwith," said the old man as he began to cut away Jeffrey's bloodied clothing with a curious pair of polished steel shears, "I had heard of your presence from the innkeeper and was looking forward to your visit. It troubles me greatly that it is under such circumstances that we meet." He didn't look at Desmond as he spoke but intently regarded his work. He was dressed in a long robe or dressing gown of some exotic brocaded material that Desmond surmised to be oriental. This had been thrown on over a high-collared white shirt of obviously fine linen. The Baron had expected no visitors. As he worked the housekeeper returned with two large candlesticks, each holding several tall church candles. These considerably lessened the darkness in the room, whose white walls reflected the candlelight from the luster above as snow augments moonlight.

As Jeffrey's garments were removed and discarded by the housekeeper, the seriousness of the wound to his thigh was all too apparent. A jagged rent marked the leg from just above the knee to just below his groin. At its midsection it appeared to be very deep, and a heavy flap of flesh sagged forward in a flow of dark blood when Desmond's makeshift bandage was removed. A gasp of stifled pain was forced from Jeffrey's mouth, and Desmond, turning his eyes away from the blood, grasped Jeffrey's cold hand. He looked down into his friend's pale face and started to see the blue eyes open and stare directly into his.

"He is awake, Baron!"

The Baron barked a short order in his native language to the old woman, who exited the room and returned shortly with a flask. This she handed to Desmond, telling him in German to make his friend drink. He did so, and Jeffrey took the liquid with some difficulty, gasping slightly. Without glancing over, the Baron said quietly, "It is an aqua vitae combined with an opiate, to ease his pain. He has suffered a terrible shock."

As Desmond watched Jeffrey's face, he could see the features relax as the pain lessened. The tawny gold of his skin had paled to ivory, and dark circles underlined his eyes. He looked up at Desmond and spoke haltingly, faintly.

"Where are we, Des? Am I all right?"

"Back in Tsolnay at the Baron's castle. You've a nasty rip in your leg, that's all. The Baron is a doctor; he's working on you right now." Desmond smiled, belying the fear he felt numbing his heart. Jeffrey returned the smile weakly, then closed his eyes again, seeming to fall into unconsciousness. Desmond steeled himself and turned back to the object of the Baron's attention to find that the wound had been rebandaged and a large bundle of bloody rags was being carried away by the housekeeper. The Baron looked at him only briefly before attending to Jeffrey's less severely damaged arm.

Desmond was struck by the old man's large brown eyes, so dark as to appear nearly black. Within them he saw such wisdom and sympathy, even pain, that he wondered at it. Who was this aristocratic landowner, lord of a prosperous region, who took in foreign patients and cared for their wounds without so much as a protest? He seemed to look at Desmond and Jeffrey as old friends in need rather than as strangers who had stumbled through their own ignorance into his presence. Desmond had never known a nobleman in his country to show the slightest interest in medicine or chemistry, yet this one showed all the evidence of one who has studied the subject for years. He acted as one who knew exactly what must be done, without hesitation or fear.

His slender, pale hands moved over Jeffrey's injured arm with exquisite gentleness, cleaning the wound and wrapping it in fresh swaddling. Jeffrey lay, unclad but for some unsoiled remnants of his underclothes, upon the smooth surface of the wooden table like a sacrificial offering to an unknown deity, and the Baron worked over him with the reverence of a priest.

Finally, having finished with Jeffrey for the moment, the Baron turned to Desmond with a sigh and motioned to his own bandaged arm. Desmond pulled back.

"There's no need now. Jeffrey—Mr. Chapman—must be taken care of before I am attended to."

"I have done what I can for now, Mr. Beckwith. Surely you must be in pain. You have lost a good deal of blood yourself." The Baron spoke softly, with a weariness that seemed born of sorrow, not fatigue.

"Done with him? But how could you be? Mustn't he be stitched up? The wound was very deep." He faltered slightly. "I—I saw, before I looked away." He bowed his head, ashamed at his own weakness. The touch of the Baron's hand on his shoulder raised it.

"Let us go into my study, Mr. Beckwith. Mr. Chapman will be in good hands with my housekeeper." This lady nodded benevolently at Desmond as he allowed himself to be led away by the Baron's grasp.

Back up the winding stairs they went, Desmond following the fluttering tails of the Baron's silken robe. Presently they turned down a short corridor, and the Baron motioned Desmond into a small, low-posted room lined with bookshelves below an ancient carved and painted wooden ceiling. A writing table piled with papers stood before the two small leaded windows. Desmond sat heavily in the chair, a curious paneled affair piled with velvet cushions, indicated by his host. The Baron remained standing, pouring two fine Venetian glasses of a dark golden wine and offering one to Desmond, who accepted it gladly. It burned gloriously in his throat, unlike any he had ever tasted. Immediately he felt the blood return to his cheeks, and his heart's pounding lessened. At last the Baron spoke.

"Mr. Beckwith, I am afraid that Mr. Chapman's wounds are very bad indeed, at least the one to his leg."

"Yes, Herr Baron, I understand that. That is why I thought you would want to stitch it closed, rather than just bandage it."

"It is not so simple. Not only has Mr. Chapman lost a great deal of blood, but a major vessel in the leg has been severed, perhaps more than just one. If I were to try to sew the wound closed, he would bleed to death in but a few minutes."

Desmond said nothing but looked at the Baron's dark, worried eyes with growing panic.

"In any case, it is beyond my skills—indeed, beyond any surgeon's skills—to repair such fragile and delicate things as the blood vessels. All we can hope to do is to keep the wound bandaged and tight, minimizing the further loss of blood."

"But I don't understand. Can such a wound heal without surgery?" Desmond knew little about the surgeon's art but was well-aware that it was an art far from perfect.

"Perhaps. We can at least hope that it will. The human body is a remarkable machine, given time and luck. Mr. Chapman is a young man in good health."

"You're saying there's nothing you can do," Desmond said leadenly. "Jeffrey is going to die, isn't he? Isn't that what you're telling me?"

The Baron grimaced at these words but came over to Desmond's side and placed a hand on his shoulder.

"I am sorry, Mr. Beckwith. There is a chance, of course, for the wound to mend. But I have seen many such wounds over the years, more of them caused by the tools of war than by wolves. We can bind them, even suture the skin to make it look as if we have repaired the damage. But for the most part we can do nothing to stop the inevitable. I am very sorry."

Desmond sat motionless, his eyes downcast, staring blindly at his hands in his lap, where they lay folded. Jeffrey was going to die. For now he lived, yet his body was torn, and no mortal power could undo the damage, could do anything but delay the end. And Desmond would be alone, truly alone; more alone than in his solitary childhood. He raised his hands slowly to his face, pressing them against his eyes and mouth to stifle the sobs of fear that threatened to burst forth into the silence of the ancient castle. A touch brought his face up, and the Baron asked him, "Would you like to go to the chapel?"

"What for?"

"To pray, of course, Mr. Beckwith."

"Pray? Pray to a God who is about to take my Jeffrey's life from him? You yourself have admitted there is nothing we can do now but wait and hope."

"And pray, Mr. Beckwith."

"And does your God, Herr Baron, answer your prayers?"

"Sometimes he does. But if he does not, he gives me strength. That is another reason for prayer—to endure in times of darkness. Those are perhaps the prayers I have needed most in my life." The Baron spoke very softly, as if thinking aloud. There was no reproach, only some surprise in his demeanor.

"Then you go, Herr Baron. Pray for my Jeffrey and pray for me as well. I cannot find it in my heart to pray. I would sell my soul to Satan himself if it would save Jeffrey."

Desmond's head again dropped to his chest as silent tears coursed from his eyes and fell to his clenched hands.

For a long moment the Baron did not move, and Desmond could feel the dark, sorrowful eyes upon him. Then the Baron spoke again.

"You say you would sell your soul to Satan, Mr. Beckwith. Would you be willing to do so with Mr. Chapman's?"

Desmond looked up at him in wonder. "What do you mean, unless you are yourself Lucifer?"

"No, Mr. Beckwith, I am not the Fallen One." The Baron, who had leaned forward in posing the last question, straightened to his full height. No sign of age crooked his back or diminished his noble carriage. "But there is one way, one slight chance, that we might save your friend's life; but I warn you that it might be at the peril of his mortal soul."

Desmond almost laughed in spite of his anguish. "You are a Baron and a doctor, Herr Tsolnay; are you now a wizard too?"

"I am not jesting, Mr. Beckwith." The Baron's face had taken on a deadly serious air. "How old would you say me to be, Mr. Beckwith?"

"How old? Perhaps 70. You are very vigorous, Herr Baron, but your face shows your age."

"Look carefully upon this face, Mr. Beckwith. Look at these hands, this frame, these eyes. In this mortal coil and with these eyes, I have lived through the passage of nearly 300 years, all told."

"What? How could you? You must be mad!" Desmond was astounded and for the moment drawn out of his sorrow by the old man's astonishing claim.

"How could I, Mr. Beckwith? I am one of the undead. I am immortal, ever-living. I am a vampire." The Baron spoke with a strange, quiet pride tinged with sorrow. There was no hint of madness in his eyes, only sincerity and candor.

"And what is a vampire, Herr Baron?" Despite his surprise Desmond felt compelled to ask, curiosity overcoming his scruples.

"A creature not unlike man or woman yet entirely different from them. We live as humans do, for indeed we are made from humans. Yet we live by blood, the blood of living humans. This blood grants us eternal life even, perhaps, as it steals our mortal soul from us." The Baron bowed his head at this, and his hands fell limply to his sides.

"How do you know you have lost your soul?" The pain in the Baron's voice had aroused Desmond's compassion.

The Baron looked up at him with a slight wry smile. "Ah, that, as Hamlet said, is the question." He turned and strode to the writing table again. "I have never *known*, one way or the other. For this reason I built the church in the village and the chapel in this castle. For this purpose I pray to God every day, as I have for the past three centuries. Never may I escape the apparent irony of my needing human blood for my body and the blood of Christ for my soul. Every day I ask the same question: If one is doomed to live forever, can one have a soul?"

"Can nothing kill you, Herr Baron?"

"Yes, I can be killed, and those of my kind have been killed before me. That is my one hope—that I still have my soul and that by living my eternal life as I do, I somehow ensure its safety should someday my immortality be breached."

"And even if I can bring myself to believe you, Baron Tsolnay, how can this save Jeffrey?" Something in the Baron's tone made

Desmond disregard the apparent impossibility of what his host had said. The old man was dead earnest, and it brought a strange kind of hope to Desmond's heart.

"My blood might be able to save him, if we have not waited too long."

"He must ingest your blood." Desmond made a statement, not a question.

"That is right, Mr. Beckwith. As my blood was transformed so long ago by that of a Turkish vampire, so might that of your Jeffrey Chapman be changed by mine."

"And what will this do, exactly, Herr Baron?"

"Exactly, I am not sure. I have never done this myself but have only experienced it from the other side. If it works, it will change him, first of all, into a creature like myself. He will be immortal, for good or ill. The more important fact at present is that his immortal body will begin to heal rapidly and with a completeness that no modern-day surgeon could accomplish.

"And then why do you fear for his soul? Have you become a child of Satan's dark dominion since your transformation? Will Jeffrey become a thing of evil?"

"No more so than I. I have no more acquaintance with the Prince of Darkness now than I did in the 15th century. If Satan allows his captives to do more good than evil in this world, then perhaps I am in league with him. I pray to God fervently that this is not so and at times even feel somehow that I am correct. But I do not know."

"Then I see no terrible risk. We must do it if it is the only chance we have." Desmond rose steadily from his chair, his voice firm.

"Do you understand, then, Mr. Beckwith?"

"As well as I can, Herr Baron. Let us make haste." Quickly they made their way back down to the surgery, where the motherly housekeeper was seated on a stool by the dying man's side.

"Leave us, my faithful woman. We have work to do." The Baron spoke rapidly, in German, with the command of a general. The old woman left.

The Baron looked closely at Jeffrey's pale face and turned briefly to Desmond. "He is very near death. We might be too late."

"We cannot! Hurry, please!" Desmond felt his panic returning.

Matter-of-factly, the old man removed his robe and handed it to Desmond. He then rolled up his sleeve and went to one of the high shelves, whence he took a glass beaker and a small scalpel. Without the slightest hesitation, he opened a vein in his arm and held the wound over the beaker as the blood spurted like liquid fire into the clear vessel. Desmond didn't move a muscle from where he stood and watched, transfixed.

When the glass was half full with dark red fluid, the Baron raised the wounded arm to his mouth and sucked on it but a moment. Desmond was amazed to see, when he lowered his arm, that the wound was all but invisible. Desmond gasped in spite of himself.

"The vampire's saliva is a remarkable healing agent on minor injuries. This I have used to good advantage over the years." He next moved quickly to Jeffrey's side and signaled to Desmond.

"You must assist. Hold your friend upright. He must swallow."

Desmond did as he was told, eliciting a groan from Jeffrey as he raised him to a sitting position on the table.

"Hold his head up, Mr. Beckwith," the Baron commanded quietly.

Again Desmond did as he was told, and the Baron held the beaker of blood to Jeffrey's drawn bluish lips. Only half conscious, Jeffrey resisted, then, drawn perhaps by the warmth of the blood, drank with surprising readiness.

"I do not think he understands," remarked the Baron. "*I* was not so acquiescent."

Jeffrey did not quite finish the beaker, and when he choked slightly the Baron took it away and signaled for Desmond to lay him down. Desmond did so and then seated himself on the stool left by the housekeeper. He took one of Jeffrey's hands and held it, watching the young man's face intently. The Baron moved up behind him and stood silently, also watching.

They stood like this for nearly an hour, and Desmond became aware of a clock ticking away somewhere in the shadows of the room. Somewhere during their ordeal it struck 11 o'clock, and Desmond started to realize how little time had passed since their return to the village.

Jeffrey's face had not moved or changed since drinking the Baron's blood. Desmond looked up at the statue-like nobleman, whose grimly set features sent a chill of apprehension through his body. Suddenly there was a slight sound, and Desmond looked at Jeffrey to find his blue eyes wide open and mouth smiling faintly.

"Jeffrey!" Desmond all but whispered the exclamation and leaned close to his lover's face.

"Desmond, I'm sorry," Jeffrey whispered ever so faintly, squeezing Desmond's hand.

"Don't say such silly things, dear friend. You mustn't apologize. The Baron has given you some special medicine that will make you better; you must wait..." Desmond froze. The blue eyes into which he had been staring were still upon his face, but they no longer looked at him. The hand that had feebly held his own was lifeless in his grasp. The Baron's hand gently gripped his shoulder.

"We were too late, Mr. Beckwith. He is gone."

Desmond looked wildly up at him. "But he spoke to me! He smiled at me!"

"He knew his time had come, Mr. Beckwith. Rarely have I seen so graceful a death. His soul is with God."

Desmond stood up abruptly, knocking over the stool. He stared unbelievingly at the corpse of his lover, not speaking as if stricken dumb with shock. Then he sputtered some meaningless words, finally forcing out of his mouth, "But we were going to save him. Your blood! He drank it."

"We were too late. He was too close to death. We tried, but we could not save him." The Baron's voice was low, heavy with a sorrow that Desmond, in his grief, didn't notice.

Desmond suddenly wheeled on the Baron. Staggering slightly, wide-eyed, he spoke with a chilling calmness. "He's dead. Then I shall join him! My life is over!" He madly tore at the bandage on his own arm, reopening the wound so that the blood began to flow again.

Turning away from the Baron, he moaned, "Jeffrey, I will be with you soon." He stumbled back to the table and bent over Jeffrey's lifeless form, sobs heaving his body as blood dripped onto the cold stone floor of the laboratory. Then his knees seemed to give way, and he collapsed backward, unconscious.

The Baron stepped to his side and knelt next to him, stroking his sweat-stained brow and shaking his head sadly.

"Poor man. I have failed you."

CHAPTER 13

Desmond awoke in a strange bed with squat, ornately carved posts of a distant era and gauzy white hangings through which he could see sunlight streaming. He was dressed in a fine linen nightshirt, and the coverlet over him was richly embroidered in silk thread. This he threw back, likewise the muslin curtains of the bed. He was in a large square room, as high as it was wide, with massive beams high up above his head and two tall casement windows with diamond-paned glass. These were open, and the sounds of birds came into the room with the warm summer breezes. He looked around in confusion for a moment, then realized where he was.

The Baron's castle, he said to himself. *And Jeffrey is dead.* He looked at his arm, which had been carefully rebandaged, but no longer felt the need to tear the wound open. The hysteria of his grief had passed, replaced by a leaden pain that he felt would never pass.

He rose and, taking from a nearby chair a brocaded silk robe similar to the one the Baron had worn the night before, went to the window. Looking out over the verdant fields of the valley, he could see the shingled and tiled rooftops of the village just below the castle walls. He could see the beautiful little church and the cozy inn, where just last evening but a day he and Jeffrey had lain safely in each other's arms. Hot tears started from his eyes, but he wiped them away angrily.

"Where is he?" Desmond looked around and headed for a low door set in the angle of the room. He found himself at the top of another winding stair, perhaps the same they had used last night. Descending it, he finally came to a corridor, and down this he passed into the great hall. It too was empty, but now the morning sun made the baroque frescoes blaze with glorious color through two enormous windows in the courtyard wall. He crossed the hall quickly, found the corridor and stairs of the past night, and thence the Baron's surgery. The table was empty, and no trace of its last occupant remained. Desmond wheeled and rushed back to the hall, where he found the housekeeper.

She anticipated his question, seeing the query in his eyes. "We have placed Herr Chapman in the chapel, Herr Beckwith," she said, indicating a pair of doors opposite.

Desmond followed her directions and found himself in a small version of the village church, more austerely designed but trimmed with lavish hangings of the past century. Before the altar was a low wooden bier, draped with a pall of black velvet. On it lay Jeffrey's body, now wrapped carefully in a spotless white shroud that left only his head, hands, and feet uncovered. His jaw had been bound with a white cloth, and the pale ivory of his face had faded even more to an ashen white. This immobile form barely hinted at the glory of the living image his face had presented.

At each end of the bier stood one of the ornate candelabra that had served in the laboratory. In them candles burned, and on the altar itself were large vases full of summer blossoms. Their sweet scent mingled with that of incense in the cool dimness.

Desmond stood for a while before the bier, staring down at his beloved's form. Finally he knelt, placing his hands in an attitude of prayer, his elbows resting on the edge of the bier. He looked up at the silver gilt crucifix on the altar and tried to focus his thoughts.

Dear God—if you exist and if you care!—why have you taken Jeffrey from me when he was all I had? To what purpose did this happen? Why did you bring me to this desolate place only to tear my heart out and throw it to the mountain wolves? Did you so hate us, our love, that you had to destroy it by destroying my beloved? Tears burned his eyes, and he bowed his head, muffling his sobs in the cool white linen of the winding-sheet.

For a time he remained like this, his wet eyes pressed into the cold and ungiving flesh beneath the cloth. He raised his head. *This is not Jeffrey,* he said to himself at last. *This is the mere husk of Jeffrey's existence, no more him than the clothes he wore. His essence, his spirit—his soul, then—is gone.* Desmond knew not if it had gone, as the Baron said, to God, but he fervently wished he could believe it to be true.

A strange coldness crept through him, quelling his sorrow and clearing his head. The sweet scents of the chapel suddenly became overpowering to him, and he rose stiffly to his feet. Turning, he started. The Baron, dressed in a trim black suit with the same simple but fine white linen as before, stood at the chapel door.

"I did not want to disturb you, Mr. Beckwith."

"Thank you. I think I am finished here."

"Please come and take some breakfast. You need strength. I have had food prepared for you."

"You will join me, Herr Baron?" Desmond asked.

"Yes, but not to eat, as you understand now. To talk." He led the way back into the hall and down the same stair onto which Desmond's room opened, to a suite of rooms apparently just below the great hall. Here the space was divided into two large rooms, somewhat lower than the hall itself. One was a luxuriously appointed drawing room in the latest French manner. The other was a rather more old-fashioned banquet room, perhaps from the end of the last century. At the long table two chairs were set at one end, and food was put out in covered dishes on a side table.

In spite of his emotions, Desmond found that he was very hungry and, no servants being in evidence, he helped himself to the varied local fare from the serving dishes. He sat in one of the stiff-backed chairs pulled up to the table. As Desmond began to eat, the Baron seated himself at the other chair, a solicitous smile on his thin lips, concern in his dark eyes.

Desmond ate in silence for a while, feeling the hearty victuals do him good even as he chewed. He glanced frequently at the Baron, but his host made no move to speak. Finally, somewhat satisfied, feeling calmer, Desmond put down his knife and fork and turned to the Baron.

"These two rooms are quite up to date and handsomely done. You must follow fashion, even in your isolation here."

"I do, although I have not traveled farther than Spalato in over a century." This reference to his age sent a shiver up Desmond's spine.

"Fortunately, it is a rather sophisticated city, and I can keep abreast of current French fashion. The drawing room is my most recent redecoration. Having suffered through the magnificent austerity of the 15th century here, I appreciate the comforts of modern taste." He beamed with obvious pride, the pride of a householder. "This room," he continued, gesturing to the chamber in which they sat, "I did perhaps 75 years ago. Its stiffness is more suited to dining—which, of course, I am little versed in—and so I let it stay."

"It is most beautiful, Herr Baron. Very different from your little study." Desmond resumed his breakfast, feeling almost normal again, distracted by the food and the conversation.

"Ah, yes, but my study is my heart—or perhaps my brain. It is easy to heat and is entirely private and thus need not be kept tidy. These rooms are my public face, like the great hall above. It is here that the villagers and visitors—at least most visitors—see me."

The last phrase reminded Desmond of why he was here, and the image of the cold white laboratory, with Jeffrey's bloodied body on its hard wooden slab, returned to him. He put down his utensils again and stared silently at the half-finished meal, fighting back tears.

Instantly the Baron was alert to his mood, regretting the inadvertent pain he had caused his guest. "I'm sorry, I've upset you again. Forgive me!"

"It's all right. I must bear my grief. As you said, I must endure." He turned his gaze, steadier now, upon the Baron's large dark eyes, seeking comfort in the pain they seemed to share with him.

"You seem more deeply affected by this than I would have thought, Herr Baron. After all, you hardly knew us."

"Even in my warrior years, I hated suffering and pain. As brutal as those times were—and as many lives as I ended on the field of battle—I never willingly made anyone suffer. That, in its day, made me notorious as a merciful commander. Some of my peers would impale their captives on blunt stakes outside their castles. I was jeered on occasion for killing the enemy quickly to spare him pain. It is all too horrible, looking back. Since then I have devoted myself to healing and easing pain. So lie my sympathies. After I returned here, facing an eternity I did not understand in this place, I made a decision: I could rule my little kingdom through fear or love. Fear works well and is far more economical, but love lasts. I chose love, and healing as a part of that. I have long used my unending life to lessen the pain of the mortal lives that depend on me. I still grieve to see others suffer. You and Mr. Chapman did not need to be friends; you are human, and that was enough for me to share your tragedy."

"You are loved, then—that much I, or we, could see from what your villagers said of you. I wish Jeffrey could have known you. He would have been as fascinated as I. He was always a greater student of human nature than I was." Desmond struggled to keep his voice even but wavered despite his efforts.

The Baron reached out and lightly touched his sleeve. "Forgive me, Mr. Beckwith, but it is clear—was clear from the moment I saw you last evening—that Mr. Chapman was more than a servant to you."

"Yes, he was, Herr Baron, far more than a servant. A great and dear friend." Desmond's eyes dropped to his plate again, and a sigh of pain escaped his lips.

"More, even, than a friend?" The Baron's eyes beseeched Desmond to speak his heart, and he could not resist the plea.

"More, even, than a friend." Desmond's eyes met his host's. "He was first my friend, in childhood, then my lover as we approached adulthood. I loved him with all my heart, Herr Baron. I don't know how I shall carry on without him by my side. Thus has your God punished us for our sin, although it was not of our doing."

"Mr. Beckwith, it is not possible for me to believe that God sees any true love as evil, no matter what the words of man might tell you. Hate is the only truly evil thing in the world. Second only to it is false love, followed by its twin, hypocrisy. If your love was true, then it was blessed."

"How do you know this?"

"I do not—I feel it, just as I feel that my soul is with me. We cannot know things like this, for all that we may read others' assurances to the contrary. We can only feel the rightness or wrongness of a thing. The most evil being on earth is so because he cannot feel anything to be wrong. I have known such men in my day."

"You do not shrink from the knowledge that we shared our lives as husband and wife do?"

"Having watched your face last night, I do not feel that the Blessed Virgin felt more sorrow as she looked on the face of her crucified Son. How can I shrink from a love that can so touch my heart? I have not known the love of either man or woman since before my transformation, but I recognize it in others. When I see it, it is a balm to my heart."

With that, as if so moved himself that he could not remain, the Baron rose from his seat. "Mr. Beckwith, I have taken the liberty of arranging for a funeral service at the village church this afternoon. I hope I have not overstepped my bounds in doing this."

"No, not at all. Thank you for taking care of this. I wouldn't have known what to do." Desmond felt a strange comfort within him and gratitude to the old man for his consideration.

"I am glad. The service will be at 4 o'clock. If you would like, my study is available to you, as are my books. If you prefer, you may stay in your chamber. My house is yours." And with these words he bowed solemnly and left Desmond by himself in the great dining room.

Desmond's appetite seemed to evaporate with the departure of his host, and he returned slowly to his bedroom. What an extraordinary life this man must have led! As Desmond surveyed the flamboyant gilt furniture of the drawing room, followed by the medieval harshness of the winding stone staircase and then by the Renaissance splendor of his airy chamber, he marveled at the man who had, entirely on his own, created this effect of generational change within the walls of the ancestral fortress he himself had built. *He is his own dynasty*, Desmond thought. *He has accepted his destiny on earth and mastered it.*

The walls of his room were covered with rough white plaster but relieved with richly hued tapestries, which Desmond took to be Flemish. In one of them he smiled to recognize the image of the Baron, standing off to one side, partly hidden by the hindquarters of a white horse. He had hardly changed in the two centuries since the tapestry had been woven, and yet he had lived already 100 years when it was created! *What must it be like*, he mused, *to live a dozen lifetimes and not grow weary of mortal existence?*

In a massive armoire against one wall, Desmond found a suit like that the Baron had worn at breakfast. Clearly one of his host's, it fitted somewhat loosely but well enough. Fresh sweet water was waiting for him on a large dressing table in an elaborate silver gilt ewer with its attendant basin. Fair Holland towels were laid by its side, along with fine soap, a razor, and a comb. Desmond quickly made his toilet and dressed himself, not without remembering that Jeffrey would have dressed him only yesterday morning. It was not the service he missed but the contact with those gentle hands he so loved. Tears once again threatened, but he stopped them with a dash of cold water and surveyed himself in the large looking glass over the dressing table. His dark, curly hair was pulled back into a tight queue once again, his face pale and drawn. In the black suit and white linen he nearly didn't recognize the laughing youth of the previous day. This man looked older, sadder, his eyes slightly red and ringed with shadows.

He retraced his steps back through the hall to the little passage that led to the Baron's study. He found the room exactly as it had been the night before, only now softly glowing in the morning sun. A white porcelain stove he had not noticed before sat in one corner.

There were perhaps a thousand volumes on the shelves of this comfortable private room—not a large library for a nobleman's house. But what books, as Desmond soon discovered in scanning the simple wooden shelves. Many of the volumes were from the 16th century—classic works in Latin and various common languages: French, German, Italian, English. An entire set of the works of Shakespeare, all from the playwright's own lifetime! Some of these were little more than cheap popular editions, some more handsomely printed volumes, but all were bound in the same deep blue leather with a curious gold crest, which Desmond assumed was the Tsolnay arms. In it was an eagle, wings outspread, below a crescent half moon. In one claw the eagle held a branch; in the other a cross.

Beyond these early works were still more ancient manuscripts, including some medieval missals and books of hours with exquisite tempera and gold-leaf illustrations on their rippled vellum pages. In addition he found shelves full of modern works from all over Europe and Britain. This explained the Baron's facility with English and his rapid understanding of foreign fashion and thought. He selected a volume with a curious title from the shelves, a small book bearing the likeness of a young Frenchman with a large nose and the words VOYAGE TO THE MOON BY CYRANO DE BERGERAC. Desmond had heard in his youth of the heretical wit of this young libertine and freethinker, but he had never read the notorious works. He delved with great interest into these pages, enjoying the old-fashioned language and the elegance of the French construction. For a few hours he forgot his troubles as he read of Bergerac's adventures, his scandalous proof of the nonexistence of God, and his mad inventions.

Desmond was thus absorbed when a tap at his elbow made him jump. It was the housekeeper, who spoke to him apologetically.

"Herr Beckwith, my master has gone ahead to the church to give instructions to the priest. He said you might follow in a quarter of an hour if you wish, sir."

She disappeared as quietly as she had come, leaving Desmond feeling abashed that the time had flown and his sorrow so easily forgotten. He replaced the book on its shelf and headed for the hall. A short flight of steps led through the massive thickness of the wall and out into the courtyard of the castle. The huge doors through which he and Jeffrey had made their last entrance together glided open with a gentle touch on well-oiled hinges. The August sun blazed full-force as he made his way down the steep stone approach to Castle Tsolnay and through the portico into the cobbled square. He was surprised to see such a bustling in the village and that all the people seemed to be headed in the same direction as he. One young woman saw him enter the square and pulled her husband back by the arm, nodding reverently as he passed. Likewise thereafter, as he walked slowly toward the beautiful little church, as people noticed his presence, they fell back and let him pass, nodding in sympathy. Some even bowed for him, as if he were some exalted nobleman.

So a stranger has died in their midst, and they have come to see him laid to rest, Desmond wondered. *They treat me like a personage. Perhaps I am, if their Baron has taken me as a friend.*

As he approached the porch of the church, Desmond saw the figure of the Baron emerge from a small house down a side street and signal to him. He changed course, heading for the doorway into which the Baron had retreated.

Once inside, he found himself in a small, low room, rather like a wareroom of a shop. There, on a pair of trestles, lay a plain black-painted coffin with gleaming silver handles and a small shield-shaped plate on its lid. On this plate was engraved simply JEFFREY CHAPMAN, A.D. 1745. The Baron greeted him with a shallow bow.

"Mr. Beckwith, I thought it would be less painful for you if we proceeded from here rather than the entire distance from the castle. Accordingly, I had the undertaker bring the coffin to the castle chapel, then back here.

"Thank you, Herr Baron, that is fine." The thought of having to make that walk behind Jeffrey's coffin made him shudder. Once again the Baron's sensitive instincts had second-guessed Desmond's own feelings.

"We can begin now, if you like." Desmond nodded, and the Baron turned to the small, black-clad undertaker and said something in a low voice in his native tongue. The little man disappeared and reappeared shortly with three strong-looking young men, also dressed in funeral clothes. At the Baron's signal, they lifted the coffin by its four handles and led the way out the low door into the village street. Desmond and the Baron, side by side, followed the pallbearers.

The somber little group entered the church, and Desmond was aware that nearby every place was filled. Many people stood without assistance. Some leaned on small chairs, while a few more prosperous citizens had more substantial chairs before which they stood with bowed head as the funeral procession passed. Desmond and the Baron took their places in the empty choir, in a pair of large carved armchairs. The coffin was laid on a low, black-draped bier before the altar. The priest who had shown Desmond and Jeffrey through the church, after giving Desmond a glance of consolation and sympathy, faced the congregation and began the prayers.

The service was mercifully short and entirely in Latin. Desmond paid little attention to the words, keeping his eyes on the black silhouette of the wooden box, in which lay Jeffrey's remains. No more would the supple arms entwine his own. Never again would he run his fingers through the soft golden down that covered those sinewy legs. Never again would those bright blue eyes taunt him, the short nose wrinkle up at something unpleasant, those white teeth flash in laughter. It was no comfort to Desmond to think of Jeffrey's soul in a better place, as the Baron had said. All Desmond could feel, even as he felt shame at his selfishness, was a wrenching aloneness that all the gentle words in the world couldn't have eased. As this sense of desolation swept through him, he bowed his head into his hands and wept silently.

The black coffin was buried in the grassy yard behind the church. Few of the villagers stayed for the interment, for this was a private matter. Only the Baron and Desmond, accompanied by the pall-bearers, remained at the graveside while the final prayer was intoned. This done, the Baron placed his arm around Desmond's shoulder, and they began their return to the castle.

"I will have a stone erected in your friend's memory..." began the Baron.

"No—I thank you, Herr Baron. I know where he lies. I would prefer no marker placed on his grave. When I return here, I will know where he is." Desmond knew that he would never come back and wanted the memory to remain only in his heart, something he and Jeffrey would share for the rest of his days.

"As you wish, Mr. Beckwith. I understand. I have sent the coachman who drove you yesterday back to Spalato to get your luggage from the inn there and bring it back here. Perhaps I am mistaken, but I thought a few days of rest here might be good for you before you resume your journey."

Desmond looked gratefully at the old man. "I have not the heart to even think of travel now, Herr Baron. If you will have me, I would appreciate resting here for a while, at least until I can bear the thought of leaving Jeffrey behind forever."

The Baron nodded, and they climbed the rest of the way to the castle without words. Desmond ascended the stairs to his room, more shadowy now that the sun had shifted to the other side of the building. Suddenly he was exhausted, and in the coolness of the tall room, he lay down on the bed and slept.

In his dreams he saw Jeffrey again, as he had first seen him 11 years earlier, a towheaded boy of ten. He was laughing and running in a green field—not the rolling acres of Beckwith House, it seemed, but a flat, featureless expanse, lushly green, having no trees or other taller flora. Desmond ran after him, joining in his laughter, reaching out to catch him and hold him. Then Jeffrey turned toward him, and the laughter in his eyes turned to fear, making Desmond look back. A great pack of hulking black wolves raced silently across the green emptiness toward them. Desmond froze in his tracks and turned to warn Jeffrey to run and leave him behind. But Jeffrey had disappeared, and the ravening wolves moved ever closer, quiet as the wind, their narrow green eyes and dripping maws growing more distinct with each advancing stride.

Then a sound: the clash of armor and the galloping of a horse. Desmond turned again and saw a richly caparisoned white horse, a crest of red feathers at its brow, galloping toward him. Its harness jangled as it came, and steam poured from its nostrils. Astride its high back was a knight, his armor glittering like silver in the sunlight, his broad sword poised to strike. The visor on the pointed helmet was down, and the polished armor hid all of the warrior's features. He lowered the sword, and Desmond could see that it was stained red, as if with blood. But the redness shimmered and moved as the charger advanced, and Desmond realized it was fire that stained the blade. He remembered the wolves and looked once more, to find nothing before him but the endless expanse of grass. A hand was placed on his shoulder, making him jump and wheel sharply, and he found himself looking up into the large sorrowful eyes of the Baron, who now stood before him in his brocaded robe. He did not speak but stood unmoving, his hand gently grasping the boy's shoulder as he stared down at him. Desmond looked deeply into the luminous brown eyes, feeling a sense of safety and calm flow through him. Then he noticed the Baron's thin, wide mouth, suddenly very red. The narrow lips were glistening in the immobile face, and a single drop of blood trickled down from one corner of his mouth, leaving a scarlet trail against the pale skin.

Desmond cried and pulled away, falling to the grass, where he buried his head for a moment to avoid the image of the Baron's bloody lips. Then he looked up and found himself entirely alone, on his stomach in the fragrant grass. He sat up, scanning the horizon, but could see nothing in any direction. He rose from the ground and started to walk, faster and faster, until he was running through the grass. A sense of urgency overwhelmed him, and he could feel a breeze pick up, coming from behind him, urging him onward. He had to find him; he must find him. But whom? He didn't know; but Desmond kept running, faster at each step. And still the wind blew at his back, pushing him forward. Then he stumbled.

With a jerk Desmond started awake to find that he was sitting bolt upright in the bed as the hangings flapped about him. The windows were open, as they had been all day, but now the weather had turned stormy. Such squalls were not uncommon in the summer in these mountains. The sky had grown black, and branches of lightning crackled their way through the heavens. Wind whipped around the walls of the castle and into his room, rattling the tapestries on their frames and giving life to the light muslin draperies on the bed. Desmond leaped from the bed and crossed to the open windows, which he closed and latched. The room was suddenly quiet.

Desmond's heart pounded madly in his chest. He returned to the bed and lay down but not to sleep. His mind reeled with the image of the dream, and it was some time before he could collect himself. Whom had he been seeking so desperately? Why had he run so? Gradually his heart slowed to its normal pace and his breathing returned to its regular rhythm. The vision of the endless grassy field danced before him. He lay in the storm-dark chamber as the thunder rumbled through the mountains and the rain drummed against the window glass.

All at once a soft knocking caught his attention. He realized that it was at his door and called out an entry. The Baron's housekeeper, holding a candlestick in one hand, came in. She lit the candles around his room—only two or three, in antique bronze holders—then told him that the Baron had ordered dinner for him and would await him in the dining room. Without asking for a reply, she left as silently as she had come.

Desmond rose again, dashed a bit of water from the gilt ewer on his face, and straightened his linens as best he could. He put on the black jacket and refastened the black silk band that held his queue. He regarded himself for a long moment in the dimly lit looking glass; then, with a deep breath, he left the room and descended the winding stairs to dinner.

The table and two chairs were as before, only now the shadowy, echoing room was dressed as if for a tiny state banquet. A row of candelabra lined the center of the polished table, and bowls of seasonal flowers were set about on the serving tables. Though only two places were set at the table, these were fitted out with splendor. A white damask cloth, crisp lines showing it to have been recently removed from its press, lay folded carefully over the end of the table where they sat. Massive silver plates stood at each place, and upon them covered *écuelles* ornately chased, bearing the same strange arms Desmond had seen in the Baron's study. The heavy forks, knives, and spoons were of the same design. An octagonal silver salt stood by Desmond's place, and next to it an octagonal caster for pepper. At each setting were two fine goblets of a pale gray-tinted crystal, each with a fluted bowl and a tapered stem as fragile as a bubble.

The Baron was at his seat when Desmond entered and rose to greet him as he crossed the shining surface of the tiled floor.

"You have rested, I hope," said the host, resuming his chair as Desmond sat down.

"Yes, thank you, Herr Baron." He motioned to the plate before him and added, "You need not have gone to such trouble over me."

"You are my guest, Mr. Beckwith, and it gives me pleasure to put on this little show for you. It has been a long time since I really en-

249

tertained in this room as I once did. Having you here provided me with an opportunity to relive some of my dinners."

"The plate is magnificent."

"Thank you. It is French, made in Paris for this room." And so saying, he removed the lid from Desmond's *écuelle* to reveal a deliciously steaming soup.

"I will be an observer only, alas, Mr. Beckwith. Please begin."

And Desmond did, enjoying every mouthful. The housekeeper appeared, bringing a bottle of chilled white wine and taking away the *écuelle* cover.

"Mr. Beckwith approves of your potage. You see, you have not lost your skill!" The old woman beamed silently before withdrawing.

"It is probably 20 years since I gave a large dinner here, and she appreciates any chance to show off her culinary expertise." The Baron poured some of the wine into each of their glasses.

"Tell me, Herr Baron, is she the only servant you keep here?"

"No, but the only one you will likely see. There are those who maintain the house and grounds, such as there are on this rock, and the groomsmen and stablekeepers. Natalya, however, is the only one allowed into my private rooms. Fortunately, I am a tidy master, and there is little enough for her to do."

Desmond took a swallow of the excellent wine and asked pointedly, "How much does she know of you, Baron Tsolnay?"

"How much? Perhaps everything, perhaps rather less. I have never told her anything in particular and can only guess as to what she may have surmised over the years."

"It does not worry you that the village people may know your secret?"

"I do not think about it. I have been here as long as any of the living villagers remember. Natalya's mother, and grandmother before that, fulfilled the position here that she now holds. It has become a tradition in her family. Her daughter now works with her, in preparation for her mother's retirement. However old I appear to be, everyone knows I should have been dead decades ago. But they have never asked me the reason. Maybe it is that they do not want to know what they suspect might be my answer; or perhaps they are happy with me and fear to upset things if they question too narrowly. I have never, to my knowledge, given them reason to fear or dislike me."

"And how many more decades do you think this can continue?"

"I cannot say. My methods would not have worked in a cosmopolitan society, Mr. Beckwith. Here we are bound as much by tradition and superstition as by religion and law. Perhaps, had I been English or French or German, I would have invented a more creative way of passing from one generation to the next. I have never found a need to do so here."

"I wonder what Jeffrey would have done had your experiment succeeded, Baron." Desmond had finished his soup and leaned back against the tall chair, his eyes on his host. They sat for a moment in silence as the housekeeper returned and took away the soup dishes. As her receding steps faded away, the Baron spoke.

"There would have been one major difference, which would have made your Jeffrey's life more complex and perhaps richer than mine, Mr. Beckwith."

"What is that?"

"I, as you can see, am an old man. I was this age at the time of my transformation. Because of it I am doomed to remain an old man through all eternity. Mr. Chapman, had he survived and become as I am, would have continued to age, although without ever losing his strength or vigor. At a certain age—I am told it is the 65th year—he would have been transformed again and returned to the age at which he was originally transformed."

"He would have regenerated to 21 years old?" Desmond's hazel eyes grew wide with amazement.

"So I was told. I have never seen it for myself."

"Who told you this, Baron Tsolnay?"

"The Turk, the man who made me a vampire. You want to know more, Mr. Beckwith." This was not worded as a question.

"Yes, Baron, indeed I would. That is, if you will tell me."

The old man hesitated, his eyes thoughtful, his brow furrowed. "I have never told anyone my tale, Mr. Beckwith. But then, I have never tried to do what I attempted with your friend. If you were to wish me harm, there is nothing I could do to make matters worse by telling you more."

"I have no wish to harm you, Baron. You can believe that I am your friend."

"All right, then. It is in fact quite simple. I was fighting against the Turks nearly three centuries ago. As I told you before, I was known—usually to my detriment—for my soft heart. Two other barons, a lone servant, and I were isolated from the rest of the troops, each of us from fairly distant provinces and principalities. The three of us were not friends, but we were all old men, though vigorous and known to be powerful commanders. Our age made us highly unusual in a time when few of our peers lived to see the passage of 50 years. Ironically—from my present perspective—our reputations as soldiers and our venerable ages made us the object of fear and superstition, even among the other noble warriors. Some felt we must have made a pact with the devil to survive so long. Between battles we were often shunned or at least left to our own devices, and thus we fell in together by default.

"After one grim day of especially appalling battle, during which our army suffered terrible losses but from which the three of us emerged unscathed, we were abandoned. Our soldiers and even our servants went with the rest of the army, leaving us alone in a foreign land. Only one servant—not my own, alas—remained faithful. Seeking some kind of safe shelter for the night, we happened upon a small band of Turkish soldiers. These we slew without hesitation but for one, who claimed to be a great wizard. He claimed to be able to give us eternal life. Notwithstanding the blasphemy of such a claim from an infidel, we spared his life, and we took him captive.

"However hostile we were to our enemy's religion, the idea of everlasting life was as tantalizing to us as Ali Baba's treasure. We set up camp and interrogated him at length. He told us of the undead, of the thirst for human blood, of the healing capacity of his flesh. At this point the more hotheaded of the three of us slashed him with his sword to see if he bled. Of course, he did, but he curiously licked the wound, which was on his forearm, as does a dog. Then we bound it for him and quizzed him further. After another hour of examination, we unbound the wounded arm, and to our amazement it was entirely healed. Such an injury, although minor in terms of battle, would have taken weeks to heal under normal conditions. We were convinced and terrified of what we had discovered. I think I was more fascinated than my peers, and as a result I was forced to be the one to experiment first. The process seemed terrifying and dangerous, as it indeed was. To begin, the Turkish vampire had to drink some of my blood to make way for his own, which I would then have to ingest. I remember the fear that shot through me when he bared his yellow fangs in the flickering firelight of the encampment."

"Fangs?" Desmond nearly gasped the word.

"Yes. At first I thought of a venomous serpent, but that is not quite the same." They were interrupted by the housekeeper's return, this time bearing another bottle of wine, red, and a platter of roast venison with vegetables, to which Desmond helped himself. When she had gone, the Baron resumed.

"So, pressed on by my compatriots, who I am sure were perfectly willing to sacrifice me should the need arise, I allowed the Turk to sink his teeth into my neck and to suck from me some of my blood. At this point I remembered little, as I swooned somewhat. I apparently went into a trance or coma, from which I awoke some time later. They had made me drink some of the Turk's blood to replace what I had lost. I had fallen into a deathlike sleep, and they had nearly killed the Turk because of it. Now I found myself wide awake and full of strength, but I thirsted. To my horror I thirsted not for water or for wine but for blood! The Turk then smiled in triumph. He then explained to my fellows that I could satisfy this thirst by taking some of their blood and giving some of my own to bring about the second transformation. After much discussion we did just that, and I recall vividly the bizarre sensation as I felt my own teeth grow before the wide eyes of the other two. One of my colleagues offered himself as the next recipient, and I first experienced the ecstasy of drinking mortal life. Then I cut my own wrist and forced it to his mouth, even as he lay in a stupor. Once he too had fallen into the death trance, which seemed less fearful now that we understood its cause, we turned to the Turk, who instructed us in the mysteries of this arcane race.

"It was he who explained the regeneration cycle and that we, as old men, would be trapped at our present ages forever. This fact, which we had not known before and that now took us by surprise, enraged the third of our party. He leaped up from his seat by the fire and, drawing his sword again, severed the Turk's head from his body before the look of surprise was off his face. Then this man, who had goaded us into capturing the Turk and who had forced me to sacrifice myself first, turned on me, snarling oaths about the devil and his followers as he brandished the bloody sword. He attacked, but I managed to kick the sword from his hand. I was startled to find that my strength was far greater than one would expect in a man of nearly 70 years, and I easily avoided him for a short while. There we were, in that smoke-filled tent, leaping at each other like caged beasts. The servant cringing in terror, the headless body of the Turk and the undead corpse of our fellow warrior lay on the ground.

"Finally, forgetting my newfound strength, he leaped upon me and tried to choke the life from me. Having no choice at last, I pushed him aside as easily as I might have a child and strangled him in a moment. It was then that I realized the extent of my power as well as its limits. Never would I die from mere injury or disease, yet always would I risk my immortality from decapitation or consumption in a fire. Although glad I had learned what the Turk had had time to tell us—fortunately, he saved his fatal information for late in his recital—my heart was heavy as I buried the two truly dead bodies and waited for the third to return to life.

"My partner awoke some hours later to learn of the hellish news I related to him. Together we traveled for many days, returning westward toward our respective homelands. The war against the Turks seemed meaningless to us now, although my comrade seemed more darkly affected than I by our new state. Where I saw it as eternal life, he saw it as living damnation. Certainly I feared for my soul, but he saw himself as already dead. Except for his servant, each of us was the other's sole companion, and together we learned the way of life we had taken upon us. We learned to hunt to satisfy our thirst, how to charm and cajole, and how to drink without killing and leave no mark, thus avoiding becoming ourselves the prey of some angry rural mob. Eventually we parted, each fearful of our lives ahead—now that these lives stretched endlessly into a future we couldn't foretell. The certainties of our mortal lives had vanished like smoke, and we were faced with an eternity as opaque as a cloudy night." The Baron stopped his narration and bowed his head.

"Does your companion survive?" Desmond was enthralled.

"Yes, at least I believe so. We have met only once since that time. It was not the happiest of reunions." He gave Desmond a wry little smile and pushed back his chair. He picked up the bottle of red wine and his glass as he stood.

"Let us go to my study, Mr. Beckwith. Bring your glass, and we can finish this bottle. Although I no longer need wine for physical purposes, it does, I find, soothe my spirit." And with that he turned and headed for the stairs, with Desmond in his wake.

Even in summer, the nights on the mountain were cool, and the porcelain stove in the Baron's study was fired up. They settled themselves comfortably, and Desmond spoke first.

"Your library is wonderful, Baron. You have treasures here."

"They are my friends, Mr. Beckwith, my only real friends. They are the only immortal remnants of human thought, and they have, some of them, lived several lifetimes in my company."

"And yet you have modern books."

"I try to stay current and truly enjoy new writers. But they too, Mr. Beckwith, will grow old even as I remain as I am."

They fell silent, and the Baron rose, going to the casement to look out over the valley. The earlier storm had blown away, and a gentle breeze hissed through the trees far below. A crescent moon gave a faint blue glow to the evening sky.

Breaking the silence, Desmond spoke, softly but distinctly.

"I want you to transform me, Baron Tsolnay."

The old man spun around, his mouth agape, his eyes wide.

"Transform you? But why, in God's name? Have you not just heard me speak?"

"Indeed I have, and it sounds to me not half as dreadful as you try to make out. I look at this room—this entire castle—I listen to your stories, see your life here, read your heart. I see nothing of which I should be afraid. The uncertainty about God and heaven and hell are not so different from the same questions I ask every day. If your immortality has not brought you any closer to understanding the secrets of the universe, neither has it taken you any further away."

"I'm sorry, Mr. Beckwith. It is out of the question." The old man turned back to the window, his back straight, hands clasped behind him.

"Yes, you can, and I beg you to do as I ask. Consider what my mortal life will be now, now that I have lost Jeffrey. What have I to look forward to in this lifetime? I will return to England, loveless and alone. My father, whom I love but who nonetheless has expectations of his own, will eventually force me into a marriage that, as you understand, will be a sham. Perhaps we will have some modicum of happiness as husband and wife—perhaps even produce children to inherit the estate and the bank. But I fear I will grow old without ever having the chance of knowing true love again. Moreover, I will needlessly make some young woman unhappy by denying her the barest conjugal affection, trapping her for her lifetime in a match of convenience."

"And how will transforming you change this?" The Baron looked down at Desmond with a slightly glazed expression, as if his mind was already hard at work to answer his own question.

"It will give me a chance to find real happiness, if not in this lifetime then in the next or the one after that. I will not have to marry—since I will be my own heir generation after generation. Thus I will be able to continue my search for someone with whom I can truly share my life, someone I can give the happiness that Jeffrey and I had."

"And you do not fear damnation, even as I do?"

"I don't believe you really do fear damnation for what you are. How could you possibly believe yourself to be evil, if what you said to me this morning was not your own feeling? Besides, I would simply be trading a soul for a soul. God has seen fit to take Jeffrey's soul long before it deserved to be taken. Why shall I not balance the account by taking control of my own soul, by becoming the master of my own destiny?"

The Baron, despite himself, smiled at this arrogance. "Ah, my young man. It is not wise to try to call God to account. Do you know what you say?"

"I do, Baron, I do. I had a strange dream this afternoon, and I am sure it was a sign. You were in it. I do not think I am here by accident." He dropped his eyes to his hands for a moment. "I do not even think, perhaps, that Jeffrey's death was without purpose, if by it I came here and met you."

Desmond raised his face again and looked intently at the Baron. They remained like this for some time: the handsome young Englishman, his cheeks flushed, his hands gripping his knees as he sat and the tall, elderly aristocrat, his white hair and pale features immobile, hands behind his back, staring down into the hazel eyes. Finally the Baron spoke.

"Another gift those of our race receive is the ability to perceive falseness in words or actions of mortals. I confess, Mr. Beckwith, I can find no flaws in your certainty."

"Will you do it, Baron Tsolnay?"

"If you truly desire it, Mr. Beckwith. I failed your Jeffrey. Perhaps I can make a difference in your life that I will not regret."

"Now?"

"Yes, if you are in such a hurry and feel yourself prepared."

"I am. I shall not look back."

Desmond picked up his glass from the writing table and held it up to his host. "To the future, Herr Baron."

The old man hesitated, then lifted his own glass and repeated faintly, "To the future."

They drained the last of their wine and went from the study down the stairs to the laboratory.

"Why here and not in my chamber?" Desmond's voice showed only curiosity, tinged with excitement.

"A precaution. I might, you see, spill."

"Ah, yes, I see." The image made Desmond's heart leap with sudden fear.

"Remove your coat, Mr. Beckwith, and lie down on the table."

Desmond hesitated before the wooden slab on which his beloved had lain just a day earlier, then quickly removed his coat and climbed up onto the table. The wine had made him slightly giddy, for which he was thankful. He lay back, staring up at the white vaulted ceiling and the unlit iron chandelier. Only a single taper, brought from the Baron's study, burned in the room. The clock ticked softly in its shadowy corner. Desmond loosened and removed his neckcloth, baring his throat.

The candle stood on the table at his side, and it dimly illuminated the entire room, surprising in its brightness. Desmond looked up as he felt the Baron approach. The old man had also removed his coat and once again had rolled up one of his sleeves. He leaned on the table and bent over Desmond.

"Are you ready, Mr. Beckwith?"

"Yes."

"Then shut your eyes and turn your head to the side."

"No. I want to see." Desmond's eyes were wide with fright, yet his face was set with a look of determination.

"See?"

"Your—your fangs. I want to see them." As he lay on the un-yielding slab, Desmond began to tremble violently. The Baron clasped each of his hands in his own, which were cool and dry. As if some force emanated from his firm grip, Desmond found himself becoming calm, his fear receding.

"So you face your first fear bravely, Mr. Beckwith. You may look if you wish. But you must then turn your head, for *my* needs."

Then, as Desmond stared up at him, the Baron's lower jaw dropped slightly, and his canine teeth began to grow and extend until they shone like two tiny knives in the candlelight. Above them the deep dark eyes of the ancient warrior looked with infinite gentleness into his own. Desmond took a deep breath, swallowing his fear, and turned his head away. He clamped his eyes shut and uttered a silent prayer as the trembling seized him again. Then he felt the warm breath of the Baron on his neck and the double pinprick of those two sharp teeth. There was a brief moment of pain, then a great pounding in his temples. Desmond's heart beat so loudly, it seemed he could hear it. Then blackness swirled around him, bringing with it warmth, calm, and oblivion.

CHAPTER 14

He later recalled that, subsequently, into this oblivion, came fire, which poured over him like liquid. It burned him to his very bones yet caused no pain. It enveloped him and rocked him in its flickering red and then gently let him slip back into the blackness of sleep. He did not dream.

He awoke gradually, as if swimming up from the bottom of a deep lake whose cool water made him tingle all over. As his senses cleared, the tingling remained; every part of his being whirred with life. Desmond sat up and surveyed the chamber. But it was unchanged. He was again in the fine nightshirt beneath the embroidered coverlet. He looked at his arm and saw there the careful bandage. This, after a moment, he unfastened and removed. Beneath it lay unblemished skin. The mark of the wolf was gone. He felt his neck. So was the mark of the vampire.

Jumping out of bed and running to the window, Desmond leaned out to look at the valley spread below him. Small white clouds sailed across the blue sky like newborn lambs. The air had not taken on the sultry warmth of midday, and he guessed that it must still be fairly early. He wondered how long he had slept and whether the transformation was complete. Dressing and shaving with haste, he hurried down the stairs to find the Baron. The drawing room and dining room were both unoccupied. No breakfast this morning—or any other morning, Desmond suddenly realized. Panic gripped him. He was now a monster, a creature more fantastical than any he had ever read of. He retraced his steps up to the great hall, thence to the Baron's study. He still found no one. His strange terror continued to grow. Everything seemed abandoned. He darted out into the castle's courtyard, where he startled a young groundskeeper raking the gravel.

The boy, perhaps 17, was so blond, and his frightened blue eyes so bright, that Desmond instantly thought of Jeffrey. The stab of pain this caused was just as quickly swept away by another, entirely unfamiliar, sensation. The summer air carried to him the scent of the boy, the scent of his blood warmed by labor. Its richness had the effect that the last evening's steaming soup had given—it made him ravenous. He was at first appalled at this new lust, so unlike anything he had experienced before. From this point forth, his fellow human creatures would also be his fount of life. Their blood would call him inexorably, and he would forever drink to the beating of their hearts. He remembered the fiery sensation of his transformation and understood what it meant.

Then he noticed that the boy was not reacting as if he had seen a fearsome predatory beast but had simply been taken by surprise by his master's houseguest at an unexpectedly early hour. He smiled tentatively at the young man and received a deferential bow in return. He calmed the groundskeeper with some pointless questions about the weather, was given a relieved smile, and turned back to the house.

Walking slowly up the entrance steps into the hall, he looked up and marveled once again at the lavish colors and flamboyant drawings that covered the walls and ceiling. Scenes of epic battle swirled across the expanses. Trumpeting angels and rearing steeds combined with valiant chevaliers, flying drapery, and tumbling clouds to create images so vivid that Desmond could almost hear them. Had these frescoes looked so remarkable yesterday? His musings were interrupted by a soft step on the polished floor, and he dropped his eyes to see the housekeeper crossing the room.

"Good morning, Herr Beckwith," she said in her accented German. "Would you wish something to eat?"

"Uh…no, thank you, not right now. Is the Baron out?"

"Why, no, sir. He is not yet up. He was very late last night, or so said the note he left me in the kitchen. He was thinking, he said. When he leaves me notes, I know not to disturb him until I see him about."

"Can you tell me where his chamber is?" Desmond felt the impertinence of the request but could not resist.

"In the tower opposite your chamber, sir. Up that staircase," she added, pointing to the one that led to the study and the laboratory. "I'm not sure I'd want to awaken him before his time, Herr Beckwith."

"If it will not get you into trouble, I'd like to see him right away." Perhaps the Baron would blame her, Desmond reasoned, if another disobeyed the orders she had been given. But this did not seem to be the case.

She answered with a tolerant smile, the sort women of her age reserved for the impulsive young. "It will be on your shoulders, milord, if the Baron is angered." This said, she continued on her way.

Once she was out of sight, Desmond walked quickly across the great room and went now up the winding stairs he had previously descended in such different moods. This staircase ended in a small landing, as did the one onto which his chamber opened. A large carved door stood at its head, emblazoned with the eagle and half-moon crest he had seen earlier. The door was shut but not locked, somewhat to his surprise. Such was the Baron's sense of security and trust in his people. Desmond slowly pushed it open, so as not to startle or awaken his host, knocking softly.

There was nothing but silence in the room, which was darkened by heavy velvet curtains at the windows. In the little light that made its way in through the drapery, Desmond could see that this room had never been updated as his own had been in the 16th century. Here the walls were entirely covered in tapestries, those of a medieval character far different from the ones in Desmond's room. There was very little furniture. A high cupboard, carved like the choir stall of some Gothic church, stood in the far corner of the room. A brass basin and ewer of simple form stood on a plain low table by the window. The only chair in the room was a high-backed rectilinear throne with a single cushion on its boxlike base. This was placed near the hooded fireplace. In the corner farthest from the windows and nearest the fireplace was a bed. There were no visible posts or woodwork, only heavy draperies, seemingly of the same embroidered stuff as the curtains. Of these only the back panels hung down, the front ones being raised up by some unseen means from the ceiling. There, lying as in state on this strange antique bed, was the Baron.

Desmond moved softly over to him. He could hear no sound of sleep—no gentle breathing or dreamy mumbling. As he approached he noted how still the Baron lay, hands at his sides, legs straight, head carefully composed on the pillow—like a medieval tomb figure. Desmond bent over him and found no whisper of air coming from his mouth. No tiny twitch or movement of the extremities gave indication of life. He was dead! Then Desmond understood at last the true meaning of the word *undead*. He must have himself slept like this last night. The sleep of the vampire.

Not knowing what to do and not wishing to leave, Desmond sat down in the uncomfortable thronelike chair and waited in silence, staring into the cold fireplace. His mind was filled with anxious questions about his new being and about the life he was beginning this morning. He recalled the sensation of the groundskeeper's scent and the miraculous healing of his arm. Images of Jeffrey came again to his mind, but the sadness that still dwelled within him did not overwhelm him. The life he had entered occupied his soul, and he found he could not look back. Jeffrey was beyond his reach now. And he himself was beyond the reach of—what? What, he wondered, would he do now? Beckwith House and his father—even England itself—seemed impossibly remote and unreal. He stood on the edge of a great precipice, the bottomless reaches of which were invisible to him. Was this a God-given opportunity he had chosen, or was it the start of a living damnation?

"I am sorry to have kept you waiting, Desmond."

At his name, Desmond jumped up from the chair, shaken. Then he relaxed as the Baron sat up on the bed and stretched in a very mortal manner.

"So you came to see me sleep?" In the dimness Desmond could make out a smile on the old man's face.

"I only wanted to talk to you—to ask questions. I didn't expect to find you so…"

"So deathlike? That is how we sleep, Desmond, how you will sleep from now on, as I have done for three centuries."

"Is it completed, then, Baron? Am I transformed?"

"For the most part. You will have things to learn, but you have changed."

"Natalya told me that you were up late. She knows nothing of this?"

"Nothing, which is as it should be, you understand. I carried you to your room and put you to bed. My mind was too full to sleep right away. I paced the castle halls and read some of my old journals until I was exhausted. You have caught me asleep because once we call up the sleep of the undead, we cannot awaken for six hours. During that time we are completely helpless, just as if we were corpses. It is our Achilles' heel." The Baron moved over to the windows and pulled aside the draperies. Morning sunshine flowed into the room. The dark tapestries revealed their muted colors to the daylight, and the window hangings glowed a deep crimson, their decoration in gold metallic thread glinting dully.

"And yet you leave your door unlocked?"

"I confess, that is not always so. But last night I felt you might seek me out this way. Perhaps I wanted you to see me, to see yourself, as we are."

"What do I do now, Baron?"

"Now you will leave me alone for a while so I can prepare myself for the day." The Baron laughed softly as he placed his hands on Desmond's shoulders, turning him around and pushing him gently toward the door. "Even the undead need to shave and wash. I will meet you in the study shortly."

Like an obedient child Desmond left and descended to the study. There he threw open the windows and stood looking out until the Baron entered, dressed in a gray velvet suit with fresh white linens.

"So," he began, "now the lessons begin. There is much to tell you, and I have never before had a pupil."

"How long will it take?" Desmond was eager but apprehensive.

"I have no idea. It has taken me many lifetimes to learn what I know, but I need not teach you all of that! My own lessons were cut short by the untimely death of my tutor, as you recall. But fortunately, I think much of what you must know is innate, in the blood. There is, however, one trial we have yet to pass before I will be at ease."

"What is that?"

"You must drink, Desmond. Last night you drank some of my blood, but you were unconscious for all practical purposes. You will have to use your own faculties to drink before I will feel secure."

"And how can I do that here?" Desmond recalled again the vivid aroma of the blond boy in the courtyard.

"The way I do and have done for centuries. With great diplomacy." The Baron paced briefly up and down the small room, his hand on his chin. Then he stopped and looked sharply at Desmond.

"I have, over the years, built on a method that arouses no fear in my people. Since I am old, my needs are less than those of a young man like you. I can withhold drink for as long as a month and not suffer. According to the Turk's brief training, you will need to drink every few days or at least once every week. This will lessen with age and then begin again when you regenerate. I have traditionally invited individual members of the village up here to dine with me, as I have dined with you, in the saloon. My ostensible reason, and this is in large part valid, is to learn from them and to talk to them. They are flattered by the attention and impressed with the setting—not to mention Natalya's food. Thus, the other evening was not so out of the ordinary for her, although she still complains that I give no grand banquets." The Baron paused here and went to the near bookshelf, from which he pulled a slim volume bound in vellum.

"I have in this book a wide array of formulas, among which are a number of quite effective short-term sleeping draughts. One of these, placed into wine or soup, will put someone in a deep sleep. I can quickly drink my fill and be resting in my chair before they awake."

"It seems rather complex. The blood loss does not harm them?"

"Not in the least, other than a residual fatigue. It would hardly be in my best survival interests to decimate my own people by feeding on them, would it, Mr. Beckwith? As for the opportunity, it is indeed there; but, as I said, life here is not as varied as that in a city. I have had to be creative. My victims, if you would call them that, think only that they have had a brief dizzy spell or a lapse of memory. If they notice the bruise on their necks the next day, I have never heard of it."

"And do you propose to do this for me?" Desmond was intrigued and amused by the old man's enthusiasm.

"Yes, but with a variation, I think. Our guest will have to remain somewhat longer in a trance, for you are not yet practiced."

"What of your housekeeper?"

"As always, she will leave the food on the serving tables and remain in the kitchen until signaled so as not to disturb our conversation." This last was spoken with a twinkle in his eye and the play of a smile across his lips.

"There is another aspect that I have to consider."

"What is that, Baron?"

"I do not take into account any needs other than the blood itself. Lust is not within the realm of my feelings, for good or ill. However, in your instance, it might perhaps be of assistance to us."

"In what way?" Desmond's eyes showed concern. Thoughts of Jeffrey swirled in his mind, and he felt his eyes well up at the idea of betraying their love so soon.

"Do not worry! I think not of any sexual union, Desmond. I merely suggest that if the source of your sustenance is also appealing to you physically, then it will help you overcome your fear. It is a terrifying thing to have to plunge your teeth into the neck of a helpless mortal for the first time. Even though your thirst may drive you forward, you were a mortal but a short time ago. Scruples do not wither quickly."

"I see, Baron. You are right, of course, although I am ashamed to admit such baseness of emotion."

"Feel no shame, Desmond. Lust may be base, but it is perfectly natural. Only when used with cruelty is it evil. In this case we will use it for your survival."

"Who shall our—our guest—be?"

"I hadn't given that any thought. Does anyone come to your mind? You've hardly met anyone in town at all, other than the innkeeper and the priest."

"Neither of them likely candidates, I should think."

"No, although the priest *has* been here for dinner."

Desmond merely widened his eyes in response, and the Baron waved him away. "Remember, priests are human beings, regardless of the impression they might try to give."

Desmond pushed this thought aside, then, hesitating slightly, said, "There was one person...this morning, in fact. I don't know if he would be appropriate..."

"Here, at the castle?" The Baron looked puzzled.

"Yes, this morning after I came down. I went out into the courtyard to look for you, and found a groundskeeper raking…"

"Jelko? A youth, very fair, rather skittish?"

"Yes, I think that was he, Baron." Desmond felt himself blushing. So vampires blushed just as mortals did!

"He reminds you of Jeffrey, doesn't he, Desmond?" A gentleness replaced the calculation in the Baron's voice, and his smile was now one of sympathy rather than conspiracy.

"Yes, or at least he did the instant I saw him. Then I was quickly taken with an extraordinary sensation…"

"You smelled him, that's all, Desmond. You caught the fragrance of his blood. That is simply your nature. Was it unpleasant for you?"

"No…well, it was strange, unfamiliar. But it was exciting and a little frightening."

"Very well, then, since that seems to be a good direction in which to start, I will have Jelko join us for dinner." The Baron made as if to leave the room, then stopped and turned to Desmond.

"I am not a snob with my people, Desmond. Jelko is not the first peasant to share my table. Remember, Mr. Beckwith, all human blood is red, even blue blood." And he left to make arrangements for Desmond's dinner guest.

The rest of the day was spent in intent conversation, as Desmond asked questions of the Baron and the older man did his best to answer them. In spite of his restricted life, the Baron had traveled frequently to Spalato and other nearby towns. He had also read a great deal and surprised Desmond with the range of his worldly knowledge. When practical considerations were set aside, their talk turned to philosophical issues, and here Desmond found the Baron thoughtful and remarkably well-informed.

"I am surprised, Baron, that you even worry about the issues of philosophy raised by mortals. Even the noblest among them could not have seen the world from your perspective!"

"You are correct, Desmond, but that assertion has never had much effect on my emotions. I have never been able to build the arrogance you might expect in someone in my position, with my background."

"But surely you feel pride, a superiority in your place?"

"Pride perhaps, and maybe even some superiority. Certainly I was not one of those debauched nobles who squandered his resources and left nothing for the next generation to build upon. After all, I am my own heir, and from this I shall never have respite. Staying here as I have, I have placed an extra burden on myself. This castle, this entire valley, has in some ways become my living tomb. I confess that in this I take a somewhat morbid pride."

"But you could leave, couldn't you?" Desmond looked with true affection upon the ancient white-haired man.

The Baron returned his look wistfully. "Yes, I could, I suppose. But what would they do without me?" He gestured in a way that took in the whole domain of which he was master. "Maybe this is my real arrogance—believing that Tsolnay could not survive were I not among them." He cocked his head to one side and stared at Desmond thoughtfully. "Who knows? One day I might leave. The world changes...I might be forced to."

"But until then you'll remain?"

"Yes, I think so. For all my doubts, I am happy here. It suits me."

They had walked through the staterooms of the castle and out into the courtyard. From there a narrow arched passage led to a small crenellated garden fixed to the side of the castle like a swift's nest. It was here they were standing, speaking in subdued tones and looking out over the valley, when the sound of a carriage's wheels grinding through the gravel reached them. Returning to the courtyard, they found the coach and driver that had brought Desmond and Jeffrey to Tsolnay two days earlier. It had been sent, at the Baron's order, to Spalato to bring Desmond's luggage as well as Jeffrey's.

"I did not know what to tell him to do with Mr. Chapman's things, Mr. Beckwith."

"Keep them here, Baron. If anyone in the village can use them, they shall be my gift." Desmond's face grew taut, and lines creased his forehead. The Baron placed a comforting arm about his shoulder and led him toward the entrance. "You have learned much today, Desmond. Rest awhile, and join me before dinner for a drink in my study. I will have your things sent up to your room."

"Rest? I cannot sleep now—there isn't time."

"Heavens no, do not call sleep now! I mean just rest; lie down, close your eyes, think about what you have learned. We sleep only when we wish to—you will learn to tell when sleep is needed." And so saying, he left Desmond in the hall and went to see about the luggage.

An hour had been set for dinner, and shortly before that time Desmond appeared in evening clothes in the Baron's study. Together they drank some fine old sherry, which Desmond had learned was admissible, as were all wines and distilled spirits. Promptly at the appointed moment, there was a knock at the door, and Natalya entered to inform them that Jelko had arrived.

"He is quite terrified, Herr Baron," she admonished with an attempt at severity, "so you and Herr Beckwith be kind to him! I don't know why you ever choose such youngsters for your little dinners; they're not ready for such worldly things."

"Don't you worry, Natalya," replied the Baron, smiling at his faithful housekeeper's maternal concern, "we will treat him splendidly. I did not choose him. Herr Beckwith did. He wanted to meet one of the townsfolk, and I could not refuse."

The old woman accepted this with good grace but remarked as she departed that her dinner wouldn't be appreciated by a callow boy.

They went to the hall and there found, dressed in his best church clothing, which was clean but none too fine, the wide-eyed blond boy whom Desmond had seen raking the gravel. He stammered out a greeting in his native language, and the Baron shook his hand firmly, asking him to speak German so that Herr Beckwith might understand them. Desmond in his turn shook the boy's broad hand, clean but rough with work. How different they were, Desmond realized, from Jeffrey's—the fingers wide and blunt, the palms callused, the nails bitten. Feeling guilty, he offered the young man what he hoped was a sincere smile and was treated to the groundskeeper's own unaffected grin in reply.

The Baron led the way down to the dining saloon, where the arrangements were as the night before, only now three places were set at the table. The boy all but gasped at the sight, and the Baron had to urge him forward to take his seat. Natalya then brought in the food, setting it on the serving tables before ladling out the soup and placing it before the three men. Then she left them alone.

Desmond noticed that this time his dish was filled, as was the Baron's. The Baron raised his spoon, to make the boy begin his own, but did not actually eat. Desmond imitated as closely as possible.

But the Baron's ruse was clever. He asked the boy many questions, urging him to talk while masking his own lack of appetite. As the boy worked at the delicious-smelling soup, Desmond was fascinated to learn just what the Baron meant to this teenager and the people of the village. The boy, remarkably, was not only literate but could speak and write German and some French. This was the Baron's doing; he had created a school many years back, bringing in a schoolmaster from Sarajevo. Even farm people and servants should read and write, he felt. He had also seen to their medical care as best he could, sending the more seriously ill to Spalato when his own knowledge failed him. When the crops were bad or water scarce, he cut back on taxes and forgave debts. When public buildings needed repair, he covered the costs himself. His concern and devotion to the people of his dominion were unheard of to one of Desmond's training, and Desmond found himself forgetting the evening's purpose.

At the Baron's elbow was a small round table set with several decanters of wine. One of these had been poured to accompany the soup, and all three men had enjoyed it. The boy was growing pink from its effects and smiled more readily now as the Baron put him at ease. Desmond was taken with his unaffected nature and at the sight of his blood-warmed flush recalled with a start the reason for his presence. Having finished two glasses of wine, the boy accepted a third. Desmond noticed this time that the Baron used another decanter and filled only the boy's glass. In all this time the Baron continued his gentle conversation, his voice soft and modulated, almost hypnotic in its soothing effect.

Suddenly, looking a bit confused, the groundskeeper turned to Desmond, his blue eyes drooping, then slumped back in his chair.

"There, he is gone for the moment. Come, Desmond, let us make ready." The Baron jumped up and went to the kitchen passage, bolting the door. He did the same for the staircase door. Turning back to Desmond, he motioned for him to place the boy on the long table, moving a candelabrum aside to make room.

As Desmond lifted the young man from his chair—a feat done with surprising ease, Desmond realized—a warm rush of his human fragrance wafted upward, making Desmond's thirst burn with sudden sharpness. Taking a deep breath to steady himself, Desmond laid the boy full length on the uncovered part of the table.

"We had better remove his jacket and shirt, Desmond."

Doing so revealed tanned arms and neck, while the boy's fair torso was untouched by sunlight. His chest was hairless, his chin nearly so, and just a trace the finest gold down glinted as the candlelight played across his arms.

Desmond stood staring down at the supine figure on the table. His thirst now raged within him, the first real thirst of his new life. He hesitated, looking over at the Baron, who stood nervously to one side like a bride's mother at a wedding.

"Just let your instinct guide you. I will be there."

Desmond looked at young Jelko. The boy's head was turned to one side, baring his neck. Eyes focused on the carotid artery, his heart pounding, Desmond bent low over the motionless figure. At a suggestion from his mind, Desmond thrilled to feel his canine teeth extend. He brought one hand up to feel their needle sharpness, then lowered his open mouth until he could feel the pungent heat of the young man's skin. He placed his lips firmly on the soft flesh, then, closing his own eyes, pressed his teeth into the sleeping mortal. Instantly a rush of hot blood filled his mouth, and he clamped his lips tightly and swallowed.

A soft moan escaped him as the blood poured down his throat. For a brief moment he fought the urge to gag, and then the blood began to fill him with a sensation of liquid fire that suffused his entire being, making his head reel. He swallowed again and again and again, until his body hummed as this new life pumped into him. Then, distinctly, he felt his heart slow and a calmness sweep over him. He knew he had drunk enough. A second wordless suggestion withdrew the miniature sabers from their mark and, his lips still firmly locked onto the boy's flesh, his tongue moved over the wound to clean and heal. Satiated, he straightened up and looked over to the Baron with triumph in his eyes. The Baron smiled broadly and came silently to him to enfold him in a warm embrace.

"You have done well, my son." Tears of a strange joy spilled out of Desmond's eyes and down his cheeks onto the black silk of the Baron's jacket.

As Desmond finished replacing the boy's shirt and jacket and cleaning up a small puddle of blood that had escaped during his feeding, the Baron alerted the housekeeper. The boy, it seems, had taken too much wine too quickly and had fainted. Natalya came clucking into the room like a mother hen, chastising her master for forgetting Jelko's youth and inexperience with strong spirits. Desmond offered to carry the boy to the room near the kitchen where the Baron suggested he be placed to sleep off the effects of the drink. As he lifted the young man once again, he noticed that the sweetness of his body no longer troubled him; his thirst was now quenched, and Jelko was once more a pretty peasant boy, nothing more.

The boy was laid on a clean bed near the kitchen, and the Baron asked Natalya to apologize on his behalf and to send him home with the remains of his dinner. This, Desmond reflected, would feed his entire family.

Together the Baron and Desmond retired to the drawing room. The Baron lit some of the candles set about the room but left more of it in darkness. Desmond noticed how he could still see far better than he would have thought in this half-light. Through the window the crescent of the moon floated in the blue-black sky. Its light reflected off the gilding of the rococo furniture, more silver than the yellow reflections of the candles. He and his mentor talked late into the night, making plans for the next few days. They would leave the castle the next day. It would be best for them to spend time in Spalato, where they could move about more freely and where Desmond could practice his lessons without the pressure of the small village about him. It frightened him to imagine any further into the future, for that would involve facing England by himself. Even his new existence could not prepare him for that ordeal.

At length Desmond began to feel fatigue, a different sort of hunger—one for rest. He bade good night to his host and climbed once more the spiral steps to his lofty chamber. There, dressed in one of Jeffrey's linen nightshirts, with the embroidered coverlet pulled up over his breast, he closed his eyes and called up from the depths of the unknown the sleep of his people.

CHAPTER 15

He opened his eyes and for a moment stared up at the sunburst pattern created by the pleated satin of the canopy lining. It was quiet in the room, pleasantly cool. The soft linen of the sheets caressed his skin, and he smiled at the sense of well-being that filled him. Suddenly a screech of brakes and a sharp blast from a car horn shattered his comfort, dragging Desmond reluctantly from the last traces of his remarkable dream.

The intrusive noise had disturbed but not awakened Tony, who grumbled incoherently and stirred. He had thrown the covers off during the night, and Desmond lovingly caressed his backside before drawing the sheets up over the sleeping form.

Then, silently getting out of the big old bed and pulling on his robe, Desmond went down the stairs to the kitchen, where Cosmo waited impatiently for her morning feeding. She meowed and purred loudly in her funny, chirruping way as Desmond opened a fresh can and spooned out the contents into her dish. He squatted down to stroke the cat's fur as it ate, Cosmo arching her back into his hand with every stroke.

"You'll never guess what happened last night, puss," he intoned conversationally as she attacked the food. "Tony knows everything. Isn't that incredible?" Cosmo seemed unimpressed with this revelation and continued her meal.

He wanted to call Roger, but since it was only 7 o'clock on the East Coast, he figured, at this hour in California, his best friend wouldn't even be able to hear the ringing. Anxious as Desmond was, he would just have to wait until later in the day. He walked out into the garden and plucked a handful of late tulips, which he arranged in a small jar and set on the kitchen table. Then he went back outside and plopped into one of the lawn chairs Tony had insisted they buy. He basked in the morning sunshine like a cat and reviewed the vivid details of his dream.

How long had it been since these memories had flooded back on him with such clarity? It must have been Tony's last request, to learn about Jeffrey, that started it. The memory of Jeffrey's death had been locked deep in his heart and had become like another piece of furniture in this house—ever present but so familiar as to hardly ever be closely examined. And now Tony would hear it all. Roger had heard the tale soon after they had returned to England, and since then it had only been mentioned in passing by either of them. Roger was a devoted friend, but he had never been the romantic that Desmond was, and he never quite understood the pain Jeffrey's memory could still bring. Desmond hoped that Tony would comprehend all this.

A shadow fell across his closed eyes, and two warm hands clamped his cheeks. "I thought all you got was six hours a day," Tony chuckled as Desmond opened his eyes and looked up into his lover's dark green–brown gaze.

"Guilty as charged, officer," retorted Desmond. "But there's no rule about resting with one's eyes closed, is there?"

"You won't really go to sleep by accident?"

"No. A very convenient trait of my kind. We sleep only when we ask for it. We can keep it up, as you recall with Roger's little French escapade, for an indefinite period. But you won't catch us catnapping."

"That must have been a preservation behavior," Tony mused aloud as Desmond stood up and stretched. "Thus, if you were being pursued or were in danger, you wouldn't place yourself at risk by sleeping inadvertently."

"Sounds good to me. You want some breakfast?"

"Sure—you're cooking?"

"I've been studying!" Desmond crowed as he led Tony back into the kitchen. Tony played with the cat while Desmond prepared poached eggs, toast, and bacon with admirable skill for someone who had never cooked himself a meal. Tony accepted this offering with pleasure, and Desmond joined him in a cup of coffee.

"How come you can drink if you can't eat?"

"It all has to do with metabolism. I still love the smell of food, though. I guess that's a human trait that I can't shake. I've experimented with it. I can't put milk in coffee, although sugar doesn't seem to hurt. Clear juices and distilled liquids are OK too. But even beef broth or clear chicken soup would make me sick. My system just isn't designed—or redesigned—to act that way anymore. And the liquids I take in come out again virtually unaltered, except for the alcohol. That gets absorbed and works in the usual way."

"Ah, that's why you're so pee-shy. I wondered."

"I suppose you'll want to see *that* too now," Desmond asked sarcastically.

"Thanks, Desi, but I'll let you keep that quirk to yourself."

"Your inquiring mind doesn't want to know?" he returned with mock disbelief.

"Maybe later—right now I'm eating!" Tony continued at his food with as much relish as Cosmo, then looked up. "So when are you going to tell me?"

"About Jeffrey? I was just thinking about that. You know, I dreamed about it all last night, the whole part of my life until I was transformed."

"You did? Was it bad?"

"No, not really, although it was like living it all over again."

"Do you dream a lot?"

"Very rarely. Twice now since I've known you."

"Is that bad or good?"

"Good, I think. It's as if my mind is telling me to get ready to tell you things. Reviewing my memory tapes, so to speak. That way the details will be fresh."

"Great, so let's start."

"Whoa, kiddo. I'm not spilling my guts to some sloppy guy who's wearing boxer shorts and still smells of sex."

"Are you objecting to my smell?" Tony feigned indignation.

"Not at all. It's just distracting. I thought we could go up to Central Park and take a long walk while I tell you. Then we can have lunch by the swan pond. This afternoon we'll do as we always do."

"Sounds like a perfect day to me," he said, wiping up the last of his egg with a crust and gulping down his coffee. Then he jumped up from the table and ran into the hall, calling as he went, "last one in the shower's a dead bat!"

They took a long, luxurious shower together under the huge nickel-plated showerhead in Desmond's bathroom. Desmond felt freer and more at ease with Tony than in all their previous six months together. Tony soaped himself, then Desmond, vigorously.

"This'll get rid of that nasty sex smell, old buddy!"

"Hey, careful! If you don't watch it, I'll want to start all over again." They shared laughter and a soapy embrace as the warm water sluiced over their bodies.

Once they had dried off and dressed, they took a cab uptown to the Vanderbilt Gardens, across the street from the Museum of the City of New York. As Desmond paid the driver, Tony stood staring up at the monumental iron gates. Beyond them the flower beds and trees were in full spring regalia, in vivid contrast to their last visit here.

"Now you understand," said Desmond coming up behind him.

"Understand what?" asked Tony.

"Why I remember when all the Vanderbilt houses stood brand new and glittering, like palaces along Fifth Avenue. Of course, they were the flashiest of the houses but not the only ones on that scale."

"It's hard to imagine what New York was really like then," mused Tony. "All we've got is black-and-white pictures."

"I can still see it like a Technicolor movie. But it seems so far away, like some memory I haven't recalled in years. The city has changed so much."

"Did you hate to see all those incredible buildings torn down?" asked Tony, turning to look at his lover.

"A little, but then I'm used to the wheels of so-called progress. Remember, I was here before the Vanderbilts even existed in New York society. When I built my house, downtown was uptown."

"Why didn't you ever move up to Fifth Avenue when your neighborhood began to slide?" They walked down the wide flight of stone steps.

"I'm a creature of habit. The house is more than I need, and it has always been comfortable, even luxurious. Moreover, the fact that it was ultimately in an unfashionable neighborhood was good for me; it protected my privacy. I've never been a socialite."

"True. But don't you ever feel trapped there—I mean, like you're tied down?"

"I've never thought of it that way. I suppose that, since it is my refuge from the world, it's also become a crutch of sorts. But I don't think I'm really trapped there. I've never seen any reason to move out. My life's in that house, Tony."

"Not all of it. Not your life before you came here."

"Good point. I sold out once, to start over, to leave my old world behind."

"Do you think you'll ever do it again?" Tony looked quizzically into Desmond's eyes, his brow knitted.

"Maybe. I can't say now. Why?"

"Oh, I'm not sure. It's…it's just that the house has always felt otherworldly to me. I didn't really understand it completely until last night, when I found out for sure—about you."

"You knew before that, didn't you?"

"Yes, but not from your own mouth. Then I realized what it was: the house isn't really alive. It's suspended in time somehow. Like you are when you sleep, alive yet dead. A house with nobody in it. Don't get me wrong, Des, it's beautiful—wonderful, in fact. But inert, as if it had stopped growing at some point. You've stopped making changes, haven't you?"

"Yes, except for the occasional rewiring and some new security things. Why change it if I like it the way it is?"

"But you *did* change it, certainly. Look at all the different things you did to it during the 19th century. But even then, they became fewer and fewer. After you put in the bathrooms in the 1880s—nothing."

"Yes, but I was different myself then. The house was new, like a toy to me. I loved to play with it." Desmond felt slightly defensive but knew that Tony wasn't attacking him. He was puzzled, wondering what Tony's point was.

"That's it exactly," said Tony, stopping suddenly. "Don't you see, Desmond? The house *has* stopped growing. You've used it up. Now it's just a shelter—albeit one you love a lot. It's just the place you sleep and sit and brood about the world. It's like your coffin, to protect you from outsiders, to keep the light of the sun off your face." The last words came out with a sort of inspired look on Tony's face, and Desmond groaned and punched him gently on the shoulder.

"Please, you sound like a junior Van Helsing! I'm going to have to stop letting you read my books." Inwardly Desmond cringed. The thought of his house as a coffin presented an unwelcome image, reminding him of Charlon's morbid mansion. He shook off the feeling. "Come on, we're not up here to talk about the house. I thought you wanted to know about the rest of my life."

"I do, I do!" Tony's enthusiasm returned, and they started again as Desmond began to reveal to Tony the vivid dream that had been his first lifetime.

They walked and walked. Following the curving paths that led them gradually southward in the huge park, Tony listened with rapt attention, occasionally interrupting to ask a question or clarify a detail. Desmond, for his part, felt an extraordinary lightness descend on him as all the memories replayed themselves through his words. The joy, anguish, and excitement of the past all flowed from him, leaving him with a strange feeling of happiness.

"And once the Baron had showed me the ropes in Spalato, I went to France. That's where I got the idea of opening a branch bank."

"And where you discovered the public gardens?" asked Tony, a sly twinkle coming into his eye for the first time in the long discourse.

"Yes. It seems that's been a universal truth since my life began, at least. Wherever there are large public gardens or parks, men who seek other men will gather, subtly but inevitably. It made quenching my thirst so much simpler. Not to mention my other inclination." Desmond fell silent, and Tony did not break it.

Then, after they had walked on a bit further, he asked quietly, "When did you and Roger finally come here?"

"A few years after we returned to England. He adapted very well to the business in London. But I found myself feeling constrained, hemmed in by the world I knew too well and for too long. I was yearning for something new."

"That doesn't sound like you, Desmond."

"You're right, it doesn't. But it was true. So I decided, with Roger's agreement, to see what we could do in America. I sold the estate lock, stock, and barrel, taking only the painting of the house as my father had built it and some books. Roger and I came to New York in 1798. We were both 30, and I was very rich, especially by American standards. We set up an office on Pearl Street—the American branch of Beckwith Bank. For the first years Roger and I shared rooms over the office. Then I moved out, leaving Roger to his busy social life."

"Hmm?" Tony's eyebrows arched questioningly.

"Yes, Tony. Roger has always been a social animal. He was always seducing women, giving parties, gambling away the night. I never really liked that, preferring to read in my rooms, perhaps host a small party of intelligent people. I never really made friends. Roger always had scads of friends swarming about."

"That's not changed much, has it?"

"No, not much. He has twice as many gay friends as *I* do. It made me very jealous at first—I was still so much in love with Roger. But I outgrew it eventually and just realized that his style wasn't mine. Lord, merely thinking about his place in San Francisco makes me tired!" They laughed together, then Desmond went on.

"I set up rooms in an elegant boardinghouse—the sort of place where young single men lived in those days. Just a sitting room and one bedroom, the one for which Lannuier made that bedroom suite you love so much. But I entertained there, in my own way. Just as I had in France. Small groups of like-minded businessmen and intellectual women. Very different from Roger's more hectic style."

"What made you decide to build the house?" Tony asked.

"I'm not sure," replied Desmond, seeming to think over his answer. "Perhaps it was just middle age setting in, my wanting something more substantial than the glorified hotel suite I was in. I was 52 when I built my house. Roger teased me, but I persisted."

"What about your second transformation—or regeneration?"

"My second, Roger's first. Unlike me, Roger was fascinated by the process."

"But he had you to look after him while it happened."

"True. There again we had—and have—different styles. Initially we went to Philadelphia in 1833, just to get Roger through his change away from knowing eyes in New York. Roger decided to just disappear and reemerge as a new person. He's always done that, while I've maintained my more complex father-to-son ploy. I had long since created the fictitious son, who appeared shortly after we arrived in England late that same spring. Once my regeneration was complete, I duly did what I'd done 44 years earlier and presented my new self with documents at the London bank. Roger, who had fabricated some new surname, was with me, enjoying being 21 again.

"We stayed in London for about a year. Then I went back to New York, while Roger returned to Philadelphia, where he set up the first of his party houses." Desmond cast a knowing glance at Tony, rolling his eyes slightly. "I think he just did it to get away from me. I've always been such an old maid in his opinion."

"I can see that," Tony put in, then dodged to avoid Desmond's playful jab.

"That's when the loneliness really began. I'd always managed to be content with Roger nearby. His being in another city made it much harder; but I got used to it. He worked hard, established Beckwith interests there, and partied just as hard. Philadelphia in the mid 1830s was a cosmopolitan city. Back in New York, I settled into my house, continuing to collect my bibelots and redecorating. It was enough to see Roger every few months."

"And you've followed the same pattern—I mean, the two of you—ever since?" Tony was asking questions like a reporter doing a serious interview, his brow knit, his eyes focused on Desmond's face.

"More or less. Of course, I would go back to France and England periodically—far less than now, since travel was so difficult and dangerous. Vampires can drown, you know. That may be the source of the myth that they can't cross moving water. Anyway, we didn't go abroad for my third regeneration, in 1877. We decided to go to Chicago for that one; and again Roger, with yet another new name, stayed. He loved Chicago even more than Philadelphia—it was so new, so raw. No one asked questions about his past. It made me shudder—so unrooted it seemed to me then."

"You stuffy old New Yorker!" laughed Tony. "No wonder you like Edith Wharton!"

"I don't think you're being fair. Chicago was a thriving place after the fire. By 1877, when we got there, it was almost as if the fire had never happened. Money was growing on trees. Not only was it the perfect place for Roger to start his new life; it was the ideal spot for our next branch office. Remember, eternal life means eternal bills and making eternal money to pay them. Roger and I have always been practical about the business."

"But you still found Chicago too unsettling to want to stay?"

"Yes. I wanted the seclusion of my little town house right here in New York. Of course, this city was hardly the provincial postcolonial center I'd first known. By 1877 things were boiling uptown, and already my neighborhood had dropped from the first fashion. Fifth Avenue, with its endless mud-colored brownstones, was the chic place to live. My street became remote and unprotected in society's view. There were too many immigrants living nearby for most people's tastes. That suited me just fine."

"And then in the 1880s the palaces began to spring up!"

"Exactly, and I watched it all from my little Gothic library."

"Did you see the Dakota go up?" Again the historian at work, Tony quizzed Desmond as they walked slowly through the meanders of the park's endless blacktop pathways.

"Oh, yes, and it was quite an attraction. Most people couldn't imagine living in such a building, nor that far up on Central Park West, which was still a mess. For most well-to-do people, sharing quarters with other families was something poor people did in tenements—or something the French did; New Yorkers all thought the French were peculiar, anyway. But we all went to see the model apartment that was set up. It had a certain appeal to me—even then. But I stayed where I was."

"When did Roger end up in San Francisco?"

"That was the next regeneration. We went out together, as usual. Another new territory to conquer for Roger's social life and our business interests. By 1921 the train service made the West Coast easy to reach, so even at that distance Roger wasn't much farther away than he had been in Philadelphia in the 1830s. And of course the telephone was an incredible boon. You can't imagine the thrill of speaking to someone who is hundreds or thousands of miles away."

"We take it so for granted today. Why did Roger stay there at the next regeneration?" Tony made some mental calculations. "It was 1965, wasn't it?"

"Why? Because by then the big cities were anonymous enough for Roger's type. He just disappeared within the same town. Moved to the house he's in now, with his green eyes, dazzling young smile, and gorgeous dark red hair. This time he went back to his original surname. Few people recognized him as the 65-year-old he'd been before, and he didn't exactly maintain the same circle of friends. Roger's always liked starting over. Occasionally someone from his past life would recognize him and tell him how amazingly like their old friend he looked. Actually, Roger learned some very interesting things about himself from those interviews."

"And you've always had a mystery son who appears just after your death?"

"Right on schedule. But you must realize, Tony, I've never had friends the way Roger did. I've never had intimates, until this lifetime. Business acquaintances, intellectual dinner mates. No one has ever really known Desmond Beckwith. It wasn't hard keeping the supposed son a secret or unveiling him after I'd transformed into my 21-year-old self. I just have to make sure to hire Roger into my firm in some capacity, if he wants it, and to sign over his estate to him."

"What do you mean?"

"Roger has always left his estate to me—he transforms first by several months. That way, once he changes, I've got to reassign it to whoever he decides his new person will be. It's always been done quietly. We both get stuck paying taxes, but that's better than the government digging into our lives."

"Is Bill Lawrence your first...uh, human friend?"

"Not human, Tony, mortal. Do I seem inhuman to you?" Desmond looked wounded.

"No, I didn't mean it that way. Anyway, you're *not* really human, no matter what you seem to me; it's not a value judgment, Des." Tony threw a comforting arm across Desmond's shoulders.

"Sorry, I didn't mean to seem so sensitive. I guess Bill and that whole group you've met are the first friends I've ever really had to call that. Even *they* don't know me well. It was all part of coming out in the '60s—the whole Stonewall thing. I felt connected with them somehow. All my years of feeling cut off from the rest of humanity, not just by my race but by my sexuality, finally boiled over. So much was going on in the '60s. I was desperate to be part of *something*. The whole gay thing just happened to suit my mood swings at the time. For once, I never really stopped to think about the consequences."

"Consequences?" Tony was puzzled.

"When I hit 65 again. What do I do, just vanish the way Roger always has? Start from scratch? When you've got ties with people, you can't start over without doing some thinking."

"So your son, Desmond the—what is it, seventh?—can take over and be their friend as his father was."

"I guess that's what I'll do. But it won't be as simple with all these people so much closer to me."

"And what about me?" Tony asked, suddenly quiet.

"That's 20 years away, love," responded Desmond, putting his arm around Tony's waist and pulling him close. "You'll have lots to worry about with me between now and then."

"But think about it, Des. I'll be 45, and you'll be 21 again!"

"And just think, when your looks are beginning to fade, you'll have a gorgeous boy to play with!"

"Will you still want me then, Desmond?" Tony's voice had grown small, childlike.

"I plan on it. What's so weird about that, Tony? I'm 45 now, and you don't seem too repulsed with me."

This happy thought seemed to cheer Tony up, and they walked on in silence for a while longer, finally reaching the end of the park at the noisy plaza in front of the hotel of the same name.

Rather than the restaurant at the swan pond, which was now far to their north, Desmond and Tony went into Cipriani's for lunch. Tony ordered a large assortment of food, and Desmond called for a bottle of wine. He felt exhilarated and exhausted, having poured out his life to his lover, this wise, handsome young man who sat across from him wolfing down a huge green salad.

Suddenly Tony stopped in mid mouthful and looked up at Desmond.

"What?" asked Desmond, seeing the look in Tony's eyes.

"I just thought of something, Des. How can I stay with you when you transform next time? What'll your friends say—you, supposedly Desmond's son, shacking up with his old boyfriend? They'll freak totally."

Despite the concern on Tony's face, Desmond could only laugh, feeling calmer and more at ease than he would have expected. He put out a hand and gently patted Tony's where it lay, still holding his fork, on the table.

"Relax, kiddo. We've got 20 years to worry about this. Let's just get through this year before we figure out the rest."

That afternoon they spent as had become their custom: Tony working on the inventory of the contents of the house while Desmond read in the library. When Desmond was sure Tony was deeply immersed in his historical record keeping up on the third floor, he slipped down to the basement study and dialed Roger's San Francisco number.

On the third ring Roger's voice answered with a brisk "Yes?"

"Roger, it's me."

"Des? And to what do I owe the pleasure? Has Tony abandoned you for boys his own age?" Behind the sardonic tone Desmond could hear concern; Roger had picked up on the oddity of the midafternoon call.

"No, quite the opposite. He likes me the way I am."

"The way you are, Des? Am I to infer that…"

"He knows, Rog," Desmond interrupted. "He knows all about me."

"Whew," returned Roger with a soft whistle, "that *is* news. When did you tell him? Or, more to the point, why?"

"I didn't. That's the thing—*he* told *me*. Last night, on his 25th birthday. He gave me a present."

"Wait a minute, you've got me a little confused. He told you and gave you a present for *his* birthday? Have you been drinking?"

"I know it sounds insane, and even more so last night. He figured me—us—out, Roger. We were both dropping hairpins, maybe subconsciously, and he picked up every one."

"How has he taken it? Strange as it may seem to ask."

"Pretty well, as far as I can see. He seems more awed by the fact that I've seen so much of the past that *he's* only read about than the fact that I suck blood to survive."

"Was he at all afraid?" Now Roger sounded like Tony, quizzing Desmond with a clinician's thirst for detail.

"Yes. At first. Terrified, in fact. I think he expected me to kill him or something because he'd outed me. That actually threw me for a loop. After all, he's read the same old stories that you and I laugh about. But to see him looking at me like that, the love in his eyes mixed with the expectation that I was going to leap at him like, like…"

"Like a panther?" Roger asked softly.

"Exactly. But I got him through it, I think. He even asked me to bare my teeth for him and wanted to watch me go to sleep. I've told him all about you, how we met."

"And Jeffrey?"

"And Jeffrey, the only person since I told you."

"His reaction to that?"

"It was all he could do to keep from crying. He really felt for me, for the whole story, Roger. I feel like I've dropped a ton of bricks from my shoulders. It's as if I've been carrying this whole house for the past century, and it's suddenly lifted. My God, Roger, it's unnerving! He's even thinking about the future—he asked me at lunch what he'd do when I transform again, 20 years from now."

"Hey, that boy plans ahead!"

"It's scary, Roger."

"To hell with scary, Desmond, it's incredibly flattering. He must love you to pieces to be worried about the future like that."

"I know, I understand, Rog. But you know how I am. It's such a switch, I don't know what to do."

"Do what he's doing. Concentrate on today, think about the future—but not too much. Do what any couple has to do—try as hard as you can to make it work. That should keep you busy until the regeneration issue comes up."

"You make a strange Dutch uncle, Roger."

"You make a strange newlywed, sweetheart."

"Are you happy?"

"Why wouldn't I be? Listen, Desi, you've carried all the burdens for both of us in the lifetimes we've known each other. I may have to get used to your *not* being such a gloomy gus. I know I'm lazy, but your happiness means everything to me, Des. If you need to shed some of your vampire guilt, *I'll* pick it up."

"What on earth are you talking about?"

"Vampire guilt, the loneliness you impose on yourself, your sense of being cut off from humanity by what you are. Your deeply introspective psyche, old friend. I've always let you do all the worrying—now I'll worry about you two, rattling about in that house, tripping over pieces of your past..."

"Oh, come on! I'm not that depressing, am I?"

"Only now and then. But the point is, I want you to think good thoughts about this relationship. It's what you've been waiting for, so make the most of it."

"I will, Dad, I promise." Desmond said this with such a deadpan expression that Roger laughed out loud.

"That's my Desmond! Keep me posted, will you?"

"Sure thing, Roger. Thanks for…whatever!"

"Anytime, chum, anytime," and he rang off.

When Desmond returned upstairs, he found Tony just coming down from the third floor.

"I'm moving along well, Desmond. A few more Saturday afternoons, and we'll have the rough list finished. It's incredible what you've got. Even without the things themselves, the documents would be an archivist's dream come true; and you've got the goods to match!"

"You're not done yet, are you?"

"No, I had some questions for you—you know, details."

"It's nice to have a living encyclopedia, isn't it?"

"Yeah, so much easier than *real* research. Did you read newspapers a lot?"

"Huh? When, you mean back then?"

"Right."

"Of course, why?"

"Do you remember things?"

"Well, some, but not everything! What are you digging for?"

"You could help steer me, direct me toward documentation for certain kinds of things that I might overlook. I just don't know how much you remember."

"Don't think I'm going to be able to revolutionize history, kiddo. Just pretend I'm a historian who's read everything. My memory's going to be full of holes, especially the nitpicky stuff you historical types seem to want. I'm sure I can help in some ways, perhaps even a great deal. But I'm not a computer of lost facts. Most of what I know is written down somewhere else already."

"That's OK. Can you come up now and help?"

"Sure." And together they climbed to the third-floor guest rooms, where Tony had printouts and handwritten notes spread out all over one of the beds.

They spent an hour or so going over the material Tony had compiled so far, preparing it to enter into the computer database. Then Tony suggested they spend their second "official" night at his place to sort of balance things—to make the weekend symmetrical, so to speak. Desmond agreed, and Tony dashed off to tidy up and prepare for his overnight guest. Desmond offered to take the papers downstairs and sat on the bed after Tony had gone, idly shuffling through the neatly ordered piles.

One sheet of paper caught his eye. Desmond scanned it once with a cursory glance and almost stuck it in with the rest of the papers, until something made him pull it back out.

It was a handwritten sheet like some of the others but covered with columns of seemingly meaningless numbers. As Desmond stared at it, the meaning of the numbers suddenly became clear to him. The numbers were dates, starting with this year and reaching far into the future. There were parallel columns, one headed D, one headed T.

"He's been calculating!" Desmond murmured to no one, or maybe to Cosmo, who had joined him upstairs and was reminding him of the empty food dish three floors down.

Tony had figured out their relative ages over the next several centuries—assuming, of course, that he was to become one of Desmond's kind this year. Desmond looked with fascination at the figures, noting that by the middle of the 22nd century, there would be a time when they would be almost the same age for almost a whole lifetime. Then, with only four years of disparity, Desmond regenerated and Tony an old man, they would suddenly be the same age. They would live a full lifetime at the same age, then the cycle would begin to retrace its steps. Desmond's hand shook slightly as he placed the paper back among the others and carefully tamped the pile together.

Tony had not mentioned himself in this light, had not even touched obliquely on the concept of his own transformation. And yet here was proof that he was looking farther ahead than Desmond himself had ever looked. The image of that endless vista forward in time made Desmond shiver. Could any love survive across the centuries? He rose slowly from the bed. Staring down the neat pile of paper for one more long moment, he turned and left the room, soundlessly descending the carpeted staircase toward his library and its refuge from the uncertainties of the world.

CHAPTER 16

May came and went, leaving behind a city rejuvenated with greenery and warmth. Desmond spent his days in the basement office, keeping his finger on the pulse of his business interests. Tony spent his week uptown at the museum helping Vivian Lake with her forays into the past of the city. He kept his own insights, newly attained, to himself while doing his best to assist his boss. Tony and Desmond met, as before, in the evening, alternating nights between Desmond's house and Tony's studio.

The weekends they passed in their habitual way, sometimes breaking the pattern to join Bill Lawrence and some of their—now mutual—friends for dinner or a movie. Everyone had noticed the change in their relationship, which is to say the more official nature it seemed to have taken on, and had also noted the change in Desmond Beckwith. The witty, intellectual, aloof man they had all known for years seemed younger, looser, more romantic than they would ever have suspected. He and Tony still appeared to guard the old brick town house—which Tony referred to jokingly as the mausoleum—like a sanctuary, rarely inviting anyone but Bill over. Those few who had at first snickered quietly about the "mother-daughter act," came to admire and like Tony, both for his own qualities as well as for his effect on Desmond.

Tony continued to surprise Desmond. He was good to his word, peppering their evening conversations with questions about

Desmond's life and lives. Most of these ceased to startle Desmond as he grew familiar with the workings of his lover's mind. He was flabbergasted, however, when Tony asked if he could accompany Desmond on his "night out," which was their euphemism for the nights when Desmond went out by himself, seeking the nourishment he needed to survive. At first Desmond balked at this—somehow his thirst and the method of satisfying it seemed personal, private. But Tony had cajoled him and finally persuaded him, for an unexpected reason. It was not, for once, Tony's insatiable and rather lugubrious interest in Desmond's vampire nature that spurred him on. Rather, it was his yearning to cope with something else—his jealousy. It was jealousy, his fear of losing Desmond, that had made him follow on that dark night when he had first seen Desmond drink. Desmond, who had known love only through Jeffrey and, differently, through Roger, did not fully understand this fear of loss. If Desmond feared losing Tony, it was to some mortal affliction, not so much to another lover. But Tony had known no love before Desmond, and he clung to his passion with the fierceness of youth. Desmond was startled to learn that Tony saw him as a Don Juan of sorts and then admitted, upon consideration, that this was not far off the truth. For two centuries Desmond had lived by himself, sexual desire and thirst for blood his only driving forces—if one discounted the business, for which Desmond had only pragmatic feelings.

And so it was that Tony began to go out with Desmond occasionally on his hunting nights, always staying in the background like some urban anthropologist, watching as Desmond approached, diverted, seduced, and abandoned his chosen resource for the evening. He would tease Desmond about his technique, something the older man had not known since his early days in England with Roger. The fact that Tony had learned how to tease Desmond from Roger made it all the more intimate.

The end of June brought another surprise into Desmond's structured world. By the middle of the month, Tony had begun making noises about taking part in the gay pride march, an annual event held in New York on the last Sunday in June. Commemorating the Stonewall riots of 1969, which had marked the start of the modern gay rights movement, the day held special import to Tony. Desmond had known of the parade—as had anyone who lived in New York—and had even witnessed its progress one or two times, but he had never considered himself part of the event. He had never quite drawn the personal connection with the marching multitudes. His own ties to Stonewall were limited to Bill Lawrence and their shared circle of friends from the '60s. Even his work as an AIDS buddy had not made the link, any more than his work with the war wounded in 1863 had attached him to the Union army. But now there was Tony at his side, pulling his arm and wheedling him playfully until he relented, much to the amazement of Bill Lawrence. Bill, seeing Desmond's resistance and Tony's earnestness, added his weight to the argument in its early stages and even requested an assignment to cover the parade for his paper from an insider's perspective. Regardless, he was surprised by Desmond's ultimate capitulation after he and Tony had worked in concert for only a short time.

Thus, a brilliant sunny June afternoon saw the three of them, surrounded by hundreds of thousands of gay men and women, walking down Fifth Avenue, which was decorated for the event with a lavender stripe. At Desmond's suggestion they had decided to march with the Gay Men's Health Crisis contingent, since it was the one group with which Desmond felt some real ties. As Louie's death began to take its place among the other varied memories in Desmond's soul, he began once again to look toward the next client to whom he could become friend, confidant, minister. Tony's presence gave him additional strength to face the sorrowful reward of helping someone else to cope with the rigors of living—and dying—with AIDS.

As the three of them sauntered cheerfully down the wide, automobile-free street, soaking up the sun's warmth and basking in the cheers of the spectators, Desmond felt himself connected to his time and place in history as he had not since before his transformation. He looked over at Bill, his close-cut curly hair graying slightly, his face still as youthful at 45 as Desmond's. Then he turned and took in Tony's lean, pretty face; his wavy, sun-streaked hair blowing back from his high forehead; and his smile flashing as he waved his free hand at sideline well-wishers. Here were two people he loved, his oldest New York friend and his lover, two mortals who shared his life more than he would ever have expected—or wished—in his past lifetimes.

He squeezed their hands, which kept his own from waving at the crowd, making them both look at him. Then he impulsively gave first Tony then Bill a kiss, to the noisy delight of one group of bystanders. Tony and Bill exchanged a quizzical raising of the eyebrows before they shrugged and settled back into their comfortable strides.

It was a very long day, the march itself followed by an endless series of speeches on West Street in Greenwich Village. This in turn was followed by the obligatory wandering about aimlessly in the hot and sweaty hordes that filled every square foot of the narrow downtown streets. Desmond took this all in stride, reminding himself that New York homosexuals were, generally speaking, no smellier and far more attractive than the mobs in Paris had been in 1793.

Eventually he insisted that Tony and Bill let him treat them to a good dinner, somewhere quiet and out of the mainstream of gay humanity. The three of them talked incessantly, reminiscing about the past—the past that Desmond shared with them. Tony was fascinated by stories of the '60s from both of the older men, and they listened respectfully to Tony's own childhood soliloquy. With all his focus on Desmond's more distant past, Tony had never really learned much of his long friendship with Bill, and he absorbed all they said with scholarly attention.

After dinner, the now dark streets somewhat less crowded and far cooler than they had been, Bill excused himself and headed back to his little aerie to write the piece for the next day's paper. Although he could send the story directly from his home computer to the *Times* editing room, he had an early deadline to meet. Tony and Desmond waved him off, then stood, uncertainly, before the restaurant.

"What should we do now?" asked Tony, although Desmond suspected there was a ready answer.

"Go home and read?" he suggested weakly. "I'm exhausted."

"Bullshit! You can't get tired that easily—I know better! Des, you could probably keep going until I collapsed, couldn't you?"

"I do get tired, you know. I do have to sleep, kid."

"Yeah, but not so early, and not after a measly day's exercise like this. I'm too geared up to relax now."

"So what do you want to do?"

"Let's go dance."

"What?"

"Dance—you know, what all those guys are doing in the bars while you're in there cruising for your dinner."

"I know what you mean, pip-squeak!"

"Most people go to those places to have fun, Des, not find their weekly intake of red corpuscles. We've never even been dancing together. Come on, let's go. The crowd will be boiling tonight. All the energy in the air!"

"All right, but where to?" Desmond offered his assent with assumed weariness, but in fact he was pleased at the idea of really being able to show off his beautiful partner this evening.

Tony named an East Village bar that was not too far away, to which they could walk in 20 minutes at a steady clip. As they walked, the night-softened air swirled about them, kicking up whirlwinds of dust and litter in the light of the streetlamps. The streets were as busy as on a normal business day, full of marchers or spectators ambling along beneath the blue-black sky.

"Des, I was thinking," remarked Tony softly.

"Yes?" Desmond replied, his voice rising ironically.

"Seriously, Des, I was wondering…"

"Wondering what? What's the problem?"

"What do you do when you get older?

"I *am* older."

"No. I mean much older, close to regeneration age."

"For sex or for blood?"

"Well, both, I suppose."

"The needs for both lessen, actually. I do age pretty well, but that doesn't make it any easier. I have to turn on the charm harder than ever. Sometimes it doesn't work, and I have to get more predatory."

"Like what?"

"I pay sometimes."

"As in hustler?"

"As in law of supply and demand. Some things never change, Tony."

"But the night you met me…"

"I'm only 45, dear heart. I *never* pay at 45!"

"When, then? Sixty?"

"Good grief, what a depressing conversation! Fifty-five, maybe. Some people actually like older men, especially handsome ones in good shape. What *are* you getting at, Tony?"

"I was just thinking, Des, that when it gets tough for you, maybe I could, you know, help you out." Tony looked down, and Desmond realized that he was blushing.

"You mean you'd pimp for me? Snare the cuties who won't look my way?"

Tony tried to protest the blunt way Desmond had worded it, but his words were cut short by a bear hug that lifted him off his feet for a moment.

"That's the sweetest thing anyone's ever said to me! I love you, you insane person."

"I mean it, Des. I'd do it."

"I know you do, Tony. So do I. Just remember, you'll be getting on in years eventually too. I may have to pimp for you."

They both laughed, but Desmond remembered the yellow paper with all the numbers on it, and a shiver trickled down his back.

The bar, once they arrived, was awash with sound, light, and the electric scent of hundreds of dancing men and women. Desmond and Tony waded in, allowing themselves to get caught up in the high spirits. Armed with a beer and a glass of wine, they moved through the flow and ebb of the mob, reassuring each other now and then with a touch or a look.

For a while they stood on the sidelines, watching the gyrations of the multifarious dancers as they followed the complex rhythms of the pounding music. Some seemed to move only from the waist up, while others concentrated on elaborate footwork. Still others, usually the younger dancers, threw their whole bodies into movement, flinging long hair and loose clothing into swirling currents of color and shape. Desmond, who had first begun this sort of dancing in the style of the mid '60s—which now seemed hopelessly dated— watched with the detached wonder of an outsider, while Tony studied the random choreography with the receptive eye of a student.

Finally, fortified with the drinks, they relinquished their glasses and took to the floor together. Desmond moved with the studied restraint of a middle-aged man trying not to look foolish as Tony turned and writhed next to him with the unconscious abandon of a gorgeous 25-year-old. Gradually, as the music and atmosphere infected him, Desmond's dancing loosened up. Tony too altered his broader movements, watching Desmond and beginning to imitate him as their bodies shifted and stretched in the wash of electronic noise. Soon they were dancing together, really together, Desmond's body keeping pace with Tony's slender frame. They exchanged looks of admiration and affection with each other, oblivious to any attention their partnership drew from the surrounding onlookers.

As one pulsating melody faded into another, Desmond glanced at his watch and was horrified—and not a little impressed—to see that he and Tony had been dancing continuously for nearly an hour. He suddenly felt drained and dragged Tony, who showed little inclination to stop, off the dance floor.

He left Tony standing in the milling crowd and made his way back to the long bar near the entrance. People were pouring into the place, fresh from the outdoor revelry that still carried on in the streets. Desmond got trapped behind a large group waiting to get drinks. As he waited, he blunted his impatience with careful scrutiny of his fellow patrons. On any typical night this bar would be full, and each night of the week targeted a different audience. Such marketing techniques apparently brought in the money.

Tonight, however, it seemed populated with a more diverse selection than he could remember. Somehow the usual rules, both social and sartorial, had been suspended in honor of the day. All genders and ages and styles were congregated under this roof. The sweater-and-slacks crowd mingled with the jeans-and-leather-vests gang; leather queens and drag queens toasted each other with daiquiris and beers. Meek young preppies, male and female, chatted with sweaty jocks, while suitless corporate types replayed the day's celebration with hairdressers and collarless parish priests. Desmond was once again struck by the fact that nothing in all his previous existence had prepared him for this extraordinary setting. This was the sort of hodgepodge society that Roger so loved and with which he filled his house in San Francisco. This was the heterogeneous and confusing "gay community" that Desmond had always kept at arm's length and which, suddenly, seemed so much a part of his life. With the specter of AIDS lingering in the shadows about them, these people celebrated and laughed together, not as in the palace of Prince Prospero, ignoring the approach of the Red Death, but as comrades in arms during a holiday cease-fire. These people were all, in their own way, fighting the same battle, and Desmond, for the first time, felt proud to be among them.

At last a space opened in front of him, and Desmond shouldered his way to the bar. He ordered another beer for Tony and a second glass of white wine for himself. As he turned, holding the two glasses gingerly, a tall young man with badly frosted hair and evident lipstick suddenly lurched in front of him, stepping heavily on his foot. In spite of the pain, Desmond managed not to spill either drink. The pale, acne-scarred face of the boy turned wide eyes on him, the red lips mouthing a silent apology. Doing his best not to wince, Desmond flashed him a winning smile and whispered in his ear as he edged by, "Careful, you'll break a heel in this place!"

It was slow going as Desmond worked his way through the maze of people, and the distance back to the dance floor seemed endless. Finally he came within sight of where he had left Tony and scanned the area for a sign of his location. His eyes tracked carefully through the assemblage of limbs, heads, and shirts until they lit upon Tony's dirty-blond hair shining in the glow of a downspot. Desmond started to move toward him, then noticed that he was deep in conversation with another man. Never having seen anyone talking with Tony this way, Desmond stopped and watched with curiosity. Tony's earlier comment about pimping for Desmond came back to him, and he found himself wondering if that was what he was up to. Or perhaps it was simply someone Tony knew. Or more likely, someone coming on to one of the cutest guys in the place—*his* guy.

Desmond moved closer. A strange sense of pride filled him as he saw how good-looking the stranger was. Tall, athletic, short blond hair paler than Tony's, nice teeth that showed beneath well-formed lips. As Desmond watched, feeling somewhat like a spying spouse, he realized that the man was older than Tony, probably nearer his own age. A strange contraction ran though him that turned to a wave of prickling heat as he saw the blond caress Tony's chest with one forefinger, making his gold chain glint in the moonlight. He was jealous! Desmond's surprise at recognizing the emotion barely kept his hands from trembling at the anger that welled up inside him. The anger was not aimed at Tony but at himself, for letting such petty mortal emotions mar the happiness of the evening. He closed his eyes, clenching the drinks, and took several deep breaths. When he looked again, the blond said something into Tony's ear and moved away from him, disappearing into the crowd. Heedless of the two full glasses, Desmond now pushed his way through the revelers to Tony's side. Tony's face lit up with a smile when he caught sight of him, then grew serious when he saw the distress evident in his lover's eyes.

"Hi! I thought they'd flushed you down the loo. Why the spooked expression?" he took the partly spilled beer from Desmond's hand.

"Who was that man talking to you just now?" Desmond asked, trying to sound casual.

"The gorgeous blond guy? I don't know. He seemed familiar, and I'd half guessed he was a friend of Bill's or yours. Don't you know him?"

"No more than you do. You think he's really cute?"

"Sure—wait a minute! You're not *jealous*, are you? My Desmond, Mr. cold-blooded immortal cool Beckwith?" Tony laughed and put his hand on Desmond's shoulder. "I'm sorry. I'll send him away. He's just gone to get himself a drink. I declined the offer."

"Did you tell him I was getting you one?"

"No, it didn't come up, actually."

"Then don't."

"Don't what?" Tony now looked puzzled.

"Don't tell him about me or send him away."

"Why not?"

"Would you like to sleep with him?" Desmond fixed his gray eyes on Tony's. There was not anger in his question. Tony hesitated a moment before answering.

"Well, I guess so, theoretically, but…"

"Then do it. You're young and sexy. There's no reason I should own your body. As long as I've got your heart." He could barely conceal a flicker of a smile at this last sentimental phrase.

"Desmond, you're kidding. We're here together tonight."

"We're together almost every night." Desmond grasped Tony's hand from his own shoulder, pulling it down and holding it.

"After all, you let me go out and fulfill my special needs without you. Why shouldn't I let you?"

"But Des…" Tony began.

"You *are* attracted to him?"

"Yes."

"If I weren't in the picture, you'd jump at the chance to sleep with him?"

"Yes."

"Do you think he wants you too?"

"I wouldn't be surprised."

"Then enjoy yourself. I admit, I was in a jealous pique back there when I saw you two talking. It floored me. I never thought I'd feel real jealousy. It never happened with Jeffrey—but that was such a different time. And Roger and I never had that sort of a friendship. All I know is that I trust you with my body at night, and I should certainly be able to trust you with your own." Desmond raised Tony's hand to his lips. Now it was Tony's turn to smile at the corny gesture.

"You're serious, aren't you?"

"Yes. Absolutely. I'll consider it training. It's only for one night."

"And you won't be mad?"

"I'll probably sulk a bit tonight. But I'll get over it. Then he took a swig from his wine and began to turn away. He stopped and looked back, raising his glass in a small salute.

"Just one thing, Tony."

"What's that?"

"Don't fall in love with him, or I'll *kill* you!" They both laughed as Desmond disappeared into the throng of dancers.

Having retreated into the shadows, Desmond couldn't resist settling himself down to watch the results of his magnanimous gesture.

Concealed from the smoke and dimness, he honed in his catlike vision on Tony, who stood, looking somewhat uncertain, where Desmond had left him. He sipped at his beer, then seemed to realize that it was incriminating and gulped it down. Shortly after this he was rejoined by his blond friend, looking, Desmond noted, even more attractive than before. He had also brought a drink for Tony, in spite of his having turned down the offer.

That is, of course, thought Desmond, *assuming he in fact did turn down the offer.*

The blond reached around Tony at this point, placing a strong golden hand on his shoulder. He pulled Tony closer to him and whispered something in his ear, making the younger man laugh.

Despite himself Desmond seethed inwardly at this, then was immediately contrite, both for having doubted Tony's honesty and for his own uncontrollable feelings. A stiff smile etched itself on his lips as he forced himself to watch the blond's increasingly blatant advances, which were now being accepted demurely by Tony—with Desmond's blessing! Finally, when he could stand it no longer, Desmond turned in disgust—again, more at himself than at Tony—and struggled to the bar to renew his drink. If he was going to torture himself, he needed fortification. Although denied the pleasures of human eating habits, he was thankful that at least the intoxication of liquor wasn't beyond his people's reach.

By the time he returned to his vantage point, he could no longer make out Tony and his companion in the crowd. The downspot had been turned over to another pretty youth, and Desmond amused himself with thoughts of his possibilities in that direction. After all, he reasoned, two could play that game. If Tony was to be allowed a generous tether, then why not Desmond as well?

Still, his eyes wandered from Tony's potential replacement in the quivering shaft of light, searching for some glimpse of his lover's sandy hair. He slowly circled the dance floor, keeping the new boy in his sights while scanning the hundreds of drinkers, talkers, and smokers as they mingled, touched, and exhaled the day's exuberance into the laden atmosphere.

He nearly stumbled onto them and only just managed to stumble backward without being seen. His heart sank, weighed down already with the unfamiliar heaviness of his jealousy, when he saw the two of them locked in a passionate kiss as they worked their way to the exit. As he watched, frozen, they broke apart. Amid his whirl of feelings, Desmond noted with some satisfaction that neither of them looked particularly pleased. Tony looked sort of pained—Desmond hoped, ungraciously, with guilt. The blond wasn't easy to read, but Desmond decided it was a peculiar grimness on his handsome features. The mob at the door advanced, and the blond put his hand on Tony's back, steering him away from Desmond.

Gulping down his third glass of wine, Desmond wheeled and zeroed in on the new boy in the spotlight, standing right where he'd left him. Steadily, Desmond made his way over and tendered his most alluring smile as he approached.

This guy was, in fact, probably older than Tony. His black hair shone like obsidian in the spotlight, and deep blue eyes looked out from under heavy lashes. He smiled coyly at Desmond's arrival and easily fell into conversation with his new suitor. Lubricated with alcohol and adrenaline, Desmond's charm flowed effortlessly, and he quickly caught the man in his spell. Banal questions were posed and answered with great charm, pink lips parting to reveal small, even teeth and a winning smile. Desmond's voice was smooth and hypnotic, charged both with lust and hunger. He artlessly ran his hand down the young man's side, feeling the ribs—he was slimmer than Tony—beneath the sheer cotton of his shirt. He ran his fingers through the silky black hair—not as coarse as Tony's and without its waves. The blue eyes lowered modestly, and the man returned his caresses gracefully, sending tiny electric shudders through Desmond's frame.

So, Desmond thought, *at least there are other guys out there who like men that are old enough to be their father.* His forefinger traced the stubble on the tanned jaw and dropped to the soft tangle of hair showing at the V of the other man's open shirt. *Old enough to be his father*, he repeated silently as his eyes fell upon something cold that sparkled beneath his fingertip.

It was a small gold crucifix, hanging from a slender braided chain, partly hidden by the folds of the young man's shirt. If it had been made of ice, it couldn't have frozen Desmond more completely.

His eyes locked onto the religious emblem as his mind scrambled in reverse. He saw again the athletic blond talking to Tony. He saw the broad forefinger play with the gold chain, a chain with a pendant crucifix just like this one. His mind's eye moved up to the handsome face, the close-cut blond hair, the broad shoulders, the all-American smile.

Old enough to be his father. Desmond had seen that man before, but not in person. He had seen him in the snapshots in Bill Lawrence's flat, standing next to his handsome blond athletic son. His son who had been the first of the vampire slasher's victims, Michael Bauer.

"Oh, my God!" Desmond gasped softly. Then, to the astonishment of the dark-haired man, who was already prepared to entrust his body to this charming older stranger, Desmond turned and pushed his way toward the front of the bar.

Desmond found a pay phone by the men's room. He dialed Bill Lawrence's number, his hands trembling.

The answer came on the first ring. "Lawrence here."

"Bill, it's Des."

"Des? Something wrong?"

"Maybe, Bill. I don't know. Something's not right."

"What are you getting at? Is Tony all right?" Bill's voice took on an edge of concern as he perceived Desmond's fear.

"That's just the question. We've been here—" Desmond named the bar "—for a couple of hours. Tony sort of got himself picked up by this man. They left together a while back."

"You're calling because Tony ditched you for someone else? Desmond, that doesn't make sense."

"It's not that, Bill. That was a notion of mine, to let him free for a night, to prove to myself that I wasn't afraid of losing him, that I could trust him. It's who he went with."

"Someone I know?"

"I think so. Michael Bauer's father."

There was a pause as Bill let this sink in.

"The murdered kid—the first one?"

"Yes."

"How do you know?"

"I didn't at first. It was only later, after they'd left, that I remembered seeing him finger Tony's gold cross—the one Louie gave me."

"Your theory about all of the victims being Catholic?"

"Then his face suddenly came back to me and that conversation we had about Bauer's father being my age—old enough to be Tony's father."

"How sure are you it's Bauer?"

"Pretty sure. Enough to be scared."

"You think Bauer killed his own son?"

"And the others, to cover up the first killing."

"Or for some other reason tied to it."

"Remember what day this is."

"Gay pride day."

"And Bauer denied to the press that his own son was gay."

"Jesus, Des. What do we do now?"

"I've got to follow them—or catch up."

"Where did they go?"

"I don't know—that's what terrified me. I hope to Tony's flat. That's our only choice. Can you get a policeman down there on a suspicion like this?"

"Could be. Yes, in fact, I'm sure that this would at least merit a squad car, on the chance that you're right."

"I know I'm right. I can feel it, Bill."

"Get going, Des. You've got to get over to Tony's. I'll be there as soon as I can."

He rang off before Desmond could speak again. Without looking back into the smoky recesses of the bar, Desmond moved toward the door. Out on the sidewalk Desmond skirted the milling people, trying to move as fast as possible without drawing attention. He didn't want to come upon them unexpectedly, had they dawdled along the way. Desmond hadn't any clear idea how much time had passed since Tony and Bauer had left. His heart pounded, and his whole body hummed with a fear he hadn't known for centuries.

As he walked rapidly down the breezy summer streets, Desmond reviewed Bauer in his mind. He had been wearing standard white sports shoes, tailored khaki slacks, and a white polo shirt. Even on this warm day, he had gotten a short khaki jacket with a ribbed waistband out of the checkroom at the bar. He reflected again with irony that Bauer was just the sort of man Tony would have been attracted to, just as he had been drawn to Desmond. The others—Desmond filed off their names: O'Rourke, Hernandez, Vitelli—had probably all been equally drawn to Bauer's young-daddy attractiveness. And he had been drawn to the crosses the three young men had worn, symbols of their faith—and probably somehow symbols of the heresy Bauer had felt compelled to avenge or punish. Desmond had no clear idea why Bauer might have acted as he had, but a chill cut through the balmy air as he realized that he had all but pushed Tony into this situation when he could have dragged him away willingly.

At last he approached the beginning of Christopher Street and turned into it. Tony's building was just a short way along the first block, so Desmond stopped at the corner and hid himself in a doorway. His heart leaped when he saw the light burning in Tony's fourth-floor corner window. They were there already. He moved out into the shifting flow of pedestrians that still filled the neighborhood. There was enough noise to mask any indoor sounds, and even Desmond's acute hearing couldn't clear a path through it.

Darting across the street, Desmond let himself in with his master key. In the small lobby the elevator was still on the fourth floor.

Desmond didn't dare call it down and risk being heard. The door to the stairway was ajar. He crept up the four flights as silently as Cosmo did, grateful to find the door on Tony's floor ajar as well. As he stepped out onto the landing, he heard muted voices through the closed door of the studio. He hesitated only a second, then stepped up to the door and knocked.

"Tony?" he called out. Instantly there was silence. He could hear indistinct movements, then, briefly, a muffled groan.

"Tony!" Desmond cried, pounding on the door. Somewhere in the back of his mind, wolves began to howl. A violent thrust of his foot splintered the lock from the doorjamb. He lurched into the room and saw that its usual neatness was shattered. The sofa bed was open, and crouching on it was Bauer, shirtless, his muscular torso glistening with sweat. In his right hand he held an ice pick. Beyond him, sitting on the floor on the far side of the bed, was Tony, eyes wide in animal fear. He looked over as Desmond entered, silently mouthing his name as the big blond turned and staggered up off the bed.

"What have you done to Tony?" snarled Desmond, his voice low and feral. He desperately wanted to get to his lover's side, but the sweating athlete stood between them.

"You killed my son." Bauer sounded hoarse and breathless.

"I never knew your son." Desmond growled as he crouched and leaped forward, catching Bauer in the midriff, hoping to knock the ice pick out of his hand. They fell together onto the sofa bed. Desmond grabbed at the pick, but Bauer kneed him in the chest and heaved himself away, rolling onto the floor near the kitchenette.

He staggered to his feet as Desmond knelt down next to Tony and took his hand. "You people killed him," Bauer gasped.

"*You* killed him." Desmond's mind raced. Where was Bill?

"What I did was an accident. He laughed in my face when I warned him about you people. He insulted our family, our faith. He disobeyed me." Bauer brandished the weapon, which Desmond could see was bloodied.

"And you used that on him?"

"It was an accident. It wasn't my fault." Bauer stared momentarily at the ice pick as if he didn't know what it was.

"But you did it again and again. Four times!" Despite his fear Desmond's voice grew hard and angry. He felt frozen in place. He didn't want to leave Tony unprotected. But how to stop Bauer?

"He was a good boy. *You* made him the way he was."

"He was born that way." Desmond saw the man's face darken, and he added softly, "You'll burn in hell for what you've done, Bauer."

The blond man roared in rage, lifting the blade to attack.

"Liar!" With a strangled cry Bauer lunged at Desmond, who let go of Tony's hand and vaulted over the bed to meet him, extending an arm to fend off the raised weapon. He caught and pushed away Bauer's arm as the two men fell with a crashing thud to the floor. Desmond felt the needle-sharp point tear through his biceps. Desmond was stronger than this hulking mortal, but his first concern was diverting Bauer's attention from Tony.

Desmond rolled and heaved the blond off him, then stumbled to his feet, glancing toward the small kitchen. Blood spattered the white Formica table, and broken dishes were scattered on the floor. Bauer hurled himself at him again, and Desmond caught him, letting them both collapse once again to the linoleum. He let the blond man struggle and focused on keeping the pick-wielding hand at a safe distance.

A long-quiescent fear swept through him as Desmond realized that he would have to kill this raging animal. He couldn't just overpower him and turn him over to the police. Desmond couldn't face an inquest and the publicity it would entail. He couldn't allow the intrusion into his private world. To save Tony, and himself, he would have to drink him dry.

A steely coldness fell over Desmond as he gradually increased his grip on the frenzied athlete, embracing him in a viselike hold. Lying full weight on top of him, Bauer struggled to move the pick toward its target and found himself immobilized.

Then, with a deep breath, Desmond raised his upper lip and bared his fangs quickly before the blond's startled blue eyes.

The look of terror that filled Bauer's face remained suspended for a fleeting moment, the bloodstained weapon poised above Desmond's outstretched arm. Then a short explosion filled the room and, without changing expression, Bauer slumped off to one side, the pick still clenched in his large golden hand.

Desmond lay stunned for a second, then retracted his fangs and looked toward the broken-in door. Two policemen stood there, one holding a pistol. Behind them he could see the curly graying head of Bill Lawrence.

"Is he OK?" Bill's voice broke the silence.

"Looks like it."

"I meant Tony. Tony!"

Desmond jumped to his feet, wincing at the gash in his arm. This would heal soon enough. Tony was his first concern. He moved quickly over to the corner beyond the sofa bed, where Tony still sat, eyes closed now as if unconscious. He was breathing, that was clear, but his hands clutched his abdomen, and dark blood trickled from between his pale fingers. Desmond looked at his own hand, with which he had held Tony's, and saw that it was smeared with blood. He knelt by the bed and placed a hand helplessly on Tony's brow.

"Call an ambulance, fast!" Bill's voice took command, since Desmond found he couldn't speak. Bill came over to Desmond and placed both hands on his shoulders.

"Looks like we barely made it. I'm sorry, Des."

"Thanks, Bill. I'm glad you're here." He stared into Tony's pale face and felt a trembling begin to move through his own frame. Tears blurred his unblinking eyes.

Once again he heard the mournful howling of the Dalmatian wolves.

He remained kneeling by the bed, holding Tony's hand until the ambulance arrived. Tony was quickly placed on a stretcher and carried down the stairs into the waiting car. Before he left the flat, Desmond looked back at the pool of dark blood that had begun to coagulate on the floor. Then he followed the attendants to the street.

As the ambulance made its arduous way past the late-night strollers in the Village, the attendants inspected Tony's wounds and cleaned him up.

"How is he?" Desmond asked, his voice colorless.

"Hard to say. Lost a lot of blood. Looks like only one wound, though. Small and deep. Bad place. He your friend, sir?"

Desmond looked up at the young man's candid, attractive face. The eyes were sympathetic. "My lover," he replied softly, feeling again the burning of tears.

"I'm sorry." The attendant looked down at Tony. Then he added, "He'll need blood. Can you answer for him?"

"What do you mean?"

"We need to give blood. Do you know his type?" The other attendant reached for a cabinet and opened it to reveal packets of whole blood.

"No, not that," Desmond said firmly, his voice steady. "Give him my blood; I'm his type."

"Sir, I don't think we can do that."

"Yes, you can, boys, and you will." Desmond began to use his vampire persuasiveness. "I'm responsible. If anything goes wrong, I'll take the blame."

"No, he won't." Tony's weak voice startled them all. "O positive is fine. You'd better hook me up fast."

As Desmond stared dumbly into Tony's heavy eyes, the orderlies did their job, then moved forward in the ambulance to leave them relatively alone. Finally, Desmond found the strength to speak.

"Why, Tony?"

"Because I'm not ready, Des."

"But I can save you." Choking desperation began to fill Desmond's throat.

"You already did save me, sweetheart. Now all you can do is transform me. And I've decided I can't do that."

"But the lists. I saw them…"

"Ah, those." Tony smiled. "Des, honey, those lists scared the hell out of me."

"Me too," Desmond confessed.

"The thought of an eternity ahead of me—on this earth—even with you…it was too much."

"Oh, Tony." Desmond's voice was a soft moan.

"It's not that I don't love you. I do, more than I'll ever be able to say." His hand moved, and Desmond took it, holding it. "I love you for wanting to transform me, for loving me enough to want me with you forever. It's just…just…"

"Just not for more than one lifetime, right?"

"Right, even for one short lifetime." Tony smiled again, as if at a private joke.

"Don't say that," Desmond whispered fiercely. "Don't even think it. We'll talk more about it later."

The sirens died down as the ambulance pulled into the hospital's emergency bay.

The emergency room was chaotic, as to be expected on a night like this, when they arrived. They quickly wheeled Tony into an X-ray station. The drivers disappeared, taking the necessary information to give the doctor. Then they moved the gurney into a corner, pulling the curtains around it to make a semiprivate cubicle. Desmond sat patiently as the plastic packet of blood continued to empty, drop by drop, into Tony's veins.

A doctor came in a short while later, scowling with concern over the wound. They would operate as soon as a surgeon was available. It was a deep pinpoint wound. No telling what sort of damage might have been done internally. He offered Desmond some well-meant but meaningless words of comfort, then vanished to make things ready.

A few minutes passed, then the curtains rustled aside and Bill Lawrence came into the cubicle.

"How's he doing, Des?" A gentle hand caressed Desmond's shoulders.

"Not sure. They're going to operate soon." The deadness had returned to Desmond's voice. He sounded tired.

They stood silently together for a while longer, both watching the shallow rise and fall of Tony's belly and the faint flutter of his eyelids. Then, without warning, Tony's big dark eyes struggled open, as if waking from a dream. He looked directly at Desmond and smiled faintly.

"Thanks, lover," he whispered. Then the eyes closed. Desmond and Bill watched as the tiny flickers around Tony's eyes and mouth were stilled, and Desmond felt the hand go slack in his tender grasp.

"Oh, God, no!" Bill mumbled, stifling a sob. Pulling the curtains aside frantically, he rushed from the cubicle to get the doctor. An ER nurse hurried in, glanced at Desmond, and bent over Tony, checking for vital signs. After a few seconds she straightened and turned to Desmond, brow knitted. The sympathy in her eyes was genuine.

"I'm sorry, sir. I'm afraid he's gone." She stood, waiting, as if expecting some response. Then, receiving none, she softly repeated "I'm sorry" and left the cubicle, pulling the curtains closed behind her.

Desmond stood up. Taking great care, as if handling a fragile package, he removed the intravenous needle. Silent tears coursing down his cheeks, he bent and kissed the lifeless lips, then lifted Tony's inert form from the black vinyl surface of the gurney.

As Bill hurried back down the corridor, the young doctor in tow along with two policemen, he was startled to find the cubicle empty, the curtains still stirring with recent motion. He craned his head around and just caught sight of someone that looked like Desmond, arms full, pushing through the double doors onto the street.

Bill ran to the doors and shoved through a group of new arrivals into the warm June night. Searching frantically to the right and left, he could see nothing but streams of passersby enjoying the gentle breezes of this perfect summer Sunday evening.

CHAPTER 17

It was well before dawn when Bill Lawrence got to Desmond's house. As he approached the high marble stoop, he realized that he'd never entered without prior invitation. He steeled himself and lifted the big brass knocker. Within seconds of his knock, the paneled door was opened.

Desmond stood there, dressed in an odd black suit with a long-skirted coat, short pants buckled at the knees, and white stockings. The white shirt had a high collar, and he wore an elaborately tied neckcloth. It was as if he were dressed for a costume party. Only his short, wavy haircut was modern. His eyes were red-rimmed but bright and alert. The hall behind him was in darkness.

"Hello, Bill. I was expecting you. Are you OK?"

"Fine, Desmond. May I come in?"

"Of course." Desmond stepped back, letting Bill enter the stillness of the old house. The ground-floor doors were closed. Only the streetlights, seeping in through the fanlight, gave any illumination. Cosmo appeared from the shadows and rubbed against Bill's ankles and purred. It was cold in the house.

Bill turned back to Desmond, who had shut the door and thrown the bolt.

"Where is he, Desmond?" Bill asked softly.

"Upstairs, in my room. You go ahead. I'm all done, and kitty needs some breakfast." He turned and melted into the darkness at the back of the house.

Shivering in the chill air, Bill climbed the carpeted stairs into the pitch blackness of the second floor. The old boards creaked with each step, as if to remind him just how long they had borne such traffic. At the top of the first flight, Bill could make out a dim glow through the open doorway of the master bedroom. He walked down the hallway and hesitated on the threshold.

Small tables had been set at each corner post of the bedstead, and on each table burned a single candle in a tall silver holder. Half a dozen more candles were lined up on the mantelpiece. The candlelight gave the white bed linens a golden radiance in the dim room. Tony lay on Desmond's bed, on top of the white counterpane, his head on one of the large square pillows. He was wrapped in a snowy linen sheet, his crossed hands, his high-arched feet, and his head all uncovered. A handkerchief was tied around his head to keep his jaw closed. Even in death, Tony was beautiful. Bill could smell incense in the room and finally made out a flowered porcelain pastille burner on one of the windowsills. A thin trail of scented smoke still issued from it.

He stood mutely in the doorway for a long moment, taking in the scene. It occurred to him that Desmond's strange costume was perfect for this tableau. Then he noticed something small and dark lying on the bed and stepped forward to look at it.

It was a book, lying open on the counterpane. Bill picked it up. It was an Anglican Book of Common Prayer, bound in dark green leather, with the name BECKWITH stamped on its front cover in gold. A silk ribbon marked the service for the burial of the dead. Bill read through the words of the funeral prayers, still familiar to him from his own Anglican upbringing in Bermuda. He was no longer a regular churchgoer but occasionally attended Saint Thomas's on holidays. The American Episcopal prayer book had been revised a decade ago and no longer had the cadences and flourishes of the old Anglican prayers. He opened the front cover of the book to find a publication date. It was a London edition, printed in 1720. Turning back to the flyleaf, Bill read an inscription written in a bold hand in rusty black ink.

DESMOND BECKWITH, ON THE DAY OF
HIS CHRISTENING
AT BECKWITH HOUSE, BERKSHIRE
AUGUST 5TH, ANNO DOMINI 1724
THE GIFT OF HIS PARENTS,
SIR CHARLES AND LADY ANNE BECKWITH

Below this were several more inscriptions.

TSOLNAY, ANNO DOMINI 1745
PARIS, ANNO DOMINI 1789
LONDON, ANNO DOMINI 1833
CHICAGO, ANNO DOMINI 1877
SAN FRANCISCO, ANNO DOMINI 1921
NEW YORK, ANNO DOMINI 1965

The first three lines were in faded black ink. The fourth was in purple, the fifth in peacock blue. The last line was written in ordinary blue ballpoint pen. They were all in the same handwriting. Bill felt himself begin to shiver violently.

A gentle pressure on his shoulder made him jump. Desmond stood beside him, hazel eyes glittering in the candlelight.

"I had to bring him here…I had to bring him home. I couldn't just let the police have him. I couldn't just let his family sweep him away. I wanted to say farewell in my own way."

"I understand, Des. I—I'm sorry. But you know the police will be here soon."

Desmond nodded. "I needed this time."

The two men hugged silently and left the room together. They went down the hall to the library, where, incongruously, a fire blazed in the marble fireplace.

"I turned up the air-conditioning," explained Desmond. "For practical reasons."

Then he handed Bill a glass of brandy and sat down, crossing his legs.

"So what happened to Bauer?" Desmond asked.

"Dead, instantly. Simpler that way, actually. The officer thought you were in danger, Des, so he fired." Here he turned to Desmond, who had moved over to the mantelpiece. "You *were* in danger, weren't you, friend?"

"Bill, that Teutonic hulk was on top of me, holding an ice pick!"

"Just checking." Then he continued. "It was an awl, actually, not an ice pick, Desmond. He had saved clippings of the three murders and those about his son's death. Mrs. Bauer had heard them arguing in the cellar the night the boy was killed. There was some scream-ing, the sound of a tussle, then silence. A few minutes later she heard the door slam and the car drive away.

"She never checked out what had happened?" interposed Desmond.

"Never left her bed. Too afraid of what she might find, maybe. About an hour later, by her reckoning, Bauer returned and came to bed as if nothing had happened. She never asked."

"Did she suspect he had killed the boy?"

"Don't know. When the story hit the press and the police called them, Bauer apparently kept muttering, 'They killed him, they killed my son.' She took that as explanation, I guess."

He finished his drink, and Desmond refilled his glass. Then, after a stiff gulp, he looked at his friend.

"So are you going to tell me what's going on?"

"I told you, Bill, I had to bring Tony back before I let him go."

"I understand that. I really do. I mean all the other things. Your outfit, for example. Tony's shroud. That antique prayer book with your handwriting all over the flyleaf." At this Desmond's eyebrows rose.

"Look, Desmond, the police will want a statement at some point. You can tailor your story to make them happy. You've got no worries there. But right now I want to know what this is all about. There was something special between you and Tony, and I never could quite see inside you two to figure it out."

Desmond said nothing but stared into the fire, eyes brimming with unshed tears. Bill leaned forward, hands on his knees.

"I've known you a long time, Desmond. In spite of our friendship, you've always been a loner. Tony was breaking down that shell that kept you cut off from us—from me. You've just lost someone you loved deeply. I don't want that pain to drive you back into your shell. I don't want you to be alone anymore." Desmond looked up into Bill's eyes. "Tell me, Des. You wanted me to see all this." He gestured down the hall.

"Are you sure you want to know?"

"Did Tony know?"

"Yes. He did."

"Am I your friend, Des?"

"Yes, always, Bill."

"Then tell me. Everything."

And he did.

Two hours later Bill's glass was empty and dry, and he sat staring thoughtfully into the dying fire.

"That's one hell of a story! More like the *Star* than the *Times*."

"It's all true, Bill. I swear." Desmond spoke softly, as if to someone bereaved.

"So you took advantage of me that night all those years back, a poor defenseless drunkard?"

"We were both drunk that night, Bill. I forgot myself." Desmond's voice was almost cheerful. Telling his tale again had lifted him out of his sadness.

Bill stood up and stretched. He moved around the room, studying it as if for the first time. He looked at the clock. "The sun will be up soon."

"That's all right. I don't have to go climb into a coffin."

"But you've got a lot of explaining to do to a lot of pissed-off men in blue."

"I'm ready to go."

"You ought to build up your strength. It's going to be stressful."

"I don't understand." Desmond frowned, confused.

Bill turned, facing Desmond. "Why don't you let me give you strength again? Like you did with Tony."

"What—you don't mean transformation!"

"No, no, not that. I'm too old to start that. Yuck, endlessly middle-aged, what a horrible thought!"

Then he went over to Desmond and, bending down, took his hands as he sat in the chair, looking intently at his friend.

"I want to commemorate this somehow. I want to give you something to comfort you and make you strong. Whether you admit it or not, you'll need it."

"Do you really want this, Bill?" Desmond asked.

"As long as it doesn't hurt much."

"It won't."

"Then do it. Now."

"All right, then."

"Where? Here?" Bill's voice was suddenly businesslike, as if he were arranging a procedure with a dentist.

"Uh, no," Desmond said, a bit flustered. "Perhaps the guest room upstairs."

"OK, then, let's go."

The silent pair climbed up to the front guest room on the third floor. Desmond lit a candle, then pulled back the covers on the simple pencil-post bedstead as Bill removed his jacket, tie, and shirt. The reporter kicked off his shoes and lay down on the bed, smiling. His dark skin, almost hairless, glowed like polished walnut against the white linens. Desmond stood nervously beside him, holding his hand, looking for encouragement.

"You never let me sleep over before," said Bill, grinning. "And don't worry about me, Desi, I've pickled myself with brandy. Won't feel a thing. Just like last time." Then he sat up partway. "I *will* sleep?"

"For a while. With all that booze, maybe a long while."

"Good. But I'll be hungry tomorrow. Will you buy me breakfast?" His words were a little slurred, his eyes drooping.

"Better than that, Bill," said Desmond softly. "I'll cook you breakfast."

"Great!" Bill relaxed onto the pillows and stared up at Desmond's face. "Thirsty, kid?"

"Yes, Bill."

"Go to it, then." Then he winked. "See you in the morning." He closed his eyes, then took a deep breath, letting it out in a long, relaxing sigh.

As Desmond bent to take solace in the blood of his oldest mortal friend, the first rays of a summer sunrise began to peep through the embroidered muslin of the bedroom curtains.

EPILOGUE

B
ill pulled the door to his apartment shut, locking it behind him. He walked noiselessly down the carpeted corridor, perhaps 40 feet, and pressed the button next to the paneled mahogany door at the far end. A small brass plate above the button was engraved in neat Roman letters: BECKWITH.

Immediately the door opened, and Desmond's smiling face greeted him.

"Surprise, surprise! You're not late, and all that way to go!" He gave Bill a kiss and stepped back into the apartment to take his dinner jacket from a bench in the entryway.

"I know, it's hard to make it on time when you live a dozen yards away," joked Bill. "Happy birthday, old man. I brought you a present." He handed Desmond a heavy package wrapped in shiny red paper with a large silk bow.

"It's a copy of Anne Rice's latest, *Queen of the Damned*. Signed."

"Really? That's fabulous. I've been dying to read it. How'd you do it?"

"Newspaper connections. Easy enough. So, how's it feel to be 50?" He gave Desmond a leering once-over. "Again."

"Not nearly as bad this time around. I feel deep maturity oozing from every pore. But not at all decrepit. Does it show?" Desmond stepped back dramatically and struck a pose. In his Armani tuxedo, the first signs of gray frosting his temples, Desmond Beckwith looked dashing indeed.

"Fabulous, Desi. Ravishing, in fact." The words were not idle.

"Let's get moving." He shooed Bill out the door, locking it behind him. Together they walked to the elevator.

As they rode down to the lobby, Bill spoke thoughtfully. "I'm going to miss having you next door, my friend."

"I'm only going to be across town, not in another universe."

"I know, I know. But it's been so lovely having you right here." Bill looked like he was going to cry.

"Oh, Bill! For heaven's sake, I'll *always* be here—metaphorically, anyway." He turned to his old friend. "Look, my dear man, I'm sorry I'm moving out of my penthouse. It just wasn't my style. I needed the change. It was great for me to come here, and I'll always be grateful to you for suggesting it. But ultimately it was just too big a change. I needed to backtrack a bit. Something more…well, more *me*." And he smiled slyly, like the cat who'd caught the canary. "And just wait until you see the new place."

The cab dropped them off at the corner of Central Park West and 72nd Street. Bill stared up, in the late-summer-afternoon light, at the immense baroque mass of the Dakota looming over the park. The exterior had recently been restored, and the sand-colored brickwork and chocolate-brown stone trim looked like new.

"I remember when they built this thing, Bill," said Desmond. "Never in my life did I think I'd want to live here."

"So why the change of heart?" Bill asked as they started down 72nd Street.

"Tony first made me realize that the old house was nothing more than my tomb. I'd stopped growing, just as the house had. After Tony died I thought living in a bright modern apartment like yours was what I needed."

"Wasn't it?" asked Bill.

"At first. But it always seemed too high up for me. I found myself yearning for something closer to the ground, more rooted somehow. Then one day—I'd been reviewing Tony's inventories, because we were in the middle of transferring the title of the house to the Foundation—and it suddenly dawned on me that I'd actually missed a large chunk of the 19th century. The most exciting part, for that matter."

They passed through a massive brownstone archway and into a paved court ornamented with raised flower beds and ringed with glass canopies set on iron frames. Desmond waved to a concierge keeping watch at the entrance and crossed the courtyard.

They started up a short flight of stone steps in one corner and pushed through a wide door set with beveled glass. Across a floor of polished marble tesserae arranged in an intricate design was another paneled door, this one newly polished and glowing in the overhead light.

Desmond stopped and turned to Bill with a wide smile. "So here's where I start reclaiming my lost decades."

He pushed open the door and pulled Bill by the hand into a high square entrance hall. It was not particularly large, but it was splendid. The walls were paneled six feet high in figured honey-colored maple with carved bands of pinwheels and flowing scrollwork. Above this the walls were papered in a large-scale print of swirling Japanese designs in gold on a dark teal-blue background. The floor was paved with brightly colored geometric ceramic tiles mimicking Middle Eastern ceramics in pattern. A fantastic chandelier, all complex angular tubing and stylized metal flowers, hung from the paneled ceiling, casting a soft electric glow. On a side table a huge arrangement of flowers filled the space with a sweet musky scent. Copper-colored, ivory, and blood-red roses, orange and yellow lilies, yellow freesia, white Japanese chrysanthemums—the effect was dazzling. A uniformed waiter came out of another room to greet them.

"Mr. Beckwith! Things are just about ready. No one else is here yet."

"Great," Bill piped up. "Where's my drink?" He walked across the hall to an arched doorway hung with heavy silk plush portieres and into a big living room. Twenty-five feet square and nearly 20 high, the room was an extravaganza of color and pattern, with a monumental carved mahogany fireplace against one wall. All of the tables, cabinets, and side chairs were angular and lacquered in a glossy black, some decorated with shallow carving, some with stylized marquetry. Several pieces also featured incised decoration picked out in gold leaf that winked in the artificial light. Overstuffed sofas, deeply button-tufted and covered in lush jewel-colored velvets and damasks, looked both forbidding and—oddly—very comfortable. Through another wide, plush-draped doorway, he could see an equally elaborate dining room. On the other side of the room, a third, smaller doorway offered a partial view of a deep blue–green library lined with shiny black glazed bookcases. The waiter returned with a tray of champagne and proffered it to Bill.

"Well, I really wanted a martini, but this will do." Then he turned to Desmond, who had followed him in. "What the hell is this? This is like a set out of *The Magnificent Ambersons*! You're still stuck in the past."

"But don't you see, Bill? I missed this part of the past. I was so weighed down with my own life that I entirely skipped the aesthetic movement of the 1870s and 1880s. I was so busy keeping the world at arm's length, keeping my little shrine to myself sacred, that I let all this slip by me. Tony helped me see that. I've restored this apartment to look the way it did when the Dakota was first built. It's the model flat I saw back in the 1880s."

"At least I don't recognize anything from the old house," said Bill, scanning the rooms as he sauntered about, sipping his champagne.

"Only the painting of Beckwith House, which is in my office off the kitchen, and some of my favorite books." He grabbed Bill by the arm.

"Don't you understand? This is a clean start. There's nothing here that I ever owned before. I've become a collector. I bought all this in the past couple of years. All of this was somebody else's, some other family's history. It's the best of both worlds for me. Everything here is old and hence comfortable for me; and everything is new to me, to my life. It may *look* old, Bill, but this is part of the world *today*."

Bill just looked at his friend, a smile playing at the corners of his mouth.

"You're getting way too weird for me, Desi."

A noise made them turn, and they saw two young men in white jackets arranging flatware on the long table in the dining room. Folded linen napkins, stacks of plates, sparkling silver, and three lavish floral arrangements filled a white tablecloth. From what he could see, Bill guessed that there would be about 30 people this evening in addition to him and his host. A bar was being set up on the sideboard by the kitchen hallway, and a large silver ice bucket sat ready to receive its load of ice cubes. Bill remembered that they were early and felt flattered that he'd been asked to come before the rest of the guests. As he looked toward the dining area, a handsome middle-aged woman in a well-tailored cocktail suit came into the room from the kitchen holding a glass of bubbling wine.

"It's a good thing you're here. Desmond would fuss at me for starting so soon, and you're my excuse."

"Always glad to be of service." Bill raised his glass.

"Vivian!" exclaimed Desmond. "You're here! They said no one else was here."

"I guess I don't count, since I'm probably the only straight person on the guest list." Then she turned to Bill. "So who's your friend?"

"Vivian Lake, this is Bill Lawrence." They shook hands with mock solemnity, trying not to spill their champagne.

"Ah," said Bill, "you're the new director at Beckwith House."

"And you're the *Times* reporter who's given us such very nice publicity."

"You're entirely welcome."

Desmond laughed lightly as they touched glasses. Together they sipped the wine as they wandered through the big rooms. Bill savored the drink in silence for a moment, then turned to Vivian.

"How *are* things at Beckwith House?"

Her eyes lit up at the question. Clearly it was a subject of which she never tired. "Marvelous! We had a board meeting today, my first. If I do say so, I think I was a great hit with the rest of the trustees."

"I'm glad Desmond finally convinced you to take the job. Are you comfortable about it?"

"Yes, I think so. I was uneasy about it because I felt I was somehow betraying the museum."

Desmond chimed in. "All I had to prove to her was that, even though Beckwith House is technically an independent entity, it's also a division of the museum. Our foundation board is entirely different from the museum's and can act only in regard to the house itself. And the museum's board can't do anything to subvert the integrity of Beckwith House. But legally the museum has title to the house and its contents and archives."

"Sounds simple enough. Why did you resist for so long, Vivian?"

"Probably because of Desmond's money."

"Ah, the root of all evil."

"Not too evil, I hope," interposed Desmond. "It's just that since I was still funding the assistant curatorial post at the museum *and* I've endowed Beckwith House, Vivian felt there might be some conflict between her and the museum administration, should any serious disagreement arise."

"How'd you resolve that?"

"I convinced Desmond to set up a trust for the curatorial position at the museum, so he can't withdraw the funding even if he wants to." Vivian's smile seemed to gloat at forcing Desmond's hand.

"And this eliminated Vivian's scruples?"

"Exactly. Now Vivian can call me anything she wants, countermand my policies at Beckwith House, ridicule me publicly…"

"Which, since everyone knows how wonderful you are, isn't very likely," said Vivian, stretching to reach an arm around Desmond's shoulders. "You're a great friend, Desmond."

"I think I owe that to Tony, Vivian. He made me realize how little I knew you, how much better friends we could be if I made the effort."

An awkward silence followed, broken by Bill, who raised his glass in a toast.

"To the fond memory of Tony Chapman."

They lifted their glasses in silence. Then Vivian turned to Desmond.

"To the birthday boy. Live long and prosper!" This time they clinked.

Desmond laughed. "Don't believe her for a minute, Bill. She knows that she'll get this apartment and everything in it for the Foundation after I die. It's in my will. She's counting the days."

"Oh, please, Desmond, you're 50 and fabulous, and you'll live to be 100!"

Desmond and Bill exchanged a look.

"Well, Vivian," said Desmond as he drained his glass, "you never know."

The doorbell rang, and both Desmond and Vivian went to greet the first guests. Bill was left on his own and took the opportunity to snoop around before the rooms got too crowded. Wandering into the library, he almost laughed to see a large and complicated television set nestled into a custom-made cabinet. He noticed too that soft classical music filled the apartment from hidden speakers in every room, evidence that Desmond had actually acquired a sound system. Tony's influence, Bill mused.

Bill thought about the other changes in Desmond over the past five years. Although still hardly a gregarious personality, there was a warmth and intimacy to Desmond Beckwith that had definitely not existed in the first 20 years of their friendship. Tony hadn't exactly transformed Desmond, but he had given him something, unshackled his soul. Since that strange evening five years earlier, Bill had become closer to this man than he would ever have expected. Even today he often found it hard to remember that his closest friend was not like him, that his closest friend would carry on his life long after he himself had turned to dust.

He caught sight of Desmond moving across the living room with a guest in tow. Dressed in sleek black evening clothes, he looked relaxed and happy. His hair was longer now, and the first gray was very becoming. But his face was still unlined, and he glowed with a healthy vigor that Bill envied. At 50, Desmond and Bill were outwardly the same age, but Bill knew his own body was beginning the slow process of disintegration that age brought to mortals. Cholesterol, high blood pressure, weakening eyesight—these were problems only he would have to cope with. There were moments when he wondered if he shouldn't have tried to convince Desmond to transform him. But no, the idea of eternity still terrified him. One lifetime was enough.

Desmond hailed Bill from the other room with comic exaggeration, calling for him to come and have another drink. Bill bowed with mock obeisance and went forward to accept another glass.

Another toast was drunk, and the two friends chatted with the new arrivals about nothing in particular as the catering staff put the finishing touches on the buffet.

Presently their talk was interrupted by Roger Deland's arrival. Roger's smooth red hair, moderately long and brushed straight back from his forehead, showed no trace of gray yet, and Bill reflected that he showed his age even less than Desmond. He had always seen Roger as a mystery, largely because of his close relationship with Desmond. It was difficult to remember that Roger was straight, and Desmond was repeatedly having to dispel the common misconception that he and Roger were former lovers. Now Roger's East Coast visits were more frequent. Tony's brief life with Desmond had made Desmond less clinging, less yearningly domestic, and it seemed that Roger relished the new easiness of their ancient friendship. Roger had also accepted Bill readily and with welcoming candor. Bill understood how Desmond could love him.

Still more glasses were brought, a fresh bottle of Veuve Cliquot opened, and still more toasts made to the new 50-year-old as people trickled into the room from the hall, oohing at their first sight of the extraordinary new apartment.

"And many happy returns!" crowed one of the guests.

Roger and Desmond laughed heartily at this, and Bill blushed, understanding the reason for their mirth.

"One of these days, you know, I'm going to lose my mind!" he said in a stage whisper to Desmond, putting the back of his hand to his forehead.

"Don't worry, dearest," Desmond interposed breezily, giving Bill a brotherly kiss and a sidelong hug with his free arm, "even if you go completely gaga, we'll take care of you."

"*That's* a comfort! I'm sure I'll be a poisonous old queer."

"Look, Bill," declared Roger, a laugh rippling through his words, "if I can put up with Desmond after all this time, you'll be a piece of cake."

Bill and Desmond exchanged a glance as they all laughed again. The subject of Bill's mortality had come up before and was not without its awkwardness among them. But Bill had made his decision years ago. Desmond had trusted him, and he would trust in return. They would take care of him, and he knew it. They were family. The warmth of this thought mingled with the tingling of the champagne and brought a smile to his eyes.

From the distance the doorbell rang again. The rest of the invited friends were arriving. The catering staff was galvanized into action, moving quickly to take their places by the bar and hefting the large trays of hors d'oeuvres.

Desmond and Bill raised their glasses to each other and to Roger, emptied them, and handed them to one of the waiters. Then Desmond clasped Bill's hand in a warm, firm grip. With a last look deep into his old friend's eyes, Mr. Beckwith turned and went alone to meet his guests.

alyson
books

B-BOY BLUES, by James Earl Hardy. A seriously sexy, fiercely funny black-on-black love story. A walk on the wild side turns into more than Mitchell Crawford ever expected. An Alyson best-seller you shouldn't miss.

BECOMING VISIBLE, edited by Kevin Jennings. The *Lambda Book Report* states that "*Becoming Visible* is a groundbreaking text and a fascinating read. This book will challenge teens and teachers who think contemporary sex and gender roles are 'natural' and help break down the walls of isolation surrounding lesbian, gay, and bisexual youth."

CODY, by Keith Hale. Trottingham Taylor, "Trotsky" to his friends, is new to Little Rock. Washington Damon Cody has lived there all his life. Yet when they meet, there's a familiarity, a sense that they've known each other before. Their friendship grows and develops a rare intensity, although one is gay and the other is straight.

THE GAY FIRESIDE COMPANION, by Leigh W. Rutledge. "Rutledge, 'The Gay Trivia Queen,' has compiled a myriad gay facts in an easy-to-read volume. This book offers up the offbeat, trivial, and fascinating from the history and life of gays in America." —Buzz Bryan in *Lambda Book Report*

MY BIGGEST O, edited by Jack Hart. What was the best sex you ever had? Jack Hart asked that question of hundreds of gay men, and got some fascinating answers. Here are summaries of the most intriguing of them. Together, they provide an engaging picture of the sexual tastes of gay men.

MY FIRST TIME, edited by Jack Hart. Hart has compiled a fascinating collection of true stories by men across the country, describing their first same-sex encounters. *My First Time* is an intriguing look at just how gay men begin the process of exploring their sexuality.

THE PRESIDENT'S SON, by Krandall Kraus. "President Marshall's son is gay. The president, who is beginning a tough battle for reelection, knows it but can't handle it. *The President's Son* is a delicious, oh-so-thinly-veiled tale of a political empire gone insane. A great read." —Marvin Shaw in *The Advocate*

TWO TEENAGERS IN 20: WRITINGS BY GAY AND LESBIAN YOUTH, edited by Ann Heron. "Designed to inform and support teenagers dealing on their own with minority sexual identification. The thoughtful, readable accounts focus on feelings about being homosexual, reactions of friends and families, and first encounters with other gay people." —*School Library Journal*

These books and other Alyson titles are available at your local bookstore.
If you can't find a book listed above or would like more information,
please call us directly at 1-800-5-ALYSON.